This book should be returned to any branch of the
Library on or before

KISMET

KISMET

LUKE TREDGET

FABER & FABER

First published in 2018
by Faber & Faber Limited
Bloomsbury House
74–77 Great Russell Street
London WC1B 3DA

Typeset by Faber & Faber Limited
Printed in the UK by CPI Group (UK) Ltd, Croydon CR0 4YY

The right of Luke Tredget to be identified as author of this work
has been asserted in accordance with Section 77 of the Copyright,
Designs and Patents Act 1988

A CIP record for this book
is available from the British Library

ISBN 978–0–571–33487–2

2 4 6 8 10 9 7 5 3 1

First published in 2014
by Faber & Faber Limited
Bloomsbury House
74–77 Great Russell Street
London WC1B 3DA

Typeset by Faber and Faber Limited
Printed and bound by CPI Group (UK) Ltd, Croydon CR0 4YY

The right of [...] to be identified as author of this work
has been asserted in accordance with Section 77 of the Copyright,
Designs and Patents Act 1988

A CIP record for this book
is available from the British Library

Monday

The bus to Kilburn is a long time coming, and while waiting Anna looks back and forth between two versions of the Edgware Road, the real and the digital. The real one, all around her, is busy shifting into its evening routine. Dozens of people are gathering around her at the bus stop, pedestrians are streaming along the pavement and clotting at the zebra crossing, cars and taxis and lorries are blocked in both directions on the road, and beyond them the Odeon is filling up with couples queuing for tickets and popcorn. Anna's attention focuses on two couples in particular, framed by the main window. One couple are tanned and chatty and their height is perfectly proportioned for the man's arm to loop around the woman's shoulder – she imagines the number 75 flashing above their heads. The couple behind them are of equal height and don't seem to be communicating at all – it appears that the man might even be wearing headphones – and she pictures a 64, before a truck lurches forwards and blocks her view.

In contrast to this raucous activity, the map on her phone is entirely empty, showing nothing but the red dot pinpointing her location and the grey and beige outlines of surrounding buildings. This is Anna's first day on Kismet, and the only match she has made was this morning in Soho Square, where she took her phone after receiving the text to say her profile was ready. The small park was deserted, but after a few minutes she saw a dark-haired man in a long coat walking around the perimeter of the square, and although she lost sight of him behind a hedge, he reappeared a moment later as a blue dot on her phone. Her excitement lasted only the time it took to press this dot with her thumb, which sadly yielded the number 54 – not enough to approach someone in a bar, let alone chase them down in the street. Since then she has checked during her lunch break and while popping to the pharmacy and as she sat at her desk, but each time there was nothing, just as there is now, during the mayhem of rush hour. She wonders if something is amiss with her profile, or if she would be getting hits if she were waiting for a bus headed to east London, and then this thought is wiped by something surprising: she can hear singing.

'Happy birthday to you.'

A young white man in a fleece and jogging bottoms is standing in front of her, with one foot off the kerb and one hand hanging onto the bus signpost. He sings at full volume, the familiar words wrapped around an altogether different, perhaps improvised melody.

'Happy birthday,' he continues, scanning his wild eyes around the bus stop, as if challenging the assorted commuters to meet his glare. 'To yoouuu!'

Everyone surrounding Anna tuts and shakes their head and turns away, but she is transfixed, sensing something staged or unusual about this performance; there is something familiar about the man's long, sad-looking face, as if maybe he is a minor celebrity, or just a friend of a friend.

'Happy birthday, dear . . .' His eyes fix on Anna at this point, and for a moment she thinks he is about to sing her name. But instead he says nothing, just stares at her helplessly,

4

as if desperate for someone to remind him of his line, before ploughing on regardless.

'Happy birthdayyyy! Toooooo. Youuuuuu.'

Silence. His eyes sweep along the bus stop once more, as if he has proved his point and shamed them into silence, and then he walks away. Anna watches him strut off towards Marble Arch, pulling a small suitcase behind him, and eventually she is jolted by the realisation of who he looks like: her dad. Not the middle-aged version, but how he looked as a teenager or young man, in those photos of him with his siblings, in his first car, at graduation, a handsome and hopeful twenty-something. The similarity is uncanny, and she watches after the singer until he is completely lost in the weave of other pedestrians, and almost doesn't notice that the bus to Kilburn has arrived and is waiting with its doors open.

Anna takes her favourite seat at the front of the top deck, and a moment after the bus chugs away she opens her contacts and calls Zahra, who answers immediately.

'How are you?' says Anna, inserting her headphones. Zahra says she's fine, that she just got home, and when she asks the same question Anna jumps straight to it. 'Something weird just happened. I was at the bus stop and this guy came and started singing at me.'

'At *you*?' says Zahra, her voice distant and echoing.

'Well, more like at the whole bus stop. But he definitely focused on me.'

'Like, a busker?'

'He didn't ask for money.'

'Was he drunk?' says Zahra, her voice louder now.

'I don't think so.'

'Well . . . what was he singing?'

5

Anna says the birthday song, and Zahra laughs and says that she doesn't understand what was so weird.

'It was like he was singing it to me.'

'Right. So you think this guy knows when your birthday is, and decided to sing it two weeks early?'

'It's in ten days, actually. But the thing is, he kind of looked like my dad.'

'Hmmm,' says Zahra, her voice faint again. 'You're the one that's sounding weird.'

'You think?'

'Much weirder than him.'

There is a pause as Anna reflects on this, and then she sighs and says that it figures, as she certainly feels weird. As the bus passes beneath the Marylebone Flyover and onto the scruffy, low-slung end of the Edgware Road, Anna lists potential reasons for feeling strange: that she didn't sleep well last night, that she had too much coffee to make up for the lack of sleep, that she still doesn't know what she's going to do for her birthday, and that she's failing at work. She doesn't add that joining Kismet has also jazzed her mood, but she does minimise Zahra's face to a thumbnail on her screen and opens the map again.

'Everyone feels like that on a Monday,' says Zahra.

'Do they?'

'Of course. Everyone starts the week thinking they're in the wrong job.'

'I see,' says Anna. 'I didn't know that.' There is another pause as the bus passes a billboard for the new Kismet Love Test, which provides a one-off retrospective score for couples who met in the traditional way. Anna considers asking if most people wonder if they are in the wrong life as well as the wrong job, but she doesn't want to go down that route, and instead asks Zahra why her voice keeps fading from loud to quiet.

'You're on speakerphone; I'm walking between the living room and kitchen. Sometimes I get home and just *pace*. The floorboards feel so nice underfoot!'

'Nice? For six months' work they should feel transcendental underfoot. Tantric, even.'

Zahra says it was worth every minute, and that they're so pleased with the results that they're thinking of knocking the two bedrooms together as well. While Zahra talks the bus stops and shuts down altogether beside the covered market, so the driver can swap with another man waiting on the street. A couple carrying large Argos bags walk past and, since Anna imagines everything and everyone in Kilburn being deficient in some way, she pictures a low number flashing above their heads, a 57. Then she looks at her phone and is surprised to see a blue dot so close to her red one they are almost touching. She taps the screen and the number 66 appears.

'Fuck me,' she says. She looks for him along the top deck of the bus, then presses her forehead to the side window. Dozens of people are walking along the pavement, but the dot on her map is static, and a little further along the road.

'What's going on?'

'I need your advice,' says Anna, angling for a view from the front window instead. 'I joined Kismet.'

'You *joined*?'

'And I've hit a 66. Should I get off the bus?'

'Anna!'

'Relax: this is just a test. Should I get off, or what?'

There is a cold silence from Zahra's end of the line. A bus

parked ahead pulls away, revealing a shelter where a dozen or so people are gathered.

'This is a very bad idea.'

'Come on, we're about to leave. Shall I get off or stay on? The number is 66. Six six.'

Zahra sighs, then repeats the number aloud a few times.

'Do you have a visual?'

'I can't see shit.'

'Then you should stay.'

'I'm staying,' says Anna, as the engine rumbles to life. 'Thanks. I've forgotten the etiquette.'

'I still don't approve. And I'm going.'

'I thought you were riding home with me?'

'I never said that. And Keir's just got in.'

'But we need to discuss my birthday. I've found proof, you know.'

'Later.'

'I'm thinking we can hire a boat?'

Her phone emits a harsh beep, the sound of a wrong answer, and the small picture of Zahra's face disappears from her screen. The bus edges away from the kerb and Anna stares out the window, trying to get a clear look at the 66, but the light is poor and the shelter crowded – the people appear like letters printed over each other on the page. The bus accelerates, and the blue dot drifts away from her red dot, until it reaches the edge of her brightly lit circle, the fixed extent of Kismet's reach, and vanishes into the shaded area beyond.

Anna turns around in her seat. Since she's almost home she decides to log out of Kismet altogether, but before doing so she pinches at the screen, making her lit-up circle shrink in proportion to the washed-out and darkened streets around it. She pinches again and is surprised that the map zooms out to show an entire view of London, her fifty-metre circle now smaller than a pinprick. She pinches again and sees the UK within Europe, then Europe surrounded by Africa and the Atlantic and Asia, and finally the round Earth floating in black space. Anna smiles. It seems ridiculous to have designed such a feature, but she thinks about the amount of money and time it must have cost, and has a sudden yearning to know more about the Kismet programmer who decided, perhaps on a romantic whim, to spend their time making it this way.

Anna is at her desk, holding her phone at a tilted angle so that Ingrid, five feet to her left, can't see the map on her screen. The circle contains her floor of the office – an expanse of almost a hundred people – a central portion of Great Marlborough Street, a slice of Oxford Street and, in fact, since the circle is actually a sphere, hundreds of co-workers on the three floors above and two below. In all this, there are no blue dots.

It is disappointing. When she last used Kismet, almost four years ago, she seemed to make at least one match every time she logged on, more often two, sometimes three. There was even one dizzying occasion, on the dance floor of a club in Hackney, when she checked her phone and the cluster of blue dots resembled a cartoon bunch of grapes. She would like to think that since then her personality has become more refined and mature, or that there are simply fewer single people, but she is nagged by a more sinister explanation: perhaps the information Kismet is compiling and sifting – the websites she visits, the playlists she creates, the items she buys, the pictures she likes, the people she befriends; in short, everything – is generating a scrambled signal, one ridden with contradictions, that will match her with deviants and fringe dwellers, reclusive creeps and sleazy older men.

'Hey, Ing?'

'Hmmm-mmm?' says Ingrid. She is typing rapidly with

all her fingers, while her eyes scan along lines of shorthand in a notebook propped on a tiny lectern.

'How long . . .' says Anna, and then stops. She was about to ask how long Ingrid was online before she met her boyfriend, but this is too personal a question, almost rude. Instead, she asks how long Ingrid's boyfriend Sam is around for.

For a moment Ingrid doesn't react at all, simply carries on typing, and it isn't until she finishes a sentence or reaches some other break point that she turns in her chair and gives her full smiling attention to Anna. She says that Sam only has one week before he returns to the Amazon for his next film shoot, and that they are squeezing every drop out of the time they have left; last weekend they rented a farmhouse and went to the third oldest pub in the country.

'They had a well *in* the pub,' she says, beaming with North American enthusiasm for the quaint English countryside. 'Like, full of water at the bottom. An actual *well*.'

Anna considers telling Ingrid that all rural pubs have wells, but Ingrid continues with a description of the house they rented, complete with heated pool; in her mind's eye, Anna sees various pictures of Ingrid and Sam and their friends messing about in the pub and jumping into the pool, imagined precursors to the real pictures she'll see later on Instagram or Facebook. Almost every week there is a gallery of Ingrid and her friends going mad at superclubs, festivals and warehouse parties, or else there will just be pictures of her and Sam lounging around their flat, enjoying outrageously healthy breakfasts, and often looking like they have just had or are just about to have sex. They probably got some ridiculous score, a 78 or 79.

'Why do you ask?'

'It's my birthday next week,' she says, ad-libbing, and Ingrid says she hadn't forgotten and that sadly Sam can't make it. Then she smiles and returns to her computer, tucking one foot beneath her other thigh, in a position that looks vaguely yogic to Anna. A second later her fingers are rattling against the keys, and her hair – a pile of hazel-brown curls – wobbles slightly as she types. Just above the collar of her white linen shirt, Anna can see the curved tip of a small tattoo that means 'calm' in Sanskrit. Over her shoulder, she sees the copy firing out across the page, something about Taiwan's tallest skyscraper. Ingrid is writing a series of articles on Asian cities, sponsored by Hyundai, and her latest piece – a feature on the insanely difficult exams faced by Singaporean twelve-year-olds, complete with example questions – went viral and made it to the top of the big board, with over ten million hits.

Anna looks up at the big board – which is visible to everyone on the news floor, regardless of where they are standing or sitting – and sees that 'Singapore Steel' is now in fourteenth place, with 1835 readers inside the story this very second, just behind a report on the launch of the new Kismet Love Test. She looks from the board down to one of the TV screens displaying rolling news, which happens to be filled with the smiling face of Raymond Chan, Kismet CEO, at his latest press conference, presumably as he denies the accusations that the retrospective Love Test will cause unnecessary disruption to people's lives. Finally she looks down to her own notepad and list of things to do, the most pressing of which is to come up with captions for a picture gallery of the world's most expensive race horses. She settles down to make a start, and as she does so a message from Stuart appears on her screen, asking her to come for a chat in the Quiet Room, 'ASAP'.

The message sets off an anxious reverberation in Anna's stomach, like the faint beginning of a drum roll. She scans the email for hints that she might be in trouble – and her memory for something she might be in trouble for – then takes her notepad and walks across the clearing in the centre of the office. As she comes into line with the glass-fronted meeting rooms, she can make out Stuart's crouched shoulders and the back of his balding head. Stuart doesn't have his own office – no one does – but in recent months he has spent so much time in the Quiet Room that everyone has gradually stopped using it for impromptu catch-ups and phone calls, even when he isn't there.

'Stuart?' she says, opening the glass door.

'Anna,' he says, without looking up from his laptop. His sky-blue shirt is exactly the same colour as all his other shirts and, as always, makes Anna feel childish in her jumper and jeans. 'You came right away?'

'You said ASAP,' she says, hovering by the door.

'Exactly: ASAP, not *right away*. But you're here now. Just let me send this.'

Anna rounds the table and sits opposite Stuart as he frowns at his keyboard. She rarely sees what an ugly typist he is, using only his fat index fingers, which float around in search of each letter before hammering it much harder than necessary. On either side of his round head she can see through the glass wall the entire floor, with the big board and TV screens at the far end and Ingrid sat in the centre, next to the space where she'd normally be. She imagines herself seen from this distance, a small blonde dot in the centre of the office, and tries to think of recent submissions that caused problems; there was an incident when she confused the princesses Eugenie and

13

Beatrice, and then a photo gallery on speedboats through the ages that was riddled with technical errors, and prompted a troll to speculate that the captions were actually 'written by a monkey'.

'All done,' he says, with an emphatic final hit. Then he looks across at her and, surprisingly, for him, smiles. It is a serene, contented expression, vaguely creepy but also reassuring, since it suggests she isn't in too much trouble. 'So then, Anna: how's your day looking? Got much on?'

'Bits and bobs.'

'Good,' he says, still smiling. 'I suppose you've seen the news?'

'Umm. I don't think so. What?'

His smile falters.

'You haven't checked your emails?'

'No. I mean yes, I have, but maybe I missed something.'

'Right,' he says, sighing, and a more familiar expression crosses his face; it is the same resigned look she detects whenever he appears behind her desk and catches her adjusting a Spotify playlist or searching for cheap flights, as if a pessimistic theory has once again been proved correct. 'If you *had* read your emails, you'd have seen a message from Romont, approving the Women at the Top series.'

He spins his laptop around on the table and Anna reads for herself the email from the marketing team at Romont, saying they would love to sponsor the Women at the Top series, and describing in gushing terms how excited they all are about it. It is surprising to read this from a woman that Anna had thought hated the idea during the pitch; she sat there with an askew look on her face while Paula and Stuart explained why a ten-article series on powerful women would be ideal to promote Romont's latest range of watches, as if she was contending with a bad smell.

'This is amazing,' says Anna, and her response appears to amuse Stuart.

'Don't sound too surprised.'

'No, I'm not. I'm . . . *impressed*. Well done. Good job.'

'It's Paula's baby, really. And it was a team effort. Yourself included.'

'Please. I barely said a word between hello and goodbye.'

'But you brought a certain energy. Paula thought so too. And we've had a little chat. We think this could be good for you, if you're ready. As lead writer.'

The atmosphere changes, as if all the air has been sucked from the room.

'Me?'

'If you're ready.'

'But I thought Ingrid—'

'Ingrid is tied up with the Hyundai series. And this will be exciting. Paula has had Clem pull some strings. We've got Sahina Bhutto lined up for the first interview. Gwyneth Paltrow for the second.'

'Sahina Bhutto?' says Anna. The name sounds almost too big to get her lips around.

Some concern must pass across her face, because Stuart explains in soothing tones that he's sure she isn't so fierce in real life, and that they have until Friday to agree on the questions, which in any case will be pegged to Romont's brand values of power, ambition and sophistication.

'There'll also be more money, naturally. Just a little sweetener, four or five K.'

'Right,' says Anna, feeling slightly dazed. 'Great.'

'You don't seem too pleased.'

'No, I am,' she says, stretching her smile into a full nodding grin. 'Uh-huh.'

'Because I need you to be up for this. Ready for this.'

'Yes.'

'You're ready?'

'I'm ready.'

There is a slight pause as he stares into her eyes, then he smiles again, the same creepy warm smile that he gave when she first sat down.

'Great,' he says, clapping as if to punctuate the air. 'It's great to have you on board. So about the launch: I just had a three-way with Paula and Romont, and we want to hang it off something newsy. Perhaps a list of the world's most powerful women, with a little bio of each. What do you think?'

'Sure,' she says, still somewhat light-headed. 'Sounds great.'

'Excellent. Get the copy done by ... what are we on? Eleven thirty? I'll tell Romont to expect the copy for sign-off by ... 5 p.m.'

'Oh. You mean *today*?'

'Of course. We'll have the guys in Charlotte work up the design overnight, publish tomorrow morning. Clear your diary, this is big.'

'The world's most powerful women,' she says, standing up. She looks through the glass wall at Ingrid and the big board and the TV screens and all her other colleagues criss-crossing on the clearing – the office appears a tangle of distractions, interruptions, eavesdroppers. She asks Stuart if it's okay to take the pool laptop to a cafe, so she can really concentrate, and he just shrugs and shakes his head, as if he couldn't begin to muster an opinion on such a trivial issue.

'But one more thing,' he says, pointing his finger at her as she goes to leave. 'Do it by continent. You know, the most powerful women in Asia, Africa, Europe. So it's not just a list of Americans.'

'By continent,' she says, nodding. 'Also, by the way . . . what do we mean by power?'

He looks at her in confusion.

'You know. *Power.* Money. Wealth. Influence. Just . . . work it out.'

'Right,' she says, nodding vigorously, as if everything is now clear, lest he ask her if she is ready again. 'Power. Got it.'

'And Anna,' he says, making her pause with the door held open. 'Congratulations.'

The word rings in her ears as she crosses the clearing to her desk, where she stands absently for a moment, her hands resting on the back of her chair. Then she goes to sign out the pool laptop from where it lives in the cabinet, and is informed by Jessica, office assistant, that the rules have changed and she isn't allowed to take it off site unless it's an 'emergency'. Anna thinks she has a miniature battle on her hands, but at that moment Paula appears and grabs her arm.

'I'm so proud of you,' she says, beaming up at her. Paula is tiny – her cornrows are only level with Anna's shoulder – but it is nevertheless overwhelming to be manhandled by her boss's boss in front of the whole office. 'You're going to nail it, I just know it.' Paula says more things like this, and Anna feels alarmed by the intimacy they imply – their only real interaction until now was at last year's summer party, where they were placed together at the dinner table, and due to some physiological fluke Anna found herself in a charming and boisterous and flirtatious mood. But before she has a chance to say something self-deprecating and witty, or even to thank her, Paula says she has to rush off – she is forever in the process of heading somewhere else – and stomps away towards the lifts. She returns her attention to Jessica, who doesn't raise another word of resistance concerning the laptop.

'What the hell's going on?' says Ingrid, when Anna returns to her desk. While putting on her coat, she tells her about the Women at the Top series and the list she has been asked to do. Without delay Ingrid swivels her chair around to face Anna and asks who the interviews are with.

'The first is Sahina Bhutto,' says Anna, trying to sound casual. 'And then Gwyneth Paltrow.'

Ingrid's eyes open wide.

'That's . . . amazing, Anna.' She smiles as she says this, but there is an unmistakable confused tightness around her eyes, as if the natural order of things has been messed with. Ingrid then stands to hug Anna, who maintains her stiff smile and wonders if she should feel offended by the younger woman's reaction, and the surprise it contains. Though maybe she will have to get used to people reacting like this. From now on, whenever she tells people she's a journalist, and they ask what sort of thing, she will mention Gwyneth Paltrow or Sahina Bhutto and it will knock their heads back slightly, as if she has suddenly expanded in front of them and they have to adjust their eyes to keep her in focus.

'Thanks, Ing,' she says, before taking her bag and walking across the clearing. There are yet more colleagues waiting by the lifts, and it is not until she pushes through to the bland stairwell that the smile drops from her face. By the time she is thirty, she will have interviewed Sahina Bhutto, she tells herself, as she swings on the railing from one flight to the next, the sound of her footsteps clattering around the bare cinderblock walls. In fact, no: by the time she is thirty her article on Sahina Bhutto will have *been published*. She tells herself that this is amazing, fantastic – uses all the same terms as Paula and Ingrid – but this does not dislodge the feeling that something is wrong, badly wrong. The reverberation in her stomach that began when she anticipated bad news is still there following the good news, only stronger now. For this is a mistake, surely, based on a misapprehension that will soon become clear to everyone. She doesn't feel ready, not even slightly.

On the ground floor she pushes through the double doors into the lobby, and the glinting surfaces of marble and tempered glass, and past the long sofas where she sat three years ago, awaiting an interview for an unpaid internship. She imagines what that younger Anna would think if she were somehow gifted a snapshot of herself today, having been made lead writer, and for the first time she gains a sense of perspective, and a dose of pride. Of course she feels unready, and undeserving. Just as she did three years ago, when Malcolm, Stuart's predecessor, asked her to take minutes in a meeting, and she didn't capture everyone's name or understand the acronyms or write fast enough, and spent the following days in a quiet panic as she tried, like some kind of archaeologist, to piece together her scribbled fragments into a coherent record of what had been discussed and decided. This memory makes her smile and realise there is nothing wrong or unexpected about being scared. How is anyone supposed to become successful, anyway, without having to undergo a series of leaps forwards that at first appear impossible, but which quickly become as mundane as everything else? As it was with taking minutes, so it will be with interviewing celebrities.

This brave thought follows her through the revolving doors and onto the street, the sudden daylight making her eyes throb. As always, the narrow pavement is crammed with dithering tourists and a much faster stream of professional types, and today Anna tells herself to walk amongst them with her head held high. She zigzags through the current of people with their expensive coats and haircuts, each one coming into focus for a fraction of a second before blurring past, and up ahead she catches sight of a young blond guy in a mustard wax jacket. His face is a mere pink smudge from her distance, but something about his shape or gait speaks to her. As he nears, a rather severe but striking face comes into view, and their eyes click as they pass, making sparks fly within her. In one fluid motion, Anna stops, turns on her heel and like a gunslinger pulls her phone from her pocket, hoping and half expecting to see him do the same. But she watches his back proceed along the pavement towards Regent Street, and when she opens Kismet the map shows nothing but the usual empty network of beige buildings and grey streets.

Five hours later, Anna is sitting in a cafe on Poland Street, wondering if Mexico is in South America or North America, or if Central America is a continent in its own right. She sits back and sucks on her pen and looks around the cafe, where five other people are sitting at individual tables behind Mac-Books of their own, and tries to subdue the familiar rising feeling of a project going wrong.

In front of her, on her screen, are the fifteen most powerful and influential women in the world, arranged neatly in a spreadsheet with a short bio and header and link to an open source and credited image. All this supposed hard work of researching and writing was complete by 3 p.m., slowed down only by the pool laptop's inability to stay connected to the internet, but the simple task of splitting them into continents has proved impossible. It hasn't just been the Mexican pharmaceutical heiress: the Russian cellist and Turkish prime minister have been equally hard to place, and the more she searches online, the more she realises that continents – those supposed building blocks of the world – are actually wispish, changeable things, about which there is no consensus whatsoever.

A bell rings as the cafe door opens, and a tall, bearded man with long hair tied into a bun takes a table by the glass shopfront, becoming customer number six. She watches him unfurl a scarf from his neck and is tempted to sneak a look at her phone, but then sees the clock above the window and that it is 4.40 p.m., and she is twenty minutes from missing her first deadline as lead writer. She tries to call Stuart again but gets his voicemail, and on the swell of panic wonders why this always seems to happen: while Ingrid and everyone else in the office gracefully rise to whatever challenge befalls them, she always buckles and becomes paralysed at the crucial moment. Telling herself to stay calm, she texts Zahra the Mexico question and then opens the Wikipedia page again. This time her eyes snag on the term Latin America, and a possible solution occurs to her: it could be done by region, not continent. Yes, of course. She looks at each woman and this option clears a path through all her niggling doubts: Mexico is in Latin America. Saudi Arabia is in the Middle East. Pakistan is in South Asia. Stuart won't mind, it's probably what he meant anyway. She gets back to work on the spreadsheet, and it is just a matter of relabelling the columns, copy-and-pasting five of her powerful women, and then the finished document is sitting in front of her, and still with ten minutes to spare.

Anna slumps down in her chair and sighs, relief coursing through her like a tonic. She texts Zahra not to worry about the Mexico question, and then, without willing it, opens Kismet. As expected, she sees the solitary dot at the centre of the map, but this time something is different: it is blue rather than red. She zooms in and sees there are in fact two small circles – a blue dot is almost entirely eclipsing her red one, leaving only a thin crescent visible. She taps the blue dot and the number 72 appears. Anna gasps and her eyes shoot around the cafe, landing on the broad back of the long-haired man by the window, customer number six. She zooms in on the map, until her screen is filled entirely with the floor plan of the coffee shop, and sees that yes, it must be him.

Anna sits up in her chair and puts down her phone and takes conscious control of her breathing. It is going to happen; he is bound to see any minute, if he hasn't already. There is turmoil in her stomach, and a powerful urge to flee. But this is a 72, and a handsome one at that, and she resolves to see it through. She moves things around on her table and fusses with her fringe and wraps her chewing gum in an old receipt that she hides in her bag. It occurs to her that she has time to check her appearance in the toilet mirror, but she decides there is no need: she is wearing her favourite charcoal woollen jumper, black jeans and her hair tied up – she knows she looks alright. The only regrettable items are her scuffed and tired boots, which will remain under the table. She places her hands on either side of her laptop and wills herself to be calm, to be cool. After a few moments there is a shuffling in her peripheral vision, and when she looks across he has turned in his seat, his eyes waiting for hers. She smiles, he stands. She looks back at her laptop, and the key stats and life stories of billionaires and politicians and scientists swim in front of her.

'Hello,' he says, standing beside her table.

'Hi.'

'I'm Thomas.'

'Anna.'

For a moment they just look at each other. He is really quite handsome. His olive skin and long hair and slightly hooked nose make him look like a pirate, but not in a bad way. And even more striking are his green eyes, which are so large and wide that it almost feels like he is glaring at her.

'You have time?' he says, and she notices an accent.

'Of course,' she says, gesturing to the seat opposite. Then, remembering the powerful women, she adds: 'I just have to send an email.'

He pauses mid-crouch, frowning.

'I go and come back?'

'No, sit! It will take literally one minute. It will be like we're having a little break. Just at the start.' She laughs nervously. 'We'll be *starting* with a break.'

Thomas nods slowly, then sits and hails the barista to inform him of his changed location. Anna swears inwardly, and then, in a single stream of thought, she drafts an email to Stella and Carl at Romont, copies in Stuart and Paula, attaches the Power Women spreadsheet and presses send. A picture of a small piece of paper appears on her screen, which folds itself into an aeroplane before pinging off into the distance. This animation loops three times before it says that the message has not been sent because she is not connected to the internet.

'Fucking pool laptop,' she says, and Thomas asks what is the matter. She tells him about her day-long battle to keep online, and how she has to send the email by 5 p.m., and he asks to have a look. He spins the computer so they can both see the screen, and after bringing up the control panel and network settings he says, 'Ah.' Then he explains, his accent now unmistakably French, that there is something wrong with the configuration, and that he can fix it.

'Yes, please do.'

'I will have to restart it.'

'That's fine. Just do it, please.'

He unticks a box, ticks another, and they watch in silence as the screen shuts down to black before gradually bringing itself to life again. When the desktop finally lights up, not only is the internet displaying full bars, but the email she had tried to send is sitting in her outbox. It is simply a matter of pressing one button, and then the paper aeroplane flies off into the distance and is replaced by a 'message sent' sign.

'Thanks so much,' she says, slapping the laptop shut. 'I owe you a massive favour already.'

'It was nothing. I only unticked a box. I'm not even good with computers.'

'Well . . . I owe you an apology, then. That was a bad start.'

He wafts this away as well and says that these meetings always catch people unawares, and that it could have been a lot worse – they could have been jogging, or at the gym, or in a dental surgery, or on a plane, or at a packed concert.

'Sounds like you've had some colourful situations,' she says.

'*Mais non*. Just examples! I have had hardly any situations at all. This is just my . . . fifth meeting.'

'In how long?'

'Six months.'

'Six *months*?' The admission is so surprising that Anna can't contain her incredulity, and she laughs out loud until she catches herself and bites her lip in contrition. But he doesn't seem fazed by her reaction, or when she has him confirm and double-confirm that it's really been that long. She sees that his eyes are always very wide, even when relaxed; the full circle of each green iris floats freely in white.

'I suppose that is not many matches,' he says, with a shrug.

'Not many, no.'

'Well . . . I take it as a compliment.'

'So you should.'

'And the good thing is,' he says, leaning forwards and crossing his meaty forearms on the table, 'that when you *do* make a match, you know it is for a reason.' He gazes into her eyes directly, then sits back and sips his coffee and adds casually: 'Plus, you save time.'

'Of course,' says Anna, smiling at him. She recognises his counter-intuitive logic as the kind she would pass off in a different context – at work, say, where she likes to be on the subversive side of arguments and to say things that make Ingrid look at her slantwise, unsure if she's joking or not. It is as if the first evidence of their compatibility has unfolded in front of her, and she thinks that she likes this French guy, likes him already. This thought feels premature, though, and she chases it away by asking if his other four matches have been with English or French girls.

'English, always. But it is not surprising. I prefer speaking English.'

'How come?'

'Speaking French is too easy. It is like—' He delivers a rapid flurry of French while moving his hand around; he speaks so fast that Anna, who spent the second year of her degree in Grenoble and was once almost fluent, doesn't catch a word. 'You see? It comes pouring out, word after word of French. It is like breathing air. With English I have to feel every word.'

Anna asks if he is in London to speak English ('no, for work'), what his work is ('sound design'), if that has to be in London ('it has to be in Soho'), and where he would live if he had a free choice ('New York'). She asks what he likes about New York so much, and he leans forwards in his chair and says: 'You ask a lot of questions.'

Without blinking Anna leans forwards as well and says: 'I'm a journalist.'

This makes Thomas smile and he asks where she writes; she names the website and he seems impressed. She pre-empts the next question by saying she is a features writer, and that this Friday she'll be interviewing Sahina Bhutto, and Gwyneth Paltrow next week.

'Who is Sahina Bhutto?'

'The architect. You must know. She built the Biscuit Tin. And that building in China that can be seen from space.'

'My general knowledge is not so good.'

'Well, she's a massive deal. And slightly terrifying. And somehow I have to interview her.'

Thomas nods slowly, his mouth downturned in an expression of sombre admiration.

'You are a real writer,' he says.

'I suppose I am. Writing word after word of English. But it's not like breathing air. It's more like pulling teeth.'

Anna feels like elaborating on this comment – the fact that Thomas reacted in a muted way to her description of her job makes her think she can speak freely about it, without the need for the effortful smile; she could probably go as far as saying that she isn't sure she's up to it, or even if she wants to be. But Thomas immediately moves them onwards by saying he likes that expression, 'pulling teeth'. He becomes animated for the first time and says that in France they would say *tirer les vers du nez* – to pull worms from your nose. Anna questions whether the two sayings actually mean the same thing, but Thomas ignores her and names other French idioms: 'to call a cat a cat', 'to put a rabbit on somebody', 'to jump from the chicken to the donkey'. Anna tries explaining white elephants and red herrings, which makes them both laugh, and they hold each other's gaze long after the laughter fades. Anna can feel a powerful stirring in her stomach and wonders if he can as well. His face is blank again, but maybe this belies an abundance of emotion. She has heard of some especially high matches where the couple sat for hours after finding each other, barely saying a word. But this is just a 72, she shouldn't get carried away.

'This is going well,' he says. 'Have a drink with me.'

The suggestion is unexpected: it is only 5.30 p.m. and not even dark outside. It would be nice to think about it, but Thomas is already pulling his jacket on. Anna watches him fasten the buttons right up to the dark hair on his neck, and says that she really should be going. But even to her own ears these words sound weak and hollow, and as he stands up she is reminded of his height, his rugged good looks, his bright green eyes; the number 72 flashes above his head.

27

'Just a quick one,' he says, wrapping his scarf around his neck. 'You did say you owed me a favour.'

They walk up Poland Street and cross Oxford Street into Fitzrovia, Thomas half a step ahead. Anna is irked by her shabby boots, which rather than a solid clop release with each step a sad squish, as if a little air is being forced out. They walk in silence until Thomas says she can start acting like a journalist again, if she wants, and she says he still hasn't answered why New York is his favourite city.

'What is not to like? I mean, it is New York. I like *everything*,' he says, pronouncing it 'ev-we-sing'.

'One thing I'm not mad keen on is the layout,' she says. 'You know, the streets and avenues, the numbers. The whole grid plan.'

'You are the journalist that answers back.'

'All those identical numbered streets, block after block after block. It's so . . . rigid.'

'I haven't thought about it. It just makes sense, no?'

'But wouldn't you find it infuriating, after a while? Having to walk at right angles most of the time?'

'It just makes sense,' he repeats, as if in conclusion. 'Everyone likes the grid plan.'

Anna feels a hardness towards him, which she welcomes as the first steady steps after a spell of dizziness. She'll have one drink, two at the most, and then leave.

'Does that mean you're excluding me from "everyone"?'

He turns away from the question into a doorway that opens to a narrow staircase. They go down to a low-ceilinged bar with chessboard tiles and green leather booths. A waiter in a bow tie takes their order and returns with two small pitchers filled mainly with ice and leaves. Anna finishes hers in four sips while listening to Thomas talk of his work and, at her prompting, his favourite sounds: a musical saw, rain against windows, a mandarin being peeled.

'A mandarin being peeled? That's not a sound.'

'My best of all!' he says, becoming effusive again. 'Like Velcro being pulled, but much softer. It has to be ripe though; there must be air between the skin and flesh. You should try.'

The waiter returns and she agrees to one more – which lasts no longer than the first – and then she goes to the toilet and realises she must quite like him, judging by the relief she feels when she sees in the mirror that her fringe has basically behaved itself. When she returns to the table a third cocktail is waiting for her, accompanied by a mandarin that he must have had the waiter fetch. She peels it close to her ear, but can't hear anything above the recorded jazz and ambient din of the place, and Thomas snatches it back and says it isn't ripe enough. He finishes peeling it and then they eat it together; the process of him passing her segments which she then puts in her mouth feels indecent, almost obscene, something the people on other tables shouldn't have to witness. This episode loosens him up further, and he even becomes chatty, until he makes a mistake: when her phone makes her bag audibly vibrate with a call or message, he calls it a baghand rather than a handbag. She laughs and he looks slightly offended, and invites them to speak *en français*.

'*Pourquoi pas?*' she says. '*J'adore parler français!*'

Thomas seems delighted, and requests that she tell him about herself. Summoning up the remains of her A-level studies and Erasmus year, Anna tells him that she lives in Kilburn but used to live in east London, that she grew up in Bedfordshire, that she has one brother, Josh, who lives in Australia, and – for no better reason than that the French words are there at hand – that her dad died five years ago: '*Mon père est mort il y a cinq ans.*' She ploughs on past this disclosure, telling him she went to university in Sheffield and spent a year in Grenoble, and that before taking up journalism she wanted to set up her own business or social enterprise. It is a sensual pleasure to speak French after so long, like opening the door onto a hitherto boarded-up part of her brain. Her tongue is loosened by booze and, with the help of hand gestures, she even manages to explain one of her old inventions, the Community Shed, a membership scheme where people would pay a small monthly fee for access to a store of high-quality DIY equipment.

'*C'est une super idée,*' says Thomas.

'*Tu penses?*'

'*Oui, vraiment.*'

Anna wonders if he is just lying to be nice, but she can't help believing him, especially when he asks questions: how much she would charge people per month, what type of tools it would stock, where it would be kept. It pleases her that he shows more energetic interest in her pet projects than he did in her professional job, and she decides this is no accident – this is probably precisely the kind of value that Kismet knows about him, about her, about them both. He asks why she never launched the Community Shed, and she stops herself about to say again that her dad died since she realises this wouldn't work as an explanation, in any language.

'*Je ne sais pas,*' is all she says. '*Sans raison.*'

He urges her to tell him another idea, and she tries to explain the online investigation she wanted to launch, to track down the owner of a suitcase that was mysteriously abandoned at Heathrow, and that she later bought at an auction house in Tooting Bec. But the thought of her father was a bump in her flow, has knocked off her fluency, and she struggles to find the words; her mangled translation must do spectacular violence to the intended meaning, for Thomas laughs out loud and says: '*Ça n'a aucun sens!*' Surprisingly, she is offended by this – it is like protective layers have been removed, leaving her sensitive to feeling mocked. Thomas must detect this dip in mood and, perhaps to make amends, he places a hand on hers and shuffles forwards so that their knees connect beneath the table.

'*Maintenant*,' he says, looking around for the waiter. 'We go for food, no?'

Anna considers their joined hands and touching knees; from these two points of contact an electrical charge is running along her limbs to the base of her stomach. She imagines going with him for dinner, for drinks, and getting a taxi back to his.

'I can't.'

'I know a great place,' he says, clicking his fingers for a waiter. Anna tries to rediscover her recent excitement, and focuses on his raised arm and the muscles that undulate beneath the thickly knitted jumper, his green eyes, his height, the number 72. But these observations bounce off glass, create no feeling in her other than guilt.

'I have to go.' She checks her watch and sees that she really does: somehow it is 8.17 p.m. She grabs her coat and bag and slides from the booth.

'But,' says Thomas, seeming innocently and profoundly confused, 'this is going well.'

'Yes,' she says, sliding her arms into her jacket. Then she

sighs and says: 'It *is* going well. *But* . . .' She delivers the word slowly, trying to allude to a whole world of invisible considerations.

'Ah,' he says, seeming to understand. '*But.*'

'Yeah,' she says, taking a £20 note from her purse. 'Another time, maybe.'

'*D'accord*,' he says, slapping his knees and rising from the booth. She tries to put money into his hand and onto the table, but he refuses to let her, and after kissing him on both of his hairy cheeks, she turns and makes for the narrow staircase.

Anna walks to Tottenham Court Road, in the same thoughtless, almost trancelike state she often experiences in the wake of an intense encounter. The sound of her boots thudding against the pavement fills her empty mind and appears to grow louder until it is almost the only thing she can hear. On the tube she swallows one of her pills with a glug of mineral water, and then watches an abandoned newspaper spread across the empty bench opposite her. The sheets are being fluttered by the wind whistling along the carriage, and eventually the breeze gains enough purchase to turn the page entirely, creating the powerful impression that an invisible man is browsing the paper.

Sooner than she'd like, Anna emerges onto Kilburn High Road and walks south beneath the cavernous, dripping railway bridge. It is only just 9 p.m., but the street is dark and quiet and asleep; most shops have their shutters pulled, other than the twenty-four-hour petrol station and the giant pub that Anna has never considered setting foot in, which is alive with football screens and shouting men. She turns onto Cavendish Road and, after a five-minute uphill trudge, onto Mowbray Road, her own terraced street. It is tempting to keep going and do another loop around to the station to walk off the buzz of the cocktails, but she is already late, and after pausing for a moment with her key pointed in front of her, she turns the lock and enters. The front door opens onto a tiny hall space and two more front doors, and she opens the one straight ahead, for the upstairs flat. She creeps up one, two, three steps, then hears the living-room door open.

'There she is,' says Pete, appearing on the landing above her. She reaches the top of the stairs and turns to face him.

'Here I am.'

The landing light isn't on, and Pete's broad frame is backlit from the living room.

'I was getting worried,' he says, crossing his arms and leaning against the wall. He is wearing the same stone-washed jeans and T-shirt as he does on almost all study days, since he doesn't feel the cold, and his stubble has grown curly and tangled, has crossed the threshold between stubble and beard.

'Worried?' she says, unbuttoning her jacket. 'How come?'

'You didn't answer my calls. Or get back to me about dinner. I was picturing worst-case scenarios. Blue flashing lights. A policeman knocking on the door.'

Anna looks fixedly at the pegs on the wall above her and feels like the worst kind of actor – a mere puppet aping the actions of a human – as she takes off her coat and hangs it up.

'Not quite as bad as that,' she says, trying to sound casual. 'Just a quick drink with Zahra.'

'Oh yeah? And how is Zahra?' He says her name with a slight emphasis that makes Anna look at him suddenly: his face is blank, and his broad shoulders seem to span the width of the hallway, blocking her path. For a paranoid moment she wonders if he might somehow know everything, if he has been tracking her movements, but she quickly rejects this as baseless, the product of alcohol and guilt.

'Zahra's good,' she says, as nonchalantly as she can. 'She's busy. Her and Keir are knocking through another wall in their flat.'

'Another one?'

'I know, right? It'll look like a sports hall when they're done with it.'

'If it's standing at all.'

Anna is smiling now, and Pete smiles back in return. It feels like a physical dose of relief to see that he believes her, and has no reason not to. She steps towards him and at once Pete's broad torso swings aside, showing itself to be less a barrier than an obliging gate; he angles his face downwards to tickle her cheek with a kiss as she passes. In the living room one of his textbooks is flattened on the sofa beside the remote control, while on the television a contestant in some cooking show is looking fearful as the judges discuss her chocolate mousse. Anna goes to the corner between the bookcase and sofa and plugs her phone into the charger that shares a socket with the freestanding lamp. She checks to see if Thomas has already messaged and is pleased to see he hasn't, since Pete has followed her into the room, and now asks if she wants any of the leftover dinner.

'What is there?' says Anna, still holding her phone with her back to him, wondering if it might be better to simply keep the thing switched off.

'What do you want it to be? Would you prefer meat or fish?'

'Fish.'

'If you'd said meat, would you prefer white meat or red meat?'

Anna switches off her phone and turns to Pete, who is leaning against the door jamb, a hint of mischief around his mouth. He is often playful and energetic on the evenings of his study days, when she imagines he probably doesn't say anything to anyone, other than the few words that are necessary to buy things in shops.

'Hmm. White.'

'If you'd said red meat, would you prefer lamb, or steak?'

'I'd take the lamb.'

'If you'd said beef, would you prefer steak, or some kind of mince-based, sauce-drenched, overly spiced meatball thing?'

'Steak,' she says, and he claps his hands.

'Well, my darling, tonight you are in luck.'

She rolls her eyes but can't help smiling as she walks past him towards the hall, and in actual fact the idea of a meaty, salty steak chimes with some boozy craving. But in the kitchen she is surprised to find a big bowl of green and beige stuff, in which thinly sliced steak is mixed together with numerous pulses and leaves and tiny seeds and that fancy grain dish that Pete and Zahra are always raving about – pearl barley or quinoa or giant couscous – but that obscurely reminds Anna of frogspawn. Pete has followed her and is once again watching from the doorway.

'It's cold?' she says.

'It's a salad.'

'What are those red things?'

'Pomegranate seeds.'

'And those little tendril bits?'

'If you don't want it, it's fine – I can have it tomorrow for lunch.'

She stirs the intricate mush with a wooden spoon, and decides that she doesn't want it; she feels guilty to realise that she'd rather eat nothing at all.

'I might just make something quick and simple?' she says, grimacing as she looks at him, as if for permission. 'Maybe some noodles?'

'Noodles!' he repeats, as if he finds the word amusing. She says again that she'd like something light, and shrugs, averting her eyes. He sighs and after a pause in which she can almost feel him manually overriding his annoyance, he says it's fine, that he can have it for lunch tomorrow. It is a long moment before he speaks again, during which time Anna switches on the radio and opens the fridge and cupboard, gathering a pack of dried noodles, a red onion, half a yellow pepper. As she takes a chopping board and begins dicing the onion, Pete begins telling her about his day, and how the head teacher of a school in Acton where he did work experience has offered him a job once he passes his exams, if he wants it. On Radio 4 is a panel show about the ethics of placebo medicine.

'That's . . . good,' she says, taking the wok from the dish rack and putting it over a high heat. Her answer lacks conviction so she repeats that it is good – *really* good – and realises she will have to tell him her own news from today; for some reason the prospect makes her suddenly tired.

'I had some news as well,' she says. 'At work we pitched for this series to Romont, you know, the watchmakers. For a whole series on powerful women. And they, like, have asked me to lead on it . . . '

She flicks her eyes at Pete and he nods and says, 'Yeah? So that means . . . '

'It means I'll have to interview all these big-shot women. Starting with Sahina Bhutto. And the week after that, Gwyneth Paltrow.'

'Gwyneth *Paltrow*?'

'Uh-huh,' she says, continuing to fuss around the stove, pouring water from the boiling kettle, adding chopped pepper to the wok, not making eye contact with Pete.

'It's just . . . it's incredible, Anna.'

'It should be good,' is all she says, and then begins pushing vegetables around the wok with a wooden spatula; the onions are already beginning to colour at the edges and oil is spitting up at her. She doesn't look away from the stove, as if the process requires her full attention, since she can tell that Pete's eyes are searching for hers in emotion. A moment passes, then he clears his throat and asks when 'all this' is starting; she says she'll interview Sahina this coming Friday, and the article will go live a week later.

'On your birthday?' he says, and laughs. 'How about that?'

Anna says nothing. She picks up a packet of noodles and tries to open them, but the plastic slips through her greasy fingers.

'This is a massive achievement, Anna,' says Pete. 'A real milestone.'

'Not really. I'm pretty sure it was my boss's boss's idea to give it to me; I don't think Stuart would have wanted to.'

'Well . . . better to be liked by the big boss than the little boss.'

'But I think she only likes me because I flirted with her at a party last year.'

Rather than respond, Pete just smiles at her in a knowing, patronising way, as if it is typical that she would downplay something like this, to try and squirm away from receiving any praise. Anna would like to say more – how for some reason she isn't proud or even pleased – but she doesn't have the words at hand to explain such a statement, or the energy to find them. Again she tries to open the packet of noodles, this time with her teeth, but the plastic refuses to give. Her fingers smell of mandarin peel.

'About your birthday: have you sent the invites yet?'

'Just a save-the-date email.'

'But it's next week.'

'I know when my birthday is.'

The boiling water is turning over furiously in the pan, and the vegetables in the wok are beginning to char. Anna takes up the carving knife and decides to stab at the noodle packet instead.

'I was thinking about what food to get in. How about something Spanish-themed? Maybe we could start with gazpacho, and then perhaps one of those spinach and ricotta tartlets, before a big paella?'

The knife slices easily into the plastic wrapping, but it becomes stuck on the glued seam of the wrapper and refuses to go further. The water in the pan will soon burn away to nothing. She grips the knife and pushes harder.

'Or maybe a big seafood thing? A series of platters. Smoked fish. Dressed crabs. Crayfish, langoustine, mussels. Though you'd have to decide soon, so I can speak to the fishmongers. How many are we expecting? Eight? Or else I could get up early and go to Billingsgate on the day, and then—'

'Oww!'

38

Anna drops the knife on the work surface and grips her left wrist. The blade cut through the plastic and into thin air, slicing the tip of her left index finger on the way. She holds her hand up and looks at the scarlet bead that has sprouted, which trickles down her finger.

'Careful!' says Pete. She goes to the sink and he steps towards her, turning off the hob on the way. 'Are you okay?'

'It's just a nick,' she says, holding her finger under the cold tap.

'Let me see,' he says, laying a palm on her back.

'It's *fine*,' she says, with edge. 'Just give me some space.' His hand flinches from her back. There is a moment of hesitation, then she hears him step out of the kitchen, walk along the hallway and close the living-room door. She looks down at the brushed steel sink, watching the blood turn to rusty streaks before disappearing down the plug hole.

Two hours later, Anna and Pete are sitting at their usual ends of the living-room sofa, as another edition of *Newsnight* – which Anna watches daily, in an attempt to persuade herself that she isn't missing anything – rounds off to its dreary conclusion. To her right, Pete has been slipping steadily towards a horizontal position and yawning regularly, and he slips yet further as she takes the remote and switches to BBC News 24, but doesn't rouse and leave the room. To her left, above and behind her shoulder, her phone is charging on the bookshelf, switched off and inert, yet emanating a dense presence. The story comes up about the new Kismet Love Test, and the face of Raymond Chan fills the TV, saying with a smile that the accusations are preposterous, that they haven't done anything wrong – she switches to Al Jazeera instead. They watch the weather man talk of a mini spring heatwave heading for the UK, then Pete makes a final exclamatory yawn, slaps his hand on the arm of the sofa and announces he is off. Anna says she will be up in a minute, that she wants to watch the headlines. This is not entirely untrue, but as soon as she hears Pete finish up in the bathroom and then scale the ladder to the loft bedroom, she takes her phone and switches it on. She senses that Thomas will have sent a message – and knows that the curiosity will interfere with any attempt to sleep – and indeed when her screen comes to life it makes the distinctive, attenuated buzz of an incoming Kismet message.

Thomas 72: *Nice to meet you tonight, shame you leave so soon. I can't stop thinking about you! It was worth the wait for match number 5! Dinner at weekend? T x*

Anna reads the message a few times, and the idea of meeting him again stirs the embers of her earlier excitement. She raises her fingers to her nose and finds they still smell of mandarin peel, even after a shower. And she is also struck by the surprising idea that spending the night with him might be a pragmatic, even prudent thing to do. Perhaps going through the motions of meeting up, getting drunk, going to his, getting naked and then having sex – those routine steps that seem so complex and audacious with a stranger – will flush all the doubts from her system and leave her calm, clear-headed, decisive. Kismet doesn't have any profile pictures, and she tries to bring forth an image of Thomas in her mind. She see him standing before her at the cafe, and when he helped her connect to the internet, but this just directs her thoughts to the Power Women lists, and Thomas is immediately forgotten: instead she wants to know if Romont have replied to her email, and what they might have said; a chirpy, positive appraisal of her spreadsheet will be a much better way to round off the day, and send her towards a contented, satisfied sleep. She logs out of Kismet and opens her work emails, and at the top of the inbox is a red-flagged message from Stuart, sent at 6.27 p.m. It is a three-sentence note, addressed to the Romont marketing team and with Anna in CC, assuring them there must be a 'simple explanation' and promising it 'won't happen again'. Anna flicks down to the previous message, from Carl at Romont, sent at 5.33 p.m., thanking Anna for the lists but wondering if she could double-check if Mexico really was in South America.

'What the . . .'

Beneath Carl's message is Anna's initial email, sent at 4.59 p.m. She opens the attachment and sees the fifteen women split into six continents – North America, South America, Europe, Asia, Africa and Australasia – without any of her final rearrangements. For a moment she feels indignant, as if she has been the victim of some unfair technical malfunction, enacted by a malign authority that deliberately tripped her up. It is impossible: she remembers making the final changes, Thomas coming over, it failing to send, restarting the computer. But did she save the changes? She must have done, surely. Though maybe not. In fact, since the changes aren't there, almost definitely not. That is all there is to it: simple human error. Like the time when the plagiarism filter caught her out for foolishly lifting a line from Wikipedia, or when she misidentified a rare species of tropical frogs as toads. Just a simple, human error.

Her heart is beating painfully in her chest, and she wants to make amends immediately. She writes an email to the whole team, apologising for the mix-up, saying she attached the wrong document. But she realises it will look crazy coming so late, and deletes it. Then she begins writing a shorter note to Stuart, with Paula copied in, to say sorry and that she'll sort it first thing. But even this will look crazy, and will ultimately achieve nothing. So instead she deletes this, and sits there, until the screen on her phone switches itself off and she lets it fall into her lap.

A moment later, Raymond Chan appears on the news again, denying any wrongdoing. She turns him off too and sits in the half-dark, the room's furniture faintly lit by the orange streetlight filtering through the blinds. The clock on the wall shows it is one minute to midnight. The end of yet another day, she thinks. But it doesn't feel like it; her heart is thumping and her nerves are frayed and her eyes are wet with tears. Sleep is hours away. It's not the end of the day: it's the beginning of the night.

Wednesday

On Wednesday evening Anna runs herself a bath. It is easily the most appealing of the methods for inducing sleep she has read about on NHS Choices, including breathing exercises and drinking warm milk and doing press-ups and having sex. She gets in and gingerly attaches her expensive Swedish headphones – principal gift of her last birthday – to the laptop placed on the tiles, from which Spotify offers up recommended tracks based on her own personal playlists. Spotify has an uncanny knack of anticipating her moods. Most nights – whether she is in the bath or lying on the sofa or merely sitting in the dark – she can close her eyes and imagine she is within a pitch-black chamber of music, the insistent beat and soaring chords of some minimal dance track opening up landscapes of emotion within her, whole rolling storm clouds of feeling. Or else some unexpected classic from ten years ago will pitch her deep into a remembered situation, of playing DJ at one of the countless impromptu after-parties they threw in the flat she shared with Zahra in Hackney. Anna would usually position herself behind the laptop on the kitchen counter, combing playlists for the track so timely and welcome and familiar that it brought hoots of pleasure from the four-person dance floor – the Minuscule of Sound, they used to call these parties – and other slumped bodies, long since unconscious, were suddenly reanimated and leaping around in delight.

But tonight it doesn't work. Each song that Spotify suggests is either timeworn and overplayed – its magic long since depleted – or unknown and obscure, and she keeps reaching out of the bath and skipping to the next track. Even when she does find a song she likes, it doesn't transport her anywhere; she remains doggedly lying in hot water, her face flushed and beaded with sweat, and surrounded on all sides by concerns, worries, unpleasant memories. Even her toes poking out of the milky water at the far end of the bath are a provocation. For how many times has she reflected on their chipped blood-red nail polish, half grown out, and decided to repaint them? And how many times has this decision been overtaken by a much more pressing concern, as it is tonight, when the memory of being called into the Quiet Room pops into her mind. Stuart didn't get mad or raise his voice at her for sending the wrong Power Women list, as she had feared, but in a way it was worse how he described the situation as 'embarrassing' – for Stuart being embarrassed seems a form of torture – and had her reaffirm that she was 'on top' of the Sahina interview, and really was 'ready for this'. This meeting left her in an agitated mood that continued until lunch, when she had an ill-tempered WhatsApp exchange with Zahra after she asked her advice about Thomas 72's invite to dinner. Worst of all was coming home to Pete, who once again had cooked her dinner, and lying to him about a plan to meet up with Caz and Hamza on Saturday night. Getting the words out was hard enough, but even worse was the enthusiastic way he accepted, as if his only concern was for her to be happy. Just remembering the trusting way he smiled is enough to make her guilt gather to an agonising pitch, and she thinks that maybe she can't go through with it, she just can't.

To try and shake off this feeling she removes her head-phones, yanks the plug, climbs out of the bath, pats herself dry, takes a pill, brushes her teeth. While doing this she tells herself that she has little to feel guilty about anyway: this is just a test, after all, and nothing has even happened. And if she does feel guilty, isn't that a good thing as well, proof she isn't serious?

Somewhat calmed, she steps shivering out of the steamed bathroom and climbs the ladder to the loft bedroom. It is not yet 11.30 p.m., but Pete is already heaving in sleep. Anna pulls on her vest and shorts, ties her damp hair in a bun, switches off the side lamp, slips into bed and closes her eyes.

She doesn't sleep. Or she does, for a moment, only to experience a sudden sensation of falling and then waking again with a jerk. Then she lies there, wide awake and newly energised, as if her few seconds of sleep were a power nap. She turns onto her left side but can't get comfortable; it feels like her muscles and blood and bones are charged with a sour energy, as if on a deep level her body knows something is awry. To discreetly masturbate would help distract her mind and dissipate some tension, but she knows she won't make it: she had a glass of wine before her bath, and one drink is enough to stop her coming, though Zahra and Pete both separately insist that this problem is merely in her head. But then, Anna always counters, what *isn't* in her head? She turns again onto her back, this time with the duvet and pillow configured in such a way as to give back the sound of her own pulse, and then onto her right side, so she is facing Pete, his silhouette just visible in the navy-blue dark. As if in response to her shifting, his breathing changes: his lips part and his tongue clacks softly with each breath. Anna thinks of what Ingrid told her, that her and Sam's default sleeping position is to lie with their bodies entwined, her head on his chest and his arm looping around her back. She tries to remember the last time she and Pete slept like that, or if they ever did, and at that moment he snores. It is a singular snore, one long strangled breath that rattles in his mouth, but it is enough to make the number appear unbidden in Anna's mind – 70 – and she sighs and is up and out of bed and getting into her dressing gown, her hope of sleep abandoned.

In the kitchen she reaches to the back of the cupboard for the bottle of expensive whisky, hailing from the mystical-sounding island of Jura, a Christmas present from Pete's parents, and pours herself a finger with a clink of ice. She has made good use of the bottle in recent weeks, halving its contents through these solitary midnight nips. She wonders what Pete will think when he sees it, and is always tempted to refill the bottle with a quick blast from the cold tap. But to do so would be to cross an important threshold and admit there is a problem, which there isn't, and so the untampered bottle goes back into the cupboard.

She picks up her laptop from the bathroom on the way to the living room, bundles herself into a ball on the sofa and spends an hour researching Sahina Bhutto. Most articles contain a cursory overview of Sahina's background and main projects – the Biscuit Tin and the stadium in China that can be seen from space – and then pick up the same anecdotes that underpin her fearsome reputation: the time she made an aeroplane turn around in mid-air because she wasn't happy with the flight attendants, and when she dissolved her old firm because they failed to secure a contract. These stories are repeated almost word for word in *Time* and *Newsweek* and *Vogue*, and it feels as if the primary research method was to steal facts from one another. Anna digs deeper, and on the third page of search results finds something interesting – on the RIBA website there is a research paper called 'Sahina Bhutto and the Modernist Condition' by a student from the University of Ohio, which is authoritative, meticulously researched, and dredges up all sorts of information from Sahina's youth in Pakistan and first jobs in America. Anna is inspired to draft ten new questions, and she decides that whatever she does, and however excruciating the interview, she will not simply churn out a repeat of those other mainstream articles. Hers will be different, fresh, revealing, insightful. Maybe if she manages this she will impress Stuart and Paula, who will forgive her for the spreadsheet mix-up, and see that she is ready after all.

She refines the questions and sends them to her work email. Then, feeling like she has achieved something, she goes to the kitchen for another whisky – two fingers this time – and decides to find something relaxing or interesting to look at online before trying to fall asleep again. Her web browser refreshes to a news digest site, with the suggested stories based on her search history. She hesitates before clicking on a story about celebrities with surprisingly high IQs – mindful of what such a selection might do to her Kismet profile – and instead goes to Facebook. She scrolls down through posts and hits Ingrid's pictures from her weekend in the country-side. There are over twenty new photos, and Anna studies each one, beginning with shots from the back seat of a car whizzing along a grey motorway. Then the collected group are in scarves and hats, hiking across a muddy field. Then they are dancing in front of an open fire in a timbered, low-ceilinged living room. Then they are swimming at night in the indoor pool – the place must have been really swish –

and there is a mid-air portrait of each person as they jump spread-eagled into the turquoise water. The final pictures are of a more wholesome dining-room scene, perhaps a hungover lunch the next day, and the sight of a candlelit cake being carried into the room makes Anna experience something akin to a full-body internal wince.

Her own birthday is nine days away. She looks up from the computer screen and across the dark living room to the narrow dining table, and imagines seven or eight friends crowding around it. She imagines them leaving at the end of the night, and being left alone with Pete. The idea releases a bass note of dread – much worse than anything to do with work, or anything at all – and her mind is sent again to that Sunday afternoon a month before, when she was alone in the flat, scrambling around like a crazy person, emptying drawers, pulling cushions off the sofa, turning pockets of hanging coats inside out. All she wanted was a cup of tea. But when the kettle boiled she had found there was no milk. So she had thrown on lounge pants to run to the shop, only to find no more than 27p in her purse, bag and coat, not even enough for a half-pint. Anna hated this: the ramshackle corner shop was just over the road, a minute round trip, while the cash machine was on the high road ten minutes away. She began scouring the flat for change, working through every drawer in the kitchen, every coat in the hallway, then moving to the living room, continuing even when she realised the man in the shop would surely let her pay later, for a principle seemed to be at stake: there had to be money somewhere in the flat, there *had* to be. In the bedroom she fingered through the little dish of leftover foreign coins from holidays, then worked through the pockets of all the clothes hanging on her clothes rail, finding nothing but dry-cleaning tickets and spare buttons. Finally she arrived at Pete's clothes, which appeared like a topological presentation of his existence, beginning with the casual jumpers and T-shirts and jeans of his new student life, then moving on to the rough fleeces and sweaters adorned with the logo of the garden centre he used to work at, before finally landing on the shirts and chino trousers and suits from his time with a global engineering firm. As she patted down one of these suits her hand found an alarming lump within the silken folds of fabric, and inside she discovered a small velvet box, along with a receipt from a jeweller's on Hatton Garden. Spare change and milk and the rest of the world were forgotten, as she knelt on the floorboards with the box in her palm. Of course she knew what it was, but that didn't take away the ceremony of the act. She took a deep breath and prised open the lid, and saw herself opening the box as she did so, as in some ways she still sees herself opening it, as if since that moment a month ago she has been in a constant fixed state of looking down upon that simple gold band, with its diamond glinting in reflection of the colourless sky.

Anna is still staring at the dining table, and imagines Pete at the end of the party, getting down on one knee. He will produce that same little box from his pocket, and then gaze up at her, the dazzle of the jewel reflected in his hopeful eyes . . .

No, she can't have a dinner party. She needs to cancel the whole thing, throw off his plans. She swallows the last of the whisky – now diluted with melted ice – and searches for 'boat hire, London'. The first option is fantastically, almost comically expensive, as are the second and third, but then she finds a company in Little Venice that offers a weekday special rate of £200, which seems doable. Her birthday is on a

Friday, and it's not too much to ask people to take the day off work, or call in sick, or, in Hamza's case, to carry on being the bums that they are. They could start in Little Venice and sail all the way through Camden and Islington to Hackney Wick, where they would go for a proper night out at Colorama, if it's still there. Yes, this is good. She can almost see the photo album already.

It is 1.40 a.m. Her mind is still turning, but the whisky is doing its work – a warm inner glow and surface fuzziness – and she should at least try and sleep. She brushes her teeth again and then scales the ladder, which she can now do effortlessly and without thinking, even when carrying two cups of tea. She drops her dressing gown and shivers as she gets into bed; the sheets are cool while Pete, deadweight in sleep, is radiating heat. Feeling guilty, she backs her bum into the warm nest of his lap. His arm falls over her like a latch, then his breathing stutters and stalls.

'Hmmmph?' he says.

'Sorry.'

'What?'

'Nothing. I've been downstairs.'

'What is it?' he says, sounding worried.

'It's nothing. I just couldn't sleep.'

A pause, then he sighs and rolls away from her onto his back.

'Now *I'm* awake,' he says.

'Sorry. I tried to be quiet.'

'Did you try not to touch me as well?' He sounds cranky, but this is how she likes him: there is weight in his voice. The whisky has put her in a generous mood, and also made her fearless.

'I've been thinking about my birthday,' she says.

'Oh?'

'I want to cancel the dinner party. I want to hire a boat.'

'A boat?' he says, his voice sharp with concern.

'A narrowboat. Or is it a longboat? You know, a canal boat.'

'You're not serious.'

'We can sail around for the day, pack it with food and booze . . .' And drugs, she suddenly thinks. How long has it been since she last had a pill or a line? At least one year. Perhaps two. Could it even be three?

'Sounds cold,' says Pete, who can get through most winters without having to resort to a coat.

'It's often warm on my birthday. Late March can go either way.'

'Sounds expensive, then.'

'It's not so bad, on a weekday. Two hundred pounds.'

He scoffs at the price, says it is a complete rip-off, and Anna thinks of the receipt she found alongside the ring, for six times that amount. Where did he find the money? The story is that he is a student and hard up, so much so that they couldn't take a winter holiday this year, that two-week dose of warmth and light that had seemed like an annual indulgence but was shown by its absence to be more of a medical necessity. And yet he bought the ring. Because being broke for him – and most other people she knows, Zahra included – does not really mean being broke; it is more like a game, and in many ways a satisfying one, which he can call off at any time simply by ringing his parents.

'I don't mind paying for it,' she says. 'If people think it's too much.'

Silence for a moment. She can almost hear his thoughts

circling around, groping for some innocuous reason to undermine her plan.

'This is crazy,' he says. 'We're having a dinner party. Everyone's happy with the dinner party idea. Now go to sleep.'

Another moment's silence, then Anna says, 'I want a boat.' This sounds involuntarily childish and makes her giggle, the seriousness of the conversation dispelled. Pete also laughs, and for a moment they are laughing together. Perhaps it is the whisky, but Anna feels a surprising tenderness for him – and for the idea of them as a unit – and, experimentally, she tries to coax this feeling by kissing the soft globe of his shoulder.

'And I'm not tired,' she says.

'What can I do about it?'

'I don't know. Tell me a story.'

'No.'

'Tell me a scary story.'

He says nothing, but she feels his body, where her feet, knees and forearms are touching him, go tense with concentration.

'I know: tell me about the shark.'

'Again?'

'I love it. Tell it from the start. In detail.'

'Alright,' he says, sighing. There is a long pause, then he begins, in a croak barely above a whisper. 'I was in Koh Phangan, living in a little bamboo hut. At the end of the beach was this lip of black volcanic rock that jutted into the sea, and beneath it the water became really dark and cool. Every morning I'd dive off and make a lotus flower at the bottom for a minute or two.'

'How old were you? When was it? Give the details.'

'It was my gap year. I must have been eighteen or nineteen. So one morning I was down there and I saw this fish swimming towards me. It kept coming for ages, then I realised it was a lot further away and bigger than I thought. It kept coming and growing, and coming and growing, and eventually I saw it was a shark, a tiger shark. He was huge, at least three metres, and coming right at me.'

'I love this story,' she mumbles, already drifting away.

'I was utterly helpless,' he says, his hands carving shapes in the half-dark. 'But then something strange happened. Maybe it was the lack of oxygen, but I suddenly became completely calm. I realised there was nothing I could do about it. I was beneath a ledge, with no air in my lungs, but since there was nothing I could do, there was nothing to worry about. The shark angled right up to me, a few feet away, staring. I stared right back, fearless. I swear he sensed it, my lack of fear, and respect passed between us, from one strange animal to another. Then he banked away to his left, looped around and swam away again.'

'Just floated away.'

'I scrambled out from beneath the ledge and burst from the water, panting, gasping, amazed to be alive.'

Anna shuffles further into his warmth.

'Floated away,' she whispers.

'It was like we doffed caps at each other.'

'Yes.'

'Top o' the morning.'

'Just floated away.'

'Exactly. Night.'

'Night.'

Thursday

On Thursday the weather is as bright and warm as the forecast promised, and on her way to an al fresco lunch Anna is pleased to pass people in their shirt sleeves and T-shirts, their bare arms swinging in the mild air for the first time this year. The sunlight burns through the fog of fatigue and alcohol that has clouded her morning. At the corner of Dean Street and Berwick Street she meets Zahra, who has them walk all the way to Old Compton Street to find a new Japanese place she has been raving about, before taking their ramen pots back to the little park in the centre of Soho Square; on the journey neither mentions Kismet or Pete or Thomas 72, and Anna takes this as a tacit agreement to keep things light, to not repeat the argument they had on WhatsApp the day before. When they reach the square they find that so many other people have had the same idea that the lawn is almost invisible, replaced by a dense carpet of office workers as they crouch over burritos, gözleme, katsu curry, fried noodles, pie and mash, tortilla, roti and countless other unidentifiable and perhaps unnamed dishes. They find a spot at the edge of one of the quadrants of lawn and go to work on their ramen pots, but have to sit so close together that their crossed knees are touching. It is a nice feeling though, and the sensation of Zahra's elbow and shoulder rubbing against her as she eats stirs up a memory in Anna.

'Hey. Do you remember that time it was as busy as this, and we ended up sitting with our backs to each other? And I had that idea for a big elasticated piece of fabric – a sling, ba-sically – that would wrap around two people, so they could both sit upright while still facing each other?'

'I have no idea what you're talking about.' Zahra is lean-ing over the pot rested between her knees; she uses a cupped hand as an extra barrier between her wet noodles and her dazzling white shirt as she lifts her chopsticks to her mouth.

'You *do* remember. We were sat almost exactly here. Or maybe it was in Hoxton Square. Anyway. "Slinghy", I called it. Because it was a sling, and because it would be a bit like sitting opposite someone in a dinghy.'

Zahra's eyes narrow to squint behind her square glasses as she chews.

'I remember one about leasing a sheep to people so it could cut their grass.'

'While entertaining the kids. *Another* great idea. Some-times I think I should try resuscitating one of them.'

'Maybe you should. Get yourself a second income.'

'Yeah,' says Anna, flatly, the thought of paid work and jobs sending a shudder through her. 'Though I should prob-ably try and not throw away my current income first.'

'Don't be silly,' says Zahra. She puts down her chopsticks and reiterates that Anna shouldn't worry about that shit, that the Power Women list was just some throwaway clickbait, and that the Sahina interview is the real thing – the *exciting* thing – the thing that will finally make her a successful jour-nalist. Anna keeps her eyes averted, and all she can muster when Zahra finishes is a hum of agreement.

'Don't sound too excited,' says Zahra, and Anna spins her head in all directions to make sure they are only surrounded by strangers.

'Do you ever feel like a fake at work?' she says, beneath her breath. 'Like everyone else is really doing their job, and you're just pretending?'

'That's called being an adult.'

'Or like you're being tested for something? Something that maybe you didn't even want in the first place.'

'Trust me, everyone feels like this.'

'You know what it reminds me of? It reminds me of running cross-country.' This makes Zahra's head jerk in confusion, and Anna describes in detail the feeling of representing her school at these big races when she was twelve or thirteen, always in the freezing cold, standing at the start line surrounded by hundreds of horrible strange children from other schools, feeling physically sick at the prospect of doing badly and not placing in the top ten, and at the same time knowing she wouldn't feel the slightest hint of pleasure if she came first, because it would only mean running more races.

'You're just nervous!' says Zahra. 'It's going to be fine. Nerves make you perform – you just need to nail the questions, then memorise them.'

'Yeah . . . In fact, I should head back and work on them. I've got the list down from thirty to ten.'

'What? I haven't even finished my noodles. We've been, like, forty minutes. And it's way too nice to take a short lunch.'

'Maybe you're right,' says Anna, thinking she can always stay late tonight if necessary. She resolves to push Sahina from her mind for the next twenty minutes, and tilts her face towards the sun and leans back on her palms; the warmth feels like a faint even pressure on her pale skin. 'We did it, Z. We survived another winter.'

'Steady on.'

'It's true. I can feel it. I can even *smell* it.' Anna inhales through her nose and tries to engage with the positive feeling she had on the walk to the park, but as she projects her thoughts forwards in time, rather than excitement for the warm bright months ahead, her imagined future stops with a thud at her birthday dinner party, just eight days away, and being left with Pete at the end, and once again she is kneeling on the floorboards in the bedroom, looking down upon the ring. A shiver runs up her arm and she realises the ground beneath her palms is spongy and damp; winter is lurking just beneath the surface. She isn't listening to what Zahra is saying – something about there being no leaves on the trees – and, unable to respond, they lapse into silence, a silence that Anna senses will mark the end of their attempt to keep things light and friendly; she can no longer hold the heavy stuff at bay, it looms too large in her mind for her to think or talk around.

'I found proof,' she says, eventually. 'He's definitely going to propose on my birthday.'

'Proof? You told me you already knew.'

'Not a hundred per cent. Now I've seen a text to his brother, and he really, definitely is.'

'You checked his *phone*?'

Anna says she couldn't resist, and relays the five-text exchange almost from memory: Pete asking his brother Bean if he was keeping the ring in a safe place, Bean asking if he was nervous, Pete saying he had it under control, and Bean joking that he should serve it to her in meringue, to which Pete said haha. Zahra listens with her lips queasily askew, the freckled skin around her nose crinkled in disapproval.

'What does this mean, anyway?' she says. 'It's hardly new information.'

'It means I have to cancel the dinner party.'

'Cancel it?'

'I'm thinking of a boat trip instead.'

'What the fuck have boats got to do with anything?'

'Because it will be a big event! I will invite people from up north – Gaby and Alice and that lot – they'll have to stay over. We can really go for it – drink all day, go out in Hackney at night, have a walk and pub lunch the next day. Pete won't propose in the middle of all that. He'll have to reschedule.'

'Until, like, a day later.'

'No way. People wait for special occasions. Holidays, anniversaries, birthdays. Where was it Keir proposed?'

'Lake Como,' admits Zahra. 'But a *boat*? Won't it be cold?'

'Of course not. Look at today.'

Zahra sighs and repeats that today's heat is a sneak preview, not a seasonal change.

'No way, it's spring,' says Anna, pointing, as if in evidence, to the timbered hut at the centre of the square, where a man in green overalls is taking a padlock from the door.

'That's a gardener,' says Zahra. 'Not Old Father Time. Look at the forecasts. It'll be raining next week.'

'I don't care if it snows – the boat's perfect. I've already asked Hamza to get us some drugs. But Pete thinks it's crazy coming from me. You need to text him, tell him you think it's a great idea.'

Zahra turns her head away from Anna towards the short road that gives onto a portion of Oxford Street. Anna looks at the side of Zahra's freckled, narrow face and marvels at how she is urging her to contact Pete. Until recently she contrived to keep them apart, because she found it alarming how well they got on. Every time Zahra came around

58

they swapped recipes, discussed botany tips and made each other laugh by moaning about their respective independent schools – which are part of the same foundation or academy or linked in some way that Anna has never quite understood – while maintaining a level of eye contact that was borderline inappropriate. But these feelings have faded over the last six months, largely because Zahra has been busy knocking down walls at her own flat rather than hanging around theirs, and then disappeared entirely when she found the ring. Now she almost misses her jealousy, since it was proof she had something she couldn't afford to lose.

'I'm not sure,' says Zahra, finally.

'About the boat?'

'About the whole thing. I think it's time you stopped . . . playing games.'

'Games? You were the one that said I should get perspective.'

'I didn't think you'd take it this far. I didn't think you'd actually . . . meet people.'

'Jesus. Look out, everyone: she's going to *meet* people.'

'Alright then. Date people.'

'They're not real dates. It's just a test.'

'A test for what? What do you even want?'

Anna could answer this question, for she has posed it to herself recently. She has managed to bring into focus a vague ambition which she has carried within her for many years. She can see herself in her thirties, living in a villa in Greece or Italy or the south of France, picking up freelance writing and copy-editing work online, chipping away at some project or other, maybe doing part-time waitressing at a local bar or restaurant. She would take advantage of the occasional cheap flight back to the UK to see friends and family, but otherwise just exist simply, cheaply, creatively, within sunshine and light, and not have to grit her teeth each October when the clocks change and all is plunged into darkness. But how does Pete fit into this idyll? Good question. And where are her babies? Thrown way off to her late thirties, to her last years of fertility, for when she is Ready.

'I don't know,' is all she says, deciding not to attempt another dreamscape after the cross-country analogy. 'But I just have doubts. He's only a 70, remember.'

'I can't believe you're bringing the number into this.'

'That's easy for you to say. You've got a 76.'

'And I never think about it.'

'Exactly. You can afford to take it for granted. With me, it's like the number flashes above his head every time he snores or, you know, gets all excited about some new greengrocer. And then I'm left stewing for hours afterwards, wondering if I switched off too quick, if I should have held out and made more matches. Do you remember the state I was in when we met? My dad had been dead for three months. Three months! And what if that whole thing threw me off course? And since then I've just been drifting?'

There is a pause – the same concerned, thoughtful pause Zahra always leaves when Anna mentions her dad, or when conversation otherwise brushes up against the idea of fathers. When she does speak again it is quietly, with her professional lawyer's pragmatic tone, saying that Anna shouldn't lose sight of the fact that Pete is funny and handsome and smart and thoughtful, and that millions of girls would kill for what she has. These words come a little too easily, Anna thinks, and she is tempted to respond by saying that several hundred thousand of them are probably better suited for him than her

– Zahra included. But she doesn't want the conversation to go any further; they are merely repeating the same arguments as they did over their phones yesterday and in the pub last week.

'Look,' she says, now with a businesslike, summarising tone herself. 'I'm not ungrateful. I understand he's a great guy and whatever. I probably will decide to go through with it. But I'm looking for something. And you've got to help me. Just text him about the boat. Please. And I won't ask anything else of you.'

Zahra turns her head one way and then the other, before sighing in resignation – Anna smiles to see she is relenting, grudgingly.

'I can't believe you read his messages,' says Zahra, standing up and unfolding her prim little tweed blazer.

'I'm a terrible person,' says Anna, standing as well; she feels her backside in search of a damp patch, and finds one. 'And I'm going to be late. I haven't got time for coffee.'

'Come on, just a quick one. You can get it to take away.'

Anna wavers between competing impulses for a moment, then decides she will definitely stay late tonight to finish the Sahina questions, for as long as it takes. Plus she needs the caffeine to power her through the afternoon.

'You're a bad influence,' she says as they head off. 'For all your supposed virtue.'

At the gates of the park they struggle to fit their ramen pots in the overflowing bins and have to leave them on the ground instead, complaining how hard it is to be good citizens. They wander down Greek Street and into a cafe, and Anna goes to the counter while Zahra takes a stool at the bench along the glass shopfront.

'Look at this footfall,' says Zahra, nodding out the window, when Anna returns with the coffee. The stream of people hurrying to work for 2 p.m. is three or four thick, and blocks their view of the shops facing them from across the narrow street. 'You must be getting hits.'

'You'd think, wouldn't you? But it's a desert out there. See for yourself.' She takes her phone from her bag, opens Kismet and hands it to Zahra, who almost snatches it and holds it to her nose. Anna is reminded of when Zahra was using it – back when they lived in east London, not long after it was launched, during her month-long search for Keir – and Anna would often grab the phone from her; nothing is more fascinating than someone else's phone when they are using Kismet.

'I can't believe it,' says Zahra. 'There's nothing!'

'I told you. They're all in bloody relationships. Kismet needs to extend the circle. Make it a hundred metres.'

'As if,' says Zahra, pinching at the screen and flicking it around. 'I heard Raymond Chan say they were going to make it smaller, to stop people fishing. Apparently in Tokyo people stand all day at busy junctions waiting for hits.'

'Hmm. Do you think it's weird that he only seems to do interviews and press conferences? Raymond Chan, I mean.'

'When you get senior enough work is just interviews and press conferences. Hey: no wonder you're not getting hits. It will know you've got a boyfriend! It's only going to match you with freaks, or other cheating scumbags.'

'I did worry about that. But the French guy wasn't a freak. He was nice. We had things in common. He was funny, and sexy.' Zahra asks how so, dubiously, and Anna describes how he looked like a pirate and does an impression of him talking about the sound of a mandarin being peeled, which succeeds in making Zahra laugh. 'I'm telling you. He was a good one.

Kismet understands me. The real me.'

'You still shouldn't see him again.'

'I think maybe I should have sex with him just once.'

'A wonderful idea,' says Zahra, still with the phone up to her nose. 'What could possibly go wrong?'

'Just one harmless night of being fucked by a pirate.'

'More likely, you'll have the kind of awkward sex that reminds you of what you've got.'

'Even better,' says Anna, with a shrug. 'I'm serious, though. Pete really has changed. He's only twenty-eight, and it's like his main ambition in life is to sit down. If you ever came round you'd see for yourself. Why don't you come round this weekend?'

The question appears to make Zahra stiffen and her eyes become unfocused, as if her thoughts have been sent elsewhere. After a moment she springs back to life.

'It's two already; now *I'm* going to be late,' she says, putting Anna's phone on the counter. She gulps the rest of her espresso, kisses Anna on the cheek and says she's the one that's changed, not Pete.

'He has! He's training to be a teacher, for God's sake. At least when he worked at the garden centre it was a stop-gap.'

'The country needs teachers,' says Zahra, grabbing her bag. 'Maybe we could go out for brunch instead this weekend?'

'It also needs traffic wardens. Traffic lights. Yes, brunch. Of course.'

Zahra kisses her on the cheek again, says good luck for the interview tomorrow and is gone. Anna picks up her phone from the counter and sees that she does have a match, a blue dot on Old Compton Street. She presses it and the number 51 appears. She almost laughs, it is such a low number – two points lower and it wouldn't register at all. She wonders what he must be like, to be deemed so perfectly incompatible. Perhaps it would be one of those guys that she has found herself sitting next to at dinner parties or at work that she has nothing to say to. The kind that has no interest in music, has no creative hobbies whatsoever, has a preoccupation with making and hoarding money that is almost primal, and that likes nothing better than to talk about house prices and mortgages and pension plans. Anna tries to visualise such a man, and this time she does actually laugh, to realise she has mentally sketched a perfect likeness of Keir. She watches the blue dot crawl like a bug across her screen, and thinks, yes, that is what the 51 would be like. But then would Kismet know her well enough to score so accurately? Of course it would. It knows every song, every website, every liked post, every shared photo, the playlists she makes and the food she orders for delivery; in short, *everything*, measured down to the nanosecond and micro-pixel. When is she more honest than when browsing around the internet? It knows her as well as her best friends. Even more so. Maybe it knows her better than she knows herself, she concludes, while considering walking down to Old Compton Street and meeting the 51, just to see if in their extreme incompatibility she might learn something about herself. But the time is 2.09 p.m. and she has to go back to work on her questions. Though maybe, she suddenly considers, it would be better to walk up to the RIBA library on Great Portland Street and do some research there. She can't decide what to do, and these competing ideas hold her in stasis, sitting by the window and watching the clock on her phone, which seems to hang on 2.09 p.m. for an incredibly long time before finally, mercifully, becoming 2.10 p.m.

Anna is surprised to find that Sahina Bhutto's new firm is in Vauxhall, that part of London she has always found the most unsightly and obscurely depressing. She arrives over an hour early, planning to eat something, have a strong coffee, memorise her questions, and to buy some deodorant – her stick ran dry two days ago, and she has repeatedly forgotten to replace it on her hurried journeys from home to office, office to home. She walks in a loop around the station, but the only cafe with any seats is a shabby place almost within the bus station. She takes a seat and looks at the laminate menu, at fried sandwiches and all-day breakfasts, and, wanting something light, since her stomach is alive with nerves, she orders the muesli with granola and yoghurt. This arrives piled up in a tall glass with a long spoon, with red berries on top; she feels the eyes of the men in the room on her, no doubt marvelling at this smart young woman digging into a lunchtime ice cream sundae. She pushes this to one side after a few mouthfuls, then flattens the list of questions on the Formica table top.

Yesterday afternoon she sent Stuart her final suggested ten questions, as agreed, but it wasn't until this morning that he called her into the Quiet Room and said they weren't quite right, weren't quite right at all. They sat together for an hour and talked through each one, and she watched in silent dismay as with hits of his fat fingers he deleted the product of her late-night research – the mentions of Sahina's childhood in Pakistan, the references to her early projects in the US, the allusion to her controversial partnership with the Saudi royal family – and replaced them instead with the three Romont brand values, one of which he demanded appear in every question, and, with a final patronising flourish, marked in bold where it did. Gone from his voice was the reassuring tone of a few days ago. Now he spoke of her thirty minutes with Sahina as a fragile, volatile thing, during which no risks whatsoever could be taken.

She reads each of the ten questions out loud and then turns the page face down and tries doing so again. What is the most *sophisticated* building that you've built? Why are there so few *powerful* women in architecture? What advice would you give – she flips over the page to check – what advice would you give to *ambitious* young female architects?

She repeats this process until she can reel off most of them automatically, helped along by a coffee in a mug the size of a bowl. She has to use both hands to pick it up, and she is pleased to see that after twenty minutes of sipping it still isn't halfway drunk, that it is really two or three coffees, a day's worth combined. This provokes a thought in Anna, and she watches the buses roll in and out of the station, wondering how much of her life she spends sitting in cafes, drinking coffee. This gives rise to a vision of every coffee she has ever drunk, gathered together into one brown, frothy pond. How big would it be? Maybe it would even be the size of a lake. She then imagines all the bread she has eaten, and eggs, apples, and wine, and then a new idea hits her, her first invention in months, even years: there could be a theme park of human consumption, made entirely of super-size installations that

66

represent the aggregate consumption of everyday items. A hillock of bread. A river of milk. A pyramid of toilet rolls. It would be at once an entertaining spectacle, a comment on wastefulness, and also a philosophical take on how our bodies are tiny vessels, mere needle eyes through which an endless conveyor of resources is slowly threaded . . .

The idea holds her in a trance, and when she snaps out of it she sees it is 2.16 p.m. and she really should be going. She folds up the questions, leaves the cafe and edges across half a dozen pedestrian crossings, her feet pinched by the shiny brogues that have never been comfortable but are at least much smarter than her tatty boots. She makes two futile attempts to find deodorant in off-licences along Kennington Lane, and then turns down the industrial side street, arriving at the sign 'Lambeth Civic Architecture' with a fresh coat of sweat in her armpits.

She hovers at the gate for a moment, catching her breath, looking up at the sign. It is a white rectangle of plastic on the large, wooden gate, with the simple words printed in an art-less, sans serif typeface. The banality of the logo is reassuring to Anna. She had expected to be confronted with some architectural marvel, a design of glass and chrome, but instead there is just innocuous normality. It is a reminder that the people inside are just that: *people*. The kind that breathe air, drink water, say hello, goodbye, thank you. They will show her in, ask if she wants anything, take her to Sahina, and even she will adhere to the basic principles of decency. All Anna has to do is say the questions, and the fierce convention of courtesy will prise Sahina's lips open, and she will get her story.

Anna pushes through a small door within the large wooden gate and into an enclosed yard containing two renovated,

67

high-windowed warehouses. She walks to the one on the left, which bears a larger version of the sign on the gate, and presses the buzzer. After a few moments the door clicks and is opened by a short middle-aged woman, her wrinkled brown face flanked with long dark hair.

'You must be Anna,' says the woman, smiling, extending her hand, and it takes Anna a second to realise she is speaking to Sahina Bhutto herself. 'You're lucky. You caught me on my lunch break.'

'Hey. Hi,' says Anna, finally shaking her hand. 'Yes. Hello. Nice to meet you.' Anna steps up into a dark and cluttered hallway that reminds her obscurely but powerfully of where all the coats were kept in her primary school. This gives onto a vast, open-plan workspace the size of an aircraft hangar, with whitewashed cinderblock walls and dozens of tropical plants ballooning from window ledges and between the partitioned pods. Perhaps a hundred or two hundred workers – all of whom seem surprisingly young and fashionable and attractive to Anna – are spread throughout the space, either in chatty clusters around tables or individually behind giant Macs or those big angled drawing boards. Several of these young polished architects pass Sahina as they shuffle along the centre aisle, and each time she says '*Ciao*, darling' or 'Hello, sweetie', followed on occasion by a 'mwah' kissing noise. Some of them look up at Anna as she walks along, two steps behind Sahina, and she meets their gaze with that inane pinched half-smile she does when inadvertently making eye contact with someone at work. Her eyes drift away from them to the far wall, where the words 'Never Stop Exploring' are painted in foot-high black letters, beneath a vast clock whose hour hand is probably bigger than one of Anna's arms.

'And how is dear Clem?' says Sahina, as she leads Anna into a pod in the centre of the open-plan space, beside a desk bearing a half-eaten sandwich. 'A great friend of mine, though sometimes we don't see eye to eye. In fact, we never do. But that's why we like each other; our sparring sessions keep us sharp. You know him well?'

'Oh, I don't know him at all,' says Anna, sitting opposite Sahina; in the next pod is a baby-faced young man with round glasses and blond hair in curtains, and she is slightly alarmed that he is well within earshot. 'I got into the same lift with him once, that's about it.'

Sahina smiles at this, then bites into her sandwich; she apologises and says that she has to leave at 3 p.m. for a meeting with the Chinese ambassador, so she must eat this now. Anna says that's fine and starts setting up. By the time she has taken out her Dictaphone and pen and folded the list of questions into the centre of her notebook, Sahina still hasn't finished her first mouthful. She takes another bite, then another, giving the impression of someone trying to finish in a hurry, and Anna pretends to fidget with things while watching her chew. Sahina doesn't look so good. Her neck is a smooth expanse of skin stretching from her chin to her collarbone. Her eyes are these huge complex things, the surrounding skin so wrinkled she almost looks like a stone sculpture that has started to crack. She takes a final bite and wipes her hands on a napkin and says through a full mouth that they are the best tramezzini in London, that she has them biked over from Soho, that the cafes in Vauxhall can't be trusted to fry an egg.

'They haven't quite mastered cereal either,' says Anna, before explaining about the cafe by the bus station serving her granola and yoghurt that looked like an ice cream. Surprisingly,

Sahina laughs out loud. It is a deep guttural laugh that makes the loose skin on her neck wobble and her eyes close, and appears somehow directly connected with the underworld. Then she clears her throat, says that she likes that, and leans forwards in her chair and says, 'Now then, sweetie, what are we going to talk about?'

Anna is thrilled. It is a delight to make Sahina laugh and to be called sweetie, and on a wave of excitement a raft of possible questions bubbles up within her: why does she have so many plants? Why did she form her new firm in Vauxhall? Why are all her staff so young and attractive? Why is the sign on the gate so bland? What is the origin of the mantra 'Never Stop Exploring'? These questions fill her mind to such an extent that they have nudged away the memory of the first question that she actually has to ask, and she slides the piece of paper from her notebook and has a look at the list one last time.

'Right,' she says, squiggling on a blank page to test her biro. 'Can you ... er ... tell me what it's like being a *powerful* woman in an industry dominated by men?'

Sahina looks up from the notebook and considers Anna blankly.

'You mean compared to being a powerful man?'

'Er. Yeah.'

'You think I know what it's like to be a man?'

Anna chuckles, hoping this is a joke, but Sahina's face remains blank. She is sitting stiffly straight in her chair, as if a rod is stretching her back to its maximum length. Her fingers are knitted together on her lap.

'No. Sorry. I mean: what's it like being *surrounded* by men, to feel that you're, you know ... outnumbered?'

Sahina shrugs this question away with a tiny lift of one shoulder. 'How do I know? I only have one experience. What can I compare it to?'

Anna instinctively jots down the answer in her notebook in longhand, before realising she hasn't received an answer, or not one she can use. She considers rephrasing it more subtly, but fears she'll get the same response. She decides to move on, but she feels rattled by Sahina's reaction, and the memory of the second question isn't at hand. It is something to do with sophistication. Why are women architects not thought of as sophisticated, something like that. But this doesn't sound right. Her pen hovers over her notebook as she struggles to remember; a bead of sweat escapes her armpit and trickles down over her ribs.

'Do you think one of the main issues in architecture is that women lack sophistication?'

Sahina's chin falls downwards and she says: 'Pardon me?'

'Ambition!' says Anna. 'Sorry, I misspoke. Do you think that women lack *ambition*?'

Sahina continues frowning at her, then says, simply, no, she doesn't think that. Anna writes this down, then moves to the next question. To make sure this time she slips the folded list of questions from within her notebook and has a peek.

'Why do you think,' she begins, noticing that Sahina is looking down at her notebook with wide eyes. 'Why do you think so few women become *powerful* architects?'

Sahina is frowning at Anna now, her lips askew with distaste.

'These questions of yours,' she says, nodding towards the notebook propped on Anna's knee. 'Are they *all* going to be like this?'

71

'Um. Like what?'

'About women.'

'Um. Yes. I mean, kind of. The series is about women. Did your assistant not say?'

'Not my assistant!' snaps Sahina, with such venom that Anna shrivels inwardly. 'We do not have assistants. Or managers. Just *people*. You spoke to Vicky, she does communications. What do you mean, it is about women?'

'Um. It's called Women at the Top. It's about . . . women who are prominent. Leaders in their fields. Such as yourself.'

'I am not a leader! What did I just say?'

'Sorry. I mean . . . *famous* women.'

Sahina now leans back and peers at Anna slantwise, leaving a pause that gives Anna time to reflect on the fact that she is losing control – this isn't good, isn't good at all.

'And who is behind it?' says Sahina, her big eyes narrowed. 'Where did the idea come from?'

Anna considers saying that the series was devised by Paula, Head of Digital, a black lesbian, but there is a hint of mischief in Sahina's eyes that makes Anna sense she might know the answer to this question already. Her eyes are so clear and liquid and alive compared to the surrounding craggy skin that Anna thinks suddenly of rock pools, and those perfect glassy ponds within the jagged black stone. She decides to tell her, in the most offhand, matter-of-fact way she can muster, that the series is being made in collaboration with a sponsor.

'A sponsor?'

'They pay for the advertising space around the article. We retain full editorial control,' says Anna. Sahina asks who the sponsor is, and laughs when Anna tells her.

'Romont!' she repeats. 'The watch people. Very good. I hear the watches are very nice. I've never had one. Have you?' Anna shakes her head, then looks at her own digital Casio: the time is 2.46 p.m.

'It's good to know where you're coming from,' says Sahina, shifting around in her seat. 'Clem didn't say you'd be representing the watch people. Now, carry on: you were saying about the women.'

'I'm not representing anyone,' says Anna. 'Like I said, they have no—'

'Yes, yes,' says Sahina, flapping her hand about, and urging her to forget all about it and carry on with the questions. But when Anna does so, and begins repeating the question about why so few women become leading architects, she cuts her off.

'Stop,' she says, with the authority of a referee. 'You're doing it again. You're asking me about something I am not. You should ask that question to someone who isn't an architect. You, for example.'

'Me?'

'You are a female. You are not an architect. Why are you not?'

'I don't know,' says Anna. 'Lots of reasons.'

'There's your answer. *Lots of reasons.* Write that in your little book.'

On principle, Anna doesn't write it down, and instead searches for the next question, a good, solid one, that will regain control. She cannot remember it; her thoughts are scattered.

'But maybe you should have been,' continues Sahina. 'An architect, I mean. Maybe you would like it more than what

73

you're doing now. Maybe you would have been good at it.'

The stress within Anna is raised another notch. She looks down at her notepad and feels like Sahina's cunning, narrow eyes can see right into her soul, and the truth that she doesn't belong here. Is this a panic attack? For a strange moment she considers running away, but tells herself to calm down and keep going with the damn questions. Her memory has been completely wiped, and she takes out the piece of paper again. The page quivers in her hand and the printed words jumble into a kind of word salad, the emboldened brand values floating free of the rest. She shifts around in her chair, tries to shuffle herself out of this panicked and confused state, but only succeeds in releasing a small cloud of body odour from within her armpits. It is a meaty, stale smell, and it reminds Anna of being in the cafe in the bus station. How nice that was, she realises, sitting there, thinking up her idea of the amusement park of piles of rotting beef, streams of sour milk, a house built of mouldy cheese. That is where she really belongs – sitting in a drab cafe, surrounded by the lost and unemployed, coming up with ideas that make no fucking sense.

'Whenever you're ready,' says Sahina. 'What's the next question Romont has given you? If you want, I can read from the list myself? I know what they want.'

This time Anna's stress hardens into annoyance. She is annoyed at the list of stupid questions, at Stuart for deleting all the good bits, at Sahina for suggesting that she can't think for herself. She reaches down for her bag, takes out her mineral water and has a sip and then puts the bottle away, along with the list of questions. Then she zips up the bag and looks at Sahina and attempts a smile.

'Sorry about that,' she says. 'I had a moment. Now then:

which of your buildings do you think is the most sophisticated, in terms of design? The Biscuit Tin, the Mujahi Doheen, or maybe one of the early ones from Washington State?'

Sahina appears startled by this name-dropping and blinks a few times. Then she composes herself and, finally, begins speaking. She says that the main purpose of her career, to the extent that one exists, is to rid architecture of silly concepts such as sophistication, which only try to make buildings more important than the people that use them. This sentiment completely contradicts the Romont brand values, but it feels good to be writing in her notebook again, and while jotting it down Anna formulates her next question; she has six minutes left, and resolves to keep Sahina speaking, no matter what. Anna asks what advice Sahina would give young people who want to become architects. Sahina aims her eyes up at the network of air ducts and metal tubing, and says pithily that they should just *be* architects. Anna writes this down as well, thinking it could be a nice ending line, and then as she is about to ask a question about Islamic architecture, they are interrupted.

'Sahina?' says a voice from behind Anna's shoulder. 'Sorry to butt in like this. I need you to confirm something. Right now.' A young Asian guy is holding an iPad and a small digital pen, aiming both at Sahina.

'Excuse me,' says Anna. 'We're right in the middle—'

'Sorry, these are the last seats on the flight to Beijing,' he says. 'They will only hold them another five minutes.' Anna watches in disbelief as Sahina takes the iPad, fishes some glasses from a pocket and peers down her nose at the screen. It is 2.57 p.m., and Sahina seems to be in no hurry whatsoever. She even asks jokily if the young Asian guy would like to go in her place.

'Sure, I could make the final pitch,' he says, with a giggle. 'I just say the building will be fabulous, right?'

'No, not the building,' smiles Sahina; 'say the people you're talking to are fabulous. Most government guys wouldn't know a tasteful building if it was built around them. Which it probably could be, given how long they sit around.' She winks at Anna as she says this. 'No, the trick is to make *them* feel special. Flattery, after all, is what most big business comes down to.'

She signs the iPad, and Anna has nothing to do but write down exactly what she just said about tasteless government officials. Then the young man walks away and Sahina asks: 'Now, where were we?'

It almost doesn't feel worth trying to keep going, but in the faint hope that her next meeting will be delayed, Anna asks a question about ambition in young architects. Sahina makes a speech about young people being too fixated on certain goals, says that they should explore, do interesting things, go on adventures, and that when she was young she walked across a desert. She says that all young people should walk across deserts, that the only aspirations they have are set by Kismet and a few other major corporations. Anna writes all this down, and follow-on questions queue up in her mind – what did she eat in the desert? Where did she go to the toilet? What desert was it, anyway? – but before she can ask any of these, she hears a clack of footsteps approaching.

'It's time to go, Ms Bhutto,' says another colleague, this time a black man in a suit.

'Please,' says Anna, desperate. 'Can I just have a few more—'

'Sorry,' says the man. 'The car is waiting.'

'I'm sorry too,' says Sahina, pushing her large body to her feet. 'But that went well, didn't it?' She pats Anna on the head as she passes, and then is gone. Anna looks down at her notes. The page is an illegible scrawl. She looks up and the baby-faced guy is looking at her from the neighbouring pod. He smiles at her and shrugs, as if to say: what did you expect?

Five minutes later, Anna is standing outside the front gate. She steps one way and then the other on the pavement, and then leans against the brick wall. She is dazed, and isn't sure what just happened, or what she should do about it. After Sahina left she remained sitting until another staff member, a woman this time, appeared to usher her out. This woman said various things that Anna didn't hear, and when they reached the front door she was surprised to find she could barely talk – her farewell came out as a garbled hybrid of goodbye and thank you. Now she wonders if she should go back in and demand ten more minutes with Sahina – she can wait around all day if she has to – and that this time she answer her questions properly. While she considers this, the small door in the gate bearing the plain sign opens, and two young men step out, no doubt employees of Sahina, sharing a joke as they do so. One is of south Asian extraction and wearing tight-fitting green trousers, the other is a freckled redhead who is making wisecracks in an Australian accent. More striking than their looks is the easy grace of their movements: as they depart along the pavement they project the same effortless finesse as everyone else in the building, as if their entire being is lubricated in health, happiness, money, success – in a word, class. She realises she was completely wrong when she thought, on her way in, that the people inside were just people. They are intelligent and successful people, overflowing with the attributes that she lacks. This makes Anna realise that she can't storm back into the office and request more time, because the only person at fault was her. She hadn't memorised the questions well enough, lost her composure too easily, was unable to regain it once it was lost. In short, she wasn't good enough, and doesn't belong in there. For years she has masked this at work, but Sahina could see it immediately – she is just a middle-England no-body, acting the part of young media professional. And now she has to return to the office, with a handful of illegible notes, and her shortcomings will finally be exposed to all.

Anna feels she might cry. But she also breathes and has a sip of water and in time succeeds in making herself calm down somewhat. Maybe it wasn't so bad. The thing she said about the desert was interesting enough, as was the stuff about young people being too beholden to Kismet and cor-porations, even if it probably goes against the brand values. She will listen to the transcript, reread her notes and see what can be salvaged. She isn't sure she can face Stuart just yet though – he will no doubt summon her immediately to the Quiet Room for a debrief – and she wonders if she can go somewhere else. A man in a T-shirt and hi-vis vest walks past, swinging his bare arms, doing that walk that construction workers often have, as if their whole bodies need to collabo-rate in shifting those massive, mud-caked boots. The sight of him reminds Anna it is a pleasant day. The sun is warm and the air is still and the distant buildings are pleasantly misted. It occurs to her that she could walk too, along the Embank-ment and through Whitehall and Trafalgar Square; the fresh air will clear her head, and help her think of something to say to Stuart. Yes, she decides, she will walk.

At that moment, the small door in the gate flies open again, and a different class of individual appears beside her: he is tall and suited and middle-aged, and looks in a hurry. He sets off in the same direction as the construction worker, then looks back and straightens up when he sees Anna standing against the wall. His hand is clutching a phone, which he holds up to his nose before looking back at Anna and smiling.

'There you are,' he says, in a clipped accent, taking small, slow steps towards her on the pavement. He is smiling at her with anticipation and happiness in his eyes, as if she is a close friend. 'I thought I was going to have a chase on my hands.'

'Sorry,' she says, shaking her head at him. 'What's going on?'

His slow, floating approach is halted five feet from her. The smile fades from his long, clean-shaven face, and a dark crease appears between his eyebrows.

'Oh. You haven't seen it?'

'What are you talking about?'

'Sorry,' he says, shaking his head. 'I thought you'd . . . well, anyway, you'd better take a look.'

He lifts his phone up towards Anna. She glances at the man's face – he is now wearing a grave, almost pained expression – and then down at his phone, which is shaking slightly in his hand. The glare from the sun obscures the screen and all she can see is the reflected outline of her own head. Then she recognises the familiar road layout of Kismet, and two overlapping dots.

'The thing is,' he says, 'we've got rather a high match.'

As he says this her eyes trace the outline of a number above one of the dots: 81. The sight makes her head recoil and in a continuation of this reversing motion she takes a step along the street, away from this tall, suited man, and squints at him through the lens of this alarming information. He must be in his mid-forties, at least. She fishes her phone from her bag, opens Kismet and presses the dot on her map; the number 81 flashes on her screen. It has to be a mistake – it is the highest score she has had with anyone, ever. It is the highest score she has even *heard* of anyone getting.

'I assumed you'd seen it,' he says.

'No,' she says, looking both ways along the street. She feels dizzy again, and reaches out to steady herself against the wall.

'Is everything all right?'

'I'm fine. Sorry. You've caught me at a funny time.'

'We needn't do this right away.'

This. What is this?

'No. I'm okay. Just . . . ' She takes a deep breath and looks down at her smart black brogues; opposite her feet are his brown suede shoes, and her eyes trace upwards to see he isn't as smart as she first thought: his trousers are khaki, his jacket is made from a crumpled linen material similar to her own, and he isn't wearing a tie. His hair is dark and close-cropped, with grey around the temples, and his square-jawed face is irrefutably handsome, though in a generic kind of way: he looks like the sort of middle-aged actor you see in adverts for credit cards or razor blades.

'The way you were standing there, it was as if you were waiting,' he says, his smile causing lines to crease around his blue eyes. 'My name is Geoff.'

The name is so surprising and disarming that Anna makes a short, spluttering laugh.

80

'Geoff,' she repeats, smiling back at him. She says her name is Anna, and for a moment they just stare at each other. She imagines the number 81 flashing above his head, and this sets off a silent explosion within her chest. She wonders if his face only seems generic because he is the kind of man she has never considered herself with, and if it would be different if he belonged to her; surprisingly, the idea makes him seem more attractive already. She still thinks there has been a mistake, that it must be a Kismet misfire, but this makes meeting him seem like a good idea, a harmless diversion. He must take her silence for hesitancy or concern, for he says that maybe they should do this another time, if she'd prefer.

'It's okay. I'm fine. I have a few minutes. Let's do something.'

'Excellent. Let's do something.' He looks up and down the street, as if searching for inspiration, then at his watch. 'It's just gone 3 p.m. I suppose it's too late for coffee. And too early for tea. And *far* too early for the pub. It's that time of day when no one wants anything.' He makes an unfurling motion with his right hand as he says this, and she notices his accent is layered: there is a semi-posh coating above a regional base, though she isn't sure from where.

'I was going to walk along the river,' says Anna.

'That sounds nice.'

'If you want to join me?'

'Absolutely.'

'Great.'

'Great.'

They stand for a second longer, as if neither is sure how to go about putting this plan of theirs into action. Then they turn and begin walking slowly along the pavement, side by side.

81

Anna is taller than average but only reaches up to his shoulder – he must be at least six foot four. They walk in silence to the end of the side street and turn right onto Kennington Lane. Anna can hear her smart pinching brogues hitting the pavement, and for some reason they bring the face of Sahina into her mind and she feels a lurching dread, and all of a sudden isn't in the mood to speak to a stranger. But just as she is about to belatedly take him up on his offer to postpone, he breaks the silence and asks if she works in one of those warehouses.

'Just visiting, thankfully. There's something about Vauxhall that bums me out. I feel like it's not designed for humans, or something.' As if to support her point, they reach the first of the pedestrian crossings which take them across the thundering, four-lane gyratory that threads through the arches beneath the railway tracks. They shuffle across two carriageways, through a dank foot tunnel that smells of urine, then across another two lanes.

'See what I mean?' she says, when they finally reach the pavement on the other side, beneath the MI5 building. 'Vauxhall is fine if you're a car, or a bus. But if you're a human you've had it.'

Geoff makes a speech immediately, as if he knew she was going to say this, and has prepared a response.

'Vauxhall is a piece of infrastructure, first and foremost,' he says. 'And recently I've decided that infrastructure is the best monument to a city. Sewage plants. Power stations. Motorway flyovers. These are the most awesome testaments to a city's combined weight. Not some poncy cathedral or art gallery. Near Bow there is a field of electricity pylons that stretches for miles.'

This eccentric speech surprises Anna – especially coming

from someone who looks like a male model – but she imagines saying it herself in a different context, and realises that it is the kind of thing she would be glad to come out with.

'I suppose there could be something sublime about a field of pylons,' she says. 'But Vauxhall? It's just a few gay bars and a roundabout.'

Geoff releases a titter of laughter, but says nothing in return. They walk for a few steps in a silence that seals off the previous conversation, and then he starts from scratch by asking who she was visiting in the warehouse. Being reminded of the interview is almost physically unpleasant, and with a reluctant huff she admits that she is a journalist, writing an article on Sahina Bhutto.

'Me too!' says Geoff, brightly. 'I'm a journalist, I mean. I haven't interviewed her. I see her from time to time – my business partner has a unit in the next warehouse. On sunny days she sits on a deck chair out in the yard. She seems peculiar.'

Anna says she certainly is that, and decides it might be cathartic and productive to relay the whole story: she tells him about her working for the website, being given the Women at the Top series, her boss changing all her questions at the last minute, and Sahina basically refusing to answer any of them. By the time she finishes the pavement has widened onto the tree-lined Embankment, with the lampposts carved into ornate fish where the narrow upper section bulges into the lower trunk.

'But she was saying things?' says Geoff. 'She wasn't sitting in silence.'

'Yes, she was saying *things*.'

'There you go. Just build it around whatever she said.'

There is something annoyingly matter-of-fact about the

way he says this; Anna had merely wanted to vent, not to invite him to problem-solve.

'But she didn't say the *right* things. She barely answered the questions about the brand values.'

'The what?'

Anna sighs and explains about Romont and the three values. Geoff looks concerned; the dark crease has returned to his brow.

'And what happens if she doesn't speak these values?'

'They won't sign it off. They won't pay for it.'

'So it's an advertorial, then?'

'No,' she says, sharply. She tells him that they retain editorial control, and that sponsored content is a major part of pretty much all websites and magazines these days, that three of them work on the desk, and that there is nothing new or unusual about it.

'Perhaps I'm out of touch,' says Geoff. 'But this isn't journalism.'

'Excuse me?'

'It's advertising, clearly.'

'Huh,' says Anna, indignant. 'So I'm not a journalist?' Her tone makes clear that he is on the brink of causing serious offence, but he doesn't flinch or hesitate for a second.

'I didn't say *you* weren't a journalist. Just that *this* isn't journalism.'

'But this is all I do.'

'In that case . . .' He shrugs and looks forwards along the Embankment. Anna marvels at how calm he seems, as if nothing has happened. It is like he is deliberately trying to piss her off and abort the situation. She is offended, but decides not to take it personally. He is obviously the kind of strong-willed man that never modifies opinions to accommodate someone's feelings – wouldn't even think to do so – and that nothing anyone says, no matter how well-reasoned, would make him question his own. In other words, he's a prick.

They walk past three of the fish lampposts without talking, and as it becomes clear that Geoff isn't going to say anything to make amends or restore levity, Anna decides the 81 must be Kismet misfiring. He is an arrogant, middle-aged prick, whose good looks seem intrinsically linked to, or perhaps the cause of, his noxious personality. Maybe Zahra was right: Kismet knows about Pete and is matching her with someone equally deceptive – this guy probably has a wife and children in some great big house in one of those awful-sounding Surrey towns, Esher or Epsom or where have you. She wants to tell him right now that this isn't working, and simply walk away. But there is nowhere to walk to, besides turning and heading back towards Vauxhall, and the nearest tube station is Westminster, half a mile further along the Embankment. She may as well keep walking until then, and have it out with him in the meantime.

'So you're a *proper* journalist, then?'

'Not any more. I used to be, after a fashion.'

Anna asks what the hell that means, and he says he was a reporter in Ukraine and Chile and Uganda, and that he was also a talking head on an Argentinian current affairs show, where he presented a segment called *La Duenda La Britannia*. His Spanish accent is so strong and surprising that for a strange second it feels like a third person is walking with them.

'I did write for the *Evening Standard*, back in the nineties.'

'And now?'

'*Now*,' he says, and then pauses, close-lipped, deliberating. 'Now I'm working on something quite different. An investigation.'

'About what?'

There is another pause, then Geoff says, 'I'd rather not say.' He speaks with such gravity that Anna laughs out loud.

'What, is it some kind of secret?'

Geoff doesn't contradict her, or react in any way at all; he continues staring ahead with his fixed, earnest expression.

'No way? It *is*?'

'It's sensitive, is all,' he says, half-defensive. 'It's not illegal. I just can't speak about it.' It is like he is talking about something from a Cold War-era spy novel, and Anna laughs again and says that her lips are sealed.

They return to silently walking, but her anger and annoyance have diffused; there is something boyish and ridiculous about his talk of a secret project that makes him harder to dislike. Westminster Bridge and the Houses of Parliament are still crouched in the hazy distance, looking like paper cutouts of themselves, and she decides to make use of the few minutes remaining.

'I was planning an investigation of my own once,' she says. 'I wanted to reunite a lost suitcase with its owner, using only the contents as clues, which I'd post on Twitter or a blog.'

'I'm listening,' he says.

She tells him that dozens of suitcases are abandoned on the carousel at Heathrow each year, and if they remain unclaimed they go to an auction house; a few years ago she went and bought one.

'Can you imagine doing that? Leaving the airport without your suitcase?'

'I suppose you'd need a good reason.'

'I have an image of someone waiting at the carousel,' says Anna, 'and getting a text that makes them turn around and just *run*.'

'Would have to be some very bad news, I suppose. Perhaps their husband or wife had been in an accident.'

'Or some really good news. Maybe their wife had gone into labour. Either way, there's a *story* at the heart of it. And that's what I wanted to get to.'

They have stopped walking and are leaning against the stone balustrade beside Westminster Bridge. They are both quiet for a moment, and look across the river to the Houses of Parliament.

'I really like this suitcase idea,' says Geoff. 'What happened to it?'

'Well, my life changed a few years ago. Something happened. It made me drop a few things.' The way she says this demonstrates that it was a major life event, and Anna feels the gravitational pull of the conversation shift, but Geoff's reply is blunt; it strikes her that he has no tact.

'And you didn't take it up again later?'

'By then I had a job. I haven't had time.'

'No time? *Really*? Couldn't you *make* time? You still have the suitcase?'

'Yes, I still have it. But it's way too late. It's like, four years ago.'

'Nonsense. The delay just makes it more interesting; it's a demonstration of the internet's capacity to cross gulfs in time and space. How the past is still with us, in digital form. How it's not even *past*. That's what makes the idea so *modern*.' He says more things like this, and is being arrogant and a little pretentious, but she doesn't mind so much, because he reiterates, repeatedly, that he thinks it's the best idea he's heard in ages. She believes him, and it occurs to her that the Kismet score isn't a complete misfire. He goes off on a tangent and talks about big data and a supercomputer – owned by some of the largest companies and most powerful governments – that is sluicing the entire data of the internet, transmitted in real time as some horrendously vast torrent of numbers and digits and symbols. He rotates his right hand around as he speaks, and she realises he reminds her of someone; perhaps a minor film actor, or an academic delivering a TED talk.

'They call it the pipe,' he says.

'They call what the pipe?'

'The supercomputer. That's their cute nickname for it. Not that they've worked out how to use the data it produces – the stream is too fast, too complex, billions of digits a second. At the moment they are employing mathematicians to just look at it, and think about how they might *begin* to map or filter it all.'

Anna stands there, her palms flat on the cool mottled stone of the balustrade, looking down at the grey-brown water below, and imagines the physical facts of her current situation translated into digital format – the GPS co-ordinates of her position, the person she is standing with – and then pulsing away from her and joining the run-off from the other people walking along the Embankment, until it becomes a flowing stream of numbers, then a surging river. She continues thinking about this until Geoff pushes up from the balustrade, and she stands and follows him across the road.

In silence they weave through tourists gathered at the base of the London Eye; on the esplanade there are stilt walkers and jugglers and a jazz band. Geoff and Anna both slip their jackets off – he carries his over his shoulder, suspended from a hooked finger in a manner that is old-fashioned and quaint. Without agreeing to do so, they drift towards the railings in front of the Oxo Tower and come to a stop there. Anna stares at the water flopping about below, the sunlight sparkling on the momentary crests and troughs. There are dozens of squawking seagulls circling and plunging, and young children are playing on the small strip of sand as if it were a beach – a second after thinking that it looks like the seaside, she detects a low-tide smell of the sea.

'I can smell salt. But that's not right, is it?'

'No, it is. The water here is brackish.'

'Brackish?'

He explains that the river is tidal until Twickenham, and that brackish water is the resultant mix of fresh and salt water, with the concentration increasing towards the sea. He moves his hand around again and, with a jolt that is neither pleasure nor pain, Anna realises who he reminds her of: her father. It is a curiously neutral revelation, and doesn't set off the bottomless, vertiginous feeling she normally gets when reminded of him, as if a trapdoor within her has fallen open.

'Not sure I can smell it though,' he says.

Geoff closes his eyes and inhales deeply through his nose, but then his mouth goes askew, as if he has smelt something unpleasant. Anna breathes through her nose again and she can smell it too – something warm and meaty – and then clamps her arms to her side, knowing it must be her armpits. She takes a half-step away from him on the railing and can feel the beginning of an awkward silence. But then she thinks about the number 81, and decides that if it were true, an issue as trifling as body odour couldn't derail things. And if it's wrong, then none of this matters anyway.

'I think you're just smelling me,' she says, pinching a corner of her shirt and bringing it to her nose, breathing in her tangy smell of onion. She tells him about the deodorant stick and how she sweated during the interview; for the first time he looks genuinely concerned, empathetic, a gentle smile curling his lips.

'I've been in this situation many times,' he says. 'Before big meetings, interviews. Public toilets are surprisingly effective. Just a bean of handwash and a blast of dryer. Works every time.'

'Well, I do need the toilet,' she says, turning to look at the cafe on the balcony of the Oxo Tower. She hands him her jacket and walks inside and up the stairs. In a cafe toilet she checks her phone and sees it is almost half past four, and that she has drifted way off course; there is little point in going back to Soho now, but she doesn't feel guilty about taking a couple of hours off – she'll be working on the article all weekend, she knows she will. She sends a message to Stuart saying she has gone home to write up the transcript, and then switches it off. Then she undoes her shirt and washes her armpits, splashing water up from the little sink. She pats them dry with paper, but obviously not thoroughly, for when she puts her green shirt back on two shapes like ink blots spread from beneath her arms.

On the riverside she finds that Geoff has vanished; he has taken the opportunity to do a runner. But no, wait, there he is, twenty metres further along, reading a metal sign attached to the railing and holding her jacket in a bundle pressed to his side; seeing him with a possession of hers makes him seem more familiar somehow, as if he is a possession of hers as well.

'How'd it go?' he says, as she approaches. She lifts an arm and he laughs at the dark stains. Then he leans down and takes a piece of her shirt between his fingers. She doesn't resist, and she feels a weird disturbance in her stomach as he sniffs at the fabric.

'See?' he says, already walking away. 'Works every time.'

They both put their jackets back on and walk quietly through the tunnels beneath Blackfriars and Southwark Bridge. The sun is beginning to dip, and the slanting rays fidget and dazzle against the glass towers of the City.

'Have dinner with me,' says Geoff, as they approach London Bridge.

There is a long pause as Anna considers what to say.

'I can't.'

'You have plans?'

'No. I'm not doing anything. The thing is, I just—'

'I understand,' he says, cutting her off, and saying he has work to do anyhow. She is almost certain that he doesn't understand, and that he assumes she is just being prudent and well-behaved on a first meeting, but she allows the conversation to lapse into silence. Either way, he doesn't appear too bothered – maybe he doesn't take the system so seriously, or is just playing it cool.

'I'm actually just going home,' she says, in a lament. 'I have no plans at all. Other than work.'

'Ah, to go home,' he says. 'The English equivalent of being marooned.'

'When I was younger, having no plans on a Friday didn't mean not doing anything. It just meant not *knowing* what I was going to be doing.'

'When you were younger!' he says, turning towards the car park by Southwark Cathedral, where a family of tourists are getting out of a taxi. He says he'll get that cab, and then walks over and speaks to the driver for a moment, before coming back.

'Well then,' he says, standing squarely in front of her, his hands in the pockets of his chinos. With sudden courtesy he says it was nice to meet her, that he hopes she has a good weekend and that he looks forward to seeing her again, if she'd like. 'Should we exchange numbers?'

'No,' she says, surprised by his ignorance. 'It knows we've met.'

'It knows? This is all new to me.'

'Of course. I'll be in your list of contacts, under Anna 81.'

'Anna 81,' he says, and smiles. 'It knows a lot, doesn't it?'

'Yes,' she says, smiling back, imagining the number flashing above his head. 'Apparently it knows people better than they know themselves. According to Raymond Chan, that is.'

'Oh yes. That guy. I suppose I'd give him that one. Although it isn't saying much. Most people don't know themselves at all.'

They smile at each other a moment longer, then he makes a little shrug that ushers the farewell ceremony to a close. Now is the time to tell him that she won't see him again, that she *can't* see him again. But he is already leaning down for a goodbye peck on her cheek and is then walking off towards the taxi.

Anna climbs up the stone steps to London Bridge, her head feeling curiously empty. She pauses on the final step, watching the stream of people walking along the pavement towards the station; there are so many of them it is like an alternative river running perpendicular to the Thames. She wonders if these meetings with Sahina and Geoff will make it easier or harder to sleep. She checks her watch and sees it is 5.07 p.m., the start of rush hour. Like a car at a junction, she waits for a gap in the rapid procession of commuters and then finally steps out, having to do a little run in order to keep pace with the surging crowd.

Sunday

On the 21st the clocks go forward, and the additional hour of afternoon light, along with the unseasonably warm weather, feels like a gift from upon high, an invitation for people to enjoy themselves, to celebrate. Anna stands at her living-room window, surveying the scene on Mowbray Road. David, the elderly Jamaican from the flat below, is leaning against the front wall while speaking on the phone in a lilting accent or perhaps even patois; the smoke from his cigarette is rising straight and silver, like a pencil line up into the sky. Further along the street, three children are riding around in circles, the oversize frames of their bikes glinting in the sun, and their shouts arrive at Anna's ear with remarkable clarity, as if there is no air or atmosphere to restrict the sound waves. A family is also walking past with a buggy and a toddler sitting on the father's shoulders, and all these things – even the new tomato plant that Pete has installed on the windowsill, which is giving off a fertile, greenhouse smell – seem to correspond with each other, as if they are different ways of expressing gratitude for this archetypal Sunday afternoon, and their collective victory over a bleak and dark winter. Anna stands there musing on this, her fingers running up and down the tomato plant's prickly stem, until she snaps out of it, remembering she is in the middle of something.

She pushes the dining table against the front wall, rolls up the rug and goes to retrieve the suitcase from the space beneath the boiler. She heaves it into the centre of the living room, and then steps back from the case and looks at it, as if for the first time. It is large, heavy, musky-smelling, and made of a dark and scuffed plastic material, polyester perhaps. The only remarkable thing is the lack of distinguishing features: there are no buckles, side pockets, brand names. It is by no means a classy or expensive-looking piece of luggage, yet its having remained closed for so many years gives it a special potency – it almost appears to throb with its own dense energy.

Anna takes a photo of the case using her old digital camera, since her phone is charging upstairs. She takes more pictures from all angles and a close-up of the remaining stub of the snapped name tag, then puts her camera down and crouches beside the case on the balls of her bare feet. There are two zip tabs, and she unzips one around to the left, the other to the right. Already a smell is leaking out, a stronger version of musk; it is like she has cut into a wheel of cheese. She ignores this and, after a moment's pause, flips the lid. Before her eyes can make sense of the dark contents, a rotten smell fills her nostrils and she is standing up and turning away, her hand covering her mouth.

'Mould,' says Pete, leaning against the doorframe. Anna looks at him for a moment, wondering how long he's been standing there watching, and then back at the case. The black contents appear to be various items of clothing pressed together, and she pinches a crease gingerly, like someone retrieving a soiled nappy. A pair of black jeans peels away from the rest, releasing a cloud of dust and a dank, wet stench.

'Ewww,' she says, dropping them and shaking her hand.

'Mildew,' says Pete. 'Really quite a lot of mildew.'

'Why don't you do something useful? I need rubber gloves, freezer bags and the laundry basket.' Pete salutes, and by the time she has opened both sash windows he is back with the required items. Anna spreads yesterday's *Guardian* across the table and, wearing the gloves, removes each item of clothing: a heavy knit fleece, two wool jumpers, a dark grey hoodie, another pair of jeans, five T-shirts, and what seems to be the main source of the smell: a pair of swimming shorts that are entirely consumed by a pale mould as thick as moss.

'Some of this stuff would fit me,' says Pete, behind her, and she tells him to shoo. She takes a photo of each item and checks the pockets before dropping it into the laundry basket. As she works though the contents her imagined person at the carousel begins to take shape: it is a man with a penchant for wearing black or dark grey, and while everything is an M size, the cut of the T-shirts and vest suggests he has big muscles. In the jeans there is a torn piece of newspaper crumpled into a tiny parcel. She unwraps it and finds a dried piece of chewing gum and half a sentence of what looks like Spanish – *quando você encontrar a melhor maneira* – and a date: 12/02/13. She photographs this and puts it in a freezer bag, as she does with the other small items lying loose in the case – flattened packets of aspirin, swimming goggles, a pocket calculator, some pens and pencils, a torch that still works. She takes all the clothes to the kitchen and puts them on to wash, cleans her hands, makes a cup of tea and brings it back to the living room, where she sits sideways on the sofa with her laptop. Her computer and digital camera take a moment to become reacquainted, but soon they transmit data back and forth, and when the first pictures appear she feels a sudden dose of pride.

She is *doing* it. Not thinking or talking or planning, but actually *doing* it. It is the final culmination of the last two days, which have been simultaneously enjoyable and relaxing and productive, and where every hour has been squeezed for its usefulness; it feels as if, for the first time ever, she has realised what weekends were designed for.

On Friday evening, after leaving Geoff, Anna returned home to find Pete sitting on the sofa, with one of his textbooks beside him. Her guilt this time manifested itself as a sudden and overwhelming tenderness for him, which prompted her to hug him for a long time. He immediately knew something wasn't right and she told him, not untruthfully, that the interview had been awful, just awful. Pete succeeded in making her calm down – he has always had a knack for doing so, even during their early days, shortly after her dad died – and persuaded her to come with him to the new Vietnamese in Kentish Town, where they could 'talk it out'.

During dinner they discussed nothing else. She relived the interview in excruciating detail, explaining how Sahina refused to answer her questions until the very end, when her answers went entirely against the brand values the article has to promote. When she finished Pete didn't give any direct advice, but instead told her about a 'thinking tool' called the 'problem-solving loop', that might help her find a solution. She knew he was feeding her techniques from his textbooks, designed for slow or unruly fourteen-year-olds, but it still gave her cause for a little optimism.

For the rest of the evening she sent Sahina's quotes and the Romont brand values around the problem-solving loop, and must have continued doing so while she slept, for when she woke on Saturday morning the answer was there waiting for her: she would do both. Her article would juxtapose the undeniable success of Sahina's career – which epitomises the Romont values – with the subversive things she was saying during the interview, and by flitting between these two apparently contradictory narratives, she would demonstrate a complex, conflicted character. Anna jumped out of bed and in her vest and shorts she scribbled this into her notebook, right there on the floorboards of the bedroom, as if worried the idea might evaporate or fly away. After breakfast she went to work properly, writing up the transcript and chopping it into segments that spliced into chunks of Sahina's back-story. By lunchtime the skeleton of the article was in place, and she was so excited that she decided to give herself the rest of the weekend off, and go for a run. She made it twice around the Heath, bought a newspaper on the way home, and after a quick shower began cleaning the entire flat. She moved the hoover and cloth and spray from room to room, scrubbing and dusting herself into a state approaching euphoria. She barely thought of her phone, or Kismet, or meeting an 81, and when she did it was to congratulate herself for not thinking about it. She didn't pause until she rediscovered the little dish of foreign coins in their bedroom, which had been hidden beneath a lingering Christmas card from Pete's parents. She sat on the bed and fingered through the dusty forints and rupees and kroner and euros and quarters, all overlapping and mixed together. A rapid slideshow of images rushed through her mind: hotel rooms, beaches, tuk-tuk rides, jungle passes, mediaeval city squares, day-long bus journeys, haggling in souks, aggressive stray dogs, airport lounges, and of course restaurants – endless, countless restaurants. These snapshots could not have been more varied in terms of climate and colouring and content, yet all seemed to equally capture the tantalising sense of being *away*, and free, and alive, and were also linked by the presence of Pete: he was there in each scene, curiously always to her left and just out of sight, but a solid reassuring presence, their union a fulcrum around which the rest of the world was made to pivot.

She put the dish back and carried the hoover down the ladder. Pete was beginning an elaborate dinner – he'd bought a whole duck from the local butcher – and Anna stood within the kitchen doorway and watched him.

'What?' he said, when he noticed her standing there. She had no trouble formulating her thoughts into words – she was thinking how clever and skilful he was, how good he was at so many different things – but she kept these to herself, preferring to try and convey the same ideas telepathically; he smiled as he moved around the kitchen and called her a weirdo, as he grated and chopped and peeled, and it seemed like he understood.

The next morning she cancelled brunch with Zahra so they could have a lie-in together, and when she did finally get out of bed she didn't really get up, just sat on the sofa in her dressing gown with a coffee and the various sections of the *Guardian* spread around her. Not that she read any of them. Instead she sipped her coffee and took to studying Pete again, this time as he set up the tomato plant on the window ledge. There was something mesmerising about the way he knotted the fragile stem to the bamboo with little pieces of string. His fingers worked delicately yet decisively, simply yet skilfully, and she found herself thinking of all the hours and weeks and years of practice that had gifted him with this deft touch and instinctive knowledge, at the garden centre and before that, growing up at his parents' house in Hampshire with the acre of land out the back. Conversely, she thought of all the time she had allowed to slip through her fingers, as she agonised over what seemed like major decisions between various directions in life, when in fact there was nothing stopping her doing any of the things she might like to. She could still have fun and go out and do what she liked, while also slowing down and having a secure home life. She could work hard and be a successful professional while also making a go of her side projects. She could explore the world while also making a nest for herself. All these things were there for the taking, if only she made use of the ample time and benefits and privileges at her disposal. She resolved to start doing this, from that very moment.

Anna uploads the pictures to a new Instagram profile and links this to a Twitter account, which she considers naming @the_pipe, but quickly decides to call @a_hard_case instead. She uses a photo of the unopened case as the profile picture, and drafts a series of tweets that explain the concept and focus on two major clues: the scrap of newspaper with the date, and the curious variability of the clothing, as if the user was prepared for all climates. After a while Pete comes in and sits on the end of the sofa, taking her bare feet into his lap. He asks for an update, and she tells him the newspaper is in Portuguese, not Spanish. He is holding one of his textbooks, but she can tell he just came in to speak to her.

'Won't Zahra see this and know you lied to her about brunch?'

'She'd have to follow me first. The only thing she thinks about is knocking down walls. No one will follow me, most likely.'

'Maybe not. But the important thing is you're doing it,' he says.

Anna nods and realises she is rubbing her heel absently against his crotch. She removes her feet from his lap and begins writing a tweet of all the countries that speak Portuguese, then Pete shuffles and clears his throat.

'She texted me yesterday.'

Anna stops typing and looks at him.

'Zahra did?' she says, and he nods. The old jealousy expands within her, as if a candle in the vicinity of her heart has been breathed on and briefly flares. 'Why?'

'She said we should hire a boat for your birthday.'

'Oh,' says Anna, her jealousy deflating. The feeling was surprising in its strength, reminding her of that time last year she came home and found Zahra already in the flat, carrying the sick bonsai tree she hoped Pete could cure; it is refreshing to feel this again, like the restoration of her appetite after an illness. 'Did she?'

Pete puts down his textbook and turns his whole body to face her.

'Look: it's your birthday, and if a boat trip is what you want, then we should do it.'

Anna looks down at her laptop, then at Pete, then at her forgotten, now tepid cup of tea. The reasons that made hiring a boat seem a good idea feel distant and obscured, like the half-remembered fragments of a dream.

'I'd forgotten all about it.'

'Even so, if that's what you want, we should organise something now. It will be expensive, and perhaps it will get booked—'

'No,' she says, shaking her head. 'It was a silly idea.

Hamza was the only person who liked it. A dinner party is fine.'

'Just fine?'

'*More* than fine,' she says. She imagines the dinner party, and Pete getting down on one knee afterwards, and as always it creates a sort of inner chaos, but this time not in a bad way. It will be fine. Everything will be fine. 'It'll be good. Great.'

He slumps back into the sofa cushions and releases a massive sigh.

'You should send out the bloody invites, then.'

'I will.'

'It's five days away!'

'You're like an old woman, you are,' she says, kicking him softly with her heel. He catches her foot in his hand and places it in his crotch again. She doesn't resist, indeed pushes downwards into the fleshy contents, which stir and harden in response.

'You almost done?' he says, looking at her, his voice thickened. She looks back at him and resists the urge to pull her foot away, to nip this in the bud.

'Just a minute. I need to write out the countries that speak Portuguese.'

With one hand Pete presses her foot downwards, with the other he begins kneading the smooth pliable flesh of her calves and then thighs, the pads of his fingers still dark from pressing soil. Anna tries to block out these fingers spidering around her legs, and looks at the list of countries. Wikipedia taught her there are nine, but in her list there are only eight – Cape Verde, Timor Leste, Guinea-Bissau, Mozambique, Brazil, Angola, Equatorial Guinea, and São Tomé and Principe. The final one eludes her. Pete's fingers are already teasing the hem of her knickers beneath her shorts, sending a shiver up through her groin. Then he puts his textbook down and gets up on his knees and comes towards her, a great dark shape blocking her view, and she looks up at him and smiles, remembering the Portuguese-speaking country she couldn't remember: Portugal.

Twenty minutes later they are upstairs, lying on their backs, atop the sheets. Pete made it all the way to being naked, Anna still has her knickers on. Anna gazes up at the Velux window; although it is almost 8 p.m. it still frames a rectangle of bright pink sky, as if the light itself is stubbornly refusing to dissolve into night. Pete is breathing heavily, every other breath a sigh through his nose, and she knows she should speak first.

'I'm sorry,' she says.

'Don't be.'

'I did want to. In my *head* I wanted to. But when we actually started . . .'

She searches for a tactful way to put it, and then he supplies a more honest formulation.

'If the feeling's not there, it's not there.'

Anna props herself up on an elbow and lays a hand on the flat of his hairy chest and looks down the length of his naked body; his deflating cock has fallen sadly onto its side.

'It's not like there's a reason. Not a conscious one, anyway.'

'I know,' he says. 'These things come and go. In phases.'

'Like that time last summer,' she says, surprising herself. 'When you didn't want to so much.'

Her saying this makes his head jerk; it is a sudden trespass into something they never discussed at the time.

'Yeah. I don't know. I suppose I didn't. Sure. Maybe I didn't.'

'That wasn't for any sort of reason, was it?'

'No,' he says, immediately. His head has turned further away from her, towards the exposed brickwork at the far end of the room.

'I thought at the time . . . that maybe you fancied someone else.'

'Really? Why?'

She could add that it was Zahra whom she suspected. But she picks a generic version instead.

'I had this idea in my head of some girl . . . You know. Someone sophisticated, smart, successful. Someone like your ex.'

His hand searches for hers, which it squeezes.

'Those girls! They're like . . . automatons compared to you. I grew up surrounded by them. You're different. You're *real*. Honestly, there was no reason. Just like with you. There is no reason, right?'

'Well,' she says, gingerly edging further into the unspoken void between them, 'I have been stressed recently. With work. And, you know . . .'

'Have you been thinking about your dad?'

'No. Not really. I think that maybe . . . I think winter gets me down.'

He turns onto his side and kisses her cheek, until she turns her face to meet his and they kiss properly. His lips are fuller than hers, and her mouth tends to become wet. They hold the closed-mouth kiss for a long time, then follow it with a flutter of short kisses and then rest their foreheads against each other and she looks down into the strange flesh canyon formed by the opposing flanks of their bodies. She should really follow through on what she has started, and tell him about the pills she has been taking since January, and how a loss of libido is the second most common side effect, after batshit crazy dreams. But Pete will overreact, will become upset and concerned, will start treading even more softly around her, as if she is at risk of killing herself. No, she won't tell him, she doesn't want to disrupt the moment. But she will tell him. Soon.

'You're a good guy, you know.'

'I know.'

'And sex isn't everything.'

'Of course not. Let's do something else instead. What do you want to do?'

'Tell me a story.'

'No.'

'Tell me a story from one of our holidays. I know: tell me about Margate, what you did on the train.'

'Margate wasn't a holiday.'

'We stayed the night.'

'Only because we missed the last train. You can't go on holiday by mistake.'

'Well. It *felt* like a holiday. We were in a holiday mood.'

Pete grumbles that a holiday is a thing, not a mood, but then there is a pause and she can tell he is gathering his thoughts. He tells her about their first date outside of London – their fifth date proper – and how they met at London Bridge and caught the train to Margate, where they planned to walk on the beach, visit the art gallery and eat fish and chips. On the train journey Pete opened his backpack, and Anna noticed a book inside.

'*The Alchemist*, by that Brazilian guy, Paul something. You asked if I was reading it. I said I was about to start, that a friend at the office had given it to me. I asked if you'd read it, and you said you didn't rate it, that it was trite. I nodded and looked down at the book, turned it in my hands a few times. Then I stood up, opened the carriage window and threw it out.'

Anna laughs. She always laughs at this story, no matter how many times she hears it; she can still see the book rushing backwards from the window, its pages flapping like the wings of a desperate bird.

'The woman sitting opposite us told me off. She said it was dangerous and wasteful. I tried to explain to her that it was trite, which made you laugh out loud.'

Anna remembers the woman's face, and continues smiling long after Pete calls her a weirdo, gets out of bed and announces he is going to use the leftover duck to make hoi sin wraps for supper. He climbs down the ladder and a moment later she can hear him moving things around in the kitchen. She continues staring at the window in a drowsy trance, until she is startled by a sudden buzz from the far corner of the room. She sits upright and looks across to where her phone is charging on the little footstool beneath the window. In the evening gloom it appears excessively dark and dense, almost like an absence of light or negative matter, its presence intensified for having not being checked for five or six hours. It occurs to her that the message will be from Geoff, and she experiences this possibility as a physical feeling, a tingling that spreads across her whole body.

She rolls off the bed and creeps half-naked across the room. She takes up the phone, types in her passcode and swipes through to the last page, where the Kismet app hides. She has one new message.

Thomas 72: *Salut! How is your weekend? Shame to not see you. Like to meet up this week? xxx*

Anna logs out of Kismet and lets her phone hang at her side. Then she just stands in the centre of the room; the excited feeling dissipates like the slow trailing off of sound after an explosion. From her upright position the angled window gives a very different view: instead of clear sky there is a tangled view of roofs, terraces and TV aerials. There is no denying that she feels shunned and slighted, and she tells herself she shouldn't, that there is no way he was an 81, no way. He is probably a 65 at most, and is currently pretending to be a family man in deep Surrey, playing with his kids and lying through his teeth to his poor wife. She continues rationalising his lack of contact until the fact that she's even bothering to rationalise gives rise to a corrupt and unclean feeling, which sharpens into guilt when the smell of frying duck seeps through the open hatch.

'Stop fucking about,' she says.

She logs back into Kismet and deletes the message from Thomas. Then she opens contacts, selects Thomas 72, presses delete, confirms the deletion. Without hesitating she does the same with Geoff 81. She considers deleting Kismet altogether, but knows this is a faff: to cancel without having found a partner requires a series of confirmations and double-confirmations and password entries and secret-question answering. She decides to do it at work tomorrow, and instead opens her emails, gets into bed and begins tapping out an invite to her birthday dinner party, this Friday at 7.30 p.m. She addresses it to Caz, Hamza, Zahra and Keir, Ingrid, Bean, Toby and Cecile, copies in Pete, and presses send.

Anna drops the phone and with a sigh falls down on her back. It is done. She feels no great sense of relief or anxiety or deliverance, feels nothing really, and just lies there looking at the window that displays the same unbroken segment of sky, only darker now. From downstairs she can hear something sizzling and the regular clatter of the wooden spatula against the pan, until this suddenly stops. It sounds like something has distracted Pete from his cooking, and she pictures him down there, perhaps checking his phone after an email notification. He will read the message she has sent, and she imagines the warmth and relief spreading through his entire being as he realises, in a way beyond his conscious awareness, that she has chosen far more than the dinner party, that she has chosen him.

Monday

After five days of clear blue skies, the new week begins grey and overcast. But Anna doesn't mind; she wakes early and in the same energised spirits that have carried her through the weekend. She catches the bus on Kilburn High Road when it is not even 8 a.m., and the upper deck is filled with a colourful array of cleaners and construction workers, rather than the usual monochrome professional types; she thinks this time she will beat Ingrid into work, surely. As the bus rumbles and coughs and splurts its way into central London, and the buildings grow tall and grey to match the sky, she contemplates what to tell Stuart about the interview; she decides to say it was a 'bumpy ride', but that she got there in the end.

In the office she strides through the empty atrium and rides the lift to the third floor, where she finds Ingrid sitting with her headphones in and one foot tucked beneath her, her fingers scuttling against the keyboard.

'Fucking hell,' says Anna, dropping her bag heavily onto her chair.

Ingrid pulls her headphones out and greets her with a beaming smile.

'Do you live here, or what?'

Ingrid says that in Canada this wouldn't be considered early, and that rather than spending the weekend in the office she has been 'crazy busy', covering the tube map with activities in honour of Sam's final days in the UK. While Anna takes her coat off and gets settled Ingrid tells her about the meal they had at the top of a skyscraper near Liverpool Street; Anna has her usual premonition of seeing the photo gallery, but this time doesn't have to wait, since Ingrid grabs her phone and brings up the pictures. Anna can't help feel envious of the view of the city from that height, with Ingrid and Sam surrounded by the other smiling couples, in front of ornate dishes of Asian food, half a mile in the sky.

'But what about you? How was your weekend?'

'It was great. Really great.'

'I bet it was. The last weekend of your twenties! Did you go wild?'

Anna inhales to speak, then pauses. The last weekend of her twenties; she hadn't thought of it like that. She realises that Ingrid will be surprised to hear that she spent it working on the article, cleaning the flat, opening the suitcase, and hanging around with Pete; the wildest thing she did was go for a run.

'Not wild, no. Do you ever have a nice weekend, even though nothing much happens?'

Ingrid nods and says 'sure' with a little too much emphasis, and Anna doesn't believe her. She would like to explain her discovery of what a weekend is for, and the inspiration this gave her, but she doesn't know how to begin. With dismay it occurs to her that the conviction she felt yesterday – as well as the blissful contentment – has already faded, is now slipping into the past, dissolving into a mere memory. She imagines watching Pete cooking the duck, and this time the image conjures no profound emotion; instead the number 70 flashes above his head.

'But next weekend is the big one, right?' says Ingrid. 'I can't wait. We're going to have so much fun.'

'Yeah. It will be good.' Anna senses that Ingrid will ask more questions about her dinner party; the prospect of answering them makes her feel tired, and she swipes the seldom-used cafetiere and walks off before she has a chance to ask. The kitchenette is empty and it is a relief not to have to make small talk with anyone, but the pleasure is soon replaced by a concern that she is inherently antisocial, or is becoming that way. With a litre of black coffee she leaves the kitchen and heads back between the HR and sports departments, which are both filling with people yawning and sipping themselves to a state of wakefulness. When she comes in line with her desk she sees that Stuart is perched beside her computer talking to Ingrid. He is telling her about his weekend, and going for a drive with his young family; only when Anna places the full cafetiere on the desk does he notice her.

'There she is! Our girl in the field. Have a good weekend?'

He is trying to be friendly and casual, but there is something awkward about it – his backside is just a few inches from her keyboard and mouse, leaving her nowhere to sit down. There is always something forced and itchy about his little trips from the Quiet Room to chat to them. His talk of his wife and twin babies brings to mind the alarming fact that Stuart is married, that Stuart has sex. There was one time, during a free bagel morning, when he came over and ate a bagel amongst them, and a dollop of cream cheese fell from his mouth onto Anna's keyboard.

'We missed you on Friday,' he says. 'Thought maybe you'd run away.'

'Sorry, it was cheeky of me. But the interview lasted over an hour, and then I went to a cafe to write up my notes, and by the time I finished it was almost 5 p.m. and I thought there was little point coming back to the office.'

Stuart watches her say this. He is about the only person in the office to dress smartly, and his hands are deep within the pockets of his suit trousers, where they turn coins and keys around noisily. Anna isn't sure what to do with her arms all of a sudden; she loops them around her back, the fingers and thumb of her right hand linking around her left wrist, as if one arm is putting the other under arrest.

'So it went well, then?' he says, sounding more sure-footed talking about work, his voice in a lower register. 'She must have had a lot to say for herself, if it overran.'

'It was a bit of a bumpy ride,' says Anna, regaining her composure. 'But we got there in the end.'

'Bumpy ride? What do you mean, bumpy ride?'

'You know . . .' says Anna, her mind scrambling for the right way to put it. Stuart's eyes are narrowed, as if trying to peer through to what she is really thinking. She always senses this with Stuart, even when trying to correct for her natural pessimism, and it makes it impossible to think under the heat of his gaze. But before she has a chance to say anything, she hears the rapid tick-tock of footsteps on the tiles, and turns to see little Paula approaching.

'Is this guy giving you a hard time?' she says, grabbing Anna by the forearm. She nods towards Stuart, who raises both palms in a gesture of innocence.

'Anna was just telling us about her interview with Sahina on Friday.'

'Oh wow!' says Paula, her eyes wide. 'How'd it go?'

'Great!' says Anna.

'Of course it did!' says Paula, shaking the flesh on Anna's

forearm. 'Every time I see an interview with her, there's always a zinger of a quote. Something bold, brassy, surprising.' She looks to Stuart and then to Ingrid as she says this, and they all agree, the four of them making a loose circle of nodding people. What kind of a situation is this?

'Did you get many zingers?' she says, smiling at Anna again.

'Oh . . . sure. There were zingers.'

'Anna was telling us', says Stuart, his dark eyes gleaming, 'that they were speaking for an hour.'

'Well . . .' says Anna, wishing she hadn't said that.

'Amazing. I knew you'd nail it. Tell you what: why don't we expand the article, make it long form. Would be a shame to waste it, if you got such good stuff.' Paula looks at Stuart, who nods with his mouth downturned, seeming to agree while still digesting the idea.

'We could get new stills as well,' adds Paula. 'Send a photographer this week.'

'New stills?' says Anna.

'Why not? Let's push this into four-wheel drive. Really launch the series with a bang.'

'Um,' says Anna, feeling the same tightness in her chest as during the interview. 'It might be, like, hard for her to find the time. She's pretty busy . . .'

'Oh, it would be an extra ten minutes, max,' says Stuart. 'Not much to ask after an hour-long interview, is it?' He is still smiling, but she detects something else in his eyes, something slick and knowing, not dissimilar from the way Sahina looked at her – the feeling of being led into a trap shivers through her. She tries to think of a tactful way of backtracking, of bringing up the fact that Sahina's answers went against the Romont values, but her mind feels jammed by the way they are all staring at her. After a while she just nods, says great.

'Wonderful,' says Paula, and with a final squeeze of Anna's arm she says she is late to see Clem, the website's CEO, and is then rushing away across the clearing. Stuart finally stands upright from her desk, and Anna is able to fall down into her chair. He hovers for a moment longer though, rattling off a list of particulars to Anna: two thousand words, copy to him by midday Thursday, run a draft by him on Tuesday or Wednesday, he'll have Jessica call Sahina's people to arrange the photos. These details wash by her in a blur, then she is watching him walking across the clearing towards his desk, and it is Ingrid's voice that is struggling to get through to her. She looks at her keyboard and the patch of desk where Stuart's arse has been resting.

'I'm really pleased for you, Anna.'

'What? Yeah. Great. Hey, coffee!' She plunges the cafetiere and pours a cup, which she sips at and then grimaces, her lips curling in response to the bitterness.

'Urgh. What is it with the coffee in this place? You need milk and three sugars just to take the edge off. Never drink the coffee they give us in the building. That's the golden rule. Why did you let me forget the golden rule?'

She stands up, puts her coat back on and asks Ingrid if she wants anything from the 'outside world'. Then she crosses the clearing, imagining the curious eyes of Ingrid and Stuart like a physical pressure on her back, pushing her out the door.

By 3 p.m., after seven or eight hours of chewing her pen and scribbling in her notebook, Anna has a revised plan in front of her, and persuades herself that she can still do this. She will inflate the usable quotes, and stretch the whole thing to two thousand words. She'll include more back-story, go deep into her childhood and initial projects, before snapping back to a vaguely contradictory statement that Sahina made, such as that young people shouldn't be ambitious at all, but should walk across deserts to escape the polluting influence of corporations. She can make the article work, she tells herself, even if it takes every hour of every day. She can, because she must.

In reward for reaching this relatively calm plateau, she goes for a walk and has a late lunch in Pret a Manger. Then she comes back to her desk and rewatches Sahina's TED talk from a few years ago, the fourth most-watched presentation on the TED website. For some reason the video won't stream properly; the red line indicating the position in the timeline keeps catching up with the grey line that measures how much has been streamed, and in the subsequent moment of buffering Sahina is frozen in some inglorious pose, with her eyes closed and mouth open. Anna asks Ingrid, who is deep within a work trance of her own, if the internet is having an off day, and she confirms that it is. But when Anna flicks across to the most-watched TED talk ever, by Raymond Chan, the video streams fine. The talk was given six months after Kismet was launched, and Anna has already watched it several times. His hair has changed but his face and glasses look exactly the same. He begins by revealing the scientific findings which prove that Kismet couples are over ten times more likely to make a serious commitment (cohabitation, children or marriage) than couples that meet traditionally, with the odds growing exponentially in correlation with the Kismet score.

'And the most beautiful thing about the algorithm', says

Raymond, his mouth stretched into its permanent smile, 'is that it *learns*. Each couple that reaches commitment feeds a new template of compatibility back into the system, which helps make future matches more accurate, which then feed the system again, in a benign cycle of learning and improvement.' He explains how the algorithm gathers millions of indicators of people's KAPO (knowledge, attitudes, practices, opinions) which give the most accurate reading of a person's 'true personality'; as he says this the vast screen behind him shows a scrolling series of millions of dots and dashes, a codification of someone's character. Next he explains the meaning of the word 'kismet' and how the technology will never be used to interrupt the normal flow of people's lives – on the contrary, since Kismet has access to people's routines, it will be able to spot anyone who is obsessively trying to make matches – 'fishing', he calls it – and intervene.

'We are not here to play God,' he says, wrapping up. 'Only to help people find the love that's right there in front of them.'

The video finishes and Anna sits back, scans her eyes around. She looks up at the TVs showing rolling news and half expects to see Raymond's face there as well, but it isn't. Kismet does appear on the big board though, twice, both stories that Anna is already familiar with. In one, Raymond is defending accusations of hypocrisy, since he hasn't used the Love Test technology with his wife of twenty years. The second is the guy in Austria who is making a legal challenge for Kismet to release the data that makes up his profile, saying that the aggregation of his online behaviour 'belongs to him'. Raymond hasn't deigned to comment on this story, and it is an unnamed Kismet spokesperson who brushes aside the argument, saying that to release people's profiles would be to gift the algorithm to their Silicon Valley competitors and that, more importantly, their data policy is clearly explained in the Ts and Cs. This talk of data makes her think of what Geoff 81 said about the pipe, and she remembers her Twitter account and suitcase project, and goes to have a look at it. She is surprised to find that other people have been looking at it too. She has 67 followers already, and twelve retweets. One of them, @DeepBlue1977, says the use of *voce* instead of *tu* for the second person singular suggests African rather than Brazilian Portuguese. Another, @Victoria_Applepie, says there was a massive flood in Mozambique at the date of the newspaper clipping, and that perhaps they were an aid worker?

Anna sits back, amazed. People are actually helping her; the pipe is working. She can almost feel her photos and words spreading through the internet, reaching more people, filtering along pipe after pipe, slowly covering the world. She writes a personal message of thanks to every new follower who has taken part, and then searches for 'internet all the data the pipe' but nothing relevant comes up. She wonders if her searching for the pipe might be detectable to one of the mathematicians paid to look at the pipe, and what they would think, to know that someone is thinking of them while they sit there looking at the endless deluge of data. The thought makes her smile, and she has a sudden, powerful urge to express this idea out loud, to Geoff, thinking that he would almost certainly reply with a ready-made speech of his own. At that precise moment her phone rings within her bag, and for a panicked moment she thinks it must be him. But then she remembers that she deleted him, and when she retrieves her phone she sees the freckled, bespectacled face of Zahra.

'Drink after work?' says Zahra, as Anna walks across the clearing to the landing.

'Can't, I'm slammed.'

'Just quickly? I want to speak to you about your birthday.'

'You're speaking to me now.'

Anna leans her elbows into the sunken window frame at the end of the landing; she is surprised to see the tops of umbrellas floating along the alleyway below, since it doesn't appear to be raining.

'So you've made a decision,' says Zahra, eventually. 'The boat is off?'

'Yes. The boat is off.'

'And the dinner party is *on*?'

'Yes,' says Anna, a trace of irritation in her voice. 'The dinner party is *on*.'

Zahra makes such a big sigh it sounds like she is blowing down the phone.

'This is great, Anna. I'm really pleased for you.' She says more things like this, sounding puffed up with a delight that Anna feels is excessive, even suspicious.

'So you didn't match with anyone else?'

'No. Well, there was one guy. It was nothing.'

'What score?'

'Like, 65 or 66. I don't even remember. It was nothing. You were right – my profile was screwed up.'

'Of course I was right. I've been telling you from the start, Pete is great.'

The familiar old jealousy flares within Anna, and she wonders if it is possible that Zahra's enthusiasm and encouragement should make her concerned. Though maybe this idea is completely irrational. She isn't sure, and just thinking about it makes her head hurt; all she wants is to get off the phone.

'Yep, you were right about everything. Even the weather. Look: we couldn't take a boat out in the rain.'

'Is it raining? It's hard to tell from the tenth floor.'

'Rain is actually hard to see,' says Anna, though she is learning this herself at the same time as saying it. 'You can see where it lands, and the things it hits, but when you actually try and look *at* the rain itself, it's hard.'

Zahra laughs and says she sounds like a fridge magnet. Then she asks Anna to meet tomorrow instead, and Anna says maybe. After hanging up she continues standing with her elbows on the window ledge, looking through the glass. Eventually she decides that yes, you can see the rain – it is like a faint reverberation in the air, a transparent shifting that hovers on the brink of perceptibility, as if the air itself is being rustled.

Tuesday

Anna is alone in a wine bar on the Strand, sitting at a high, narrow table beside a floor-to-ceiling glass wall that makes her feel she is in a tank. On the other side of the window, homebound office workers are struggling against the confusing weather; a fine misty drizzle is falling, which is simultaneously heavy and light, while the air is mild to the point of being warm, almost tropical. Some commuters are responding with raincoats and umbrellas, some with a folded newspaper raised above them; most are simply walking with their heads lowered, resigned to getting wet.

Her phone is on the table in front of her, and with fingers that feel strangely hollow she sends a message to Pete saying she's meeting Zahra for a quick drink. Then she looks again through the glass, and the sight of a tall, dark-haired, suited man on the far pavement causes electricity to branch through her.

But it isn't him, and her startled nerves relax. The strength of her reaction is alarming, and she reminds herself that her being here is of no consequence, that she doesn't have to be here at all. It is less than an hour since he called her at work – thus proving that he could still call, despite her deleting him – and asked blithely if she was 'hungry, thirsty or both'. She isn't sure why she agreed. She supposes it would be good to thank him for the encouragement with the suitcase project, though that hardly feels like a reason.

In fact, the sensible thing would be to get up and walk out. Just as this thought is about to be translated into action, she sees another dark-haired man hurrying along the far pavement, and this time it is him, her 81. He jogs to make the final beeps of a pedestrian crossing, disappears from view for a moment, then reappears in the centre of the bar, where he stops and casts his eyes about. She gives him a little wave and he approaches.

'Hello, Anna,' he says, planting himself at the end of her table, hands on hips. He is wearing a grey business suit that is much sharper than what he wore on the South Bank, but is still tweedy, vintage-looking.

'Hello, Geoff.' She pivots on her stool to face him and they smile at each other.

'Nice suit.'

'Thanks. It's my lucky suit.'

'Oh yeah? You think something good will happen if you wear it?'

'Of course. Though, in this instance, the good thing has already happened.'

They continue smiling at each other, but neither extends a physical greeting. She feels a pang of regret about her appearance, since once again she hasn't had the chance to choose her outfit; she is wearing a heavy-knit burgundy jumper, her unwashed hair is tied up, and on her feet are the oafish boots. Nevertheless, his bright blue eyes still seem to appraise her with interest, even excitement. His long, rectangular face is beaded with moisture, either from exertion or the rain, which he wipes away with his hand. There is something ridiculous about how handsome he is.

'You can sit down, if you like?' she says.

'Maybe,' he says, and she realises his smile is fixed. 'If you'd like me to.'

'What do you mean?'

There is a pause, then he says: 'You deleted me. On the app.'

'Oh.' Anna can feel herself blush. 'You can see that?'

'Your name, Anna 81, became faded in my list of contacts. I found out that means you deleted me.'

'Sorry.' Anna looks at her hands twisted together in her lap. It is embarrassing, but seems a good opportunity to come clean. 'It was nothing personal, it was just—'

'Please, don't apologise. It should be me apologising. I was advised not to call, but then . . . something made me think you didn't mean it.'

'What made you think that?'

'My little finger,' he says, holding up a pinkie, as if it is his source of intuition. Finally he sits down on the other side of the table, barely wide enough for two plates. The white sky and vast windows are filling the bar with an even, pale light that casts no shadows, and Anna notices that his irises aren't simply blue, as she'd thought, but are flecked with yellow around the pupils, like the flares during a solar eclipse. They continue gazing like this, until Geoff does something surprising: he leans forwards and kisses her cheek. Anna is stunned; they have already been together for several minutes, and the kiss, outside its ritual place, feels shockingly intimate. She laughs awkwardly and feels her face flush again, and it's a relief when the waiter arrives with a menu, which Geoff scans before saying something in French. She takes the menu and finds the bottle he ordered, the Chassagne-Montrachet, for £220.

'We're celebrating,' he says, as she gawps at the price. 'We've had good news on the project.'

'Your secret investigation?'

He nods and looks away from her, squinting at the glass wall beside them.

'What does that mean? You've had a breakthrough? You've cracked the code?' She says this with a light scorn that he doesn't acknowledge.

'I wouldn't go that far. But it's a promising development.'

'And it's still a secret?'

'More than ever, I'm afraid. It's a sensitive time.'

'Is it to do with the pipe you were talking about?'

He looks back at her and smiles, and she senses it is.

'I really can't say.'

'You've tapped into it somehow, haven't you?'

'Wait and see.'

'That means I'm right,' she says, cheekily, and he shakes his head and tuts, his expression further confirming that she's on to something. The waiter returns with the bottle in a bucket of ice and two glasses which, after giving Geoff a taste, he fills.

'Congratulations, I guess,' she says, raising her glass. 'Let's drink to mysterious achievements. To boys and their toys.'

'No. Let's drink to success. To the feeling, rather than the specific prize. I've always found it tastes the same, no matter what you've achieved. It's like the world is on your side, like it wants to be your friend. Cheers.'

They chink glasses and a flurry of personal successes – passing her second driving test, opening her A-level results, being offered the initial internship at the website – flit through Anna's mind, before she sips the chill, biting wine. She holds up the glass and expects to see splinters of ice floating in the yellow liquid, then takes a second, bigger gulp.

'I'm celebrating as well, actually,' she says, taking her phone from her bag. She tells him that she finally started her suitcase project at the weekend, and brings up her key stats on Twitter: in the last day her number of followers has jumped to 179, the number of retweets to 44, and over a dozen posts are now using the #ahardcase hashtag. She shows him a picture of the newspaper clipping and says that it has been identified as coming from a Mozambique title, *Canal de Maputo*, and that on 17 February 2013, the date on the clipping, the country was severely flooded, and full of foreign aid workers.

'During the flood there were only a few flights to Heathrow a week, apparently,' she says, flicking her screen in search of the relevant comment. 'According to one guy, BAA have a database of all passengers for a certain period of time.'

'This is a good start,' he says, with a measured tone. 'Forgive me for being slow. But why are you celebrating?'

'Because I'm doing it. Because it's working.'

'Come on, now. You've barely started. Less than two hundred followers?'

'It's good for it to be small, it means I can speak to and thank each follower individually. Besides, what did you expect?'

'I expect this to be big. Really big. I'm not joking. I think you can actually find him. You just need to take it to the next level.'

'How do I do that?'

'The problem is a credibility gap. You need to gather more supporters. You have to like people who can then follow you.

Celebrities. Journalists. You have to really invest time in it. Treat it like a full-time job.' It's surprising that he knows so much about Twitter.

'I've got a full-time job already.'

'Oh, yes, that,' he says, scornfully. 'But this is real journalism. And it won't come without any sacrifices.'

'Sacrifices, yes. But not earning any money? You know, my job isn't that bad. I have quite a lot of wriggle room. And besides, how will I eat?'

'Lots of freelance journalists start out like this. You would get noticed, then start to get offered jobs. Of course it can pay.'

'I imagine those freelance journalists didn't have mortgage repayments to keep up.'

Geoff looks out the window again and then peers at Anna with his long fingers pressed to his lips, as if assessing how much he can trust her.

'You know, there is something you could do,' he says, angling across the narrow table. 'Something I could help with. A shortcut, so to speak.' He tells her there is a method for gathering extra followers, a way of exploiting a loophole in Twitter's back end, that lots of people use. 'They call it mopping up,' he says. 'We could bump you up to one thousand, two thousand followers in a few minutes.' He clicks his fingers.

'You mean creating fake accounts?'

'God, no. Something much better than that. These are real people, only they won't know they're following you.' He seems excited, and has a mischievous gleam in his eyes.

'This sounds very dodgy. Is it to do with your pipe thing again?'

'Technically speaking, everything is to do with the pipe. But the point is it isn't cheating. Lots of people do it, to take their work to the next level. And you owe it to yourself to do the same.'

Anna asks again what the hell it is, exactly, but Geoff says he doesn't want to go into the details, and changes the subject successfully by saying he is fond of Mozambique, even though he was once kidnapped there. Anna requests the full story and he begins telling her, in a surprisingly jaunty way, about when he worked for a newspaper in Malawi back in the nineties – the *Lilongwe Herald* – that wasn't published daily or weekly, but *when it was ready*. The whole operation was floored for a month by the printer breaking down, and Geoff spent the time hitch-hiking through neighbouring Mozambique, aiming to learn to surf on the way. In one town on the coast he was looking for a lift, and a young guy in startling platform shoes joined him in a bar where he was drinking a Coke, and said he could find him a lift in the morning and a bed for the night. He bought Geoff another Coke, and another, and called his friends and they all surrounded him in the bar and insisted on calling him John.

'Each time they bought me a new Coke they promised it would be the last, and that after I drank it they would sort me out with the room and the lift. Eventually I suspected something wasn't right, and politely tried to leave. But they pushed me back into the booth, told me to finish my Coke. This went on for hours, until two or three in the morning. Then they finally took me out, said they were leading me to the bus station where they would get me a lift. But instead they just took me to another bar, and ordered me a Coke.

'I must have drunk twenty Coca-Colas. In the end they

made a mistake and let me go to the toilet, and I climbed out the window and ran for it.'

'I'm not sure that classes as being kidnapped.'

'Seriously, they were terrifying. They all had these platform shoes. They were like an African *Clockwork Orange*. I even left my bag. But no, I suppose it was nothing. I've had much worse scrapes.'

He tells her equally colourful stories about when he was on a rowing boat at night on a lake in Kashmir, stoned out of his mind, and drifted into Pakistani territory, and found himself under a spotlight with twenty border guards on a patrol boat pointing guns at him. Or the time in Paraguay when he was arrested and accused of being a spy, but was released following an intervention from a hairdresser whom he'd given a large tip to. His hands move around as he speaks, and Anna becomes transfixed by his long sculptured fingers as they swoop and dip. She looks up from his hands and in the delicately etched creases around his eyes sees evidence of experience rather than age. He has *lived*. This occurs to her with the weight of revelation, and she feels a swirling in her stomach, as if the liquid it contains is being stirred. She thinks maybe the wine is getting to her, but even as she thinks this she takes another sip, and then Geoff refills her empty glass.

'You've lived in a lot of places,' she says, when he finally falls silent. He says it is because he has always put off settling down, and Anna is pleased to have impetus to make a speech of her own. She says that she was like that in her early twenties; everyone else she hung around with at uni went from being left-wing stoners and idealists to suddenly applying for law conversion courses and graduate schemes during their final year, perhaps to justify their horrendously expensive private-school educations. But Anna was content to do nothing. She moved to London after graduating, worked temp jobs, tried to set up projects and generally bummed around. Her peers complained of post-uni blues, but she loved it. She thinks maybe it was her happiest time, and managed to stretch it out for four or five years, culminating in a six-month stint in San Francisco, staying in her dad's sister's flat.

'Four or five years is nothing,' says Geoff. 'I'm still stretching it out.'

'Having said that,' continues Anna, 'having a proper job means you can take proper holidays. Go on real adventures. The Philippines, New Zealand, Iceland.'

'But only once or twice a year. That's nowhere near enough. The trick is to make your whole *life* a holiday.'

'You do realise that I'm not a millionaire.'

'I don't mean literally jetting off on trip after trip. Holidays aren't about a location. It's a *mood*. A disposition, a way of interacting with the world around you. It's not just something to be done during breaks from work; you can be on holiday while *making* money. And it can be anywhere. France, Italy, Scottish island. Even Vauxhall.'

He is turning his hand again, and his mentioning Italy conjures up in her mind an image of a life in the Mediterranean, scraping by in some whitewashed villa, doing bits and bobs of freelance work – it occurs to her that he is visualising the same thing, and she imagines an 81 flashing above his head. She would like to ask if he has ever lived in Greece, but Geoff turns around and holds his hand up to a waiter.

'Wine's done. Fancy another?'

Anna looks at her empty glass, the empty bottle, and for the first time since he arrived tries to assess her feelings.

She considers going home, but this is a momentary thought, instantly rejected on the excuse that it feels like she just got here; the hour has passed in what seems like five minutes. But equally she doesn't want to just sit there getting drunk.

'No more wine. I'd like to, you know . . . go somewhere.'

His eyes narrow; it occurs to her that he might think she is suggesting they go and have sex. It occurs to her that she is.

'I spend my whole life sitting,' she says, hastening to continue. 'At work, at home, in bars. I'd like to *do* something. I haven't been dancing in months.'

'You want to go dancing?'

'That's just an example.'

'Okay. Let's *do* something. Where are we? The Strand. Let me think.' He looks downwards and becomes unnaturally still. Then he nods and says: 'I've got it. Just the thing; short walk from here. Something a bit different.'

The bill comes and Geoff counts many £20 notes onto the table, then gives £10 directly to the waiter. This reminds Anna of something, and while sliding off her stool and following Geoff towards the exit, she thinks of how her father insisted on tipping everyone, and even once gave £2 to the fast-food boy in a service station, who merely pushed their dinner to them on a tray.

They walk east, towards Aldwych. The sky is a sagging white blanket, the breeze is warm and damp and fidgeting. Many people are on the pavement and Anna could easily be spotted by an acquaintance or colleague, but she feels absurdly invisible, as if this is happening in a different realm to her normal life. She thinks of a streamed video, and how the red line is like her conscious awareness of her actions, and the grey line is the plans and objectives that allow these actions to make sense; it feels like these two bars are moving through time together, the red and grey lines unfurling in tandem, the latter laying track that is immediately eaten up by the former, like flagstones being laid just in time for each landing foot. She smiles at herself and says: 'I'm a bit pissed.' Geoff laughs and takes her hand.

They cross Lancaster Place and Anna is disappointed when he leads her beneath the arched entrance to Somerset House.

'Don't worry,' he says, as if hearing her thought. 'I'm not taking you to look at Art.'

They cross the courtyard and go through open doors into the South Wing, where Geoff pulls her left past a sign saying 'Private'. At the end of the corridor they turn onto the East Wing, then through double doors to a stairwell. They descend four flights, until the stairs open to a basement corridor with nylon floor tiles and electrical wire tacked to blank white walls.

'If anyone asks,' whispers Geoff, 'say you work in Self-Assessment.'

Before she has time to ask why, he shouts: 'Excuse me.' The words echo around the bare walls, then a door opens ahead of them. A short, grizzled man steps from behind it, a caretaker of some kind, in a blue sweatshirt and matching trousers.

'Sorry to bother,' says Geoff, a peg posher than normal. 'We were wondering if they were open?' He points over the man's shoulder towards a set of double doors at the end of the corridor. The caretaker looks along the corridor, and then at Geoff and Anna, appearing to size them up.

'Oh, we're not going to use the kit,' says Geoff, chuckling.

'Just a nostalgia trip. Showing the new guard how things used to be.' He nudges Anna as he says 'new guard'. After a moment the caretaker nods and, in heavily accented English, says they should follow him. They walk down the corridor to the locked doors, Geoff chatting to the silent man as he checks for the right key. On the other side of the doorway Geoff and Anna are sealed in almost total darkness.

'What's going on? Why did you say I was part of the new guard?'

'Because it wouldn't have helped if I hadn't,' he whispers, feeling about on the wall. 'I had to establish you in a context he'd understand.'

'What does that mean?'

'It means,' he says, flicking one, two, three switches, 'free to those who can afford it. Very expensive to those who can't.'

A gathering electrical hum, then a green corridor appears before them, lit by a row of gold sconces. The lower halves of the walls are panelled, the upper half are floral damask wallpaper. Every twenty feet or so there is a wooden door, giving the appearance of a hotel. The smell is of dust.

'Where are we?' she says, stepping along the worn carpet. She opens the first door and reveals more darkness and a thick, musty smell. After finding a switch – an old-fashioned brass toggle rather than a plastic plate – a square room appears before her, dominated by a billiards table and an oil painting of a white-wigged aristocrat from another century.

'Believe it or not,' says Geoff from behind her, 'we're in the Staff Gymnasium of the Inland Revenue.'

He leads her to the neighbouring chambers – a table-tennis room, a fencing court and – the *pièce de résistance* – a rifle range, which to Anna's eyes looks more like a bowling alley. Geoff explains that the entire Civil Service was once based at Somerset House, and that while the Inland Revenue formally left for Whitehall ten years ago, it seemed some of the old boys didn't have the heart to give up the gymnasium and lounge.

'I was once embattled with the taxman,' he says, stepping back into the corridor. 'When I finally returned to Britain and was going to settle down, they hit me with some outrageous avoidance charges. And that's when I read up about them more, and found out about this place. It felt poetic, to fight them in court during the day and use their steam room at night. Come on, time for my favourite sort of recreation.'

The final room in the corridor is the lounge, with armchairs surrounding low tables, oil paintings bunched close together in rows, and a carpet so thick it is like walking through mud. Geoff takes a decanter from a cupboard and pours amber liquid into two tumblers. She takes a sip – the gold liquid meeting her lips with a fierce kiss – and drifts away to the other side of the lounge, settling before a painting of a bald man with red cheeks and a shining pink head, forever locked in furious eye contact with the viewer.

'This place is special,' she says, raising her voice to carry across the room. 'I'll give you that.'

'Oh, this is nothing. London is full of places like this.'

'Really?'

'Not just London, all cities. All life, even. There's treasure everywhere, if you know where to look.'

Anna steps sideways and considers a painting of a gentle, red-robed man who is staring benignly downwards and to his right, as if gazing directly into the very essence of Things.

'Treasure everywhere,' she repeats, mimicking his voice, and then laughs.

'I don't mean in an *exotic* sense,' he says. 'It's just that people live constrained lives, given what's on offer. Just think: every day you'll pass women on the street who genuinely believe they can't have an orgasm. Or that they can't be happy.'

His saying 'orgasm' seems suggestive and makes her turn, but she only sees the back of his head while he looks at a painting.

'It's not that people don't *want* to be happy,' she says. 'Or don't want to have orgasms.'

'I know that. The problem is they believe, on a very fundamental level, that it is due to a deficiency in themselves, rather than the ideology they inhabit.' He continues making this speech to the painting in front of him, saying the problem has reached pandemic levels, especially amongst people her age. 'I see people in their twenties who already think their life is behind them. They say things like "I wish I'd done this" or "I wish I'd been that." They don't realise that if they don't like their lives, they can change them. It's why so many young people take drugs.'

Again she stares at the cropped hair on the back of his neck; this time he turns to meet her eyes.

'That's not the only reason people take drugs,' she says, thinking of her pills.

'Don't get me wrong,' he says, 'I've got nothing against drugs. I used to take them as well. But they're vulgar. They offer a chemical shortcut to something that's in your mind anyway. An acid trip is no crazier than the dreams you have most nights. It's all in your head. The joy, the energy, the madness. It's all there.'

133

The fact that she takes drugs just to feel normal makes Anna ashamed, and this sharpens into a desire to defend herself.

'You sure that's not the booze talking?' she says, with edge. Geoff smiles.

'Good point,' he says, and then looks down into his glass sadly and, with an effort of self-control Anna herself feels, seems to resist the impulse to take a sip. She senses she touched a nerve and wants to be nice to him, to make up for it.

'Well, you are British,' she says. 'Our whole lives are built on booze.'

'True,' he says, before turning back to his painting and beginning another speech, about how living overseas made him more British, rather than less, since the fact became his main point of distinction. He swirls his hand around, as if explaining this to the long-dead cavalier in the picture before him, and Anna has a mischievous thought. Silently she places her tumbler on a table, then treads out of the room while he speaks on.

The lounge is not the end of the Gymnasium, as she had thought, but its halfway point: the corridor turns left onto another row of closed doors. Anna walks quickly, and then, on a rush of childish excitement at being alone in a forbidden place, she runs. After opening several doors she finds a changing room, and after using the toilet she is taken by the reflection of her face, and leans close in to the mirror. She considers the downy white hairs that give her pale skin a dusty finish; her wide, full mouth; the bulbous end to her nose; the darker patch of sun-damaged skin on her forehead, legacy of her gap year. These are painless, tender observations. Even since the age of seventeen or eighteen, when she filled out after an awkward and lanky adolescence, she has quite liked her face. Boys and men have always seemed to like it, too. She grins, to assess her wrinkles, and is reminded that her thirtieth birthday is three days away. This makes her think of Pete and the Sahina article. It all feels of distant relevance, as if it is happening to someone else, in another city or country, to someone she barely knows. It's a curious feeling, this being cut off from the facts of her life, and it reminds her of being on drugs – on *real* drugs, party drugs. She thinks of the Minuscule of Sound, and remembers having the same feeling then – at 5 a.m. the rest of the world seemed very far away, and she was free to be her best self. She remembers one time – perhaps one of the first times she took a pill – she went around the club talking to every person who wasn't dancing, persuading them to 'get involved', feeling utterly fearless and charming, in love with the world and her place in it. Yes, that's what she feels like now. But she remembers something else as well; something more distant and buried, memories from childhood. She stamps her boots against the bathroom tiles to gather sense data, and remembers that she regularly felt like this as a young girl, was often brimming with excitement and the desire to run and shout and show off, especially if her dad was watching her. There was one time in particular, when he had taken them to a giant adventure playground, complete with obstacle course and competitions, and she swung from monkey bars and rope swings and won the race she was selected in, while Josh – crybaby as ever – sulked because of their dad's obvious preference for her. It is incredible how vividly she remembers this, and she wonders if there is something about Geoff that evokes this same feeling, and if this could be the basis for the 81 score – perhaps Kismet somehow knows about this submerged feeling and how it can be unlocked. The idea is too complex to process, and she puts it aside and gathers more sense data, this time clapping her hands and inhaling through her nose; at the end of her breath she catches a note of chlorine. She follows this smell through the changing room and into an adjoining black space that she knows, even before the light flicks on, contains a swimming pool.

Anna laughs out loud. The pool is perhaps ten metres long and is covered with a dark blue canvas attached to a roller. She walks around the lip and finds a hand crank which she turns a few times, causing the roller to rotate. She kneels and turns many more times, and like a giant lolling tongue the cover retreats onto the roller. The exposed water breathes cold air onto her face.

'Anna 81,' says Geoff, causing her to start. He is standing by the door at the other end of the pool, and is almost shouting. 'I thought I'd lost you.'

Geoff hits another switch by the door and lights come on within the water, changing it from ink to turquoise.

'Just exploring,' she says. 'Looking for treasure.'

'I thought maybe you'd run away.'

'To run away, to explore. Is there a difference?'

'I suppose not.'

She thinks of something else to say, something aphoristic, and decides to venture an impression of Geoff's posh accent and strenuous, up-and-down speech pattern: 'Of *course*, you can't *get* anywhere, without *leaving* somewhere *first*.'

His grin appears tiny, seen across the length of the room.

'Very good,' he says, then stands with hands on hips. She gets the impression her playfulness has thrown him, that he is momentarily out of ideas. But at the same time he seems to stare with a new animal desire. It is as if her impudence has rankled him, but also enhanced his interest, made him impatient to get to her. He puts his hands in the pockets of his trousers and walks slowly around the pool towards her. She also walks anticlockwise around the lip, away from him, and they come to a stop facing each other across the width of the pool. He grins at her across the water.

'You know, I've always had a funny relationship with swimming,' he says. 'A love/hate relationship.'

'That doesn't surprise me.'

'That I don't like swimming?'

'No. That you've got a long-winded opinion about it.'

Geoff's grin now appears fixed. She knows she is being rude, but thinks that on a deep level he is enjoying it, is willing her on. Besides, his saying the number has reminded her she can't make mistakes; if the number is correct then her every instinct must be true.

'You're clever,' he says.

'You think?'

'Clever and funny.'

She shrugs.

'Some people think I'm a klutz.'

'I don't believe it.'

'At work, especially.'

'That's because you're in the wrong job. You're chasing the wrong spectacle, for the wrong reasons. No wonder you don't feel yourself.'

'Is that right?' she says, with mock credulity. 'And how do I escape?'

'You have to rearrange the co-ordinates of your life,' he says immediately, as if this is a prepared speech, something he says ten times a day. 'It is desire that gives shape to our existence and makes sense of the world. To escape ideology is to redraw the map.'

'Sounds doable.'

'But it will feel like destroying yourself.'

'Ouch. Does this chat often work with girls?'

'No. But you strike me as a special case.'

For a moment they just stare at each other, and there is no mistaking the desire in his eyes. She feels a familiar urge to flee, but she suppresses it and continues staring, riding the moment. It occurs to her that this was the point of the whole meeting, that this is the plan she has been working to all along, but subconsciously, only revealed to her now, and it immediately makes sense: she was going to spend the night with Thomas 72, so why not with Geoff 81? She takes off her boots then her socks; the pimpled tiles are freezing beneath her feet. Her toenails are in need of repainting. No matter. As she unstraps her watch Geoff continues walking anticlockwise around the pool; she does the same. They come to a stop at opposing ends, Anna this time by the door.

'Let's play a game,' he shouts.

'I thought we already were.'

'Let's play a different one.'

'Okay,' she says, taking off her heavy jumper, beneath which is only her bra. She feels a pang of regret for the pinchable loose flesh around her belly, no longer the effortless firm slab of her early twenties. He resumes walking, as does she, until they are facing each other across the width again, Geoff now beside her stale boots. He can probably smell them from where he stands, but so what? He is an 81, and she can do no wrong. She unbuttons her jeans and tugs the denim from her thighs and calves before stepping out of them. Her half-nakedness is enhanced by Geoff remaining fully clothed in his pale suit.

'What shall we play for?' she says, mirroring his hands-on-hips stance.

'What do you mean?'

'In your game. What's at stake? What do we stand to win?'

'Oh, everything,' he says. 'We stand to win everything.'

'Both of us?'

'Both of us.'

'And what do we lose?'

'The same. We stand to lose everything.'

She laughs at this exchange; it seems they are simultaneously talking nonsense and making code for the deepest meaning. Then she waits for him to walk again, before realising he isn't going to. He stares fixedly, and she now understands the purpose of the game: it is all about her; it is her turn to move, he is just here to watch. If she doesn't like her life, she can change it.

'Okay,' she says, emboldened by his gaze. 'I'm game.'

Without hesitation she steps forwards, pushes off her toes and leaps into the air, stretching her body into a straight line that knifes into the cold waiting water, swallowing her whole.

It is almost midnight when she unlocks the front door; the flat is dark and silent. She leaves her boots on the mat and then tiptoes up the hardwood stairs. In the bathroom she compensates for her drunkenness by taking excessive care when brushing her teeth, washing her face, drinking a glass of water. She sniffs at her damp ponytail and tries to determine whether the smell of chlorine is actually there, or whether she can only smell it because she knows it should be there: impossible to say.

There's no way of reaching the loft bedroom quietly, but somehow she climbs the ladder, flips the hatch and clambers onto the floorboards without waking Pete, who is fast asleep – his snores sound like gravel being crunched by slow steps. Still, she doesn't want to risk turning a light on and, unable to find her vest and shorts in the dark, she strips naked and slips into bed. Pete's breathing splutters as she lies down next to him; his lips smack together and he sighs through his nose. Anna holds her breath, willing him to remain asleep, but then his hand reaches for her beneath the duvet. His sleepy fingers land on her ribs and become alert, as if surprised to find bare skin. They scan down to her hip and then up to her chest, where they hesitate, as if pondering the meaning of her being naked. Then they begin kneading her right breast.

Anna lies completely still, her eyes closed.

He squeezes and pinches her nipple for a time. Then, perhaps reading her lack of resistance for compliance, his fingers trace across her belly and into her tangle of pubes, where they nestle for a moment, as if thinking. Then one finger hooks around and neatly fills the hole that, to Anna's surprise, has become moist and swollen.

'Huh,' she gasps.

His finger moves in and out and the soft friction causes a kernel of energy to sprout within her groin. Instinctively, she tilts her pelvis upwards into the press of his palm and clenches her buttocks, causing the kernel to grow until it has an insistent will of its own. She pulls his hand away by the wrist and whispers: 'Fuck me.'

An invisible rustling and shuffling takes place, as Pete removes his shorts and T-shirt with the haste of a sentry called to sudden action, after months of bored, redundant waiting. Then his full naked weight is upon her. His lips are warm and slack with sleep, his wet kiss tastes of toothpaste and something acidic, perhaps alcohol. He is already hard, and she opens her legs and after a fumbling alignment they fit together. 'Mmmmph.'

'Yes,' she whispers, her lips grazing his ear. 'Yes. Fuck. There. Shit. Yes.'

She repeats these words in random order and without meaning, only to give shape to the air being forced in and out of her. The duvet slips to the floor. Pete speeds up and the kernel in Anna's groin grows with each thrust, gaining size and weight and heat. Anna's talk is smothered by another kiss, and this time she recognises the tangy flavour on his tongue: wine. Pete has been drinking wine. This prompts an unwanted image of Pete sitting alone in the living room, waiting for her, and she is seized by guilt.

She forces her mouth from the kiss and turns her face on its side. Pete continues thrusting, he is almost there already, but for Anna it is over. The kernel and the lust have vanished, leaving only a catalogue of pleasureless sensations: liquid sloshing in her stomach, goosebumps spreading along her bare legs, the bed frame creaking beneath her, a chafing on her inside thigh . . . She is grateful for the dark, small mercy, so she can't be seen grimacing as her mind flits between the lonely image of Pete on the sofa and its counterpoint, her chinking glasses with Geoff.

He kissed her twice. First, as they climbed the stairs from the Gymnasium back to ground level, having been interrupted by the caretaker, he pushed her against the wall and they kissed in a firm, closed-mouth way that reminded her of black-and-white films. Second, after more drinks at the Waldorf, they cowered from the resurgent rain beneath the awning of a closed jewellery shop. This time it was prolonged and elaborate, a series of kisses. She stepped onto the shop's raised doorway to equalise their height, her arms around his neck.

'See me on Thursday,' he said, during a momentary break, a pause for breath.

She said nothing, just leaned her face back towards his.

'Thursday,' he said, breaking off again a few moments later, holding her at arm's length. 'We can go somewhere *really* special, have dinner . . .' And we can fuck, was the third suggestion, unspoken. He smiled and they carried on kissing, while rain drummed against the awning.

Pete makes a noise, something between a groan and a grunt, that restores Anna to the present moment: she is being fucked. Vigorously and noisily fucked. Surprisingly, the kernel has returned to her groin. She thinks again of Geoff's kiss and the kernel swells, pushes upwards to her abdomen.

'Yes,' she says, feeling she will make it after all. 'Fuck. Shit. Yes. There. Yes!'

She thinks of Geoff's tongue in her mouth, she thinks of his long fingers tucked into the arse-pocket of her jeans, and she thinks: Thursday.

'Yes!' she says, raising her legs and scissoring them behind Pete's back. This is his cue, and he lowers himself to enter from a more oblique angle, finding her spot, his belly pressing against her pubic bone. The kernel is now a hot ball of energy that begins to split, the heat spilling outwards and spreading into her chest, her legs.

'Now,' she says, clamping herself to him.

He grunts, she gasps and the word Thursday resonates through her mind as the hot energy fills her legs, her arms, her head, and then her whole body is gripped by a heat that gathers into a red blaze and then dissipates in a slow series of shimmering waves.

Afterwards, they lie together beneath the retrieved duvet. Pete's heavy arm is laid over her chest. He is clearly tired but seems to want to stay awake, to keep hold of the moment.

'And you came?' he says.

'Yep. Uh-huh.'

'But you've been drinking?'

'Yes,' she says, only now realising how rare this is. 'Funny, huh? Who knows what controls these things?'

'It's probably all in your head,' he says, shuffling closer to her.

'That's what Zahra thinks,' she says and then, fearing this could prompt him to ask about her evening, she rushes to speak again. 'I've got to sleep, Pete. It's gone twelve.'

'It's true. It's tomorrow already. Tomorrow is Thursday.'

'Yes,' she says, hearing a breathy panic in her voice. She turns away from him and rearranges herself on the pillow, the duvet folded up around her head and transmitting the sound of her rapid, fluttery pulse. Pete takes his arm back and she listens to his breath become slow and raspy, as he sinks away from her into sleep. While she lies there, alone, her eyes wide open in the dark.

Wednesday

Anna scrolls up and down the article on her computer – 'Sahina_v.6' – and wonders if she has done enough for the day. It is 7.30 p.m., and the third floor is almost empty. While the newsroom downstairs will still be ticking away, with the night shift getting into their stride, the sports and sponsored content desks go to bed for the night – even the twenty-four-hour news screens shut off at 9 p.m., leaving just the big board projecting away through the night, refreshing its stats every ten seconds, to nobody.

Ingrid is still there though, typing away; as always she is sitting up straight with her face close to the screen, and Anna feels herself having adopted a similar posture these last few days, as opposed to her usual slumped imitation – it is like her and Ingrid are nose to nose in some stationary race. Anna decides to do one more comb through the document. The structure of the article has taken shape, the overarching logic and beats; she can see them beginning to grow distinct and sharp within the swamp of words. The article begins with a summary of Sahina's supposedly cutthroat rise to the top of global architecture, rehashing most of the scary and ruthless stories Anna read about her in the other articles from *Vogue* and *Time* and *Newsweek*. Then she undermines this stereotype by zooming in to the moment she stepped from the dark hallway to Sahina's office, showing this open-plan, idyllic space in which the young, fashionable and doting staff giggle and make kissing sounds at Sahina as they pass. The article follows this same pattern, zooming out to talk of her career from a familiar cool distance, mentioning her most famous buildings and the awards she's won, before flicking to a jazzy section that seems to contradict this, such as her saying that young people shouldn't be architects, or that she doesn't want her buildings to be sophisticated. Anna has discarded all the mean bits – the stuff about the tasteless government officials and when she questioned Anna's competence – because she's decided that the main angle, the all-important scoop, will be to show that Sahina isn't such a bitch after all.

All this is in place. What isn't yet complete is the writing itself: sentences end without warning, run into each other and generally wouldn't make sense to anyone but Anna. But this is nothing to worry about. For her, making the sentences cohere and flow is one of the final, brainless elements of writing – comparable to checking for typos – that happens once the real business of threading the ideas into a logical order has been taken care of.

'Enough!' says Ingrid, pulling her headphones out and pushing back from her desk. 'You win.' Anna watches her shut down her computer and pull her coat on, accompanied by the little sighs that have become her aural trademark since her boyfriend Sam left for his latest Amazon expedition, to spend six weeks in some tree to capture a few seconds of footage of poisonous frogs fucking or fighting.

'I'm going to beat you in the morning,' says Anna, and Ingrid just laughs and says that some things are sacred, before walking off.

Anna is alone. In fact, no. She spins her chair and sees that Stuart is still in, over at his desk, his back to her. It is weird

for just the two of them to be here. Being the last two workers alone in the office has an inescapable sexual subtext, irrespective of the fact that they have zero sexual tension. It is
unpleasant to think of this, but she cannot help it. There was
that one time, well over a year ago, they passed each other
on the stairs – him going down and her going up – and in the
reflective glass of the landing she saw him turn his head and
unmistakably check out her backside. Worse still, his eyes
then clicked with hers in the glass, so he saw her seeing him,
and then turned away rapidly, already flushing with embarrassment. For the next month it felt like he only spoke to her
in person if it was absolutely necessary, didn't come over to
her desk once, emailed for everything, and she imagined him
privately burning with shame.

At that moment an email pings onto her screen, from
Jimmy in AV. Since it has 'Sahina' in the subject header she
opens it, and then downloads a file of the best stills taken
yesterday, when he went himself to Sahina's office. There
she is standing beside a plant. There she is standing beneath
the 'Never Stop Exploring' mural. There she is stood outside the warehouse in the sunshine. All are taken on a wide
lens, and Anna wonders if Jimmy was alarmed by Sahina's
skin as well, and was looking for a tactful means of avoiding
a close-up. But even from a distance, Anna can still detect
that sly aspect in Sahina's eye, the live spark at the centre of
the ruined face, and a shiver goes through her, remembering
the feeling that she could see into her soul.

Anna looks over her shoulder and sees Stuart peering
close to his screen, and supposes that he is clicking through
the stills as well. In a moment he will stroll across the clearing and ask Anna which she prefers and, as an offhand aside,

how the copy is coming along. He might even ask to have a look, and she will have to assuage his concerns about the garbled syntax, absent grammar and the sentences that run off the edge of a cliff. She imagines his arse perched beside her on Ingrid's desk, and the fact that it's just the two of them in the whole big office, and with that she is saving her document and shutting down the computer, all of a sudden unable to leave quick enough.

It is almost 8 p.m., but the bus to Kilburn is still packed with homebound workers. Instead of her usual seat at the front of the top deck, she gets the first seat behind the stairwell, in front of the CCTV monitor that cycles through a dozen or so crackly images from cameras secreted in all corners of the bus. Anna can see herself in three of them – from the front, side and back – and she is interested by the sight of herself; it is like in clothes shops, when the double reflection in changing-room mirrors gives an unexpected insight into how the rest of the world sees her.

She supposes she looks ordinary enough – perhaps a handful of the guys would look twice, but otherwise she is entirely unremarkable, an extra, a face from the crowd. But what if they knew she worked for the website, and was writing an article on Sahina Bhutto? Would they be impressed if they knew? Most people seem to be professional and successful, and half of them probably have a credential or claim to fame that is equally impressive. The CCTV video switches again to the frontal view of her, and experimentally she overlays the idea of the Twitter meme instead: she imagines herself as a quirky social media star, the young woman who reunited a lost suitcase with its owner, four years later. This time the idea resonates – she can see herself stand apart from

147

the crowd, talking proudly at dinner parties – and she takes her phone from her bag to check on her key stats. It is only an hour since she last checked, and already there are a handful of new followers; the total is now over three hundred. Today there have been several more suggestions and ideas, the most interesting being from someone called @bilboa_baggins, who says that his brother works for the Spanish airport authorities, and they keep a database of all flyers; if there really was a limited number of flights going between Heathrow and Mozambique in February 2013, then all their names should be on a spreadsheet at BAA HQ. He rounded off with an estimate that a weekly flight, using a Boeing 737, would mean there are just a few hundred possible candidates. A few hundred, she thinks. Just four days ago it was seven billion; now it is down to a few hundred, or less, considering it is a medium-sized but muscular man. She imagines how great it would be to find him, to actually find him, and how surprised everyone would be, and what Geoff said about giving the number of followers a push. Maybe she should take him up on the offer, if it really is legal, and everyone is doing it—

This thought is interrupted by her phone making the short buzz of a Kismet message. It is from Geoff 81, of course. It is uncanny how all the messages he has sent today have corresponded with her thinking about him, but then perhaps not that surprising, given how frequently, or constantly, he has loomed in her mind. She opens the message:

I'm going to take your silence as agreement. 6 p.m., London Bridge. The Tooley Street entrance, street level. Bring your laptop.

Below this are two other messages he has sent today, which

148

she hasn't answered. The first thanked her for last night, and for being such a good sport when the caretaker interrupted her swimming. The second, sent a few minutes later, told her to meet him at London Bridge, and that he would make up for the embarrassment of yesterday by taking her somewhere *really* special.

Anna wonders for the hundredth time today what 'really special' means, given his trick with Somerset House. Perhaps the country residence of the Chancellor of the Exchequer or the Lord Mayor, which Geoff somehow knows can be accessed by a key hidden in a plant pot. Or maybe an underground bunker somewhere in Kent, decked out for the military top brass and political leaders in the event of nuclear war. Most likely, she thinks, he will show her the pipe, or the place that he has managed to sluice it to, some theatre or gallery space where the entirety of the internet's data can be seen surging across a giant screen. She goes to reply to the message and then realises that he isn't asking her to. He knows she will be there. The number 81 is a proof that he knows what she thinks, that such messages aren't necessary; it is almost a cord of communion that stretches from her to him, wherever he is . . .

She tries to shake herself free of this thought and looks out the window, only for the bus to stop beside the billboard for the Kismet Love Test. The glass is beaded with raindrops, and every few seconds one of these gains sufficient mass to slide smooth and straight down the glass, warping and smearing the bright billboard lights behind it, so it looks like the colour is bleeding out of the letters on the Kismet advert. She reminds herself that he can't be an 81. It must be inflated, a Kismet miscalculation. They certainly do happen. During her twenty-minute lunch break

149

today she searched online and found dozens of stories. As well as the high-profile case of the disgruntled Austrian who is demanding Kismet release his profile data, she found many similar stories, mainly on local news websites, of people complaining about crazy scores and mismatches. Each story concluded with a generic response from a Kismet spokesperson, saying they never claimed their scores were perfect, that mismatches were inevitable, but that, on the whole, the algorithm is the best means possible of determining someone's compatibility.

The bus starts up again, the Kismet billboard slides from view, and Anna tells herself that it is a good thing if the score is an exaggeration. All she wants is one night of adventure and excitement, a birthday gift to herself, never to be repeated again. And even if the number is accurate, and he really does represent a one-in-ten-million match – she looked this up, too – then surely it is an act of moderation and admirable restraint, to only sleep with him once?

Yes, she thinks, as she puts her phone away and stands up and rings the bell, either way, it is fine – everything is fine. Then the bus stops and she skips down the stairs and onto the street, giving thanks to the driver on the way.

The flat is alive with the sound and smells of cooking. Pete prepares most of their meals, and always makes an effort on his study days, but tonight he has really gone for it. When Anna has changed into lounge pants and taken a pill, she comes downstairs and finds the narrow table in the living room set with a carafe of water and silver cutlery, as if guests are coming. He comes through with two plates, which he introduces as if he is a waiter at some fancy restaurant: pan-fried bream with garlic mash and purple sprouting broccoli. She watches him curiously as he takes a seat, and wonders if he is ramping up ceremonies in advance of her birthday. But when he smiles at her she sees an excited glow in his eyes, and decides this is more likely about last night: it is a gesture of gratitude for the sex, for the end to the bout of celibacy.

'Did you have fun then, with Zahra?' he says, taking up his knife and fork. The table is so narrow they always sit at right angles from each other, Anna at the head and Pete on the side. She notices that his facial hair has thickened since the weekend, has crossed the line between stubble and beard. It is funny how it grows uninvited, without purpose or benefit, like the weeds and nettles in David's garden downstairs. 'You certainly stayed out late. For a Tuesday.'

'It was fun,' she says, and then, before he can ask for details, tries throwing attention back to him: 'How was your evening?'

'Uneventful,' he says. 'Though it certainly improved when you got back.' He smiles at her again, and she looks down at the burnt-out eyes of her fish. 'It must have been our talk the other day. Amazing how it can help just to put things into words.'

'Yes,' she says, and then returns to her fish. Her stomach turns as she cuts through its shiny scales and pulls soft wet flesh from its spine. 'Yes, it must have helped.' She loads a fork with a wet flake of fish and a dollop of mash and washes it down with a glass of water that she suddenly wishes was wine.

'And how's the article coming along?' he says, evidently trying to keep the mood light, conversation ticking over. She tells him that it's fine, that it's coming into shape.

'Have you shown it to anyone yet?' he asks, and then frowns when she says that she hasn't.

'Don't worry. I'm on top of it. I'll give it to Stuart tomorrow afternoon.'

There is sufficient edge in her voice that Pete nods in agreement and returns to his food, which he is eating with just a fork. He likes to cut up his food at the start of a meal using his knife and fork, then pass his fork to his right hand and proceed to eat using just that, while his left arm takes a nap. Zahra does this as well, and it obscurely annoys Anna that these two people who have such a vocal passion for food don't even adhere to basic table manners.

'Do you want some wine?' she says, realising that there is no good reason to deny herself. She gets up and goes to the kitchen, where she finds a third of a bottle of white in the fridge. It must be the bottle that Pete had last night while she drank with Geoff, and this thought is like a squirt of black ink into her mood. She takes it back to the living room with two glasses, but Pete says he doesn't want any, since he had a few drinks last night. Anna nods and pours herself a glass, pretending not to notice his implication. A few moments pass, then he makes his point directly.

'You must have drunk a fair amount last night as well?'

'Sure,' she says, taking a sip and shrugging. The wine isn't nice but she enjoys the alcoholic bite at the end of the taste sensation, like a sting in its tail. He is watching her sip, and it occurs to her that he might have found the whisky bottle. 'But I've been working hard, too.'

This comes out wrong, as if she is trying to say that he hasn't been working hard, has merely been lounging around with his textbooks. But Pete doesn't respond and they both eat in silence; she senses that he is suppressing the urge to say something, and is inwardly repeating some mantra about how to diffuse the heat from conversations before they flare into arguments. Eventually he speaks again, this time about the birthday dinner party.

'So who's confirmed?' he says. She tells him and he then asks many more questions about the event – what she would like to eat, to drink, for pudding, if she wants to go shopping tomorrow night for the food she likes. Anna gives short answers to each of the questions, lacking the energy to think about any of these things, and reminds herself of what she has to tell him, of the lie she has prepared.

'About tomorrow,' she says, her fingers gripping hard around the cool metal of her knife and fork. 'I'm going to have dinner with my mum in the evening.'

'Oh yeah?' he says. Anna's face feels hot, and her heart makes the little lift that lie detectors must measure for.

'Yes,' she says, looking down at the face of her fish, its expression now seeming a fixed scream of pain, and cuts yet more white flesh from the hole in its side. She covers this with mash and says: 'We were going to have dinner over the weekend but she's busy so we thought we'd go the night before my birthday instead, just the two of us.' She puts the fish and potato in her mouth then starts loading her fork again. It is reassuring, in a way, to not enjoy lying; it is further proof that this is a blip, an indulgence.

'Sounds nice. Send her my love.'

'Will do,' she says, pouring another glass of wine. She can feel his eyes on her as she does so and, to justify the speed of her drinking, says: 'This wine is delicious.' The sound of her own voice make her feel strangely uncomfortable, and she

153

stares down into the yellow liquid until she realises that she said exactly the same words the night before, to Geoff, only that time she meant it.

In the middle of the night, Anna wakes with a gasp. She has been dreaming. Already the details of the dream have disintegrated, but she knows it included her dad in some way, and that she was on a ledge or cliff face and then falling, falling. She lies in bed and waits for the sense of danger and panic to fade from her waking mind, but it doesn't, it intensifies. It feels as if the darkness all around her is a physical force pressing in from all sides. Her breathing is short and pained, and it seems possible that her airways are closing up and that she will be choked by her own anxiety.

Anna gets out of bed and crosses the room and opens the Velux window. Cold air stings her lungs and makes every hair on her half-naked body stand on end. She takes conscious control of her breathing – in for four seconds, out for five – and the panic begins to retreat. By placing her elbows and chin on the window frame and rising onto tiptoes, she is able to stand almost comfortably, and look out across the neighbourhood. Above the opposite terrace she can see a sliver of central London, and the tops of a few tall buildings – City-Point and the Shard and that ugly skyscraper in Elephant and Castle with the wind turbines at the top – around which light is just beginning to gather. It must be almost morning. She thinks of Sheffield, and the house she shared with Zahra and Hamza in third year that was at the top of a hill; from the dormer window in her room she could see the entire city, and she often sat there blissfully watching it fade from night to morning, from evening to night. The memory is a soothing one, and her mood lifts further at the sight of a plane rising up from the west, the red wing and tail lights flashing. She thinks again of her man, four years ago, standing at the carousel at Heathrow, waiting for his luggage. He would be standing there huddled among the crowds of families and couples and businessmen, some of whom he'd recognise from the flight, watching the first bags appear on the conveyor and then more bags and wondering if this will be the time that his bag doesn't. Then he switches on his phone and it starts buzzing with a backlog of messages – from his boss, his boss's boss, his colleagues, his wife. There has been a coup or an assassination or an uprising or some other major event in X – she hasn't worked this out yet – and he is needed there, right away. He runs to Departures, learns there is one flight for X in thirty-five minutes. He thinks of his bag on the carousel, feels a sentimental pull towards a couple of garments, and then bids them farewell. He asks for one ticket to X, and without even being told the price he hands the woman behind the counter an American Express . . .

Anna is shivering now, but she is happy; the feeling of panic was merely the overhang of a bad dream. She treads back to bed, and the feeling of getting between the warm sheets is a physical delight. Pete is on his back, and snoring lightly. She nudges him, and instinctively he turns onto his side, as if even in the depth of his sleep he is sensitive to her needs, and only wants to make her happy. She snuggles closer to him and kisses the downy nape of his neck. Then she closes her eyes and goes to sleep.

Thursday

There are many places on and around Carnaby Street to buy boots, and during her lunch hour Anna moseys around several before settling on a boutique on the top floor of Kingly Court. She selects three pairs to try on, and while sitting and waiting for the shop assistant to come back with size 7s she whips a sock off and admires her newly painted toenails. The boots arrive and she quickly discards one pair that is far too pointy, and takes a long time mulling over the other two. They are almost identical pairs of black leather riding boots, and the main difference – other than subtle variations in the lining and stitching – is the price: one is £110, the other £320. In some ways they look identical, but she prefers the expensive pair, she really does, and eventually reminds herself of her pay rise and repeats a maxim she's been using in clothes shops since she was a teenager: that expensive items aren't actually more expensive, since the real cost can only be calculated much later, as a function of how many times you chose to wear the item in question, and how much you enjoyed doing so. The assistant takes away the expensive pair to box up, but then Anna can't bear to put on her old boots – which now appear ridiculously, comically shabby – and asks to wear the new ones out instead. With her old boots swinging from a giant paper bag she heads towards Soho Square, buying a curry pot on the way. It is a bit cold and blustery, and she has her pick of the benches – on a sentimental impulse she selects the exact spot where she activated Kismet and sat waiting until a 54 drifted into the park. Somehow this was only last week. She thinks about this while poking at her curry pot, but barely eats a mouthful – her insides are full of a swirling nervous energy that leaves no space for food. She manages about half before heading back to work; at the edge of the square she drops the full curry pot in a bin and, after some hesitation, stuffs her old boots in there as well.

'New shoes!' says Ingrid, when Anna arrives at her desk.

'A present to myself,' she says, turning her feet around; the boots are so dark and lustrous they appear wet. 'For the last day of my twenties.'

Ingrid bends down to touch the leather and asks where they're from, and seems to want to keep talking, but Anna puts her boots beneath her desk and makes it apparent that she has no time for chatting. She continues combing through 'Sahina_FINAL', correcting typos, deleting unnecessary words, beating the sentences into shape. But she is too excited to hold a thought in her head, and keeps losing her place and gazing absently around the office. One time she looks up, and the sight of a new Kismet story appearing on the big board makes her think of Geoff and the evening ahead of her; nervous energy rushes through her like a gust of wind and it feels possible that she might faint.

Her self-imposed deadline is 5 p.m., and at 5.04 she rounds off the last paragraph so that it at least partially makes sense, and emails the whole thing to Stuart. Then she crosses the clearing towards the Quiet Room, and taps on the glass door.

'I've sent you the copy,' she says.

Stuart is typing an email about the Longines account, she can see over his shoulder – why is it always watches? – and without looking up he grumbles that she should have sent him a draft yesterday or the day before.

'But just leave it with me. I'll come and find you later.'

'The thing is, I have to leave early today. It's my birthday tomorrow, and I'm meeting my mum for dinner.'

He types a couple more words, then gives the enter key an almighty thwack, before turning in his seat towards her. The resigned and disappointed look passes over his face, as if he should have expected this kind of niggling complication.

'Alright then,' he says, nodding to the empty chair. 'Let's go through it now.'

'The thing is,' says Anna, wincing, 'I have to leave now now. Like, this minute.'

His expression hardens into annoyance, and he asks how she still found time for a lunch break. Anna isn't sure if he really can track her movements or is bluffing, but she just apologises for being a pain and says that the article is all finished, that she's really pleased with it, and that she can come in early tomorrow to talk through any changes, with plenty of time to make edits before sending to Romont. He holds her in his narrow searching gaze, trying to discern her motive, and when he sighs and shakes his head she knows he is begrudgingly acquiescing to her plan.

'Make sure you come in early,' he says.

'No problem. Thanks.'

'Really early. Eight a.m. early.'

'Sure thing. See you then.'

He nods at the door, and she surprises herself by making

a girlish cheeky smile before turning on her heel and leaving the room.

At 5.15 p.m. Anna shuts down her computer and heads to the stairwell, her clunky laptop weighing down her rucksack and pinching the skin on her shoulder. In the ground-floor lobby toilet she fusses with her make-up and puts her hair down and wafts it around for a while until she decides to put it up again. On Charing Cross Road she catches the 176 to Penge, and takes the front seat on the top deck. She checks her phone to see if he's messaged to cancel or delay, and since he hasn't she just ends up looking at his name in her contacts and the number 81. It is a vast, towering number, and she tells herself it's okay to be nervous. She hasn't slept with anyone but Pete in over four years, let alone with someone with whom she shares the highest match she has ever heard of, anywhere, ever. Of course, the number is an approximation, and she wonders if it's been rounded up from something like 80.6284985 or down from 81.4322. Then she wonders about its raw, pre-numerical form, and remembers the image that appeared behind Raymond Chan during his TED talk, an abstract spread of dots and slashes and wingdings that covered the wall behind him like a vast constellation, hundreds of thousands of stars, each one representing a practice, an attitude or a belief, creating a map of our true selves . . .

Anna feels the dizzying energy swirling within her again, and this time she thinks she might be sick; something rises as far as her throat before retreating, leaving an acidic flavour in its wake. In fact, her nerves have crossed the threshold into discomfort – her palms are clammy and her mouth is dry, and the burbling in her stomach makes her think of the long waits before the firing gun in a cross-country race. To calm herself, she focuses on her Twitter channel and the laptop in her bag, and the prospect of her number of followers being boosted to one thousand or two thousand. What will happen? These people will share and retweet her posts and her number of followers will snowball until a breakthrough occurs – someone who works in BAA that is willing to help, or someone who was in Mozambique at that time, or maybe even the man himself. She imagines making a ceremony of returning the suitcase to him, and the story being picked up by local and even national media. Maybe she could talk to Paula about the story being put on the website? And why not, since it is just as interesting as most of the crap they write about. She can see it on the big board, nestled up there amongst the pieces sponsored by Hyundai and Longines and Samsung and North Face. It could become a little runaway hit, and Paula could take her to the airy boardrooms on the tenth floor and ask what she *really* sees herself doing in five years' time. Or maybe she could use the project and the Women at the Top series as a platform to launch herself somewhere else, maybe a job in the field or one of the major news centres – New York, Hong Kong, Dubai, Sydney; or, even better, she could go freelance, and pick up odd bits of work and chisel away at projects from some whitewashed villa in the Mediterranean . . .

This idea holds her attention until the abrupt silence of the engine shutting down restores her to her present moment and position on the bus. They have stopped moving, but the windows are steamed and she can't tell where they are: the pavement and buildings and sky appear as featureless grey blocks. The driver then speaks through the intercom, saying that regrettably they will be terminating here. A collective sigh spreads through the top deck, and then the other passengers begin filing down the stairs. Anna follows them down and onto the street, and is surprised and alarmed to be somewhere that looks entirely unfamiliar. They are on a curved and rising embankment, surrounded by squat seventies-style offices, with some taller but equally ugly buildings stacked behind them. She really has no idea where they are, and for a strange second she thinks maybe she slipped into a trance on the bus, lost an hour and followed the bus its entire route. Is this Penge? But, wait: she takes a few steps along the pavement, then the white dome of St Paul's reveals itself, with a Barbican tower peeking over its shoulder. She walks further along the pavement and tries to gain a more precise sense of where she is. Across the road is another bleak office building, and a trampy-looking guy rolling a suitcase along the pavement. She recognises him, but isn't sure from where. For a second she thinks it might be an old colleague of Pete's from the garden centre, but then she realises it is someone else: the tramp that sang to her. Yes, that's right. It's the one that looked like her dad, and sang his own unique version of the happy birthday song. He notices her watching him, and stops and returns her stare across the road. Yet she still carries on looking, held fast by the uncanny resemblance to her dad; it is almost like a young version of her father has been sent in disguise to spy on her.

'What the fuck are you doing?' he shouts.

Anna startles, and turns and hurries along the pavement away from him, her face tucked down into the collar of her jacket, and doesn't look back.

She follows signs to the Millennium Footbridge, which feels wet and rickety and hazardous, and on the South Bank turns left. Bad weather is coming up off the river; powerful icy gusts that mess with her fringe and sting her cheeks. She puts her head down and walks quickly, but each step jangles the feeling in her abdomen, which has crossed from discomfort to something even worse: a bottomless feeling like a trapdoor has been opened. Being shouted at by the tramp has rattled her, and the image of his face is locked in her mind's eye. *What the fuck are you doing?*

She climbs up to London Bridge – the heavy bag feeling like it contains a guilty cargo, a severed head – and then threads through the long queues of buses and taxis to the station. Automatic doors part for her and she steps through to the giant refurbished forecourt the size of a football pitch, the ceiling as high as a cathedral. People blur past in all directions. She worms her way through the crowd, surrounded by the din of thousands of footsteps blended into an echoing hum, above which the Tannoy announcement sounds disembodied and holy, like the voice of God. Once in the centre of the space, beneath the giant hanging information boards, she turns in a circle. Geoff is nowhere to be seen. Surprisingly, this fills her with relief. Maybe he was never meant to be here, it has all been in her imagination, and she can now go back to Pete and continue life as normal. The prospect feels extremely cosy and inviting, but then she remembers that Geoff said the Tooley Street entrance, and she retraces her steps out to the taxi rank and bus stops. She goes down the soot-blackened external staircase and lingers on the landing between two flights of stairs, which serves as a balcony overlooking the smaller forecourt for platforms 4, 5 and 6.

This time she sees him immediately, the size of a pocket lighter from her elevated vantage point. He is wearing a dark green jacket with the collar up, and it is remarkable how closely he resembles the bankers and office workers around him. For a while he remains as still as a statue, his head tilted up towards the information board, then he puts his hand in his pocket and lifts a little white something to his mouth. His square jaw works a couple of times, crushing the mint or chewing gum, and instead of freshness Anna has a proxy taste of whatever guttural flavour he is trying to conceal. Her hands are gripping the metal railing, and the sudden sense that she is on a raised platform with nothing but empty air between her and the ground causes the trapdoor within her to open again; her insides lurch.

At that moment, as if alerted by something, Geoff turns and looks up towards Anna. She backs away from the handrail and takes two steps down the stairs, her view of him blocked by the upper stairway she just came down. From her new position she can only see Geoff's feet, which continue turning a circle until they are facing the information board again; she concludes he did not see her. She edges out from behind the stairs, just far enough to see the full extent of his body and the names of the destinations as they flash onto the screens. New Cross, Lewisham, Greenwich, Charlton, Woolwich, Dartford, Gillingham, Canterbury. She imagines alighting at any of these places, and walking with Geoff along a cold wet high street, and the prospect feels too real and uncertain and dangerous. The board refreshes and she sees Margate is the next train's final destination, and she thinks of Pete throwing the book from the window and with that she is walking up the stairs and hurrying past the waiting buses and taxis, without looking back.

A moment later she is on the street and winding through

commuters towards the bridge, the horrible ominous feeling diminishing with each step. At the centre of the bridge she pauses, and finds that now the cool wind coming off the water is refreshing; likewise, even though she is on a higher platform than within the station, the flagstones and balustrade feel robust and infallible. She sinks further into this relief, until she realises there is still a live connection between her and Geoff. She pulls her phone from her bag and the thought of the imminent call makes it feel as potent as a grenade; her hands shake in her haste to turn it off, and for a moment she is tempted to fling it into the grey-green water below.

Safely north of the river, Anna turns left and walks along Cheapside and past St Paul's, loosely retracing the route of the bus that brought her east. A light rain begins to fall, and she ducks into the doorway of a pub in Aldwych, at first just for cover, but when the rain becomes heavier she goes inside. She buys a pint of lager and takes it to a round corner table, where she holds her hand out and watches it shake. A sort of adrenalised relief courses through her, as if she has had a near-death experience, a juggernaut that missed her by a few feet. It is almost difficult to believe she came so close to doing something that now, only a few minutes later, feels utterly senseless. Where did she think he was going to take her? What time would she have got back? What would she have told Pete if it was late? Would she have been able to get to work early tomorrow? Would she have been able to get to work at all? She turns her dormant phone around in her hand, as if looking for the answers to these questions in its glinting black screen and dusted silver casing. Towards the end of her pint she concludes that she has been in some kind of destructive trance, that the stress of work and her birthday and Pete's proposal and the excitement of getting an 81 and maybe her pills – or a combination of the above – have subdued her normal prudence and made her think she could somehow get away with all things at once, without anything having to give. It seems like good fortune that she has regained her clarity of mind, but she realises there was nothing lucky about it; the creeping bottomless feeling that gathered as she neared the station was her natural good sense kicking in, as it always would have done; she was never going to meet him.

The rain has stopped so she walks up Kingsway and then to Covent Garden. Two men pass her with bags of chips and she can smell the salt and vinegar; the resultant hunger pangs remind her she is alive. She decides to take herself for dinner, especially as this is what she is supposed to be doing anyway, with her mother. She walks past the windows of dozens of restaurants before seeing a fancy place called Green Rooms on Shaftesbury Avenue, that Zahra and Pete and maybe even Ingrid have all raved about. It definitely seems like somewhere you need to book, but it is still early and she is able to get a seat at the end of a long bench near the kitchen, beside a group of young people, two guys and a girl – all creative Soho types with haircuts and tattoos and high scores flashing above their heads.

Anna feels self-conscious initially, but she forces herself through this and orders the spatchcock chicken and, since a glass is scarcely cheaper and she deserves to treat herself, a carafe of white wine. She feels the fashionable people register her order and the fact that she's alone, and makes peace with this. So what if some strangers think less of her for sitting on her own? She should stop letting these things get to her. Or comparing her life to the imagined lives of others. So what if her relationship is not the most exciting and high-scoring in the world, she thinks, starting on her first glass. Or if her social life has slowed down somewhat in recent years. At least she used to go out, to excess, during uni and in her early twenties when she lived with Zahra in east London. They seemed to drink most nights, took drugs most weekends, and more often than not everyone would pile back to theirs for the Minuscule of Sound. Yes, she had her fill then, she thinks, pouring herself another glass. In fact, she had more than her fill, and it probably wasn't as great as she remembers. Sundays through Wednesdays she used to be good for little else than smoking roll-ups and drinking cups of tea. Her relationship at the time, with a guy called Ed, was subject to the usual complications and bullshit. There would be times of deep depression, and others when she would get carried away in the same manner as she has these past weeks. Back then, her mania was more often centred on ideas or inventions; in contrast to her uni colleagues – who, despite their privileged backgrounds, had en masse panicked at the prospect of not being on some kind of professional or educational advancement scheme – she had made no effort to establish a career and was still powered by the notion, instilled in her by her dad, that she should be doing something enterprising or altruistic or creative, or preferably a combination of all three. She had it all mapped out. Supported by temp work and the occasional cheque and messages of encouragement from her dad, she worked on ideas, and the plan was simple: she would keep churning them out until one was good enough to launch, which she would do using crowdfunding. The business would start slowly, but after a few years would flourish and she would sell it on, and then start another business, or buy a property somewhere – in Greece, she hoped – or write a book, and by the time she was thirty she would be a standalone success story, someone who had branched off at right angles from her peers and yet somehow made it all make sense. Her best idea, by far, was the Community Shed. One day she bought a crap hammer for £3 so she could hang a picture, and was overwhelmed by the idea of every flat in their council block having its own crap, barely used hammer, and the notion for the Community Shed popped into her mind, complete at the moment of inception. It would be a wonderfully stocked, communal tool shed that could be accessed by members, who would pay a small monthly fee. She was so jazzed with the idea that she spoke about it constantly, even at parties and clubs, to the mixed amusement and embarrassment of her friends. She got as far as drafting an application for crowdfunding, but then she took off to San Francisco. Before she has a chance to dwell on the reasons for not having picked it up again, a plate floats down from over her shoulder and her chicken is laid before her.

It is a whole small chicken pulled out to a butterfly shape and flattened, sprinkled with pomegranate seeds; it looks alarmingly like roadkill, the grill marks reminiscent of tyre tread. But it tastes good and goes perfectly with the crisp cold wine. Zahra and Pete were right about this place, and if she were indeed having dinner with her mum this is where she would bring her. She feels guilty for using her as a false alibi, and decides to call her. She cannot turn her phone back on, so she dials her mum's old landline number into her work phone.

'Darling?' says her mum. 'How are you? What is it? What's wrong?'

Anna puts her on speakerphone and says that nothing is wrong, that everything is great, that she just wanted to say hi. The waiter asks if everything is okay and she says it's great.

'Are you in a restaurant?' asks her mother.

'A very nice one.'

'On your own?'

'No, you're here with me.'

There is a pause as her mother processes this. The fashionable young people really are now looking, but Anna doesn't care. She tells her that she has to work early in the morning, that she is having a dinner party in the evening to celebrate her birthday, but that she isn't making a big deal out of it. There is another pause at her mother's end of the line.

'Is everything okay?'

'Why wouldn't it be?'

'You sound a little . . . *funny*. You used to be so excitable on your birthdays.'

'I'm being responsible. I thought you'd be pleased.'

'I am. I just want to know you're happy.'

'Happy,' repeats Anna, with a scoff. She makes a speech about how happiness is an overrated concept, and at the very best a fleeting emotional state, and that being content is much more important. 'Am I wrong?'

Her mother changes the subject, asks if she's called her brother recently, and Anna says she's called him the precise same number of times that he's called her. Then there is a pause. She can see her mother clearly in her living room in Bedfordshire, the television on mute, a programme lined up for 9 p.m. Eventually her mum tells her that she loves her, that she should call Josh if she has a chance, and that she'll see her over the weekend. Her final comment is that she is sure Anna will have a great day tomorrow – a really great day – and Anna wonders if maybe she is in cahoots with Pete about the ring, if everyone in her life has been plotting and scheming behind her back for months.

It is dark by the time she pays up but doesn't feel so cold, and she decides to carry on walking. She goes up Shaftesbury Avenue and onto Dean Street, the Soho lanes transformed into their garish night-time mood, the taxis and rickshaws now sharing the roads with staggering groups of drinkers and tourists. She passes a cocktail bar that looks strangely familiar, even though she's never been there, and curiosity takes her inside. At the bar is a ginger, bearded guy covered in tattoos, and when he greets her in an American accent she realises he is one of Ingrid's friends, that she's seen him in dozens of pictures in this place and at pubs and parties and festivals and wherever. Anna keeps her amusement to herself and sits on a stool and orders a Bourbon Sour. When it arrives she raises a silent toast to her mother, who means well and in fact does well and has always been lovely. Then she raises a toast to her brother Josh, living in Australia, and decides she will try to call him, despite it being *her* birthday, her thirtieth at that. Does he even know? She forgives him for being so distant and self-centred, and orders a second cocktail, which she raises for Pete and Zahra, for always being there. Why is it they always come together in her mind like that? A thought of one is usually followed by the other; it has been this way since her very first meeting with Pete, in a pub, when they were both shy and tongue-tied and Zahra did the speaking for them. They've been linked in her mind ever since, but this is a good thing; she loves them both, and she's been stupid to let jealousy get in the way in the past. Then

she drinks to everyone else who has been with her throughout her twenties, including her colleagues at work – they're a
good bunch, really – and to the owner of the suitcase, wherever and whoever they are. So what if she never actually finds
them? She's proud of the Twitter feed, regardless of it only
having three hundred followers; it is cute and fun and – who
knows? – maybe the spirited little band of investigators will
somehow find him. Her final sips are dedicated to all the
other inventions and project ideas that once filled her heart
and, for a time at least, made her think she really was going
to be some kind of freelance entrepreneur: the Cycle Line,
her idea of ripping out the Circle Line – since it is useless
anyway – and having a subterranean cycle tunnel instead; the
rental service that would allow people to have a sheep for the
weekend, to cut the grass and entertain the kids; the Slinghy,
her two-person hammock; the hollow chopsticks that would
double up as straws when eating ramen; the app that would
replace business cards by providing a one-button means of
exchanging contact details; the karaoke machine that would
teach people languages through translations of their favourite songs; those two inventions that went off the scale of
her sense of the possible: a device that would home in on
the source of a bad smell, and another that would somehow
list the contents of her fridge while she paced indecisively
around the supermarket. And of course to the theme park of
human consumption, an idea that isn't even a week old. She
hasn't thought of it since the moment of inspiration, and it
is already on its way to being forgotten. Even after a week
it feels like a ridiculous notion – who would want to pay
money to walk around amid stinking mounds of beef and
butter and cheese? But she dedicates her final sip to the idea,

silly though it was, and drains the glass while thinking of all the other ideas that she has forgotten over the years simply because they were forgettable.

Anna leaves the bar, her mood now lifted to something approaching elation. She drifts into Chinatown, and on a nostalgic whim she buys a pack of ten Embassy No. 1 and a box of matches. She stands in the doorway recess of a closed shop to smoke one, and the process is as nostalgic as she'd hoped; the sensation of peeling the cellophane wrapper and then pulling off the gold foil to reveal the rows of orange teeth short-circuits her mind back to being a teenager, to standing in the bus shelter in the Market Square. The smoking itself isn't as pleasant – the smoke feels too real and overwhelming, like having straw stuffed up her nose – but then something nice happens. From along the road she can hear banging drums and whistles, and these are followed by dozens of people with coloured masks and paper lanterns. The procession undulates up the road and past Anna, teams of masked dancers holding up a long dragon with sticks that itself appears to be dancing. This world, she thinks.

Where to go next? She considers going to Soho Square to perform a ceremony of cancelling Kismet for good, but she supposes it will be locked up by now. Instead she heads south along Wardour Street, and it isn't until she reaches the gaudy expanse of Piccadilly Circus that she realises where she should go. She walks the length of Regent Street and then on to Great Portland Street, before pausing by the turning to Little Titchfield Street. It is a narrow and dark street, the only activity being a bar called, simply enough, Social. Anna hasn't been here in years, and as she approaches she is almost surprised to see it is still doing lively business. A handful of people are smoking behind a velvet-roped area, and flashing lights and pumping music are pressing up against the steamed front window. Anna plants herself in the road directly in front of the entrance, and remembers standing in the exact same spot four years ago, while watching the gangly figure of Ed, her ex, approaching her along the street. They hugged for a long time – it had been six months since she'd ended things and taken off to San Francisco – and then awkwardly shuffled into the bar.

Anna steps into the roped-off smoking area and puts her face to the misted glass. Her idea was to sit in the same booth where she and Ed sat that night, but the re-enactment isn't going to work: so many people are dancing in the middle of the bar that she can't even see through to the leather booths at the back. She supposes that she could go and dance herself, since she was lamenting just earlier how she never does this, but stirring up the memory of being here with Ed has killed off any such desire. That night they'd had the place to them-selves, and immediately after sitting down she told him her news: her dad was dead. He'd died two weeks previously, a few days after she returned from California. Ed was shocked, and listened in silence as Anna told him the whole thing. How he'd died on a Tuesday morning, while walking in the South Downs with wife number three. After a steep hill he announced chest pains and the desire to sit down. A minute later he slumped over, closed his eyes, and that was it. He was fifty-seven. On that Tuesday, and during the long days that followed, Anna assumed the role of the clear-headed organ-iser, while her mother and brother and wife number three all went to pieces. She took charge of the death certificate and calling his friends and family and organising the funeral. She didn't feel grief or shock, didn't feel anything really, other than pride at how efficient and decisive she was being, as if this were a performance on his behalf, a final chance to show off to him. It was only after the funeral – during which she didn't cry – when days began to resume their normal shape that she thought of herself, and called Ed.

Once she'd finished saying all this Ed hugged her for a long time. Then he said some nice things – the same nice, reassuring things that most people seemed to say – and hugged her again. During their second drink she persuaded him that she really was okay, and that they could speak about other things. So they discussed instead her time in San Francisco, the short films he was making, their mutual friends. They laughed a little and she edged around the booth towards him, but her warmth wasn't reciprocated. He was polite, sure, but he was as stiff and cold as a closed door. During the third drink something twigged, and she asked if he was seeing someone else. He said that he was, that she was called Catherine, that he'd met her on Kismet. The news hit her like a dazing blow to the head, and the rest of their drinks washed by in a trance, until they were saying goodbye on the pavement. Then she was watching his lanky frame proceed away along the street, and she was walking in the other direction, alone, towards Great Portland Street.

Anna steps out of the smoking area and walks back to Great Portland Street. She turns right and walks slowly, her eyes scanning for visual cues. Just before the junction for the next side road she sees the pavement is skirted by a waist-high, mottled white wall – as if it has been pebble-dashed and then painted – above which is a thick, closely-cropped hedge, the kind that would be much too sharp and dense to

173

thrust your hand into. Yes, she thinks, plucking off a small waxy leaf and squeezing a drop of sap out. It was right here that it happened, that the full weight of her dad's death finally hit her. She could see him clearly in her mind's eye as a young or youngish man, sitting in the driver's seat of his first car, grinning. She could see him as an older man in his little study, where he would stare out at the garden for hours on end. She could see him walking up the hill, holding a hand up to his chest. And she could see him cold and lifeless in the box. Dead.

Anna began to cry. It started slowly, but then it grew stronger and stronger, until she was doubled over, weeping and sobbing on the street. She told herself to stop, but it was as much use as telling a wound to stop bleeding. The memories of him kept flowing through her, whirling and chaotic. She cried for the man he was and also the man he never quite managed to be; for the dozens of projects and hobbies and ideas that had seemed, to her at least, such an impressive cluster, but which in the end delivered so little that at his own funeral he was described as a supply teacher. She cried for all this, but she also cried for herself too. For the fact that the bottom had fallen out of her existence and that now she had nothing – no dad, no boyfriend, no job, no money – and that she had been labouring under a delusion for years, the delusion that she was special, that she was destined for great things, that somehow the world wasn't going to get her in the end. On and on she cried, as strangers walked past, and all she could do to salvage some dignity was to stop herself making a noise. Not a sob or a moan, just tears in full flow, and a face distorted and a body buckling back into the sharp hedge, every time a new image of him appeared in her mind.

Tonight, however, it isn't like that. Anna looks at the flagstones, the white wall, the hedge, and decides that she feels fine. There is no bottomless feeling in her stomach; there is no feeling at all. In fact, she looks back at that night with something almost like gratitude. It was a wake-up call, in a sense. It was for a purpose. Because it was where she started to realise something she's forgotten these last weeks – she didn't want to be like him. In a way he was just a big kid. Always dreaming, always changing his mind, always putting his energy into the latest idea; he simply never struck a deal with the great unforgiving world, never took stock of the people around him and his given talents and tried to make the best of the situation at hand. And, while her life might not be as adventurous or exciting as he seemed to think it would be, at least she has the basis for contentment, which is more than he ever did. And, ultimately, it is contentment that provides a platform for us to take advantage of happy moments, when they arrive, not to constantly chase them. Just like tonight, she decides, feeling her light adventurous mood returning. She gives one last parting swipe to the hedge, and then turns around. She walks back towards Social, thinking that maybe she will go dancing after all.

2

Friday

Anna wakes and finds she is contained within a box. It is a small box, not nearly long enough for her body, and her legs are bent and her neck is cricked. In the distance she can see some pale strips of white light, otherwise all is darkness. She pushes her head up and her feet down, trying to break through the soft walls of the box, but they do not give. Panic begins to gather, until she makes sense of the cushions beneath her, recognises the strips of light as venetian blinds and realises she is on the living-room sofa.

Why is she on the sofa? She doesn't remember going to sleep here and can't think of a reason why she'd want to, and it strikes her as unfair and somewhat cruel that she is not comfortably in her bed upstairs. But then she closes her eyes and she *is* upstairs, pleasantly spread-eagled on the double bed. She rolls around, luxuriating in the space and cool sheets, and when she finally reaches the edge she gets up and pads on bare feet across the bedroom, which is now the size and proportion of a vast, open-plan office, and lifts the hatch and begins descending the ladder. The metal rungs narrow and soften into a climbing rope, and she finds herself swinging in open blue sky. Carefully, her grip strong and true, she lowers herself downwards, hand over hand, all the way down to Bedford High Street, bustling on a Saturday afternoon. She is in town with her dad to buy new school shoes, Doc Martens, but her dad has stopped to chat to a man she doesn't know. Anna is embarrassed by her bare feet, and isn't sure how to engage with the adult conversation; should she look back and forth between the speaking faces? Or just stare forwards gormlessly, like a child? In the end she looks up, and her dad starts singing the Happy Birthday song, and the other man claps and then she drags him onwards and they are finally in Clarks. She hurries along the wall of shoes, and her worst fears are realised: the Doc Martens she wants are not on sale. For weeks she has agonised over whether to buy Doc Marten boots, which have been adopted with cultish fervour by the cool girls at school, or to simply replace her dull Clarks slip-ons, and she was delighted to learn of a compromise: a low-cut version of Doc Martens, the shape of a regular shoe, yet with the distinctive yellow thread around the top of the sole. But the assistant confirms they have none in stock, and in fact he hasn't even heard of them, and now Anna's dad is hurrying her to decide between the full-on boots and prim shoes, and it feels like a momentous decision – a choice between how she'd prefer to be derided in the playground, as a try-hard or a geek – and at once the aggregate torment and shame of thousands of little slights and digs overwhelms her, and she bursts into tears, right there in the middle of Clarks. But when she opens her eyes the walls of the shop fall down and it is a happier time: Anna is running and skipping through fields in much smaller shoes, with Velcro straps and little ladybirds on the side. Her dad walks behind, and is singing again. Anna's brother Josh is with them as well, in the form of their first dog, Rufus. The field slopes to a river bank, and Anna skims stones and balances on a branch and wants her dad to see her showing off, but has lost sight of him. Downstream a culvert protrudes from the muddy bank, and instinctively she knows he is in there and goes down and climbs inside. She has to crouch to fit in the tunnel, her neck cricked and knees bent, splashing through puddles towards a murmur that gathers in volume, and eventually there is a pinprick of light that grows until she emerges onto a metal balcony overlooking the sheer flank of a dam. Twenty metres to her left, a huge cylinder of white water, as wide and fast as a train, is roaring out of the dam wall and then arcing down to the reservoir, where it turns to white smoke, a rapidly churning cloud.

'Anna! Up here!'

She looks up and sees her dad is on a higher balcony, connected to hers by a rusty ladder.

'Come up! The view is incredible. You'll love it.'

The ladder is out of reach, so she climbs onto the metal handrail of the balcony. She balances on tiptoes and stretches towards the first rung, her body flattened against the sheer wall of the dam. Then a gust of wind gets between her and the stone and she slaps at the wall but grabs nothing and her foot slips off the handrail and she is falling, falling—

Anna gasps and sits upright. This time she is fully awake, and reality is restored around her. She is on the living-room sofa, wearing her bra, knickers and socks. There is a sharp pain behind her eyes, her guts feel watery and unsettled, and her tongue is almost entirely dried out from sleeping with her mouth open. The venetian blinds look like a stack of glowing white spears, and the floor beneath the window is a guilty arrangement of the half-empty Jura whisky bottle, a packet of Embassy No. 1 and a lighter. Her coat, shirt, jeans and boots are spread across the floor, in a twisted approximation of her body shape, and it is only when she sees her phone lying face down beside the sofa that she remembers: it's her birthday.

Anna falls onto her back and raises a hand to her aching head. Memories of the previous day chase each other across her mind, and she releases a long animal moan. Running away from Geoff at London Bridge. Talking to her mum on loud-speaker in the restaurant. Drinking cocktails alone. Visiting the spot where she broke down on Great Portland Street. Returning to Bar Social and lurking like a creep at the edge of the dance floor. At that point the memories unspool and dissolve, and she isn't sure if she ended up dancing, and what time she left, and how she got home, and how long she stayed up with the whisky and cigarettes. It is worrying and confusing, this absence of time, but not more so than having left Geoff at the station without a word. She has a vision of him waiting below the information board, and it seems amazing that she left him there without even a text of apology. Anna reaches for her phone – thinking she should at least respond to whatever messages he has sent – but it is turned off and the screen doesn't light up when she presses the button. She remembers the battery was about to die, and tosses the phone aside and picks up her watch instead. The time is 11.14 a.m. For a moment she just looks at this, her body entirely still, thinking it can't be the time, it just can't be. Then the full weight of the fact gathers within her, slowly, like a rollercoaster that pauses at the crest of its initial climb before gravity takes hold and the carriage descends into free fall.

'Fuck.'

Anna is up and on her feet, eyes wide, heart pumping, and within two seconds she devises a plan: toilet, shower, clothes, run to the tube, at her desk in forty-five minutes. Even before these thoughts have passed through her mind she has peeled off her socks and knickers and bra and then runs naked along the hall to the bathroom, the liquid contents of her stomach churning nauseously. She steps into the shower without waiting for the water to warm up, and thirty seconds later is out again, bundling together her discarded clothes in the living room. Upstairs she throws on a low-risk combination of clothes: black turtleneck jumper, black jeans, her hair pulled up in a ponytail. Then she grabs her make-up bag and heads down the ladder again, thinking she will have to try and apply it on the tube.

In the hallway she picks up her bag and coat, and then steps into the kitchen for a glass of water. What she finds in there makes her stop still. The room has changed, is filled with unfamiliar shapes and arrangements that her eyes struggle to make sense of. The small table has been brought into the centre of the room, and is bearing a colourful array of items: there is a carton of orange juice, a full cafetiere, a rack of toast, a bowl of fruit salad, a concertina of envelopes, and, in a central position between cutlery and cups, a plate covered by another plate. On the fridge blackboard is a note in Pete's distinctive, dyslexic handwriting: 'Happy Birthday Sleepy Head! Enjoy your breakfast!' She puts her finger to the cafetiere – it is stone cold – and wonders what to do with all this stuff. She doesn't want any of it, not a drop or a bite, and feels a surge of annoyance for once again being presented with something she didn't ask for. She supposes she should throw it away, and removes the plate covering the other plate, revealing scrambled eggs and smashed avocado on some fancy toast. A blast of sulphuric gas fills her nose and tugs at her stomach, and this time she raises a hand to her mouth, knowing she will be sick. She runs along the hallway and falls to her knees beside the toilet, opening her mouth as a fountain of hot sludge reverses up and out of her. She takes a few sharp breaths before heaving again, releasing another stream of liquid acid. She spits, gasps for air. The third heave delivers only viscous, stringy goo, the fourth just air, and then it is over. Anna rests her forehead on the toilet seat, her body twitching. Within the yellow-brown grit filming the water are some pomegranate seeds that had cushioned her chicken so pleasingly last night, like a bed of rubies. She ponders these for a second before pulling the flush.

She hurries along Mowbray Road and then Cavendish Street, breaking into a little run when she crosses roads. The sharp ridges and eaves and chimneys of the passing houses are crisply defined against a blank, white sky. Her birthday sky. She thinks of her dormant phone in her pocket, and all the birthday messages that will have arrived from her mum and aunts and maybe even her brother. Amongst all these will be the messages from Geoff last night, most likely of confusion or concern or perhaps even recrimination. It is weird to think that he probably sent the first of these while standing on the train station platform a few minutes after she fled, and since then this message will have been patiently waiting to be read. Where has it been since then? Has it been bouncing between masts and pylons, waiting for her phone to come to life so the radio waves can be reconstituted into digits, letters, words, meaning? This thought accompanies her along the high road, and at the station she strides through the cavernous ticket hall and up to the open-air platform, where she sees the next train is in three minutes. This is exactly what she'd hoped for – not a significant delay, but just enough time to buy a coffee from the kiosk built into the station house. It feels like the first good news of the day.

184

'Tall Americano,' she says to the young black guy tucked behind a bank of muffins and nut bars. 'With an extra shot.'

'The Americano has two shots already.'

'I know. I'd like an extra one.'

The guy eventually does as he's told, and Anna takes the brimming cup and a fistful of sugar sachets to the platform edge; the train is due in one minute. She steps to the wall of the station house and places the hot paper cup on the sloping ledge of a bricked-up window. Delicately, she pinches off the lid and shakes a sugar sachet. The board now says 'Train approaching'. She bites the sachet but it slides through her teeth. She bites again forcefully; the whole sachet splits and sugar granules fly out over her hands and sleeve and onto the floor.

'Shit.'

She can hear a gathering thunderous rumble, and a snapping noise like electrical wires being whipped. She looks at her coffee again and the steaming cup seems to throb with a totemic energy. If she manages this, everything else will fall into place. It all depends on whether she can get a second sachet open smoothly, and she does, and then pours it into the coffee as the train crashes in beside the platform, accompanied by a gust of warm wind. Anna stirs with the wooden splint and then replaces the plastic lid, but it doesn't seem to fit, and she can't push too hard with the cup balanced on the sloping ledge. Behind her the train has stopped, then there is the pneumatic hiss as the doors are sucked open. Discarding the lid, Anna picks up the paper cup and turns towards the train, but the doors are not where she expects them to be. Rather than directly ahead, the nearest door is at least ten metres to her left. Trying to stay composed, she begins angling across the platform, the steaming coffee held in front of her. But then the train makes its final beep of warning and Anna rushes, jerking the cup. Scalding liquid spills over the lip and runs over her fingers, her wrist. She winces, sucks air through gritted teeth, and lets go of the cup as she makes a lunging step up to the train, just as the doors close behind her.

'Are you all right, love?'

Anna finds her balance and glances at the white-haired woman who is speaking to her, before putting her face to the vestibule window and looking out at her dropped coffee. It is amazing, the mess she has made, the impact she's had: the contents of that small cup are spread across the entire plat-form like a brown bed sheet, spawning tributaries that finger along seams in the tarmac and trickle off the opposite edge. A station official in an orange jacket is looking down at it all, as if thinking: what's happened here then?

'Have you burnt yourself?'

Anna tells the white-haired woman she is fine and looks down at her hand – there is a pink blotch on the loose flesh between forefinger and thumb, and the sight makes the burn sting for the first time. She looks up and sees the man in the orange jacket, the man who must clear up her mess, and just before the train slides away she sees him shake his head sadly, and then they are in a black tunnel and the glass gives back nothing but the reflection of her own startled face.

Twenty minutes later Anna arrives at the lobby of the build-ing, her face partially hidden behind a thick and hasty coating of make-up. All three lifts are up on the top floors, and in a rush of impatience she pushes through to the stairwell. All she wants is to get to her desk and focus on what she needs to do, but on the third-floor landing she is confronted by the small but formidable figure of Paula, waiting for the lift in a long winter coat.

'Hey!' says Paula, her face lighting up as if seeing Anna has made her day, her week. 'How are you?'

Anna says that she's great, really great, as the lift arrives with a ping.

'Are you sure?' says Paula, ignoring the lift. 'You look a little . . .'

'Well,' says Anna, rolling her eyes and whispering from the side of her mouth, trying to assume the sassy, conspiratorial persona she thinks Paula expects from her, 'I'm actually hungover. You see, it's my birthday today.'

Paula's face opens up again, this time as if she is releasing a silent scream. Then she hugs Anna and spins her around on the spot, while singing a high-pitched and strangely robotic version of the Happy Birthday song.

'So we need to celebrate,' says Paula.

'I've got to finish the article first.'

Paula asks what article, and Anna is surprised to have to remind her that the Sahina piece is going live today.

'Of course it is. In which case, we definitely need to drink later.'

'I've actually got plans already.'

'Just a quick one,' says Paula, pressing the lift button again, and this time it is less of a question. Anna says, 'We'll see,' and with a final satisfied giggle Paula pats her backside and she is released.

As she crosses the clearing she is pleased to see Stuart's desk is empty, and that she probably has time to get organised before meeting him. In fact, the whole office is half

empty, this being the day that most people, Ingrid included, invoke the right to work from home. Without taking
her coat off she switches on her computer and connects her
phone to the charger she keeps here; both screens light up
for a moment, acknowledging the life-giving electricity, and
then fall black again as they make whatever secret and minute arrangements they need to be ready. Anna becomes settled herself and waits with her hands laid on either side of
her keyboard, taking control of her breathing, looking up
at the clock on the bottom of the big board: 12.06 p.m. It's
not a disaster. Stuart wanted the copy to go to Romont for
10 a.m.; if she does a rapid edit now it can be sent for 1 p.m.,
which still gives them time to go live today. Her computer
screen lights up with its loading graphic, a wormlike line
that rotates clockwise in a visual plea for patience; before
it finishes her phone begins vibrating against the desk, the
sound running up Anna's spine. The buzzing continues for
what feels like a full minute, the notifications for backed-
up texts and missed calls threaded together. Eventually it
falls silent and she calmly picks it up. There are many texts
and notifications and voicemails, but Anna skims past these
to Kismet, which she opens. There are no missed calls, no
messages. Nothing.

The absence doesn't make sense, and she logs out of Kismet and opens it again, thinking it needs to refresh or reboot
or whatever. Still no messages. The last activity is the message
from Geoff 81 on Wednesday afternoon, telling her to meet
him at London Bridge, 6 p.m. She continues looking at these
messages – or, rather, looking at the absence of any messages
since then – until there is a shuffling in her peripheral vision.
Without turning she knows it is Stuart. And, sure enough, he

is coming across the clearing, his eyes locked on her, carrying some papers in his hands.

'I've been calling you all morning,' he says, without introduction. 'What the hell happened?' He is managing to keep his voice down, but is clearly furious.

'Sorry, Stuart. I'm so sorry. I'm having a crazy time at the moment, and last night—'

'Whoa, whoa, whoa,' he says quickly, cutting her off. He sits down on Ingrid's empty chair and rolls it towards Anna, well within range of the sickly smell – her hangover is radiating from her as a form of energy. 'I don't give a shit how busy you are. We had an agreement that you would come in early. And now we have a problem. A big fucking problem.' He drops the stapled handful of paper onto the desk and her eyes trace the familiar opening sentence of her article. 'What the fuck is this?'

'It needs more work, I know,' she says, feeling nauseous again. 'The typos and grammar are all over the place, but I can fix it, just give me—'

'It's not the typos,' he says. 'It's the whole thing. All this flitting back and forth between the past and present, long descriptions of her office. And this crap about her being nice, and attacking corporations. It goes completely against the brand values. What the fuck were you thinking?' He is trying to lower his voice, but its full volume keeps escaping like trapped gas; she senses others in the office watching them, wondering what is going on.

'I was trying something new,' she says, meekly, looking down. 'I wanted to juxtapose the public image of her, the terrifying persona, with the real person. The fact that she's actually quite nice . . .'

'So you were experimenting. Good stuff. Well done.' He sighs and shakes his head. 'Well, we can't send this to Romont. We're going to have to call Paula, tell her we need to postpone.'

'Don't do that,' says Anna. 'I have more stuff. I can fix it.'

He looks up to the high ceiling as if requesting from a higher power the patience and goodwill to have any more hope in her. Then he checks his watch.

'Show me the transcript,' he says.

'The transcript?'

'Yes, the transcript! Bring it up. Let me see it.'

She hesitates, her tired and strained mind struggling to un-pick the implications of showing him the full unedited record of the interview. She says that it's a mess, that she needs to fix it up, that he should just give her twenty minutes. His eyes become wide, as if in disbelief that she is still trying to bargain for time.

'No, Anna,' he says, smiling. He looks almost happy, and Anna thinks that maybe this is what he's wanted all along, that her promotion was just an elaborate means of getting her into this position. 'No more chances. We're going to fix this now, together. Please, bring up the transcript.'

There is nothing for her to do but take her mouse, open the 'Sahina' folder on the desktop, and open the file marked 'transcript'. Then she slides her chair backwards to make way for Stuart, who rolls Ingrid's chair behind her desk. She watches over his shoulder as he reads through the unedited transcript, feeling that he is staring directly into the private and shameful contents of her head. Also palpable is the attention of others – Jessica the office assistant, and Ben from the sports desk – who cast curious eyes towards Anna as they cross the clearing, obviously surprised by this unusual break with protocol.

'Jesus Christ,' says Stuart. 'You call this being nice?'

She peers over his shoulder and sees he is looking at the bit where Sahina accused her of being a representative of Romont.

'It reads worse than it was. You had to be there.'

'She implied that you're not a real journalist.'

'Well . . . maybe there were a few bad moments.'

'Not bad, good. This is the best bit so far. You should start with this.'

'Start with it? But she was so—'

'And this bit, about the governments. "Big business is just about flattery." She said you could use this?'

'Um. Well, she said it.'

'She didn't say you couldn't?'

'No. She didn't say that.'

'All right,' says Stuart. 'We'll use this too. This could be the headline. Right. This is what we'll do.'

He picks up the paper version of her article and begins scribbling on it, narrating his edits as he makes them, starting with the need to get rid of the stuff about walking through the desert, about the layout of her office, about her childhood in Pakistan, and especially the stuff critiquing Kismet and the other corporations. He tells her to keep the mentions of those famous stories but to take away the ironic gloss, to present them as fact. Then he makes two big scrawls at the top of the page, telling her to start with Sahina accusing her of not being a journalist, followed by the bit about government officials having no taste; he even writes out a suggested first sentence – 'Sahina Bhutto has a reputation for being hostile to journalists, but perhaps it was a first when . . .' He tells her to deliver the copy to him in an hour, polished and ready to go, and that he will brief Romont for a quick turnaround at 3 p.m. Then he is standing up and walking away, without so much as a pleasantry to seal off the conversation, without even looking at her, and shaking his head as he does so.

Anna picks up the paper, and feels she is being watched by others from around the office. She glances up, and the proof of their attention isn't that she catches them looking, but in the way they all spring into action, a sudden simultaneous jerk as they hurry to prove that they weren't.

There isn't time to feel sorry for herself. Or to dwell on what Stuart has said. There's no time for anything, in fact; she only has fifty minutes, and it isn't nearly long enough to make all these edits. But the sight of her expensive new boots glows up at her as an emblem of financial responsibility, of financial exposure, and of the fact that her only option is to make a start. All those meandering, multi-clause sentences that dip and loop around and were honed through dozens of edits are now deleted in a half-second, and it is as if they never existed. What is left in their place is empty white space on the page, and in order to thread together the remaining islands of text she comes up with the only things that the time constraint and her addled mind can generate – short, stumpy, workmanlike sentences and unavoidable cliché. She writes that Sahina has 'never been one to suffer fools gladly' or 'take prisoners', and that she is prone to 'throwing cats amongst the pigeons'. These words pour out of her without any shame, without any feeling at all, just an abstract compulsion to get the job done. She only breaks once, to get a glass of water, and walks to the kitchenette and back without making eye contact with anyone, in a tunnel of her own concentration.

After fifty minutes she has made all the changes, and as

a final gesture she adds the piece at the start deriding the government officials – careful to remove specific mention of China – and then the para about how rude Sahina was to her, starting with Stuart's suggested sentence. With two minutes to spare, she attaches it to an email and presses send. The little piece of paper folds itself into an aeroplane and flies away into the distance. She looks towards the Quiet Room and imagines Stuart slamming out of the glass door and coming towards her, this time not even trying to contain his fury. He doesn't appear; she isn't even sure if he is in there. In need of distraction, she gazes up at the big board, and sees a report on the guy suing Kismet to release his profile; the case is going to be heard by the European Court of Justice. While she is looking at this her phone buzzes against the desk, making the abbreviated tone of a Kismet message. It occurs to her that he has finally messaged her, that he decided to let last night slide – to allow whatever extreme emotions inspired her absence to pass – and is only now trying to find out what happened. She picks it up and finds it is a regular message from her mother. She hopes she is having a lovely day, and that she is happy. *Have a great birthday, darling. Lots of Love. Mum x.*

The earnest sentiment makes her think she might cry. Then she is alarmed to discover that she really is, right there at her desk. The words of the message blur behind water, and she gets up and walks quickly across the clearing, holding her breath to keep in a sob. Not until she is inside the toilet cubicle does she breathe again. She sits on the toilet and bends over double and cries, the tears coming without thoughts attached, and her body vibrating and twitching, as if from a gentle fit of retching. Then she blows her nose and wipes her eyes with a tissue – her make-up all gone to shit

– and goes downstairs and through the lobby and into the street, on the lookout for pain relief.

In the corner shop she buys paracetamol and also a can of Red Bull, which she has never liked but whose brash promises offer some hope, at least. She is embarrassed by the idea of drinking the can in the office, so instead stands tucked into a little recess between shops, hoping none of her colleagues see her. She sips the Red Bull – which has a strange, electrically charged flavour that is surely found nowhere in nature – and looks at the people walking past on the street, looks at the sky above, where the clouds are beginning to dissolve away. Her birthday street. Her birthday sky. The sight of the attractive fashionable people has an unpleasant effect on her, she feels the equal of none of them – they are all moving so effortlessly, not just along the pavement, but through space–time itself, through the continuum of their existence. They all have £60,000 jobs. £700 coats. £200 haircuts. More important than having these things is the belief that they deserve to have them, without which they would be worthless. But have they had an 81, thinks Anna. Probably not. That's one thing she can say she had, even for a short period – the highest score she's had at anything, ever. Her 81. She can see him standing beneath the information board and wonders how long he waited for. Twenty minutes? Thirty? And then he . . . what? Perhaps he knows her so well, the connection between them is so strong and clear, that on some level he knew why she hadn't come, that this wasn't a casual thing for her, that some major life event prevented her. Or maybe he was furious and is still smarting now, and is waiting for her to have the decency to apologise. Or, likeliest of all, he probably just shrugged his shoulders and walked away, already checking his phone for alternatives – Anne-Marie 67, Jess 74. This makes most sense, she supposes, given his lack of contact, and the fact that he never seemed too fussed about the whole thing. This conclusion causes an immoderate sadness to come over her, like a whole dark storm cloud of melancholy, until she literally shakes herself in an effort to shuck this off. She takes a final sip of Red Bull and crosses the road, deciding to block any thought of Geoff and Kismet from her mind, and to focus solely on it being her birthday and Pete and her imminent party; she resolves not to check her phone for the rest of the day.

Back at her desk two emails are waiting from Stuart. One is short and curt, telling her she is lucky to get away it. The other email is to Romont, with Paula in CC, in an entirely different tone; he writes that they had an amazing interview with Sahina and that Anna did a superb job with the write-up, which is attached for their approval. She opens it and reads through. Stuart has made a few more changes, mainly adding and emphasising the brand values, making sure ambition, sophistication and power appear all over the place. He has allowed her clichés to stand, and has added some more of his own. It is just a cheaper, nastier version of the articles she read in *Time* and *Vogue* and the others, and less well written. But it is done now. This is her entry to the world. She feels the heavy sadness again, and even as she tells herself not to, she reaches out and picks up her phone: there are no new messages.

Two p.m. becomes 3 p.m. becomes 4 p.m. There is nothing to do but wait. She considers eating something but the remnants of nausea still forbid it, and instead she finally sifts through her backlog of texts. She sends Pete a message thanking him for the breakfast and apologising that she didn't have time to eat it; he writes back almost immediately, saying he doesn't mind at all, that he hopes she had a good time with her mum and that she is 'feeling good about everything'. A text then arrives from Caz, saying she can't come tonight because she has to work; Anna tells her not to worry, that it's not a big deal. There are also messages from Zahra, Hamza, her aunt Ruth, and Dianne, her dad's third and final wife. She makes a point of replying to each, adding a little personalised flourish and this reminds her that she hasn't checked her suitcase project since yesterday afternoon. There are several new followers and messages, and the first one she reads makes her heart leap. It is from @DeepBlue1977 – one of her most enthusiastic collaborators – and says that he has managed to track down through a friend of a friend someone that works in BAA HQ! Anna gets a burst of hope and excitement, and this lasts for as long as it takes to scroll up to the next message from @DeepBlue1977 saying that he spoke to the BAA man, who confirmed that all passenger list data is deleted after two years. *You're too late*, he says. She scans through more recent comments, hoping that someone might have contradicted him, but it is just consolation messages from her other faithful supporters. A lump expands in her throat. She thinks of her man at the carousel, now permanently out of reach, and the vision of him fades to nothing. The final message, from only twenty minutes ago, is @DeepBlue1977 saying he hates to be the bearer of bad news and that he hopes she isn't too disappointed! It is clear that a response is required from her; the lack of any reaction is conspicuous, given the frequency and sassiness of her earlier posts – her silence suggests she is too stunned or confused to contribute, or that maybe something bad has happened to her. This thought makes her wonder if Geoff has looked at her profile in search of clues to her absence last night; maybe, since he claimed to be such a big fan. She opens her list of followers – now 564 strong – and begins scrolling through them, clicking on anyone that could conceivably be Geoff. She does this for a time before realising she is being crazed; even if he is following her, what difference does it make? She swears at herself for letting this thought creep into her mind, and returns to the task of responding to her real followers.

She begins drafting a new tweet, but doesn't know what to say. Another scroll through the consolatory messages reminds her not a single one of them said anything positive, and on a sullen impulse she decides this would be a good time to call the project to a halt. She writes that there is now little evidence to go on, as far as she can see, and they should leave it here. She writes a second, thanking those who helped her in the search, saying it was fun while it lasted, but that was all it was – she has no ambition to initiate a global lost property service. In her third and final tweet, she says that if any of them does see any more evidence, please feel free to 'take the lead'.

As she posts this the light around her desk darkens, and she has the sensation of people approaching her from all sides. She looks up and is surprised to see Mike, the head of HR, standing a few feet to her right, grinning, alongside Beatrice from payroll, Jessica the office assistant, and also Tom and Ben from the sports desk – all of them are encircling her in a tight ring. For a weird moment she feels an animal instinct to lash out at them, to defend herself and her territory, and it is only when she sees Paula bearing a small cake that she realises what is happening.

'Haaaapppppyyyy Biiirrrttttthhhhdddaaaayyyy tooo youuuu!' they begin, singing each syllable in slow motion. 'Haaaappppppyyyy Biiirrrttttthhhhdddaaaayyyy tooo youuuu! Haaaappppppyyyy Biiirrrttttthhhhdddaaaayyyy, deaaarrrr Annnnnaaaaaaaa. Haaaappppppyyyy Biiirrrttttthhhhdddaaaayyyy tooooooooooo youuuuuuuuuu!'

There is a short and diffuse applause from the small group, which Anna sees also contains Margaret from planning and Sophie from procurement – practically everyone from the skeletal Friday staff, other than Stuart. Mike is tearing black foil from a bottle of Prosecco, and Paula places the cake beside Anna's keyboard and brings them all to attention.

'I knew you guys were useless,' she says, 'but I didn't think you'd manage to forget Anna's thirtieth birthday.'

The group scoffs at this accusation, and there is a loud pop as Mike opens the Prosecco; he pours it into cups that Beatrice lines up on Anna's desk, the force of the fizzy wine almost knocking over the weightless plastic. The first cup is put in Anna's hand, and she takes a glug while looking over at Stuart's desk; she is relieved to see that he is either in the Quiet Room or out, since his joining this gathering might tip the balance between awkward and unbearable.

'To make up for being so lame, you all have to come to the pub and buy Anna a drink,' says Paula. Anna is about to interrupt and say she can't go for drinks, but Paula continues. 'And before you start making your usual piss-weak excuses, bear this in mind: this is more than a birthday celebration. Just a few minutes ago, Anna's first article as lead writer was signed off by the clients, and will be published in the next few hours.'

A murmur of surprise and congratulation spreads around

the group; someone squeezes Anna's shoulder from behind, another whispers 'well done'. Anna is surprised herself. She turns to her computer and sees there is indeed one new message, from the team at Romont, entitled 'Sign off'.

'And an interview with Sahina Bhutto, no less! Which the clients at Romont called "tough" and "no-nonsense". She might come across as a wallflower, but don't be deceived – this is going to take Anna to the top of the big board, and not for the last time.'

There is another burst of applause, and Anna averts her eyes from their congratulatory faces – rather than pride she feels embarrassment, and imagines Stuart's fat fingers tapping out the most egregious cliché: 'heads will roll'. It would be nice to disappear, to vanish from sight, but instead the applause ends and there is a silence that she knows is her responsibility to fill.

'Come on, Anna, give us a few words.'

'Remind us what it's like to be young.'

'Or remind Mike, anyway.'

'Oi!'

There is simply no option but to stand up and say something, and Anna takes the last sip of Prosecco and gets to her feet.

'Thanks, guys. As Paula pointed out, I'm thirty today. I remember someone saying this is the age when you stop messing around and start acting responsibly.'

'Shame!'

'Who told you that?'

'Never!'

'It wasn't Paula, that's for sure!' says Mike, and everyone laughs.

'Whoever said it,' says Anna, trying to smile along with the japes, 'I decided to live by it. And that is why, unfortunately, I can't come to the pub myself tonight, as I have a party at home and I have to go and prepare . . . and . . .'

The crowd emits shock and disapproval; Mike and Paula boo. They seem genuinely disappointed and confused. 'But then,' she says, making weighing scales with her upturned palms, deciding to make the disappointed faces smile again. 'I suppose I have the rest of my life to be responsible. The rest of my life, starting tomorrow.'

Just after 5.30 p.m. a group of nine gather in the lobby, then head out to the street; the sky is still light but the narrow lanes are deep in shade. Paula strings them along Poland Street, talking as much as the others combined, and regularly swiping a hand at the person she is joshing at that particular moment. It is already heaving at the John Snow, with dense gangs of drinkers spilling off the pavement into the cobbled street, and inside they have to squash themselves into the corner of the bar where all the dirty glasses are stacked. Anna is pressed up against the side of a fruit machine between Paula and Mike, who buys her a pint of lager which feels giant, undrinkable, and which she holds with two hands. He asks what she's doing for her birthday, and she tells him about the dinner party. Then he asks about Pete, and what he does, and Anna finds herself giving the standard response to this question: that Pete is training to be a teacher, though he used to work for this high-flying global firm and is an engineer 'by trade'.

'Why aren't I invited to the party?' says Paula, poking Anna in the ribs.

'I thought you'd have more exciting things to do on Friday

night,' says Anna, trying to assimilate into the cheeky persona she assumes in front of Paula. 'Hooking up with old flames. Making new ones.'

'As if! London is so boring; everyone is hooked up already.'

'Being in a couple isn't boring,' says Mike, and Paula replies that, while she'd like to defer to Mike's extensive knowledge of being boring, the truth is that being attached *is* boring, because nothing else changes.

'People go out, have a few drinks, go home with their partner. Nothing changes. *Boring.*'

Anna is conscious of not saying much and asks, just to add something, if she thinks other cities have more single people – immediately she regrets that there is nothing spirited or witty about the question. Being squashed between two senior managers is making her feel self-conscious, even more so than usual. Paula makes a speech about how Kismet isn't so big in Hong Kong or Bangkok, how you can go out and still meet someone in an old-fashioned, analogue way.

'Paula is just bitter,' says Mike, touching Anna's forearm, 'because she hasn't found the right girl yet.'

'That's not true. I find the right girl almost every week.' Anna laughs and Mike rolls his eyes.

'But you haven't settled *down*.'

'I settle down every night! Then I get up again in the morning. Also, I'll settle for that.' She points across the busy pub to a table where four men in suits are pulling on their coats.

'We won't all fit,' says Mike.

'Don't be such an accountant. We'll get cosy. If there's room in the heart, there's room for the bum.'

The whole group follows Paula to the table, Mike complaining that he isn't an accountant. And indeed they do all

fit, nine around a table for four, Anna packed so snugly between Jessica and Beatrice that it is a struggle to bring her
second pint to her lips. But it is a nice feeling, to be a group
of colleagues crammed together. Just after 6 p.m. she is given
her second pint, which goes down easier than the first, and
whoever bought the round also delivers several bags of crisps
and nuts, which are torn open on the table. Anna crunches
through handful after handful, her body applauding the salt
and sugar and grease, her first food of the day.

'Here's a question,' says Ben. 'I know you can wolf something down, or dog someone, but can you *cat* them?' Everyone groans; this is typical Ben.

'You can badger them, I know that much,' says Paula.

'Or outfox them!' says Anna.

'And then slug them, right in the chops!'

'You guys, quit horsing around.'

'Honestly, I can't bear it!'

Now everyone is laughing and trying to join in, and Anna
feels herself drifting into a blissful, liquid state. She loses her
sense of self, retreats inwardly until she feels almost like a
disembodied, floating eye watching with pleasure as her colleagues jostle and throw barbs at each other. What wellbe-
ing there is, she realises, to drink beer with these friendly,
energetic people who clearly all love each other's company,
despite barely knowing each other really; perhaps it is precisely because of this that they get on so well. She continues
floating inwards, feeling her eyes glazing over, until conversation turns abruptly to her. Paula once again accuses Mike
of being an accountant, and he tells her to stop showing off,
just because she's soft on Anna.

'As if,' says Paula. 'Anna is the straightest girl in London.'

'Hey!'

'No offence, darling. But you're as straight as the Red Arrows.'

The others laugh briefly, and then attention turns to Beatrice when she accuses Mike of being the biggest flirt in the office. Anna is stunned. The straightest girl in London. She takes another sip of lager and decides to stand up for herself.

'I've been with girls,' she says, louder than intended. Everyone falls silent and looks at her.

'*You* have?' asks Beatrice.

'Well, one girl,' says Anna, already wishing she hadn't said anything. 'Not girls.'

She takes another sip of beer and looks down in her lap. Everyone seems at a loss for what to speak about, her interruption having torn through the previous conversation.

'So,' says Paula, clearing her throat. 'When was this?'

'I'd rather not say.'

'Oh, come on. You've got to now.'

'I'd really rather not, I made a fool of myself. I shouldn't have said anything.' Rather than deter them this statement stirs their interest, and Ben says that she should tell the whole thing, that he senses this will be good. She says that she met a girl, a friend of a friend, and one night after a party they spent the night together. Beatrice asks where this was, and Anna says it was in San Francisco. Mike asks why she was in San Francisco, and she says she lived there for six months when she was twenty-five. Paula asks why she moved there, at which point Anna sighs and resigns herself to telling the whole story, from the top.

'Alright. Have I not told any of you that I moved to

America? Well, I did, just for the hell of it, for six months.'
Still they demand more back-story, and Anna quickly explains that in her early twenties she lived in Hackney with Zahra, her best friend, and was seeing this guy called Ed, but that she suddenly decided to change everything in her life.

'Everything?'

'*Everything*. So I split up with Ed and bought a ticket to San Francisco.'

'Did you have a plan for when you got there?'

'No plan at all. Or friends, or job, or contacts. The only thing was that Ruth, my dad's sister, has an apartment there, which she said I could use.'

'Handy.'

'Right. But there was a mix-up. I arrived to find a woman already living in the flat. Ruth thought I was coming a month later, apparently. Anyway, this turned out to be a good thing. I went to a hostel and asked around online, and the next day I found a room in Oakland with a bunch of art students. This is now too much detail, right?'

'If anything, not enough,' says Ben.

'Okay. So I moved into this house, which was like . . . *wow*. It was huge, on four floors, with this big open kitchen and a roof terrace. And the people were great. They'd spend their days working on paintings or sculptures, and took me to parties in the evening. I was in heaven. And the room I was crashing was best of all. It belonged to this girl called Juliette, who'd gone to Japan for a month, and it became my favourite place in the world. It was packed with books, vinyl, jewellery, antiques. Everything was so *personal*. It was like . . . it was like being in this girl's head. There were all these . . . *things*, these strange little art pieces.'

'What sort of things? Give details, examples.'

'Alright. For example, she had a tiny square canvas, a miniature canvas frame just a few inches across, like a painting for a wendy house. And a wooden clothes peg was stuck to it, gripping a shiny plastic Valentine's heart. And beneath the peg the word "remember" was painted on the canvas.'

They all frown and look at each other.

'What does that mean?' asks Beatrice.

'I don't know. That's my point, none of it made sense. But I loved it. I could spend hours in there looking around, or reading her books, flicking through picture albums, listening to old records.'

'You looked at pictures of her?' says Ben.

'Sure,' says Anna, with dignity, as Mike winks at Paula. 'Some were of her.'

'And you fancied her?' says Ben, his eyes wide, and Paula jabs him in the ribs.

'I wasn't *aware* of fancying her. I just really liked her; she seemed like a better, cooler version of me. I'd get back from work – I'd found a job in a bookstore – and would immediately want to be in Juliette's room, even if there was a party on the terrace. So that went on for a few weeks, and then . . . Then I began acting strange.'

'Strange how?'

Anna stops and has the last sip of the second pint, putting it down next to a brand new one, which she didn't notice arriving. She can feel her heart beating, and remember being in Juliette's room, and the racing feeling that was the same as being in raves, and the way she felt in Somerset House – that childish sense of abandon. It is thrilling, but also quite draining, to be telling this story aloud, for the first time ever.

'I suppose things changed when I found the book. It was a notebook. I found it under her bed. I'd begun snooping weeks before. I'll never forget it. It was a black leather notebook, and "Be Still My Beating Heart" was written on the cover in gold Letraset. Inside she'd written out hundreds of text messages, going back about a year, all between her and this guy Martin. I read it in one sitting and it killed me, the care she'd gone to, writing them in different-coloured ink, putting the date and time by each one. I also couldn't believe how similar some of it was to Ed and me – some of the arguments they had were almost identical to ours. The final messages were only a few weeks old, and that's when I realised: she'd run away to Japan because she'd split up with Martin, just like I'd run away because of Ed. It was uncanny.'

'And you thought it meant something?'

'Yeah. I mean, it felt more than just a coincidence. I felt like we were supposed to find each other. Help each other . . .'

Her voice has grown increasingly small saying this; she feels tired and now really wishes she hadn't started.

'And then what happened? Keep going. You're doing well.'

'Really,' says Jessica. 'You're good at telling stories.'

'Um. Well. Then I began acting *really* strange.'

'Details, examples,' says Mike.

'Sorry. I suppose I thought about her all the time, even dreamt about her. My aunt's flat became free but I kept paying rent to live in Juliette's room. I started counting the days until she came back, and was working myself into a frenzy. I didn't feel like she was going to replace me in the room, I felt like she was coming to *join me*. I thought, you know, we were going to be together.'

'You mean *together* together?'

Anna looks down at her lap. 'Yes. It took me completely by surprise. And at the same time felt the most natural thing in the world.'

'So? Come on, you're killing me here,' says Paula. 'She came back? You got to meet her?'

'Yeah, she came back. Obviously I had to move out before she arrived, but the others invited me to a "welcome home" dinner party they were throwing for her. I'm not sure I've ever been more nervous in my life. I almost cancelled, I don't know how many times, and on the way I stopped for a shot of tequila, just to try and calm down. Somehow I made it to Uptown, then the house, then I was inside, hugging all the others, stepping up to the terrace and there she was, sitting at the table. Not the idea of her, or a picture – the living, breathing Juliette. She looked great. She sounded . . . *great*. Even better than I expected, and I can't tell you how frustrating it was. There were ten people having dinner and she was at the other end of the table. And I was so self-conscious I could barely string a sentence together. But she was jetlagged anyway, and after dinner she went straight to bed. So I just sat there getting drunk on white wine, hating all the others. I smashed a glass and said I had to go home. They tried to make me stay but I insisted, and said I'd let myself out. But on the way down I had another idea. I didn't let myself out.'

Each of the eight faces leans closer over the table; she senses the men on the next table have cocked an ear as well.

'And then?'

'I stopped on the first floor and went to Juliette's room. The door was ajar, and I pushed it open.'

'I told you this was going to be good,' says Ben.

'It was dark, she was asleep. I stepped inside and for a while just stood there. Then she woke with a gasp and was like: "What? Who's there?" I said it was me, Anna. She turned on a lamp and glared at me; I don't think she remembered who I was. I explained I'd been staying there and she looked at me blankly and asked if I'd left something in the room. I said no, that I just wanted to speak to her. Fuck, I was pissed. She frowned but then for some reason – perhaps seeing the look on my face – said I should sit down. So I perched on the end of the bed and, you know, told her everything.'

'Everything?'

'*Everything*. Just as I told you. And in the telling I realised how crazy it sounded. I felt so stupid I couldn't look at her, and as it went on it turned into an apology. Then I felt her hand on my shoulder. She laughed and said it was fine. That it was the weirdest thing in the world, but also great, and that she was flattered. She said we should hang out sometime. I nodded and said okay, and dared to look at her. Her hand was still on my shoulder and her face was, like, right there. Then I did it. I kissed her. Just for a few seconds. The crazy thing is she didn't pull away. We held it for a moment, both with our eyes open, neither of us blinking . . .'

Anna stops, realising only now that her story is going to have to fork away from reality at this point, that she isn't going to be able to tell them what really happened. The truth is that she kicked off the story with a lie: she has never slept with a girl.

'And *then*?'

'And then,' she says, feeling herself blush as she trespasses into fiction, 'then it happened.'

'There and then? Just like that?'

'Yes, there and then. I don't think I need to draw you a picture.'

'Wow. Just that one time?'

'Yep. A week later my friends Zahra and Caz flew over, and we hired a car and went around Yosemite and down to LA. I never spoke to her again.'

'Wow,' says Mike, and Ben says he actually does think she should draw a picture. The whole table is impressed and looks at one another, exchanging fair-enough expressions. Paula apologises for calling Anna the straightest girl in London, and Mike tells her maybe she's still in with a chance. Anna lifts pint number three, already a third gone, and fills her mouth, swallows, fills her mouth, swallows. Once again the corrupt feeling of being a fake rises within her, made worse by their praise and approval.

'What is Letraset, anyway?' says Jessica.

Anna sinks into her chair, while the memory of what really happened flows uninvited through her mind: kissing Juliette. The two of them staring at each other, the moment hanging, stretching. Then she felt everything within her go cold and the familiar bottomless feeling in her stomach, as if she was on a rollercoaster that shot suddenly upwards – it felt too real, too unpredictable. Without a word she stood up from the bed, grabbed her bag and left the room. She flew down the stairs, out the front door and into the street. And never went back to the house, for shame.

'It's like Etch-a-sketch, isn't it?' says Mike.

'No,' says Paula, 'it's those stencil things with all the letters and numbers.'

'Those stencil things are called *stencils*.'

These words wash over Anna as she wallows in the memory of running away from Juliette. It is curious to remember that bottomless feeling, the same as she felt with Thomas 72, or when she went to meet Geoff last night. She has always assumed it was her dad's death that made her react to danger that way, that made her cautious and steered her away from shipwreck. But there it was that night with Juliette, months before he died, in the safest situation imaginable. She had precisely nothing to lose, and the girl she had coveted for months, with an intensity she had never known, was in her arms. And still she got up and ran away.

'Come on, Anna? What is it?'

'What? Sorry?'

'What's Letraset?'

'It's . . . it's those sheets of plasticky paper, with waxy letters that you transfer by, like, rubbing a coin on it.'

'Congratulations, you win another pint. Same again?'

Anna says she should probably be getting on, and then looks at her watch, which says 7.04 p.m.

'Shit,' she says. 'I've got to go. Like, now.' The table is shifted out and then Anna is pushing past Ben to stand up. She grabs her bag from beneath the table and while squeezing out of her space bids them all a hurried goodbye, says sorry for telling such a long and weird story and now running off; they all shout overlapping goodbyes, and without being able to acknowledge any of them she is away from the table and pushing out the door. The darkening street is clogged with static vehicles, and she walks all the way to Dean Street before spotting a cab with its light on.

'Kilburn,' she says, climbing in. 'Fast as you can.'

The driver makes a three-point turn and accelerates down

a narrow one-way lane, only to get stuck in another queue on Old Compton Street; gangs of boozy pedestrians stream around the cab as if it were a rock in a river.

'Rush hour,' says the driver. Anna checks her phone: she already has two missed calls from Pete, and a text to ask if everything is okay. She ignores the questions but says that she's on her way, and then slumps in her seat and feels the warm breeze of the heaters on her face. Soon the traffic clears and they make progress along Tottenham Court Road, the sodium glow of lampposts swashing through the car like swords of light. But then the driver turns off the main road, and Anna cringes when they pull onto Great Portland Street, directly beside the patch of pavement with the white wall and waxy-leafed hedge. She is embarrassed to recall how she stood there last night, drunk out of her mind, feeling pity for her dad. How ridiculous, to pity someone whose only aim was to live without hypocrisy and in keeping with his true desires, irrespective of what anyone else thought. She hasn't followed through with anything that she wanted to do. She never set up her projects in time. She didn't sleep with Thomas 72. She didn't even dare spend the night with Juliette. She has always lacked the courage to live the life she wants, and accuses people like her dad of being careless and childish because it is easier than accepting that she is essentially gutless. This thought evokes a vivid image of Geoff standing beneath the information board, which blends with her half-remembered dream featuring her dad, and diving into the swimming pool in Somerset House, and breaking the kiss with Juliette, and her man with the suitcase at the carousel. These thoughts must hold her in some kind of trance, for the next thing she knows she is thrown against the door as the cab turns off Kilburn High Road, and a moment later they are idling outside her house.

The two front windows of the flat are dimly lit, like a cave with a fire deep within, and when she opens the door she is surprised by how dark and silent it is. She can barely see the stairs, and the only sounds as she climbs are her clopping boots and her own heartbeat. At the stairhead she turns to face the living-room door; pale light is leaking around the edge of the rectangular frame, like the flares around a solar eclipse. Anna takes one, two, three steps and pushes into the room; it is like opening a door to a storm.

'Happy birthday!'

Seven people are facing her, all with their arms raised above their heads, clapping, their mouths opening and closing.

'Thought you'd show up, did you?'

'What time do you call this?'

'We thought you'd run away.'

'The cheek of it!'

Anna's eyes snap between the cheering faces: there is Zahra in a tight-fitting green dress that makes Anna aware of her humdrum jumper-and-jeans attire; her fiancé Keir is in a pink shirt beside her, his white teeth gleaming; Pete's brother Bean has a new beard and makes a wolf-whistle with his fingers in his mouth; Toby and Cecile are clapping in a restrained, muted way; Ingrid is smiling but looking out of place, clearly a stranger in the room; and finally Hamza is floating above them all, standing on a chair. All these thoughts flick through her mind in the second it takes her eyes to scan across the room from left to right, and then there is a cracking like gunfire, and green, red and pink ribbons of party poppers arc towards her. The floor shakes as Hamza jumps from the chair, and he comes at her with his brown arms outstretched, his bottom lip overturned in a pantomime expression of sorrow.

'She's bewildered!' he says, gathering her limp body in his arms, and then she is rapidly hugged and kissed in turn by the others, who queue up behind him. Then they are seated along the table and Anna is standing alone, leaning against the arm of the white sofa, looking across the room. It is weird to think this is the same room that she woke up in this morning. The long dining table has been brought into the centre of the room and is covered with a white tablecloth, and the only light is from four chunky candles spaced along its centre, amongst the jagged landscape of glasses and crockery and cutlery. Outside the range of the dim candle glow, the edges of the room are lost to shadow, besides the rectangular glow of Pete's iPad, which is sending forth some inoffensive acoustic ballad.

'Where is Pete?' she says. Everyone at the table smiles, and at that moment Anna senses a presence behind her. She turns and sees him standing in the doorway, although it is a new version of Pete, so unfamiliar that for a fraction of a second she wonders if it really is him. For the first time in years his cheeks and chin are pink and clean-shaven, and his tawny, shaggy hair has been slicked to one side with some kind of product that makes it appear black. His eyes haven't changed though, and are narrowed slightly as they search for reassurance that she is okay, that everything is alright; she smiles at him and his eyes widen, relaxing.

'See, guys?' he says, stepping forwards and taking Anna's hands in his; his white shirt is rolled up to the elbows, and his forearms are coated in flour. 'I told you she hadn't abandoned me.' He pulls her onto her toes for a kiss, his big lips wet against hers, then puts his arm around her shoulder and turns them both to face those sitting at the table, who now form a gleeful little audience. 'And I want to start with an announcement. As well as Anna's birthday, we have something else to celebrate. Get your phones at the ready. Just under an hour ago, Anna's first article as lead writer, an interview with Sahina Bhutto, was published.'

Pete takes his own phone from his pocket and holds it up for the group; ready on the screen is a tiny image of Sahina's smirking face, followed by Anna's byline. Impressed and surprised noises ripple along the table, and people start grabbing at their phones to look themselves. Pete brings Anna in for another quick kiss on the cheek, before letting her go and disappearing into the dark hallway.

'This is amazing, Anna!' says Bean, before passing the phone to Cecile.

'She's doing Gwyneth Paltrow next!' says Zahra.

'Dark horse, you are.'

'Why didn't you tell me about this?'

'As in *the* Gwyneth Paltrow?'

'I've shared it already.'

'You're a *proper* writer, finally.'

Anna takes her seat at the head of the table, and with each utterance the corrupt dirty feeling intensifies. She wants to say something to excuse herself for the clichés and the ugly short sentences, but it is effort enough just to maintain a smile, and she looks instead at her hands in her lap – the knuckles are white where her fingers are twisted together.

'This is great,' says Ingrid, who holds up her phone the longest, giving the article a professional appraisal. 'It's a really bold style. Anna!'

'Stop it, guys, she's embarrassed.'

'She's alright.'

'Look at her, she's overwhelmed!'

'She needs a drink, is all,' says Hamza, and then he disappears to make her an Old-fashioned. Anna smiles at each person, to prove she's fine; in the dim candlelight only the front of their faces and torsos are clearly visible. Zahra is sat immediately to her left, and on an instinctive impulse she checks to see where Pete is sat in relation to her, a throwback to the jealousy she used to suffer at social events and double dates; she is relieved to see the empty chair at the other end of the table that must be his. A silence gathers, which Anna decides is hers to fill since she hasn't spoken a complete sentence since arriving. She lays her hands on the white tablecloth and tries to think of something funny to say. Her first impulse is to be self-deprecating about her appearance, and explain that she didn't have time to shower and change, but she rejects this idea, since it might cross the border between comic and tragic.

'Sorry for being late,' she says, finally. 'But I had a drink with work people and . . . what can I say . . . I like them better than you guys.'

They all smile and good-naturedly dismiss this suggestion, apart from Keir, seated to Zahra's left, who is glaring at her.

'Forty minutes we were holding those damn party poppers,' he says, shaking his head, not trying to hide his annoyance. Zahra puts a hand on Anna's forearm, as if in apology for her fiancé, and says they had fun chatting amongst themselves.

But Keir persists. 'How can you be that late to a party in your own house?' His pink shirt is rolled up to the elbows, and he plants his heavy and strangely hairless forearms on the table. He isn't a huge man, barely more than six foot, but always spreads himself to appear bigger, sitting sideways on chairs or back from tables, as if he doesn't fit in the available space. 'We all thought you'd run away.'

'Who ran away as a kid?' says Zahra, sitting forwards to block Anna's view of Keir. 'When I was six I ran away with just my cello, who I called Bruno, to go and start a new life in America. We made it to the end of the street.'

People take Zahra up on this challenge, and Anna is pleased to see attention drifting away from her. Toby says that as a teenager he spent the night outside a closed train station in Oxfordshire, and used a bin liner for a sleeping bag. Bean says he once spent the entire night in his tree house as a seven-year-old, and no one in his family – not Pete, not his parents – noticed he was gone. At that moment, as if responding to his name being mentioned, Pete kicks the door open, and he and Hamza carry in two laden trays. A bowl of red soup and a hunk of focaccia are placed before Anna, who also receives a cocktail in a pitcher, garnished with ice, green leaves, a glacé cherry and a slice of orange.

'The soup is cold,' says Toby, more in confusion than complaint.

'It's gazpacho, you klutz,' says Cecile, his wife, and Anna thinks of their number, 73. They are the only couple, besides Zahra and Keir, whose score she knows for a fact. 'You'll like it. It's basically a Bloody Mary in a bowl. But without the celery, Worcester sauce, cucumber, parsley.'

'And vodka,' says Hamza.

'Which I'm surprised you can taste,' says Keir, 'with all that other crap.'

'Depends how much you put in,' says Hamza, and everyone laughs. Pete, standing at the opposite end of the table
from Anna, brings them to silence by cracking a spoon against
his glass. He really does look strange; his white cotton shirt is
buttoned right up to the pink skin on his clean-shaven neck.

'I'd like to raise a toast to Anna. For staying alive for
thirty years, for managing to arrive at her own party, and
for becoming a famous journalist. Cheers.' Everyone clinks
glasses, but Pete remains standing, and with a soft downward movement of his hand he brings them to silence. It is
surprising how smoothly he can work a room, when he has
to; it seems to go against his nature, and she attributes it to
his private-school education, thinking it is a skill all of them
were given, whether they liked it or not. He smiles down at
Anna with a hint of mischief in his eyes. 'And I also wanted
to tell Anna about the schedule for this evening. You see, I
thought it would be a shame, on a night as special as this,
for us to talk about the weather and holidays and jobs and
house prices and the usual crap. So, in order to give the night
some structure, I asked everyone to come prepared with
their favourite story – their favourite *Anna* story.'

'Fuck off,' says Anna, as everyone beams gleefully in her
direction. 'I vote we talk about holidays and the weather. I
vote for that.' No one is listening to her; they are already
noisily debating who should go first, as excited as children
around a campfire.

'Zahra, you should.'

'Mine's too serious, let's do a fun one.'

'What about Pete, since he's already stood up?'

'Don't be a klutz, Pete will go last.'

'Hamza, yours will be funny.'

'Yes, Hamza!'

This enthusiasm is repeated from all corners of the table and Hamza, rolling his eyes and displaying a reluctance that Anna thinks is disingenuous, relents.

'Alright, I'll do it, as long as we can start eating.'

He looks to Pete, master of ceremonies, who nods and raises two upturned palms, prompting the others to bend over their soup; they dunk their spoons and tear at bread with an eagerness that makes clear how hungry they are, and renews Anna's guilt for being so late. She looks down at her own bowl and the red mush breathes cold air onto her face; she reaches for her cocktail instead, and is surprised to find it already half-finished. The iPad is now playing a Beach Boys song, and she wonders what the hell playlist this is.

'I feel bad telling this story in front of Pete,' says Hamza, between slurps of soup. 'Since it involves other guys.'

'Don't tell it, then,' suggests Anna.

'Or another *guy*, to be precise.'

'I didn't think she was a virgin when we met,' says Pete, and Toby says, 'Shame.' Pete ignores him, and adds: 'Just keep it PG.'

'All right, here goes.' He puts down his spoon and rubs his hands together. 'As you already know, me and Anna went to Sheffield together, and were in the same halls. I met her in the very first week, and I liked her immediately. She was quite nerdy – not obviously fashionable or cool – but she had this sharp, sarcastic wit, and always acted like she was half above it all, as if she really *was* the coolest but only she knew it. So we started hanging out, and I would drag her around to gay bars, club nights, house parties; grown-up stuff, not the student bullshit. But it was hard work: she was the kind of fresher that went home at midnight because she had lectures in the morning, or would refuse a drink because she was starting to "feel drunk". *And* she had a boyfriend from home at uni in Nottingham that she went to see every fortnight.'

His voice is accompanied by the clatter of spoons against ceramic and the occasional slurp. Anna is enjoying the story so far, and decides to try and eat something as well. She dunks her spoon and lifts some soup up to her face; it is thick and blood-red and thins to pink water at the edges. It tastes slick and salty, and her instinct is to spit it out, but she forces herself to swallow. It slides down her throat and she grabs her drink to wash it away; the table fractures into a kaleidoscope through the glass of her upended pitcher.

'All this goody-two-shoes nonsense felt like a waste to me,' continues Hamza, 'and I made it my mission to loosen her up. The boyfriend in Nottingham didn't last until Christmas, which helped, and she soon realised that lectures were pointless and stayed up drinking with the rest of us. But the holy grail was getting her to take a pill. She resisted for months, but by halfway through the second term, she agreed to come to a rave.'

'No,' says Anna, realising what story this is. 'You cannot tell this story. It's my birthday, and I forbid it.'

Hamza folds his upper lip over his bottom one, in a childish expression of penitence, and an excited murmur spreads across the table.

'You've *got* to tell it now,' says Keir, and others concur.

'It's the *best* story,' says Hamza, as if the matter is out of his hands. 'And half of them know it already. I'll keep it PG, promise.' His wheedling voice is given physical form by his fingers, which knead the flesh of her forearm. Anna scowls at him, but he blows her a kiss and looks along the table again.

'The rave was called Headcharge, in some part of Sheffield that looked like it was trying to go back to being a slum. As you can guess from the name, it wasn't a light-hearted event, but Anna approached it like a science exam. She'd read up on all these forums about ecstasy and MDMA, and on the way to the club she decreed she would take just half a pill and only drink water, no booze. She followed this strict rule, and after a few hours, while me and the others were off our faces, she was complaining that nothing had happened. We tried several things to make her come up – dancing to spread the chemicals around her system, having intense conversations, making her drink lots of water; it was like trying to cure a kid of hiccups. Eventually she admitted defeat and agreed to take another half. This one I bought from some dude in the club, and *wow*. It had a little Ferrari symbol on it, and fuck me – after thirty minutes I was rinsed, and somehow lost track of Anna. I shat myself, trying to find her. Then eventually I spotted her, dancing *on the stage*.' Hamza is jigging his hands above his head to mimic her dancing, and the first volley of laughter flies from all sides of the table.

'On the *stage*?'

'With, like, forty other people,' says Anna, with a tut. 'The stage was *part* of the dance floor. Come on Hamza, keep it real.'

'I waved at her across the club and she gave me these two massive thumbs up. When I made it to her she hugged me and told me about this energy that was flowing through her, making her excited for "things to come". I took her out for a cigarette, hoping to calm her down, but the opposite happened. She wanted to speak to every other smoker, and not just speak to them – she was like a stand-up comic, going around and working the audience, obliged to make fun of everyone. And they loved it! Soon I lost her again, and hours passed – you know how it goes – and when I next saw her she was with this guy, slightly older than her and a bit edgy-looking. They weren't kissing or dancing, but were going around the rave trying to, like, *give* people things. Cigarettes, sweets, chewing gum. It was like a game they were playing. What did you call it?'

Anna looks at him with thunder in her eyes, and says: 'Free tuck shop.'

'That's it! Free tuck shop. They thought it was the funniest thing. Eventually it was 6 a.m. and Anna was still with this guy. We all wanted to keep partying, and decided to go back to our halls. Anna and the guy came in our taxi, but when we got to halls they stopped to smoke outside. And – Pete, put your fingers in your ears – we didn't see them again that night. I didn't see her until dinner the next day, which was breakfast for us, and we went to the pub after. I asked her how it went with matey, and she said it was "fine, fine". Then she made this hundred-mile stare, and eventually said . . .'

Hamza pauses, allowing the words to gather weight, while mimicking her dreamy gaze.

'"I think he stole my iPod."' Another flurry of laughter, this time mixed with concerned inhalations, especially from Ingrid and Cecile and Bean, newcomers to the story.

'He *stole* from you?' says Ingrid, but Anna doesn't look at her; she is staring darkly at Hamza, who ploughs on.

'I was furious,' he says. 'I said we should call the police right away, or at least call the guy and tell him what a fucking dick he was. But Anna was weirdly reluctant; she said we couldn't call him, because he "didn't have a phone", and that she didn't want the police involved. "I just want to draw a line beneath it," she kept saying. I pushed the issue as far as I could, but eventually I gave up and we moved on. If I ever brought it up, she'd say she didn't want to talk about it. Eventually the whole thing was forgotten, until one day Anna and me were walking down to the city centre. To give blood, if I remember rightly. We were on West Street, when suddenly Anna gasped and turned around, grabbing my hand. She dragged me the way we had just come, and when I turned around I could see why. There was matey, sitting on the street, *begging*.'

No laughter this time, just a horrified gasp.

'*Begging?*'

'He was begging!' Hamza has his hands on his slick black hair, as if to help him comprehend, even after all these years. 'He was a homeless guy!'

'He wasn't *homeless*,' says Anna. 'He was probably just pretending.'

'He had a dog on a piece of string!' says Hamza, and now everyone is laughing, even the girls. They are all so excited they begin talking over one another, each trying to make a joke.

'I hope you didn't still give blood,' says Keir.

'I knew you were into giving to charity, but that's a bit much.'

Pete is joining in the clowning: he has put his fingers in his ears, and now takes them out and looks around as if he hasn't heard a thing.

'It strikes me as ironic', says Anna, raising her voice above the din, 'that when I've walked around town with most of you fuckers, you always say that a beggar probably *isn't* homeless, that he's playing the system. But when I have sex with one, they *definitely* are.'

No one reacts to this, they are all clapping in the direction of Hamza, in appreciation for the story.

'And what if he *was* homeless?' continues Anna, this time directly to Hamza. 'He's probably less skanky than most of the guys on Grindr.' Again no one reacts, and Hamza signals that he wants to wrap up.

'So, I suppose the moral of the story is', says Hamza, the words interleaved with the last splutters of laughter, 'that in just over ten years, you've gone from sucking off a homeless man—'

'Hey, keep it PG,' snaps Pete, though he is smiling as well.

'Sorry. You've gone from *fellating* a homeless man, to interviewing one of the world's leading architects. And for that fact alone, I'm proud to be your friend, and think you deserve a round of applause.'

Everyone claps and cheers, and Hamza bends down and kisses the top of her head. She sits still, smarting from the story, while around her there is a flurry of activity. Her barely touched bowl of soup is taken away, people go to the toilet and drinks are refilled; on his way to the kitchen Pete plants another kiss on her head and whispers, 'You're a good sport.'

A few minutes later he returns with the second course: ricotta and walnut tartlet. The pastry and cheese is more inviting than the cold soup, and she decides to eat this course, or to make a show of trying to; she can feel Pete's eyes on her from the other end of the table as she slices and lifts a small flaky triangle to her mouth. As she slowly makes her way through the tart, the table breaks into two conversations: at her end, Toby, Keir and Zahra are talking about knocking through walls in their respective flats. At the other end, people are quizzing Bean on his plans to open his own bar. The iPad is playing something that sounds like Coldplay. Anna half listens to both conversations while she chews and sips, and Keir's description of their open-plan kitchen/living room reminds her of how long Zahra has been wrapped up in her building projects. She challenges herself to pinpoint when Zahra was last in her flat. She can't quite remember, but knows it was some time last summer, during Pete's final months at the garden centre, and that strange phase when he seemed to go off sex. She is watching Zahra from the corner of her eye as she thinks this, and then sees a furtive glance along the table between her and Pete. The look is remarkable because it is so fleeting – a mere fraction of a second, as if they are strangers – and Anna experiences the old familiar jealousy. She tells herself this is a good thing, the restoration of a healthy appetite, and then this thought is halted by Hamza hitting his hand on the table next to her.

'Knocking *through*,' he says, so loud it makes Anna jump a little in her seat. 'It's all I hear about. In pubs, restaurants, parties. People are always talking about knocking walls down. It's an obsession.'

Every head turns to him in surprise.

'It creates light and space,' says Toby. 'Of course people like doing it.'

'They like *talking* about it more,' says Hamza. 'Anna, why don't you knock some walls down, now that you're a proper grown-up? How about that one – you could have an open-plan living room/bathroom.'

'That would be a bit *too* open-plan,' she says. 'Since the ceiling would fall down as well.'

Everyone laughs, except for Keir, who is peering at Hamza across the table.

'You've never owned a flat, have you, Hamza?' he says, making it sound like a curious abnormality.

'Nah,' says Hamza, not looking at Keir. 'I don't want to be burdened with a mortgage.'

'So you pay off someone else's mortgage instead?'

Zahra is pulling at her glasses, indicating her desire to speak; Anna thinks someone will have to intervene, since Hamza and Keir have a history of locking horns.

'If people want to have mortgages, they can,' says Hamza with a shrug. 'I prefer to be mobile.'

Keir grins. 'In case you need to leave some place in a hurry?'

Hamza grins back. 'Or get some place in a hurry.'

'I would like it, sure,' says Anna, trying to suck attention away from the two boys. 'But I wouldn't want to spend nearly as much time as you guys took to do it.'

'What do you mean?' says Keir.

'I mean, the best part of six months. It's crazy, really, to let it take over your life for so long.'

'Are you nuts?' he says, laughing. 'It took two weeks.'

Anna turns in confusion to Zahra, who has a frozen expression on her face, and then averts her eyes downwards. When she looks up she says: 'Let's have another Anna story.'

'Yes,' says Pete, at the other end of the table. 'Another Anna story. We need to get through them, it's almost nine. Who should go now? Bean, why don't you?'

Anna is still confused by what Keir said about the building work taking two weeks, but the moment is dragged onwards

225

as the table deliberates who should tell the next story. Zahra suggests Ingrid, who has barely said anything all meal, but she winces and shakes her head.

'I haven't prepared one,' she says, and Pete interjects, his mouth full of tart, saying it is *his* fault – he meant to get hold of Ingrid's contact details but forgot. Nevertheless, the whole table remains focused on Ingrid, and she is asked about working with Anna, working at the website generally, her first job at the *Toronto Evening Post*, her flat in Hackney Downs, her boyfriend Sam. Cecile asks about Sam's job making nature films, and Anna senses she is trying to get a feel on what score they got; perhaps she guesses that, based on Ingrid's looks and personality, it is something ridiculously, sickeningly high.

'But Anna's the better journalist,' says Ingrid, clearly trying to shove attention back down the table.

'That's one hundred per cent not true,' says Anna.

'It *is*. She's really versatile. Look at the Sahina article: it's so punchy. So *tough*.' The mention of Sahina's name makes Anna grimace inwardly – she sees Stuart's fat fingers and the phrase 'takes no prisoners' flashes through her mind.

'It's not so great,' says Anna. 'I doubt it will do very well.'

'Course it will. Sahina is clickbait. It will top the big board.'

'If it does or doesn't, I don't really mind. I mean, I don't feel personally . . . *invested*.'

Toby asks what she means, and she tries to explain – as tactfully as possible – that it is almost more like advertising than journalism, since the message is pegged to brand values; ideally she would be writing something that is an expression of herself. The whole table is silent, and looking at her as if they don't understand what she's saying.

'Like the suitcase thing?' asks Pete, who appears as confused as the others. Once again Anna finds herself cringing, this time at the thought of her man at the baggage carousel, now forever out of reach. Toby and Bean both request explanations, and she has to tell the story from the top: the auction house in Tooting, the bags left at Heathrow, the segment of newspaper from Mozambique, the Twitter channel, the interest from someone at BAA, her idea of the person running from the carousel.

'But I left it too late. All the records are wiped and there's nothing else to go on.'

She looks around the table as she delivers this gloomy analysis, hoping that someone will contradict her and say there *must* be loads more evidence, in a whole suitcase. Her eyes settle on Pete, who is smiling affectionately along the table, as if he finds her project charming and endearing.

'The good news is I get to keep the clothes,' he says, and everyone laughs. 'Some of the stuff's not bad.'

'And anyway,' says Keir, smiling at Anna, 'there's no money in something like that, is there? It's just a hobby.'

'Of course there's money in it. Not right away. You have to build a base first. Get yourself noticed. But lots of investigative journalists start with a project like this.'

'Is that what you're saying? That you'd like to be an investigative journalist?' There is something dismissive about this question, and Anna stares squarely at him and says, 'Yes, I would.'

'Haven't you left it a bit late?' He says this with an amused snort, and she wonders if he's already pissed.

'In what sense?'

'Late to change your career. I mean, you're *thirty*.'

For a moment Anna thinks he must be joking, and releases an indignant sigh. Then she shakes her head and looks around the table, expecting to see her own incredulity reflected. But instead they are all listening with perfectly neutral expressions. Pete in particular is blank-faced, and in no way appears about to jump to Anna's defence; for all she can tell he agrees with Keir.

'What's *wrong* with people in this country?' she says, louder than she expected. 'How can *thirty* be considered too old to change career? When are we supposed to make our minds up on what we want to be? When we're straight out of university? Or maybe sooner, before we decide what to study. Or even what we do for A-levels. That sounds about right – let's have our sixteen-year-old selves decide on our future. And what's the worst that could happen if we *did* change career? Even if we went back to school or did another degree? All we'd lose is a bit of income for a few years. So what? Who cares? We live in one of the richest countries on the planet, all with families and friends backing us up. Why not take *risks*? I'm telling you: if dead people could hear you saying that thirty is too old to change career they'd worry for your sanity. It's *bullshit*. Sorry to shout, but it is. Total bullshit.'

Anna falls silent, and sees that her hands are shaking. There is an itchy, awkward pause, until Keir clears his throat and says he was 'only joking'. Anna sees that Pete is staring at her with a familiar concerned expression, as if her earlier unspoken reassurance had been misleading, and then he breaks the silence by asking if anyone can help him clear the table. They all seem willing to help, and there is a chorus of scraping chairs and crockery being stacked. Anna sits still as the table is transformed around her, taken aback herself by the speech she made. It felt like the words were not entirely hers, as if her body became a temporary vessel for the voice and opinions of another.

'Maybe we should step out for some air,' says Hamza, gripping her shoulder. 'What do you say?'

It's nice out on the street. The night air is cold but clean, with no breeze, and the streetlights are giving off more glow than the candles in the living room. Hamza peels the cellophane from a packet of Marlboro Lights and aims them at Anna.

'Have you given up giving up?'

'No,' she says, sliding one out. 'But now I don't smoke, it's okay to have one every now and then.'

Hamza laughs and offers the pack to Zahra, who shakes her head and looks away, her arms crossed tightly against her chest; Anna wonders why she followed them out. Then her cigarette is lit and she is lost within the sensations of the first pull: the crackling sound, the orange glow, the heat in her throat, the rippling grey cone she exhales. It would seem that the cigarette she had in Chinatown last night has paved the way for her enjoying them again, since this one is delicious.

'You really kicked off there,' says Hamza.

'Yeah . . . He touched a nerve, I suppose.'

'Don't get me wrong, I was right behind you. I still haven't decided on my *first* career.'

'That's because you've got money,' says Zahra. 'Your dad's money.'

'And you're a pauper?'

'I'm dependent on a wage, as is Anna. Without it I couldn't pay off my mortgage. People get priced out of London all the time.'

'Please! You're a lawyer, for Christ's sake. Don't make out you're financially precarious, it's offensive to people that actually are. It's just an excuse to never take risks.'

'You can be dependent without being precarious. If I quit my job and opened a cafe or started making jewellery and it went tits up, I'd lose my flat. It's as simple as that.'

'Well, I see things differently. And by the sounds of it, Anna does too.'

'Anna is just seeing a haze. She's drunk.'

'Hey! I'm not drunk.' But at that moment, as if prompted by their words, a dizzying energy swirls up through her, and Anna has to shuffle her feet to find a new balance.

'Babes, you're smashed,' says Hamza. 'You're even more wasted than Keir. But we can straighten you out. Here, take this.' He hands his cocktail to Zahra and pulls a tiny plastic bag from the coin pocket of his skinny jeans.

'What?' says Zahra. '*Really?*'

'Of course. It's her thirtieth. And she asked me to.'

Zahra turns her scowl to Anna, who shrugs. She can faintly remember asking Hamza to get drugs when she was still planning the boat party; the memory has the porous and dubious quality of a dream. Hamza has a dab and hands the bag to Anna, who holds it up to her eye – from close range the contents look like a sample of dirty snow.

'This isn't a good idea,' says Zahra, placing her hand on Anna's forearm.

'Relax,' says Hamza. 'It's a pure mellow high, nothing speedy. And it will sober her up.'

'That's the oldest lie in the world!'

'Stop saying I'm drunk, both of you. I'm *fine*. I'll just have a bit.' Anna prises open the baggie and licks her little finger.

She tries to take a small dab, but her finger is a crude instrument, and when she transfers the crystals to her tongue the chemical bitterness is revolting; she snatches and gulps at Hamza's cocktail to wash it away.

'You can put the girl in Kilburn,' says Hamza, returning the baggie to his pocket. 'But you can't put Kilburn in the girl.' He flicks his cigarette into the road and steps back through the gate, and Anna feels a sharp tug on her sleeve.

'I want to talk to you,' whispers Zahra. 'Alone.'

Hamza turns at the door and, seeing them both hovering by the gate, lifts one eyebrow knowingly and disappears inside.

'What's wrong?' says Zahra, her eyes blinking up at Anna from behind their glasses, as if searching out the answer to her own question.

'Nothing's wrong. You're the one being weird. What was all that about Keir saying your kitchen took two weeks?'

'Ignore Keir. You know how proud he is. But listen, what is it? You seem so . . . *fraught*. You're not eating anything.'

'I had some nuts in the pub.'

'And how are you feeling about . . . you know? About Pete?'

'Fine,' says Anna, looking down at her new boots. 'I mean, it's going to happen, isn't it?'

'That's all you feel? *Fine?*'

'Uh-huh,' says Anna, weakly, still looking at the ground, suppressing a sudden desire to tell her about Geoff. Zahra tuts and takes both of Anna's upper arms in her hands, shaking her a little.

'It's not fair, how this happened. It's so shitty that you found the ring. No one should have this long to think about it. People should have two minutes, max. If I'd known that

Keir was going to propose a month in advance I would have shat myself. And when I said you should get perspective, I didn't think—'

'I met someone,' says Anna, the words just popping out. 'On Kismet, the other week. An 81.'

'An *81*? What the fuck? What happened?' Zahra's face is aghast, and Anna glances up at the dimly lit window before gathering the energy to tell the whole story. But when she starts speaking she is surprised to find the story is over almost as soon as it has begun. She had only two meetings with Geoff, the South Bank and Somerset House, five or six hours in total, with no sex, no hotels – not even a shared meal.

'You didn't sleep with him?'

'I don't even know where he lives.'

'And you're not going to see him again?'

'No way. I mean, I totally stood him up at the station. Not that he cares. He didn't even text to ask what happened.'

Zahra nods sadly, and they stand in silence for a time.

'I'm sure he wasn't really an 81. I think you were right – doing this behind Pete's back screwed up my profile, matched me with creeps. He's probably got a family in Surrey, or wherever.'

Zahra nods and repeats the number 81 quietly, and says it still must have felt like a big deal. Then she looks up at the window and says they need to go in.

'You should have told me.'

'I know, but I'm okay now. It's just been stressful. I feel better for talking about it.'

Zahra rubs her arm and smiles.

'You'll be okay, I know you will,' she says, before rising up on tiptoes and kissing Anna plumb on the lips.

In the bathroom Anna splashes water on her face and sits on the closed toilet. She takes her phone from her pocket and reads a new text from Pete. It is a long message saying he hopes she's alright, that he knows 'how hard today must be for her' and that if she wants he can cut the dinner party short so it is just 'the two of them'. She puts her phone away and for a moment ponders the tomato plant that is being stored in the bath; it is a soothing sight and reminds her of the previous Sunday she had with Pete. Anna gathers herself and goes back to the living room, where Pete is serving the main course. She goes to him and interrupts by kissing his cheek, and he turns to kiss her fully on the lips. She senses the rest of the table watching, probably interpreting her gesture as an apology for her outburst, or at least a demonstration that she intends to play nice from now on. As she goes back to her seat she is drawn to the iPad, which is playing something by Corinne Bailey Rae, and sees it is a pre-packaged Spotify playlist called 'Perfect Dinner Party'. Jesus Fucking Christ. She logs onto her profile and puts it on to random select, and Pete doesn't say a word – he doesn't care about the music, is just aware that it is useful to add ambiance, like a sort of carpeting in the air.

No sooner is she settled back in her seat than a steaming plate of seafood pasta is set before her, creamy ribbons of tagliatelle with shreds of lobster and a powerful scent of lemons. She resolves to eat the whole dish this time, and ventures a first bite, washed down with wine, while trying to tune into the various conversations crossing the table. Keir and Toby are discussing holiday destinations and Ingrid appears to be explaining to Cecile how far she is along the process of becoming a British citizen. Through these two conversations, Pete and Zahra's eyes lock again, and this time they begin talking – she asks him where he bought the seafood, and they discuss a fishmonger in Kentish Town. They begin naming other food shops in northwest London, and as always they agree on everything; all conversations between Zahra and Pete involve them discovering that they like exactly the same things, which is of course just a vicarious means of saying they like each other. Anna feels jealous again, and this time she remembers precisely when Zahra last came round. It was after the Notting Hill Carnival. Yes, that's right. All four of them had gone, but Keir left early and Zahra ended up coming back to theirs. They stayed up drinking and eating takeaway, until Pete and Anna went to bed and left Zahra to pass out on the sofa. The next morning Anna had to go to work – since UK Bank Holidays count for little at the website – and she remembers the acute anxiety of leaving Pete and Zahra in the flat together, him upstairs and her on the sofa, both half-naked and hungover. The discomfort stayed with her all day, and she decided to be especially watchful the next time they were all together. But the next time never came. Just a few days later Zahra announced that they had begun tearing up their kitchen, and this building process seemed to absorb all her spare time, and amazingly she hasn't been around since. Anna thinks of what Keir said about the knocking through only taking two weeks, and wonders if Zahra might have had a reason to lie but this thought is interrupted by Bean, who suggests it's time for another Anna story. Cecile is selected, and she tells her anecdote while people continue eating. With her voice only just carrying over the sound of cutlery and masticating jaws, she describes when Anna took her out on a 'big night' during second year, and how, when it was time to get a taxi home, Cecile found Anna with another small brunette girl under her arm, who she thought *was* Cecile.

'What can I say?' says Anna, as everyone claps and says well done to Cecile. 'You've got one of those generic faces.' Hamza makes the delighted squeal he does when a joke grazes the threshold of being rude, and then suggests they crack on with another story, since it's almost 10 p.m. Zahra is selected again and this time agrees, on the basis that they clear the dirty plates first; Anna is surprised to have her half-eaten bowl taken away from her, until she notices that all the others are empty.

Once the table is cleared and crumbed down and every glass is refilled, everyone nudges their chair back from the table and points it towards Zahra who, as if responding to the air of expectancy, stands up.

'I don't really like public speaking, but here goes. Right. Okay. Now. Some of you will remember the flat that Anna and I shared in east London.'

'I remember the rats,' says Hamza.

'I remember going to dinner and using a Frisbee as a plate,' says Cecile.

'There was *one* sighting of *one* rat. But yes, it wasn't the classiest residence. It was on an estate in Hackney, and let's just say it wasn't unusual for our route home to be blocked by police tape. But we had the *best* time back then. The very best of times. Some of you will also remember what Anna was like in those days. We were all wide-eyed and ambitious, but she was especially so. She didn't have a proper job, just did temp work and spent her time writing blogs and coming up with ideas for inventions, projects. Her favourite one was the Community Shed.'

'The Community Shed!' exclaims Hamza. 'I remember that fucker.'

'The community what?' says Toby.

'The Community *Shed*,' explains Anna. 'It was going to be a community membership scheme, where people pay a monthly fee and get to use hammers and drills and ladders and whatever, all stored in an accessible location. Like Streetcar. But a shed.'

'That would never work,' says Keir, and Zahra slaps him on the arm and says she's telling the story.

'Anyway,' she says. 'Anna used to talk about this idea a *lot*. Even at the pub or during our parties – we called them parties; really it was just five or six people dancing around a laptop in the kitchen. The Minuscule of Sound, she used to call them. But Anna would always become euphoric. I re-member one time she said our flat was the "centre of world consciousness".'

Zahra leaves a pause for some sniggering, and Anna points out that she was quoting Ginsberg. She remembers the precise moment she said those words, seven or eight years ago, and her physical sensations at the time: straining jaw, fluttering heartbeat, cold sweats. She realises she isn't just remembering these; she is reliving them, right now. The drugs are starting to do their work, and she looks at Hamza, to see if she can detect any visible signs, but his eyes are locked on Zahra.

'One night about six of us were partying in my bedroom until well into the morning. At one point Anna got up and left the room – to use the toilet, I assumed. But when Caz went out a while later, she returned and said that Anna wasn't in the flat.' Zahra is pulling faces and doing voices now – so much for not liking telling stories. Toby asks if he should

236

brace himself for another tramp blow job, and there are a few seconds of laughter that stops suddenly. Everyone focuses on Zahra again – their candlelit faces remind Anna of children listening to a ghost story.

'We went looking for her. She wasn't smoking on the walkway balcony, and we walked around for a while until Caz was like: "Look! There she is!" And there she was, standing in the kids' playground, three floors below us, talking to two young mothers with prams. We went down there, and as we approached we could hear her asking if they had a hammer, a ladder, a paintbrush. She was pitching the Community Shed.'

A collective gasp goes around the table, and then everyone looks at her, their eyes wide in shocked delight.

'She was doing *what*?'

'While you were on drugs?'

'What time of day was this?'

Zahra looks as if she is trying to suppress her own laughter, and holds out a hand to indicate she isn't finished. 'The two women looked totally confused. Me and Caz both took Anna by the arm and gently led her away, and out of the playground. We gave her a glass of water and put her to bed, and she kept saying they loved the idea, that they wanted to invest. "I was just spreading the love," she said. Then she closed her eyes and said it a couple more times – "spreading the love, spreading the love" – and then she fell asleep. The end.'

'You're a maniac,' says Toby, looking at Anna with a humorously bewildered expression, as if he now has to reappraise everything he thought he knew about her. Bean and Ingrid and Cecile – also strangers to this story – are looking at her with milder versions of the same expression, and then everyone turns to Zahra, who is still standing, and begins clapping. Zahra does a little curtsy, then lays her hand flat atop Anna's head.

'Those were the most fun years of my life,' she says, patting her hand. 'And I'm so proud of what you've achieved since then.'

The applause moves up a gear, and is spiced with a whistle from Bean and a sentimental 'ahhh' from someone, probably Ingrid. They are all projecting warmth towards her, but she doesn't receive it. Something about the story has left her feeling peeved. It is a story about her, apparently, but she felt shut out of it; or, more accurately, she feels trapped within it, her role limited to something comical and hapless.

'Don't you think it's a good idea, though?' she says, when the clapping dwindles and Zahra retakes her seat. 'There's definitely a gap in the market for something like that.'

Everyone is smiling at her, but for some reason no one says anything – it is like she is a child asking a question relating to some fantasy world or endearing misapprehension, which is charming and cute but doesn't require an actual answer. Worst of all is Pete, at the other end of the table, who is smiling contentedly, as if he finds Anna's eccentricities wryly amusing, nothing to be taken seriously.

'I'm not joking,' she says. 'Think about it. Every house on this street will have its own hammer, which it uses once every two years.'

'A hammer costs £5,' says Keir, slightly slurring his words.

Anna is ready for this objection, and says: 'Yeah, a really crap one, made in some Chinese gulag.' But before Keir can respond, Toby interrupts and with unusual intensity asks Zahra *whereabouts* in Hackney their old flat had been; using her hands to draw a map, Zahra explains it was tucked in behind Mare Street, equidistant between London Fields and Victoria Park. Toby makes a satisfied 'ahhh', and then Cecile asks Ingrid where that is in relation to her place. Ingrid does her best to explain, and is helped out by Pete, who then tackles questions from across the table as to the relative locations of other places in northeast London: Dalston, Homerton, Hackney Wick, Clapton, De Beauvoir Town. Toby then asks about house prices, and the whole group begins a lively discussion about which of these areas are affordable, which ones used to be and which ones never were; even Hamza is getting involved.

Anna looks between them all in wonder. Not one of them considered her idea worthy of serious discussion, and yet when it comes to the prices of houses in areas of London they have no connection with – have probably never even been to – they are suddenly talking over one another in eagerness to share the latest opinions, rumours, statistics, theories. It would appear that understanding the housing market is of fundamental importance to them, on a par with having a stable and well-paying professional job, taking decent holidays twice a year, and – she imagines – having some kind of plan for where the inevitable kids will go to school. These are the building blocks of a successful and happy existence; anything outside of this, such as her ideas and inventions, is just a shot in the dark, something that should be out of your system by your mid-twenties.

'Is Victoria Park Village affordable?' says Toby, and Ingrid asks if he is making a joke.

Anna looks about the table, between each of her closest friends and her boyfriend – soon to be fiancé – and marvels at how different they must be from her. All of them went to fancy private schools, and probably have hundreds of thousands of pounds waiting for them when their parents drop off, if not sooner, and have the backing to be whatever they want to be. And yet they all steer precisely the same course, more or less, living out their days as lawyers, teachers, consultants, seeming determined to consign themselves to grey mediocrity. They must be so averse to the bad things that can happen to people – unemployment, money troubles, parental disappointment, depression, loneliness, death – that they are not willing to take the slightest risk. In a word, they are scared. In another word, they are cowards.

'Leyton and Walthamstow,' says Pete, sagely. 'That's where people are buying now.' This is pooh-poohed by Cecile, who says that Walthamstow is cooked already, and that people are going as far as Woolwich or West Ham.

Maybe she's being harsh, thinks Anna, pouring herself a new glass of white. They are not cowards. For one thing, Bean is opening his own bar and Hamza is basically a bum. And the rest of them, who are taking the nine-to-five route, aren't doing so because they are shrinking away from their deep desires; the sensible route for them *is* their deep desire, the product of common sense. She is the only one who was raised to feel a vague duty to make her life extraordinary, and therefore has to grapple with these questions at every turn. And it is therefore only her, she realises, finishing her wine with a hefty gulp, who is the coward. And what a coward she is! Despite all her talking and thinking, she has taken no more steps towards her ambitions than the people surrounding her. The idea Zahra presented of her in the story – as the quirky idealistic airhead – is the real her; it is her private version of herself that is the fantasy. She never did set up the Community Shed crowdfunding page. She never did open the suitcase when there was still a chance of finding the owner. She never did sleep with Juliette in San Francisco, or with Thomas 72, and she certainly didn't take the chance to be with an 81. Put simply, she has never dared to be true to herself, and never will be.

The next thing Anna knows, she is being shaken by the shoulder.

'Anna should do one,' says Hamza.

'What?' she says, unsure what he is talking about. Time has slipped forwards since she was last cognisant of the entire group; they are no longer talking house prices, or anything at all, and are instead looking along the table at her expectantly.

'You should tell *your* favourite Anna story,' says Hamza, giving her shoulder another shake. His jaw is slightly askew and his pupils are dilated; there is no doubt that he is feeling the drugs, too.

'Um,' she says, sitting up straight, trying to shuck off the melancholy that shrouded her last train of thought. 'All right. Just give me a minute.' She takes a deep breath and lays her hands flat on the tablecloth; just beyond her fingertips is a half-pint glass full of a layered creamy pudding, perhaps panna cotta. She doesn't know when this arrived, and notices that everyone else has finished theirs.

'Is she asleep?' asks Ingrid. Everyone laughs at this, but Anna carries on staring down at her hands, trying to direct her thoughts inwards and back in time, her mind working at half speed.

'What about the time the Moroccan man tried to buy you for thirty camels?'

'Or when you missed the flight to Scotland and tried to run through security?'

'Or when you thought you were having a heart attack and called NHS Direct?'

More tittering; she ignores them all. She sifts through and discards any story that reaffirms their idea of her as clumsy and naïve; she wants to parade her best self – fearless, imaginative, enterprising.

'I know,' she says, slapping the table. '*This* is my favourite story. Sorry if you've heard it before. So: for my mum's fiftieth birthday we planned to go to Paris for the weekend, as a family. This was during second year, so I got the train from Sheffield to Bedford one Friday, and was going to stay at her house the night before. It was while eating dinner that I realised there was a problem: I'd left my passport in Sheffield.'

A collective groan throbs around the table.

'But that's just the *start*. Listen. So there I was, eating Chinese takeaway with my mum and brother and aunts, while privately having this miniature freakout. What was I going to do? The whole trip had been booked, and our train from St Pancras was at eleven the next morning. I slipped upstairs and called my dad, who lived in Cambridge at the time. I only wanted a sounding board, but he immediately had a plan, and told me what to do.'

Anna pauses and looks around the room, refastening the attention of all her listeners. She is enjoying the physical act of speaking – the air in her chest fluted into words and sentences – which is making her feel simultaneously more and less sober. The obscuring fug of booze has retreated somewhat, leaving her more sensitive to the heart-pumping, joyous rush of the drugs. But she is concerned to see that Ingrid and Bean and Toby are frowning, perhaps in confusion, and she thinks maybe her speech thus far has been

garbled nonsense. Then her eyes land on Pete, who is smiling and nodding in encouragement; she knows that he understands her story and why she is telling it, and is sharing
in her excitement.

'A few hours later my mum went to bed,' she continues.
'I couldn't have told her the plan; she wouldn't have let me
do it, would have thought it was too dangerous or not even
possible. So I waited thirty minutes and then crept out of
the house to the main road, where my dad picked me up.
He drove like a maniac, and by one we were on the M1, by
two we were past Nottingham, by three thirty we were in
Sheffield, pulling up at the house. My passport was in the
little shoebox I kept all my personal crap in. Love letters.
Birth certificates. Do you remember?'

She says this to Zahra, who says that of course she remembers it, since Anna woke up the whole house.

'Then we were on the motorway again! We only stopped
once, at a service station, where Dad had a coffee and we
mucked about on some fruit machines. Otherwise we just
kept heading south. I tried to take over the driving, but he
said I should sleep. So I did, or pretended to while watching
him drive, my eyes half-closed. It was starting to get light,
and I remember seeing his silhouette against the brighten-
ing sky, and wishing we would never reach Bedford: I would
have been happy heading south forever, down to the coast,
into Europe, I didn't care . . .'

Anna is casting her eyes beyond the table, beyond the
room and even the city, and making a sweeping gesture with
her right hand towards some imagined horizon. She can almost feel the blood racing in her veins, and remembers the
feeling of being her best self, the same as she felt in Somerset

House, at the Minuscule of Sound, or showing off for her dad as a child.

'Of course we did reach Bedford, and he dropped me off. I snuck into the house and tiptoed to my room, where I lay on my bed for twenty minutes, listening to the birds, until my mum knocked on my door and said "wakey wakey". For the rest of that day on the Eurostar and in Paris everyone kept telling me I looked tired, but I told them I didn't feel it. And it was true. I felt great. As happy as I ever have. That's it. The end.'

Everyone smiles and claps, but there is no laughter or warmth in their reaction.

'A lovely story,' says Cecile.

'Great,' says Bean. 'Really, really great.'

Ingrid mutters something equally generic, and Zahra says that her dad would be really proud of her. The response is far more sombre than she anticipated, and she realises that people are being polite and sensitive, are treading carefully now that she's brought her dead father into the room and laid him on the table for all to see. She looks beyond them to Pete, whose reassuring smile has evolved into something heartfelt and tender, with his head cocked to one side. He raises his eyebrows, as if asking her a question, and she senses he is repeating his offer to curtail the dinner party if she likes, so that it can just be them. She decides that he doesn't understand, after all; his reaction is not to join with her excitement, but to feel sorry for her like the others. Only drunken Keir is willing to release the tension.

'I thought you were going to say you arrived in Sheffield without your house keys,' he says, laughing at his own joke. 'Or that you came home with someone else's passport.'

Zahra scowls at Keir, as does Pete.

'There's no need for that,' he says, and Keir holds his hands up.

'Sorry, Anna. I shouldn't joke. I know how hard it was for you.'

'It's all right,' she says, for the first time this evening feeling some affection for Keir. 'I don't mind joking about it. He wouldn't mind, either.'

'No. It's poor form. And sorry for taking the piss out of your career plans – I wasn't trying to be a dick.'

'No worries. I'm sorry for taking the piss out of your kitchen plans.'

'You were right to! It didn't take two weeks, it was a month, at least. I had sawdust in my hair, my teeth—'

'Shut up, Keir,' says Zahra, in a furious whisper. 'It took much longer than that.'

'No it didn't. We had it ready for Christmas. Look, I can prove it.'

He reaches for his phone, and Zahra slaps him on the forearm.

'Just shut up. You're confused. And drunk.'

This time Keir stops. He appears to have been reduced through drink to an almost bovine stupidity, and glares at Zahra like a child that doesn't know why they're being punished.

'Ready for Christmas?' says Anna. She looks at Pete, who appears unaffected by Keir's statement. He is studying his wine glass, as if something of urgent importance is taking place within the empty vessel. She looks at Zahra instead, who appears flushed and fidgety and is pulling at her glasses. Then it happens: Pete and Zahra glance at each other. Their eyes meet for the smallest fraction of a second, but it is never-theless highly charged. His eyes are slightly wider than usual and seem to communicate alarm, as if some conspiracy is un-ravelling before them. Then they both turn away again, Pete back to his enchanting wine glass, Zahra with a smile to the whole table.

'So what was everyone's favourite Anna story?' says Zahra. 'The Anna story of the Anna stories?'

Anna pushes herself to her feet.

'Excuse me,' she says, and staggers away from the table.

In the bathroom she turns the light on and off again, pre-ferring to sit on the toilet in the dark; the sink and bath appear like icy fossils of themselves. Muffled conversation is seeping through the wall, the voices of Keir and Hamza car-rying twice as clearly as the others'. Anna is drunk and feel-ing the drugs – even sat still she senses a shifting movement, as if she were on a small boat at sea – but she tries to con-centrate on what just happened in there. She thinks of what Keir said about the kitchen being done by Christmas, and the little glance that Pete and Zahra shared, and the conclusion is irrefutable, even to her addled mind. They have been in cahoots, and must have agreed to match their stories as part of a plan to . . . what? To keep themselves apart, because they could no longer control their feelings for one another. Not since that morning after the carnival, when Anna left them alone and hungover together. When something *did* happen between them.

These thoughts envelop her in a coldness. She takes her phone from her pocket and it lights up like a torch, the brightness making her eyes throb. In her photo stream there are several pictures of them all from around that time last summer. There is one of Zahra holding her bonsai tree. There are several from the carnival itself, including a selfie of all three of them holding cans of Red Stripe; perhaps Anna is just squinting, but there is a definite tension on her face compared to the other two, who are smiling unreservedly. It is as if that earlier version of herself knew more than she thought, or more than she dared to think. Because in a way it feels like she has known all along, on a level of knowing so deep it is possible to discount or ignore. And there is almost a grim pleasure in finally being proved right, like pulling out a sore tooth that has been nagging for years. Yes, she's known all along. Zahra and Pete have always just clicked. They have such similar backgrounds and taste, and identical orthodox visions for what they want in the future. Whereas Anna has always been struggling to keep up, straining herself to match with their ideal. And while doing so, she has been drifting away from the life she really wants, and has alienated the people she should be with. She imagines Geoff standing beneath the information board, and before she can stop herself she closes her photo stream and opens Kismet. There are no new messages. Then she opens Twitter, and sees that some of her followers have responded to the last message she sent, agreeing with her decision to shut it down. But she has a new message too, one from an unknown follower called @21_yerffoeg, at 6.44 p.m.

Don't give up, there's tons more evidence. Look at the name tag on the handle, it has the start of a logo. Go forensic, just don't give up!

There is a photo attached, and it seems that her new follower is the one to have gone forensic; it is one of the first pictures from her Instagram gallery, showing the snapped plastic name tag with the beginnings of a grey circular logo on it, perhaps a company emblem. Anna experiences a tiny sparkle of excitement and hope, and she decides to send a thank-you message to this follower immediately. Their profile picture is the cartoon shape of a new user, and they are only following one person, her. She looks at the name again – @21_yerffoeg – and as the letters rearrange themselves she feels the bathroom and the building and the world turn around her as well. The graphics on the screen shake within her hand, and are then blurred by a film of tears. Her 81. He hasn't been in Surrey with his wife, or taking other women to Somerset House; he has been thinking of her all along.

This thought is abruptly halted by a knocking on the door.

'Anna?' It is Zahra's voice. 'What's going on? Are you sitting in the dark?'

'Just a minute,' she says, returning her phone to her pocket. Then she switches the light on, blows her nose, takes conscious control of her breathing and repairs her make-up in the mirror. When she opens the door Zahra doesn't replace her in the bathroom, but takes hold of her upper arms and asks if she is okay.

'I'm fine.'

'Are you sure?'

'Yes.'

'Sorry about Keir,' says Zahra. 'You know how proud he is.'

Anna squints at her in the dim hallway light. She isn't sure whether to believe her or not. She retains a masklike expression, and eventually just nods and gives a hum of assent. Zahra appears to accept this, for she takes Anna by the hand and leads her back into the living room, where Pete is

stood pouring champagne into a long line of flutes. Anna retakes her seat and her stomach crunches when Toby whispers
something to Cecile about a taxi: it is almost time.

'We can only fit in one more Anna story,' says Pete. 'And
that's going to be from me.' He puts down the champagne
bottle and begins passing the bubbling flutes; they float
around the table from hand to hand, the first one arriving at
Anna. She holds it to her nose and sour bubbles leap into her
nostrils; she puts it down again, deciding she wants to sober
up a bit – she wants her nerves to be sharp.

'Obviously I've had longer than anyone to think of a story,
and that's why I have to apologise for this not being a funny
story, or a particularly good story. In fact, it might not class as
a story at all.' He smiles genially as he says this, again showing off his innate public speaking skills, and Anna is struck
by how unfamiliar he looks with his hairless pink chin and
slick black hair. It is only a tiny imaginative effort to pretend
that she doesn't know this man, that it is a stranger talking to
them; she thinks of the glance he shared with Zahra, and realises that it might not require any imagination at all.

'At first I was going to speak about the first time we ever
met, in a pub in Islington. I approached and lingered awkwardly, and it was Zahra that had to do most of the talking
between us. I thought I'd blown it, that she didn't like me,
until Anna went to the toilet and Zahra said that she must
like me, because she'd sent her a text while the three of us sat
there to ask if her fringe was "behaving itself".

'Then I thought I was going to speak about the first big
date we went on, to Margate, when she spent most of the time
talking about how weird it was to be going out with a guy
who was younger than her. Then I thought maybe it should

249

be a story from one of the holidays we've taken. Morocco, Sri Lanka, Vietnam; my favourite being when Anna navigated our car straight into a forest fire in California. So I had all these ideas, and then just the other day, as I tried to work out which story to tell, the most ordinary weekend came and delivered the very, *very* best moment of being with Anna.'

He stares at her without blinking, and she can see the dazzle of a jewel reflected in his damp eyes. Could it be that he is going to do it here, now, in front of everyone? She glances at the pockets of Pete's jeans; she thinks she can see a bulge that could be the ring box, but it's hard to tell in the flickering candlelight.

'It was just last weekend. She came home after the interview with Sahina Bhutto all stressed, and then we went out to dinner in Kentish Town and talked about it. The next day we did lots of things, boring things – went for a run, cleaned the flat, cooked dinner – but for some reason it just felt *right*, everything came together. And then the next day Anna opened the suitcase. And I stood there, by the door, watching her open it. And even though that project didn't work out, there was something about her willingness to have a go, to get excited about something so unusual, that slayed me. This is what I've always loved about her. She has this edge, this quirky quality I don't see in anyone else.'

Anna's face is burning with the belief that Pete really is going to do it here, now, in front of everyone. There will be no waiting until afterwards and going down on one knee – he will pull the box out in a moment, ask the question, and everyone will hold their breath until she says . . . what?

'And last Sunday, watching her open the suitcase, I realised again what I'd already realised many times before. But

each time it hits me like new knowledge, a revelation. I realised I wanted to spend the rest of my life with you.'

Anna stares up at him, her body frozen with panic. She
isn't ready. She needs more time, needs to think straight about
Pete and Zahra and other things besides. Pete moves his hand
downwards towards his pocket, but rather than reach into
his jeans his fingers swoop up his champagne flute, which he
holds above his head.

'To Anna,' he says. 'Happy birthday!'

The others raise their glasses, echo his happy birthday, and
drink. A second later they are all talking amongst themselves,
and when Pete sits down Anna knows that normal time has
resumed, and she has survived.

Anna's body goes slack in its chair. It is a dazed feeling of
relief, similar in intensity to the sensation she had the previous evening when she fled from London Bridge, as if a
hurtling juggernaut has only just missed her. The feeling is
short-lived, though, as she soon realises that the juggernaut
has not missed her – its arrival has only been postponed for a
short period of time. In fact, it has only been delayed by a few
minutes, given that everyone is now up and out of their seats,
and the party seems to be over. The main light is switched
on and everyone looks squinty and overly lit as they pull on
their jackets and scarves. The girls circulate around the room
hugging each other, while the boys shake hands and bid each
other hearty farewells. In order to extract a little more time
Anna attempts to get some new business started – she asks
Bean for a detailed update on his bar, suggests Toby and
Cecile stay for a nightcap, and tries to get Hamza to go out
for a cigarette. But they are all pulled irresistibly to the door
by the arrival of taxis, and there is time only for goodbyes,

and each person queues up to kiss and hug Anna in turn. Zahra whispers 'good luck' into her ear, Hamza puts the Marlboro packet and lighter into her hand. Then she experiences another time slip, because the next thing she knows she is looking down from the front window to where all seven of her guests are standing in a loose circle on the pavement. It feels peculiar and somewhat sinister, to be looking down at miniature versions of the people that seconds ago had so noisily surrounded her.

'And then there were two.'

Pete's saying this causes her to start; she didn't know he was standing behind her. He is watching her, his hands clutching the back of a chair. She tries to smile at him, then returns to the pavement where a people carrier has arrived; pocket-sized versions of Keir, Zahra, Toby and Cecile climb in, while Hamza, Bean and Ingrid walk off towards the high road. Then there were two, she thinks, and from the corner of her eye she sees Pete edging his way towards her around the table. She carries on staring at the taxi, as Toby slides the door shut to encase them within the cab, and Pete encircles her from behind in a hug.

'Baby,' he says, nuzzling her neck above the collar of her jumper; his shaved chin scratches like sandpaper. Who is this man? He asks if it wasn't so bad, after all, and she is daunted by the prospect of having to speak. She feels like a block of ice in his arms, rigid and lifeless. 'It was good,' is all she can organise herself to say.

His legs and torso are pressed against her back, and she tries to detect the lump of the ring box in his jeans. He sighs through his nose, and she braces herself for some emotive declaration, some highly calibrated statement to propel them towards the fated moment, but instead he says: 'I'm going to put some dishes on to soak.'

'Okay,' says Anna, quiet as a trapped bird.

'Then it's time for your present.'

She nods, and the weight of his body is lifted off her back; she watches him rounding the table and leaving the room, and as he crosses into the hallway her voice is restored and she says: 'Wait.'

He stops and turns, one eyebrow raised.

'I'm going to step outside for a moment. For some fresh air.'

His eyes narrow slightly, before he smiles.

'Whatever you want,' he says. 'It's your party. But don't be long.'

'I won't,' she says, trying to smile back. She waits until he has closed himself in the kitchen, then she grabs her bag and goes down the stairs.

The night air is so cold and clean and refreshing that for a moment Anna is fooled into thinking she has sobered up entirely, and would be fine to drive a car or give a speech or do anything at all. But when she lights a cigarette she realises she is still firmly within the grip of the drugs: the hot smoke is far too delicious, releasing a voluptuous tingling sensation along her veins and across her skin. She smokes with metronomic regularity, losing herself in the plumes and swirls, until she is struck by two anxious thoughts: one, that the cigarette is almost finished already; two, that Pete is probably watching her from the living-room window, just as she was watching the others a few minutes ago. But these are irrational concerns: if she is enjoying smoking, she can simply have another cigarette. And if she doesn't want Pete to watch her, she can simply move.

Anna walks down the street. At the corner of Cavendish Road she drops the butt of her cigarette and crushes it beneath her foot, and then places a fresh one between her lips. Simple as that. She is also pleased with her new position and vantage point, but what if Pete saw her move, or comes down to check on her, and sees her standing twenty metres up the road? She walks further, turning left onto Cavendish Road and then right into Brooklands Court where she perches on the front wall of a seemingly deserted house covered in scaffolding. Now she is properly tucked away, and the feeling of being off the map gives her mood another lift. How easy it is, to satisfy your desires. All you have to do is look inside yourself, focus in on what you really want, and act accordingly.

At that moment her phone buzzes within her bag. Her first thought is that Pete must be calling her, though it seems early for him to reach out in concern. Could it be from her 81, following on from his Twitter message? She pulls it from her bag and finds a message from Ingrid, giving thanks for this evening and saying her friends are lovely. She doesn't reply, and instead opens Twitter again and rereads the message from Geoff; she imagines him combing through all the pictures on her Instagram feed, and with a pang of guilt sees him standing beneath the information board at the station. How callous she was, to leave him there without even saying sorry. He deserves an apology at the very least, and without thinking too much about it, she opens Kismet, finds Geoff 81, goes to write a message, before cancelling and pressing 'voice call' instead. The phone rings five times, two reverberating trills of unequal length, before an automated voice tells her to leave a message. She hangs up.

Anna holds her burning cigarette up to eye level, and

guesses at how much life is left in this one – three drags, four at most. Of course, she could just light another, and then another, could keep smoking until the pack is empty, at which point she could walk to the high road and buy more. She could spend the rest of her life doing nothing but smoking, if that's what she wants, and at that moment her phone lights up and vibrates in her hand. It is a voice call, from Geoff 81.

'Geoff!'

'Hello, Anna,' he says, after a pause, his voice sounding clipped and grown-up.

'Hey. Hi. Hello.'

She is walking again, with no destination in mind. She turns off Brooklands Court onto Cavendish Road; at the bottom she can see the glowing shopfronts of the high road. There is a silence, and it takes her a moment to realise he is waiting for her to speak.

'I suppose I should say something, since I called you.'

'That's the convention, yes.' It sounds like he has an ice cube in his mouth.

'Well . . . I just wanted to say sorry for last night. It was a crap thing to do.'

'These things happen,' he says, immediately. 'When you're as old as me, you become inured to things happening.'

There is a pause until Anna thinks of another thing to say: she thanks him for the tweet and the clue, and says that she will follow it up.

'Ah, now that *is* important,' he says. 'Standing me up is forgivable. Giving up that project would not be. It would be a terrible shame, for you and your followers. But mainly for you.'

Anna repeats that she will definitely follow it up, and then

they fall silent again; she notices she is leaning against someone's wheelie bin. It is apparent that Geoff isn't going to hold
up his end of the conversation, and Anna considers rounding
things off. But she doesn't want to do this, and asks what he
is doing instead.

'I'm looking out the window. Having a drink. You sound
as though you've had a drink yourself.'

'Well, it is my . . . I mean, it is Friday,' she says, catching
the word 'birthday' just in time. 'Who are you with?'

She can hear Geoff take a sip of his drink; ice cubes clink
about. Then he says: 'I'm alone.' The news that he isn't with
his family in Surrey is a sudden, unexpected relief.

'What can you see out the window?'

'All of London. The whole damn thing. You see, it was
misleading to call it a window. It's a wall of glass, and really
quite high up.'

'What floor?'

'The twenty-second.'

'Whoa.'

'I can see everything northwest of Elephant and Castle.'

'Elephant and . . . Wait, are you in that crazy skyscraper,
the one with the wind turbines?'

'I am indeed. Do you know it?'

Anna is delighted by the coincidence, and explains that
it is the only building she can see from her bedroom when
standing on tiptoes. She says that she is obsessed with views,
and he says he is too, that it is the sole reason he picked the
place. This time the coincidence doesn't surprise her at all.
It is the least she would expect for an 81; if the number is
accurate they should have all the big things in common. She
watches a man walk past on the high road, his body appear-

ing black against the gleaming shopfronts, and decides to give Geoff a test.

'Can I ask you something?' she says. 'My friend had this idea for a project. Tell me if you think it sounds any good. You know how people all have sheds and drawers and cupboards full of hammers and nails and ladders and half-empty paint pots and crusty paint brushes and all this other stuff?'

'It sounds familiar, yes.'

'How often do people use these things? Like, never, right? And yet everyone has them. But what if you had some kind of local store that people could access as part of a membership scheme, a shed-like thing with high-quality tools and stuff, that they could pay a small monthly fee to use. Like Streetcar. But a shed.'

Geoff laughs, and says it is an excellent idea. He asks questions and picks holes in the plan – how would they protect the sheds from burglars, and how to deal with the inevitable Sunday afternoon surge in demand for tools – but he reiterates that he thinks it's a great idea.

'You think it would work?'

'Of course. It's the best type of business – one that strives to make money *and* make the world a more efficient place.'

'That's it!' she says, excitedly. 'That's exactly it!' She is walking again now, still on Cavendish Road but further uphill. Her phone makes the beeping noise that indicates another call is trying to get through. She ignores it and waits for it to stop beeping before speaking again.

'It was my idea, really.'

'I know it was.'

She laughs and says: 'I know you know.'

Anna stops and perches on a low wall; the rapid walk

uphill has made her dizzy. She waits for her heartbeat to slow down but it doesn't; it is not exertion but excitement that is making it pump. The same rushing excitement she used to feel at the Minuscule of Sound, or when she and her dad picked up the passport, or when she and Geoff broke into Somerset House. While she thinks this the line is silent, but Geoff hasn't complained; it is like he understands and welcomes her reflective moments, as if they have achieved comfortable silences already.

'So . . . tell me what you can see from your window.'

He says immediately it is just so many lights, and that it's better in the day, when the city spreads out like an ornate Persian rug. His words remind her of the imagined manifestation of her Kismet profile, a spread of thousands of dots on translucent paper, each one a co-ordinate of her personality. She further imagines Geoff's profile – an equally complex constellation – being laid over hers, and the two corresponding in such a way that many of the starlike dots are doubled in size, providing an invitation for lines to be drawn between them, tracing a new sign of the zodiac.

'It sounds dreamy,' she says.

Geoff clears his throat, then says: 'Why don't you come and have a look?'

The idea makes Anna stop still on the pavement.

'Come and have a look?'

'Yes.'

'You mean *now*?'

'Why not? I could do with some company.'

She sighs and says, 'I *would* like that. A lot.' Her emphasis suggests a 'but' is around the corner, though Geoff doesn't let her get to it.

'So would I. And it's a very simple thing, if you want to do it.'

Anna runs through the idea in her mind: walking to the high road, jumping in a cab, riding to Elephant and Castle, sailing up to the twenty-second floor, being with her 81.

'Just think,' continues Geoff. 'If *you* want to do it, and *I* want you to do it, then it would be perverse not to do it.' Her phone makes the beeping noise again.

'It might feel like a big decision now, but it really is a small thing. A simple thing, if it is what you want. What are you afraid of?'

'Nothing,' she says. 'There's nothing to be afraid of. I'll do it. I'm coming.'

'Good,' he says, as if this was a matter of course.

'I'll come! I'm coming!' she says, taking big strides down the slope, her voice wobbling with each step. Geoff checks she knows the address, and tells her what to say to the concierge.

'See you soon!' she says, and then hangs up. She looks down at her phone and knows that any second Pete is going to try and call; the device feels as potent and dangerous as it did last night, when she considered throwing it in the Thames. Before switching it off she has to tell Pete something, though. She imagines him in the house, pacing back and forth in the living room, wondering where she has got to. Her heart goes out to him, but only so far; she thinks that on some level he already knows that it wasn't going to work, just like she always knew about him and Zahra. She sends him a one-word message – *sorry* – and then a four-word message to Zahra – *I couldn't do it*. Then she turns it off and continues towards the high road. It occurs to her that the traffic might be clogged, or she might struggle to find a taxi at this time, and will have to turn her phone on to summon one. But then, as if the world is just sitting around waiting to collaborate with her plan, the very first vehicle that approaches her is a black cab. The letters TAXI are glowing orange, and as she raises her hand it obligingly slows to a halt beside her.

Thirty-five minutes later she is sailing upwards in the lift, the display panel flickering through the floors as her stomach drops. On the twenty-second floor she finds door number 176, and is about to knock when she decides to get rid of her chewing gum; on the landing she finds an ankle-high chrome bin. Then she knocks. The door clicks, then swings open to reveal Geoff.

'Anna 81,' he says, softly, as if in reverence. He is wearing a white shirt, untucked, and tan chinos. So handsome, she thinks. Every time it surprises her.

'Hello, Geoff.'

He steps aside to let her in and they walk along a short hall-way that opens into a sweeping living space; to the left is a sunken, carpeted lounge area, to the right a glistening kitchen, all brushed steel and glazed tiles and the wall painted jet black. They hover on the threshold between the two rooms. He must be quite rich. She always assumed he had money, but not this much money.

'I'm pleased to see you,' he says, nodding slightly.

'I'm pleased to be here.'

They say this formally, as if performing a ceremony; she is glad she got rid of her gum. She feels awkward, and the sensation passes through her of reality not matching anticipation, or the real situation being *too* real. She looks down at her new boots and tells herself to ride this out.

'So you wanted to see the view?' He extends his arm towards the kitchen and she sees that the black wall is actually a continuous expanse of glass. She walks towards it, and at first the window gives back the reflection of the kitchen and her own approach, but then she sees beyond this to countless white and yellow lights, as bunched and layered and numerous as stars in a clear night sky. The sudden awareness of height and distance makes her stomach turn over, but not in a bad way. She steps right up to the glass and after a few moments the landmarks make themselves known amid the twinkling chaos. The London Eye is a thin purple disc standing on its side. The Palace of Westminster is an amber mass stretched along the river. St Paul's is a tiny white-tipped helmet, nestled within taller shapes.

'You can see everything,' she says. She is facing northwest, and off towards the glimmering horizon is Kilburn. She guesses where it is, then blots it out with a thumb pressed against the glass. How incredible, to think the room, house and suburb that so completely surrounded her are now behind her thumb. It is a change of perspective akin to having flown into space, and in a way she has: she has flown into space and landed on a new planet, planet Geoff.

'Do you have any children?' she asks.

'A daughter,' says Geoff. She can see him reflected in the glass, leaning against the kitchen table, watching her. 'Her name is Clara. She's eleven. She lives in Argentina with her mother.'

Anna nods, says nothing. For a moment she is daunted by all the things she doesn't know about Geoff, and thinks maybe he wants it like this. He wants to keep things light, superficial – he has no idea what day this is for her, what she has just done. She watches his reflection for signs that he is annoyed by her question, and in contrast he rises and approaches her. She reaches her hands out behind her to welcome his, and in a flourish of co-ordination they fit together: she loops his long arms around her waist like a belt, he pulls her back towards him, takes some of her weight, and then kisses the back of her head, sighing through his nose. Yes, yes, the touch, she thinks, sinking back into him. She can feel his breath on her ear and his steady heartbeat pressed on her back, the vibrations humming through her like faint electricity. Their shadows in the glass are now a single column. And yet it is not a sexual longing she feels, or not precisely. It is deeper than that, their touch satisfying a much deeper shared hunger. And it is this sensation, more than anything else, that proves the validity of the number: they are in no hurry. She looks at their reflection in the glass, and the number 81 flashes above them.

'What do you think about Greece?' she says.

'The country?'

'Yes.'

'It's one of my favourites. I've always wanted to live there.'

Anna laughs. Geoff asks why, and she says it doesn't matter. Nothing matters. She leans back into him and feels herself sinking, floating downwards; still standing, she falls into a sleep that is not sleep but something else drowsy and tranced, until Geoff suddenly dredges up a forgotten phrase from her childhood.

'Come on,' he says. 'Time to hit the hay.'

'My nan used to say that.'

'Mine said "time to take you up the wooden hill to Bed-fordshire".'

She laughs, says she *is* from Bedfordshire, and then admits to being tired.

'It's been a long day. Just a moment longer.'

They continue standing, and she thinks it has indeed been a long day; its beginning feels as distant as the furthest twinkling lights, or even the stars above. But it is about to come to an end, as all days must. She isn't sure of the precise time, perhaps it is 1 a.m. or 2 a.m., but that is irrelevant. Days aren't measured on clocks, they are expanses of consciousness cut into shape by sleep. And this day, her thirtieth birthday, is about to end, and her youth is about to end with it. Her youth, all that fumbling and fear and self-deception, is packed away. And life – her *real* life – is about to begin.

3

Thursday

Mozambique has been host to many large-scale calamities, but the floods of 2013 were particularly disastrous. A prolonged rainy season and successive typhoons meant that two great rivers – the Limpopo and Zambezi – burst their banks and turned their sprawling basins into lakes the size of Belgium. Half a million people were made homeless, thousands drowned, and some unfortunate souls were eaten by farmed crocodiles that used the rising water to swim free of their cages. The UN decreed the emergency a 'Level 3', which means that most humanitarian agencies – Unicef, WHO, UNHCR, WFP – have to react in some way, as does a little-known branch of the UN network, the United Nations Humanitarian Air Service, or UNHAS, a fleet of light aircraft and helicopters that can be deployed to extreme disaster situations where normal infrastructure has been knocked out.

Anna stops reading to have a sip of coffee and look up at the big board. Her Sahina article is still at number six, with 5068 current readers. Ingrid is sitting next to her, with her headphones in and her foot tucked beneath her bum; the uppermost curl of the tattoo meaning 'calm' is just visible above the collar of her shirt, which stands in contrast to the fact she's seemed tense and agitated all week. Across the clearing, Stuart is sitting at his desk, presumably because someone from on high, perhaps even Clem himself, has intervened to stop him using the Quiet Room as his own personal office. It is a typical Thursday afternoon, just gone 3 p.m. She has been in her thirties for almost a week.

Anna opens Instagram and finds the close-up photo of the broken name tag that Geoff told her to focus on. On Monday she tweeted the picture with a zoomed-in inset of the beginning of the emblem, and a new follower, @cloud_ nine, posted a picture on the #ahardcase thread of a name tag on his own suitcase, containing a complete version of the same grey emblem, along with the UNHAS logo. 'How many people would use UNHAS during a single disaster?' she asked him, during the excitable follow-up exchange. 'A few dozen, max,' he said, and added that UNHAS probably had a record of all passengers. She had him reconfirm this, unable to believe her luck – she could now see her man standing at the carousel, clearer than ever. She can picture him at Heathrow, abandoning his suitcase and running to catch a flight to Nepal because of an earthquake, or Iraq because of a wave of displaced people, or Indonesia because of another typhoon.

Anna condenses this information into three tweets, complete with an overview of the flood that was happening in Mozambique in February 2013, and an appeal to her lovely followers to see if they are linked with anyone at the UN. After posting these she goes to the kitchen for water, where she encounters some gossip; Beatrice and Mike are in there whispering, and they happily share with Anna the rumour that Paula is set to be promoted to managing editor of the website, second only to Clem. When Anna returns to her desk she sees the number of people reading her article has increased slightly, to 5074, and these six extra readers make her feel happy and grateful, and even more pleased to have written it. Over the last week she has reread it numerous times, and on each occasion the stunted sentences seem less offensive, the clichés less clunking. Maybe her initial repulsion was due to the paranoid expectation of an angry call from Sahina's office, demanding they redact parts of the article or else remove it completely. But the call didn't come, and it has occurred to Anna that Sahina expected the article to demonise her; maybe she even wanted this. Her scary persona is half the reason she is talked about so much, after all; perhaps she sees the propagation of this myth as necessary for her global brand. While feeling at peace with the Sahina article, Anna is thrilled at the prospect of meeting Gwyneth Paltrow, and whoever the other eight women are; during a three-minute hallway chat with Paula, she said that Stella McCartney was in the frame, and maybe even Meryl Streep, if she comes to the UK to promote her new film. Women at the Top is a good thing, she has concluded. No, a great thing. She will finish the series and then use it as a basis to look for bigger and better things – field reporting jobs, an overseas assignment, a true crime investigation.

The big board refreshes, and yesterday's April Fool story – about people being able to send text messages simply by thinking about it – slips further down, overtaken by an interview with Elon Musk. At the very top, with more hits than all the other stories combined, is the live blog following the European Court of Justice's decision to uphold the Austrian High Court's ruling, and insist that Kismet allow the heartbroken man to see his profile data. The story has been an almost constant presence on the bank of TV screens, and it is there again now, on Al Jazeera: Raymond Chan can be seen speaking at this morning's press conference, for the first time ever not wearing a smile, the subtitles relaying his pronouncement that this is a sad day for Kismet, and a sad day for anyone who has been made happy by it. The Austrian man clearly doesn't agree; he is seen in the next shot celebrating outside the court-room, pumping his fist in the air.

'Cheer up, Raymond,' says Anna, reaching for her phone. She taps out a message – *Are you free?* – and a few seconds later, almost as quick as a reply in a spoken conversation, he writes back – *No, I come at a very high price.* She tells him that he's not funny, and over the course of six messages they decide that she will go to his right away, as he tells her he wants to fuck her until she forgets her own name.

She shuts down her computer and puts her notepad in her bag; already her core temperature and heartbeat are rising, to think that in thirty minutes she will be naked in his bed, entangled and thrusted about, all of her senses stimulated to bursting point.

'You're leaving already?' says Ingrid, pulling out her head-phones.

'I've done enough for the day.'

'But you've been on Twitter all afternoon.'

For a moment Anna is shocked by this insight, since the slight curve of their desk means that Ingrid cannot see her screen. But then she remembers that Ingrid is a new follower – one of several hundred from just the last few days, includ-ing a *Guardian* journalist – and will have seen all of today's tweets.

'It's getting exciting, isn't it? The net is closing. I think we're actually going to find him.' Ingrid's frown indicates that she isn't willing to share in Anna's excitement, that she genuine-ly is concerned about Anna's work. 'Seriously, though, I've done all I can for Women at the Top. The Gwyneth Paltrow interview has been pushed back until Monday, and Stuart has already approved my questions.'

'Why the delay?'

'It was Romont's shout. They wanted to keep the Sahina piece for another weekend.'

'Another weekend?' says Ingrid. She is clearly startled. A client deciding to extend an article is the ultimate sign of success, and a rare one at that, measured in a way that is only seen by senior management, and for which the numbers on the big board are just a proxy. Anna simply nods, and Ingrid seems to gather enough goodwill to smile and say congratulations. There has been a series of adjustments in their relationship this week, as Ingrid has become more and more of a peer, and Anna feels another crank towards equilibrium as she gracefully accepts Ingrid's good wishes. Then her phone buzzes in her hand: *Please don't be too long. I am walking around like a tiger in a cage.*

'So I deserve the afternoon off, right? If Stuart asks, tell him I've got to let a plumber in, would you?' She regrets saying this immediately; it is the sort of thing a sleazy adulterous boss would ask of his secretary. Ingrid's face screws up, and Anna rushes to make amends. 'In fact, don't tell him anything. I'll tell him myself. I'm coming in early tomorrow. Earlier than both of you.'

Ingrid smiles thinly, and Anna says goodbye and leaves. Even as she walks across the clearing, Anna can sense that Ingrid's smile will have been replaced by her typical agitated scowl. These past days Anna has noticed, for the first time, that when Ingrid works she is bristling with stress – if you watch her closely you can almost see her buzzing. The tattoo meaning calm, Anna has realised, isn't so much a boast but an aspiration, an elaborate note-to-self. This is one of several revisions she has made to her view of Ingrid; it is almost like some enhancing filter has been removed. She has also noticed how lonely Ingrid seems without her boyfriend, and senses the arguments and bitter resentment that must underpin his three-month stints in the jungle. Her online galleries appear different to Anna as well. The images of her friends on Facebook – this week on a walk around Victoria Park – have an irrefutable performative quality, and raise the question of why they feel it necessary to publish so many photos of themselves having fun. What are they trying to prove, exactly? And why? It feels like Anna can see the real Ingrid for the first time – complete with her frailties, anxieties – and as she waits for the lift Anna decides to be nicer to her. With each passing day she becomes more convinced that soon she will leave this place for good, and it would be a shame not to do so on a high.

Fifty minutes later she is lying beneath the duvet, her limbs feeling as slack as a pile of cut rope. She is watching the floor-to-ceiling window as if it is a cinema screen, the view of the city – which appears to her on its side, with the sky to the left – holding her attention as much as the most riveting film. She hasn't yet had a chance to test the theory that she could gaze like this all day without getting bored, but she has learnt that the view is indeed better during the day than at night. The city is spread out like an intricately woven carpet, a complex of greens and reds and greys and blacks, that partially makes up for this being the most boring stretch of London, barren of all landmarks, with nothing but bland suburbia between here and the shallow green hills on the horizon. More interesting than the buildings and neighbourhoods is the weather; from this height it is possible to watch the dark heavy clouds roll in from the southwest, bringing with them rain and wind and what feels like a premature twilight. But Anna likes it when rain smatters the glass wall – as it is doing now – since it enhances the cosiness of being in bed within a room where the temperature is perfectly consistent throughout, as if an ambient warmth is filling every nook and cranny like a liquid.

Geoff pushes the door open with his foot and carries a dainty silver tea tray into the room. He is wearing a thin gown with oversize cuffs that reminds Anna of a kimono, but is apparently from Istanbul.

'Your bedroom is on the wrong side,' says Anna.

'I beg your pardon?' he says, setting down the tray on the bedside table. She tells him that there is nothing interesting to look at, apart from the nice colours and the clouds, and he baulks at this suggestion.

'I'll have you know that some of the most important political developments of the twentieth century happened just beyond this glass,' he says, pouring green tea into two cups and passing one to Anna, who props herself on an elbow to receive it. 'The other side – St Paul's and Westminster and all – they're just distractions, that isn't where the real action happens.'

'Here we go,' she says, rolling her eyes, as if in protest at the impending lecture, but she knew her statement would elicit such a response, and wanted nothing less. He goes to the window and begins pointing at landmarks and giving a potted history of why they are significant – the Brixton riots, the Putney debates, the Stockwell shooting. His gown has fallen open and his soft penis is visible between the two hanging flanks, appearing to nod along with his talk.

'You know I can't see what you're pointing at,' she says, between tiny bird sips of the scalding liquid. 'My eyes need to be in alignment with your finger.'

'It's the stories that matter, anyway,' he says. 'Stories of rebellion, of the fringes challenging the establishment. My favourite kind of stories. I have always felt a solidarity with the fringes. The rebels. The dispossessed.'

'Is that why you live in such modest surroundings?'

He smiles at this, says touché, and then a darkness comes across his eyes and he says, in a dastardly way, that it's all the better to keep an eye on the enemy. Anna laughs out loud and says he doesn't have any enemies. While dropping his gown and getting into bed behind her – his hairy chest feels like a carpet tile pressed against her back – he explains that his fellow residents of Strata SE1, who only live so high so they can pretend to have nothing to do with Elephant and Castle, are the enemy, or close enough.

'They bring out the worst in me. Every time I see them in the lift or the lobby, I sense their self-satisfaction. They are the ultimate disciples of the prevailing ideology, and this building is the culmination of everything they've worked to-wards.' Maintaining an entirely serious tone, though Anna listens hard for signs that he's joking, he adds that he sees them walking out of the station, looking like a different spe-cies to the brown and black workers in the market. 'And eventually they probably will be, since the human race will evolve into two subsets: those able to pay £20 a month for Kismet, and those who aren't.'

'Jesus,' says Anna. 'You really are a paranoid fucker.'

'Maybe I'm exaggerating.'

'Living here to keep an eye on the enemy?'

'Let's also not forget that this was a snip. And it's a short-term arrangement; I won't be here long.'

This statement lands with a thud. In the ensuing silence Anna wonders what 'here' means in this context. This flat? This city? This country? It would be too bold to ask directly, and she searches for a tactful way of teasing out the information.

'Sometimes I think of leaving London, too,' she says. He doesn't contradict her, just begins rubbing her left shoulder. 'I'd like to live somewhere with more space, light, warmth,' she continues. Geoff hums in agreement, and she leans her shoulder into his rubbing fingers, which are forceful and systematic. She is tempted to elaborate on her last statement by saying that she would like to live in southern Europe – maybe an Italian or Greek island – and that in the vivid fantasies that have illuminated her most recent bouts of insomnia, he is always there beside her. But she suppresses the desire to say this, as she does when the urge to ask him to switch off Kismet rears up within her, usually following a particularly amusing conversation that culminates in the number 81 flashing above his head. Anna isn't one to conform to gender roles, but for some reason – maybe because Geoff is significantly older – she feels the suggestion of switching off Kismet has to come from him. In fact, she already feels she has said too much, and decides to backtrack.

'I shouldn't move abroad though. My brother moved to Australia and it would be too hard on my mum. He thought of it first.'

'How selfish of him.'

'Youngest child,' she says. 'But maybe I don't need to move anyway, it's just wanderlust; perhaps I just need a weekend away.'

This makes Geoff laugh.

'It's a tough decision: moving away for good, or going away for the weekend. Perhaps do the latter first: it will be like watching the trailer before seeing the film.'

'Exactly.'

'How about a spa break?' he says, pushing her shoulder so forcefully that she is rolled onto her front. Then he jumps up to straddle her arse, and begins chopping and slapping her back.

'Owww!'

'Go with the pain. Don't fight it, it's a *wave. Go with it.*'

'Get off me, you hippy.'

His genitals are resting on her bum like a sack of loose skin, and she wonders if they will have sex again. Surely not: for one thing, Geoff has a meeting about his project at 7 p.m. But the pads of his fingers press into her side ribs, then reach around to her breasts, pinching and pushing in a way that is just the right side of pain. She can feel the sack of skin resting on her bum changing shape, coming to life like a timelapse film of a flower blooming, and the spit in her mouth thins to a sweet water, knowing that they will.

Forty minutes later, Anna is standing at the bus stop opposite Elephant and Castle station, waiting for the 148 to Kilburn. Further along from the station is the beginnings of the market, and she watches three older women of unclear ethnic heritage – they could be Latino, or Russian, or Asian, or some modern hybrid of each – packing up their stall. One of them looks up at Anna, as if sensing her attention, then glances down again. What did she see? Just another white English girl waiting for a bus? Or does she know, perhaps in a way that is beyond her conscious awareness, that Anna has had three orgasms in two hours? It seems impossible that she doesn't look different to the grey commuters around her, or to how she looked a few weeks ago; it feels she should be glowing slightly. The 148 trundles to the stop, and its appearance makes Anna realise how much fun she is having, or, more accurately, how much fun she is having compared to the prospect of going home. She watches a few people step off, some others get on board, then the doors close and the bus drive off, while she stands still. The information board says that two other buses are due imminently, the 136 and the 341, and she goes to the big map in the bus shelter. Her finger follows the squiggly orange line of the 136 to Lewisham and then the southeastern hinterland, names she's never heard of: Lee, Eltham, Bexleyheath. This reminds her of a game that she and Zahra and Hamza and Caz used to play when they first moved to London. They would pick a random place in the city that none of them had been to, and then go there on a Saturday afternoon with the intention of exploring – though usually getting no further than the first half-decent pub they stumbled across. Tube map lottery, they called it. Her heart swells with nostalgia, and it feels like fate when her finger follows the purple line of the 341 right up to Islington. She thinks of another person and responsibility that she has been putting off, which she now resolves to avoid no longer: Zahra.

It has become habit for Anna to meet Zahra in a pub near her flat – primarily due to the supposed building works, but also to avoid Keir's lordly presence – and tonight they arrange to meet in the pub filled with taxidermy at the end of Essex Road. There is something grotesque and decadent about being surrounded by so many stuffed animals, but it is the place where Anna first told Zahra about finding the ring and her plan to join Kismet, and for this reason alone she suggests it, drawn to the idea of symmetry, completion, closure.

She arrives early, and is surprised to find Zahra waiting for her at the bar, wearing a new pair of round-framed glasses. They haven't seen each other or spoken for almost a week, perhaps a record, and for a second Anna puts aside the uncomfortable burden of what must be discussed and gives herself over to friendliness.

'Look at you,' she says, pulling Zahra into a hug. 'You look like a sexy secretary from the fifties.' But Zahra is stiff in her arms and mumbles something about the glasses being on offer, before moving the conversation on to Pete and asking how he is.

'You want to get straight down to business, don't you?' says Anna, as they take their two glasses of wine to a small table beside a cabinet of preserved butterflies.

'What do you expect? I haven't heard a peep out of you all week.'

'That's because there isn't a peep to report.'

They settle into their seats, and Zahra says she doesn't know what she means.

'Just that. Me and Pete haven't spoken about it. It's like a silent impasse or something. I came home on Saturday and we were going to chat, but then I fell asleep and since then he's been avoiding me.'

'Since then? Are you serious? He still thinks you spent the night at mine?'

Anna just shrugs, and Zahra's mouth falls open in disbelief.

'How can you live with someone and not talk about you running away like that?'

'We've barely seen each other. He's been sleeping on the sofa, and we've both been really busy with our work. It's his first exam next week.' This feels like a valid point, but it makes Zahra plant her elbows on the table and place her head in her hands.

'His first *exam*,' she groans. 'This is too fucked up.'

The intensity of Zahra's reaction is beginning to work on Anna, and she doubts her certainty that Pete is fine. But she holds her composure and explains that Pete doesn't seem that shook up, that he's good at compartmentalising, and in any case he only thinks she ran away to Zahra's on her birthday – hardly cause for a nervous breakdown.

'I know you feel guilty for lying to him, but honestly, he seems fine.'

'He's not *fine*,' snaps Zahra. 'You're pushing him to the brink. He could be about to . . . I don't know . . . to collapse.'

Anna raises her eyebrows at this possibility and shrugs, while looking deeply into Zahra's eyes.

'Maybe you're right,' she says casually, taking a sip of wine. 'I suppose you know him better than me.'

This makes Zahra flinch. 'What? No. That's not what I'm saying. But I don't think you understand anything at the moment. You're being crazy.' She says this quietly while looking away, no doubt at one stuffed animal or another, and for a moment she appears deflated. She hasn't touched her wine. Then she comes to life again, as if she has just worked something out.

'You know what I think?' says Zahra, her eyes narrowed behind her owlish new glasses. 'I think you haven't told Pete because you're not sure about this other guy.'

'Geoff. His name is Geoff.'

Zahra's face contorts, as if a bad smell has been blown across the table.

'Of course I'm sure about him. It's not even like there's a decision to be made. He's an 81, for God's sake.'

'It can't be just about the number.'

'It's not *about* the number. The number is about everything. He's perfect for me.' She explains how they are both journalists, are both obsessed with innovation and travelling the world, how they have the same subversive attitude towards pretty much everything; in short, that he brings out the person she's always wanted to be. She thinks but doesn't add – and the thought alone sends a shiver through her groin – that the sex is unreal.

'Have you switched off, then?'

'Not yet.'

'How come? If everything is so perfect.'

'We will, soon. But it has to be at least halfway romantic. It's not something you can just blurt out over breakfast.'

'And you'll string Pete along until then?'

Anna sighs and shakes her head, and makes a conscious effort to resist the urge to argue. When she does respond it is in a measured, pragmatic tone, delivering a pre-planned speech.

'Look. I know you think I'm doing something terrible to Pete. But this is for his good too. We're not a very good match. I know you think we are, but we're not. I don't want the same things as him. I don't want the same things as most people. A few years ago, when my dad died, I think I lost sight of that for a while. And since then I've been drifting. I've been depressed. And now it feels like I've woken up again.'

Zahra is looking at Anna with a concerned and thoughtful expression, even a hint of a smile; maybe she has finally managed to get through to her. Zahra reaches across the table and lays a hand upon Anna's.

'Do you think', says Zahra, in a tentative little voice, 'this is all about your dad?'

'No I fucking don't,' says Anna, pulling her hand back. 'Why does everyone always think that? This is a happy situation. I'm just doing what I want, what's good for me. Why can't you be at least a bit supportive?'

'Because you're throwing away something special,' says Zahra, in a wheedling voice. 'Pete is a great guy. I don't want you to do something you'll regret. That we'll all regret.'

This time something snaps.

'Maybe you should go out with him,' says Anna, deadpan, taking another large gulp of wine. 'Since you think he's so damn special.'

Zahra scoffs and shakes her head, and then commences to fidget: she checks her watch, checks her phone and finally takes a sip of wine. Anna watches her, remains entirely still.

'Hey, Z. How come you never come to my flat any more?'

'What are you talking about? I was there last week.'

'But *before* my birthday. You hadn't been for months and months. You used to come round all the time. Sometimes when I wasn't even there. Why did you suddenly stop?'

Zahra looks concerned now. 'What kind of questions are these?' she asks.

'Just questions. Why was it?'

'You're being weird.'

'No I'm not. They're simple questions. Come on.'

Zahra rolls her eyes, as if it is annoying to have to engage with whatever game Anna is playing.

'I don't know. Lots of reasons. We were really busy with the kitchen for ages, for one. These things don't always happen for a reason.'

'Right. The kitchen. That huge renovation. It was just strange how during my party, Keir said it only took you a month.'

'You know what Keir's like: he always exaggerates to win an argument.'

Anna nods and smiles, says that she's probably right.

'But it did get me thinking. About the last time you came round. It was after Notting Hill Carnival. You stayed at mine afterwards. The next morning I had to work and left you and Pete alone in the flat. After that, you never came round. Not once.'

Blood has risen to Zahra's face. She appears to be quivering slightly. Anna, for her part, is both thrilled and terrified. After a while Zahra raises both palms in the air.

'This is nuts. You're nuts.' She stands and takes her coat from the back of the chair.

'You're leaving?'

'I can't be fucked with this.'

'But we're having a conversation.'

'I'm not staying to answer questions like these,' she says, pulling on her coat. Her cheeks are burning red. 'And if Pete asks me again, I'm not going to lie to him. Call me when you're not fucking insane.'

With that she walks across the pub. Anna watches her

push through the door, then her eyes flick between various people who are looking at her; she realises their conversation has turned almost every head in the room. Anna locks eyes with the barman and shrugs, intimating that her unpredictable friend is out of control, though she imagines she probably looks quite distressed herself. Her pulse is thrumming through her temples, and when she holds out a hand it trembles alarmingly. This rush of pure feeling is then translated into more precise emotions as she replays Zahra's evasiveness, her blushing, her running away like that. It is a strange cocktail of feelings. On a visceral level she feels shocked and sad, for she never expected it to be confirmed so blatantly. In another, darker corner of her soul she feels grim satisfaction for being proved right. And on the highest level, the cool glass pane of her consciousness, she feels that this is a useful development: it means that her inevitable confrontation with Pete will not be a one-sided confession from her, with him playing the innocent martyr. She tells herself not to be upset, and reaches across the table and slides Zahra's barely touched glass of wine across to her, deciding to stay and drink both. But she is distracted by the ghostly print of Zahra's lips on her glass, and holds it up to inspect further. The pinkish residue of lip gloss is as finely etched as a fingerprint, and for some reason this granular evidence of Zahra's being makes the sad shocked feeling swell up within Anna, and she has to put down the glass and twist around in her seat, unable to look at it at all.

Just after 10.30 p.m. Anna arrives in Kilburn and walks to Mowbray Road. She hovers on the porch for a moment and then unlocks the door and creeps inside with the care of a bomb defuser, which proves to be unnecessary, since the flat is dark and lifeless. She should probably linger in the living room and wait for Pete to return but this is once again overpowered by the desire to avoid him, to put the showdown off for one more day. She quickly sheds her bag and coat and brushes her teeth before climbing up the ladder.

Once in bed she finds she isn't sleepy. She tries a breathing technique that Geoff told her induces sleep – in for seven seconds, hold for four, out for eight – but it doesn't work. As with other recent nights, her thoughts do not unspool into drowsy nonsense and then oblivion, but instead become more lucid and energised – she can hear his voice in her inner ear and see his face in her mind's eye, and this soon morphs into a full-colour narrative of the two of them in a villa in Greece, on the terrace at night, the stars twinkling like the co-ordinates of their perfect alignment. Even the sad remnants of her conversation with Zahra only interrupts her for a second or two, and then she is back in Greece, the fantasy floating onwards without any conscious steering. She imagines a daytime scene, her and Geoff sunbathing naked, having sex in the pool, going to a tiny beach and coating each other's bodies in grey mud which is baked to a dry crust by the sun; it is almost as if she is watching an internal film of her own construction, until the vision is burst by the scratch of a key in the front door.

Pete's footsteps have always been heavy, but it seems he is making a special effort to stomp about. He thuds up the stairs, drops something on the dining table, goes through to the bathroom, turns on taps, flushes the toilet, then plods through the hallway. Anna expects to hear him re-enter the living room and flop down on the sofa, and is alarmed to hear the ladder whine as he clasps it and begins to climb towards her. Anna turns to the wall and clamps her eyes shut, a second before the hatch opens and Pete heaves himself onto the floorboards.

He staggers about, turning on a lamp, emptying his pockets, unbuckling his belt, then falls eerily silent. She can hear nothing besides her rapid heartbeat in her ear. To make so little noise he must be standing still, probably in the central point of the bedroom where the sloping ceiling allows him to stand upright. Anna strains to hear something above the static hum and eventually makes out the wheeze of his breathing. He must be standing there watching her, and she imagines the spot between her shoulder blades where his eyes are aiming. He must also sense she isn't asleep, and is trying to decide whether to finally have it out with her and demand to know what's going on. Anna braces herself for this confrontation, and in a way wills him to initiate it; she has been ready for this conversation since she returned from Elephant and Castle on Saturday afternoon, in the same clothes as her birthday, a fallen woman in her thirties. She expected to find a shell-shocked Pete, a broken home, and to spend the day in bleak reckoning. But when she entered the flat Pete was in the living room with his textbook, and stood to face her, looking more concerned than angry. He didn't appear broken, he was still Pete; the only difference from the night before was that his stubble had returned as a grey shadow. He asked if she'd been at Zahra's, and in a moment of cowardice and fatigue she simply kept her eyes averted, said nothing and allowed the suggestion to be accepted as fact. Then he kissed her on the forehead and hugged her, told her everything was alright, and generally did his calm-down-Anna routine.

'I'll make us some lunch,' he said, and she suspected this was a ploy he had picked up from his textbooks. She remembered him saying once that you shouldn't have an emotional conversation if you are tired, hungry or angry. 'And then we'll have a chat, okay?'

Anna said that she'd like a shower as well, and he said this was fine – totally fine – that she should take her time, and then they'd have a chat. Those were the last words to have passed between them: *and then we'll have a chat.* Instead of having a meal and talking everything through, Anna fell asleep. She hadn't meant to, but she had been up most of the previous night with Geoff, and the heat and steam of the shower intensified her tiredness, and as she dried herself in the bedroom the desire to lie down and close her eyes was irresistible. The next thing she knew it was Sunday morning. She was alone in the flat. She walked around in a daze, trying to work out what happened, and deduced from the dents in the cushions that Pete must have slept on the sofa. She then found a message on a deck of Post-it notes, saying he had gone to Bean's. He had written these few words so hard that an imprint was visible on the next Post-it note, and the one after that. Since then he has slept on the sofa every night, has stayed out late every evening, and appears to have gone out of his way to avoid her, apparently trying to shame her into breaking the silence. And here he is now, standing over her, watching, saying nothing.

A full minute passes, and Pete is still standing there. Anna feels as lifeless as a fallen log, so stiff and inanimate it is strange that the air keeps moving in and out of her. She thinks maybe he is plying another technique, that he knows she is awake and will find his silent waiting unbearable. But just as she is about to sit up and say 'Fuck it,' he comes to life again. He exhales massively and drops his trousers, the buckle of his belt clattering against the floorboards. Then he staggers about, hits the lamp and comes to the bed; the mattress complains as he flops down next to her, and seconds later he is snoring. It is obvious from the stale sour smell that he has been drinking beer, lots of it, and that whatever he did in the bathroom didn't involve brushing his teeth. Now that the moment has passed she regrets not waiting up in the living room and speaking to him. She wonders if Zahra could be right, if he really is on the brink. Either way, there is no chance of her achieving sleep now, with him snoring next to her. She slithers out the end of the bed, grabs her dressing gown and climbs through the hatch.

Before setting up a bed on the sofa she decides to do some exploring and learn more about Pete's state of mind. The heavy items she heard him drop on the table are his textbooks and notepad. Anna flicks through the notepad, looking for signs of an impending breakdown, but all she finds is page after page of bullet points on educational theory, conflict resolution and conceptualisation, all written out in his fragile and wayward handwriting. Pete is getting on with things, as she knew he would: getting on with things is his way. Perhaps he is chalking up her behaviour to some kind of existential crisis about turning thirty, only vaguely related to him, or is attributing it to her dad, as everyone else seems to. She continues flicking through the pages, reassured by every blank margin, until suddenly, halfway through the notebook, there is a doodle that fills the upper corner of the left page: he has drawn the letter 'A' in ornate 3D shading.

A lump expands in Anna's throat. She takes conscious control of her breathing and flicks through the remaining pages, looking for more, blinking the blurring liquid from her eyes.

There is nothing until the last page of notes, probably from earlier that same day. Again it is a large drawing of elaborate design, only this time it is the letter 'Z'. A to Z, she thinks. Anna to Zahra. Beginning to end.

She drops the notepad and looks for his phone. His jacket pocket yields nothing but loose change and a scratched Oyster card, but there it is in his backpack, nestled along with his keys and wallet – his big three, he calls them. She takes the phone back to the living room and sits on the sofa. While punching in his passcode – 1987, the year of his birth – she questions whether she really wants to do this. It seems possible that she will find evidence that is so shocking it will blow a hole in her existence: a three-year affair, an abortion, a stream of graphic sex pictures, declarations of love. With her heart everywhere at once, she opens his messages and sees a stack of threads from Bean, his parents, his friend Finn, his other friend Matt, from her. There it is, below that: Zahra. She opens the thread and sees the messages from her birthday, with Pete asking Zahra if she'd heard from Anna, and Zahra confirming that she'd come to hers because she needed some 'space to think'. A week before that is a spate of messages about hiring a boat for Anna's birthday. Anna swipes the screen upwards and is amazed to find the next message is about the preparations for Anna's birthday trip to Dungeness two whole years ago. Between then and last month, there is just an empty white space.

For a moment Anna is flooded with relief, to think that somehow this has all been a mistake. But then her mind traces back to last summer, in search of a memory of Pete texting Zahra, or vice versa. Without even trying, she can think of a handful of examples. When they were planning a visit to Brighton. When Zahra was giving him running updates on

288

the health of her bonsai plant. During the carnival when they managed to lose Pete, and Anna's phone was dead so they had to use Zahra's to track him down. And now all these messages have been wiped away, along with what else?

She minimises the screen and then drops the phone. For a time she sits in the half-dark. Across the room, the tomato plant stands proud on the window ledge; the light from the nearby streetlamp is projecting the plant's complex, alien-like shadow onto the far wall, within a box of amber light that is the exact hue, Anna realises for the first time, of urine. Then she stands and goes to the tomato plant. Her first thought is to shred it with her bare hands, to behead the tight green bulbs, snap the prickly stem, scatter the soil across the floor. But having it smash on the ground outside seems like a better idea, and she pushes open the window. As she picks up the pot she is surprised by its weight, and almost drops it on her feet. She has to crouch to catch and keep hold of it, and then staggers backwards to find her balance and ends up sitting on the couch again, with the plant pot on her lap, her face covered in the leaves, her forehead against the stabilising bamboo. She stays in this position for a long time, her nose full of the fertile greenhouse smell, until she feels the first tear spill from her eyelid and trickle down her cheek.

Saturday

Geoff is a surprisingly cautious driver. The weekend motorway is wide open, but he remains tucked in behind lorries in the slow lane, holding the steering wheel stiffly with both hands. Anna decides that she likes this – the inconsistency with the rest of his personality adds texture – and studies his face for a time. She admires the shape of his head in profile, thinks he has the kind of powerful brow and jaw that would look good on a coin.

'Stop looking at me,' he says.

'Has anyone ever said you'd look good on a coin?'

'They haven't actually. Please elaborate.'

'I can really imagine you as a leader, perhaps during ancient times, with a laurel wreath on your head. Wearing a toga.'

'This is the nicest thing you've ever said to me. Tell me something else.'

'You drive like my grandma.'

'Now now: old ladies are the safest drivers, and pay the lowest premiums for it. If your grandmother was here she'd tell you the same thing.'

Anna says that she would indeed, that they'd probably get on well, before returning her eyes to the front window and lifting her bare feet to the dashboard. Today is the warmest day of the year so far, twenty-four degrees and rising, and Anna is wearing denim shorts and a vest top; the car smells of sunscreen. From the stereo a CD of Egyptian jazz is playing, which Anna wasn't sure about at first, but now she likes the urgent, insistent rhythm. Geoff taps his finger against the steering wheel in time with the rapid tempo. A blue sign grows at the side of the road and swipes past: Swindon 11, Bristol 66, Exeter 118. These place names remind Anna that she doesn't know where they are going, and it strikes her as interesting that she doesn't care. At first she thought he would be taking her to see the pipe – or wherever it was he wanted to take her from London Bridge – and was surprised they drove west out of London, but she soon decided that the physical destination didn't matter; what was important was the emotional objective, the fact that he would surely at some point ask her to switch off Kismet. This thought directs her attention to her phone in her bag in the footwell, and the fact that she hasn't responded to Zahra's message; Zahra said, somewhat cryptically, that she felt 'weird' about the other night, and suggested they meet up to 'talk'. Anna takes her phone and taps out a quick text, repeating the same lie she wrote to Pete on a Post-it note, that she is going to her mum's for the weekend. The message sends and she imagines it flying as radio waves through the sky, at several thousand miles an hour, before arriving at Zahra's phone a few seconds later, where it will be magically reformulated into pixels, words, meaning. She feels guilty for putting off speaking to Pete yet again, but she knows that things will have to come to a head anyway – what difference if it is one day or the next? This weekend with Geoff is just a present to herself before the ugly business begins, and means she can face the demolition of her old life knowing that the foundations of her new one are firmly in place.

'What are you looking at now?' says Geoff, pointedly. He does this when she looks at her phone: he asks what she's doing with the dismissive and scolding tone of a school teacher, as if challenging her to justify what is so interesting.

'Twitter,' she says, tilting her screen away from him. 'Reading my new messages.'

He asks for an update, and from memory she recounts her most recent interaction. She tells him that the net is closing: her new contact @cloud_nine has put her onto someone who works at UNHAS, who has confirmed that only a handful of aid workers used their service during the 2013 Mozambique floods, and that he can email another colleague and ask to mass-contact the list on her behalf.

'You're a natural,' says Geoff. 'And this is just the start. You could create a whole series like this, using the internet to connect people with things they'd given up as lost.'

'And have a global lost property service? It's hardly going to win a Pulitzer.' It is Anna's instinct to respond modestly and dampen his enthusiasm, but she wills herself to embrace it: from now on she will fearlessly strive for success, and part of this will be to accept praise when it is offered. They pass two green hills to their right, and between them she has a rare view of the distant, sun-kissed horizon, which feels like a sudden glimpse into the future. 'But, having said that . . . a journalist did email me. From the *Guardian*.'

'The *Guardian*,' says Geoff, and the car jerks as he takes his eyes off the road to look at her. 'Who?' His reaction is surprising, and she wonders if he might be jealous. She says it is someone called Natalie Ward, from the travel desk, and the concern seems to wash from Geoff's face.

'Don't know her. But that's great news. They'll probably commission you to do a regular slot.'

'Yeah, right. It'll probably be a coffee and a chat.'

'No, I can feel it. This is going to happen.'

'Well, in *that* case. If you can *feel* it.' She says this, yet still turns towards the passenger window so he can't see the smile on her face, the same half-embarrassed, half-delighted smile she used to have when her dad told people she would be a star. To change the subject, she twists around and asks if he wants anything from the back seat, where sparkling water, a bag of sweets and an expensive bottle of smoothie are strewn. Her only request for this trip – other than for it to be somewhere interesting and surprising, like their descent into Somerset House – was that they stop at a service station; not to do so would deprive the road trip of authenticity. She cracks open the bottle of smoothie, and as she brings it to her lips Geoff turns the wheel suddenly, causing a blob of juice to jump from the bottle and onto Anna's bare thighs and the upholstery between.

'Shit.'

'Sorry,' he says, 'I was going to overtake the lorry but thought better of it.'

'The seat,' she says, rubbing the dark blotch between her legs.

'Don't worry about that. Dmitri doesn't care, this is just a Volkswagen.'

She finds a tissue in her bag and scrubs at the stain, before giving up and sinking into the seat. The landscape is changing; the parade of green hills on their right is smoothing out into pale meadows, the beginnings of Salisbury Plain.

'Who is Dimitri, anyway?'

'Dmitri. Not Dim, Dm.' He makes the sound of a hum with a 'd' at the beginning. 'He's a computer programmer.'

'He's Russian?'

293

'Armenian,' he says, and she can tell he is about to make one of his speeches; he takes his left hand from the wheel and makes a chopping motion. He says he's been to a fair few places and that, pound for pound, you won't find a more intelligent nation than Armenia. 'It's a country of chess masters, rocket scientists. Powerful minds.' Anna asks how he knows Dmitri, and Geoff pauses before answering.

'I'm working with him. On the project.'

'Oh,' says Anna, feeling like the car has hit a bump. 'Your project.' There follows the charged silence that occurs every time his project is mentioned, while Anna fights back the urge to accuse him of being ridiculous and not trusting her. Between them is the pumping afro-beat, over which a singer begins wailing.

'I *will* tell you,' he says. 'But we're so close to cracking it. I want to show you when it's complete, not when it's *almost* complete. But we're talking days, not weeks.'

Anna sighs and looks out the window, and reminds herself that she has secrets too. Not just minor details, great big whopping life facts. Geoff doesn't know about Pete or the drama surrounding her birthday, and this feels like a good thing; if he did, it would clutter up and interfere with their light-hearted chatter, the good-humoured exchanges that are the essence of this new relationship. All this other stuff – their respective exes and families and individual histories and jobs and friends – feels like a meaningless pact with the outside world, mere background noise. This thought makes her forgive him already, and she considers leaning over and kissing his stubble-darkened cheek. But he probably won't welcome the distraction, so instead, to prove she's not sulking, she says she'd like to go to Armenia.

'You would? How come?'

'Nothing in particular. Just because it's a place. Because it's somewhere different. It's like you said: a holiday is a mood, not a specific location. I'd happily go anywhere. Armenia. Hong Kong. New York.' She switches to reading the road sign that is growing on the outside verge. 'Andover. Salisbury. Yeovil. Taunton.'

'*Yeovil?*'

'Anywhere. Happiness is a journey, not a destination. At least that's what I read on a Hallmark card.'

'Be careful what you wish for,' he says, indicating left. She thinks he is joking, but then he veers onto the slip road for the A303. Anna laughs, then shrugs.

'I mean it,' she says. 'Take me anywhere.'

For a while she thinks they are going to Yeovil, or that Geoff doesn't actually have a destination in mind and is making it up as they go along, but soon after passing Stonehenge he pulls a folded piece of paper from his pocket, which he gives to her and asks her to navigate. By 2 p.m. they are winding through the incredibly narrow lanes of a village called Pilton, Geoff driving too close to parked cars and clattering wing mirrors. The directions lead them onto a track between ploughed fields, and they finally crunch to a stop on the shingle drive of a red-brick farmhouse.

'*Voilà,*' says Geoff. 'You said you wanted something like Somerset House. So here is a house in Somerset.'

He explains that it belongs to a friend of his, while taking the key from beneath a large plant pot. Anna follows him inside and spins around the expansive ground floor, admiring the Aga in the kitchen, the wood burner in the living room, the terrace with a view of Glastonbury Tor, a mediaeval tower atop a hill that looks to her like an inland lighthouse. Many roll mats are stacked against the wall, and on the telephone table are piles of leaflets for Pilates, music therapy, transcendental meditation.

'What is this place?' she says, raising her voice to carry into the kitchen. She can hear him tinkling about, probably fixing a drink.

'My friend organises yoga retreats. She's in Thailand at the moment.'

'You really are a hippy, aren't you, Geoff?'

He laughs, and says: 'I'm happy to be, if the label helps. Our ideology is all about labels. The world is simply too chaotic, too raucous for our comprehension, so we label things to help get a handle on it: the stuff we like – the cool, the fashionable, the lucrative – can come to the front, the stuff we dislike – the bums, the depression, the illness – we move to the back.'

He rambles on in this vein; with him everything comes back to ideology. Anna decides to silently abandon him as he makes this speech, in a homage to when she did this in the real Somerset House, and because it is funny to leave him sermonising to no one – it has become a little thing she likes to do.

On the upper floors there are single rooms, double rooms, en suites, twin rooms, and a room with no furniture that is perhaps left empty for soothsaying or meditation, or is just being decorated. Anna picks the one that feels like a master bedroom, with large windows looking out across brown fields that stretch as flat as the ocean to the shimmering, hazy horizon. She kicks off her pumps, drops her denim shorts,

peels off her T-shirt and bra and knickers, and climbs between the cool sheets, waiting to be found.

Sex with Geoff is usually a sensual, almost tantric affair,
but today – perhaps because of the head of steam he devel-
oped during the long drive – it is hurried, almost frenzied.
He pins her legs up so that five toes are pressing into each of
his shoulders, and fucks her vigorously in this one position.
Just before they finish, he jams a finger into her arsehole,
while using the other hand to softly press on her windpipe.
Then it is all over, and they are lying on their backs, panting
at the ceiling.

After a few minutes, apropos of nothing, he says, 'You're
a dirty bitch,' and Anna slaps him in the face. It doesn't connect as well as she'd like, so she tries again with her other
hand, but he catches this, and they begin wrestling.

'You disgusting old man,' she wheezes, as she tries to pin
him down. His arms are long and wiry, but she gets within them and for a time it feels like she's winning, but then
he twists her around with an arm up behind her back, and
eventually they both fall slack again in a top-to-toe position,
laughing and moaning. Her head is rested on his pale thigh
and her eyes are level with his slack penis, now a darker hue
than when erect, and thicker-skinned. She suddenly thinks
of her idea for a theme park of human consumption, and
wonders if it would be possible to represent the totality of
someone's sex life in an installation. A water fountain where
the liquid looks like semen, representing the totality of a
lifetime's ejaculate? Or maybe one of those fairground elec-
tric chairs, only powered by the energy of five thousand orgasms? She shuffles her head closer to his cock, close enough
to smell her own residue, and then takes it in her mouth, with

the vague idea of cleaning it. Geoff mirrors this gesture by burying his head between her legs, and gradually she can feel his cock pumping up with blood, one pulse at a time, until it is long and hard and filling her wide-open mouth. They stay in this position for a long time, Anna sucking and slurping with the same lazy persistence you'd use on a gobstopper or a stick of rock. Eventually she loses her sense of the context altogether – of what she is doing or who she is with or where they are – and becomes an empty vessel for what feels like disembodied consciousness. She looks at the window and wonders how the glass feels encased within its wooden frame, what the shaggy clouds feel like being blown across the sky, what the walls felt like being splattered and smeared with wet paint. This last thought restores her to the present moment and Geoff's licking, and she realises she is about to come, again. Anna is embarrassed – an orgasm seems a vulgar interruption to an innocent, childish game – and she would like to abort, but already the tip is too steep. But as the first tremors reverberate through her, Geoff's cock starts to spasm in her mouth and, amazingly, having floated as separate as planets for twenty or thirty minutes, they come at exactly the same time.

In the late afternoon Geoff takes the car and disappears for two hours, returning with two bottles of red wine, a bag of vegetables, and a whole rabbit he bought from a hunter. He skins the animal himself, but his ambition exceeds his skill in the kitchen, and Anna does most of the cooking. It is just warm enough to sit on the terrace in jumpers, the sunset making a silhouette of the Tor, and while eating they tell each other stories, one long one each, delving deep into unknown terrain. It begins when Geoff says, without any precursor, 'I hate the countryside.' Anna laughs at the sudden remark, and he makes a speech about how the country, while ostensibly providing space and privacy, does precisely the opposite: it is almost entirely demarcated land, covered with fences and 'No Trespassing' signs, where governments and corporations can get away with their most audacious schemes and experiments, and where the harsh, scrutinising glare of village life makes it impossible for individuals to be the least bit subversive. 'I grew up in Gloucestershire,' he says, as if this explains everything. To capitalise on his effusive mood, Anna asks him questions. She asks if he went to private school, and is glad when he says that he didn't, though he says that he went to the kind of former grammar that may as well be private. He surprises her by saying he didn't go to university, as he was a rebel and failed his exams, and that he thought his family would never forgive him. She then asks about his daughter – who he hasn't mentioned once – which leads on to talk of the young girl's Argentinian mother. Anna asks if they were married, and he says they weren't, but that he was engaged to an Indian woman called Bhavna, who he lived with in London; he seems to gulp after saying her name.

'We don't have to talk about this,' says Anna, her interest creeping into jealousy.

'I don't mind.'

'Maybe *I* mind.'

'Well, indulge me. I want to talk about it. And it was twenty years ago.' He puts his knife and fork down, and says that he lived with Bhavna for a year in Brixton, while he was a trainee reporter with the *Evening Standard* and she worked as a junior doctor. They wanted to get married and decided to fly to Assam, where they would introduce Geoff to the extended family, gain approval for the marriage, then follow through with the ceremony, all in a two-week swoop.

'The trip started well. The Dhars seemed to accept me. Like me, even. But on the third afternoon things became complicated. The mother took me for a private cup of tea. "I don't care that you're English," she said. "And I don't care that you're not Hindu. All I care is that you visit the sage." And that's when she told me about Kundali. Have you heard of it?' Anna shakes her head, her mouth full of rabbit stew, and Geoff explains that it is a form of precision astrology, where a sage will use the birth details of an engaged couple – the location, date and time – to generate a number based on planetary alignment and the resultant levels of various energies: *vasya, yoni, tara, bhakoot, vasri.*

'This all seemed like nonsense to me, but Bhav's mother took it very seriously. She told me that when she was growing up, her elder sister wanted to marry a boy in their small town, but the sage said they had a dangerously low level of *mangal dosha*, and that the marriage would upset the gods so much that one of them would be dead within six months. They married anyway, and four months later the groom was killed in a car crash. She told me all this in one sitting, over a cup of chai, and I had no choice but to agree to see the sage the next day.'

Geoff looks away from the table and shakes his head.

'The results were not good.'

'They weren't?'

'Twenty-two out of a possible thirty-six. Apparently Bhav had low levels of *mangal dosha.* Which wouldn't be too bad, but I had no *mangal dosha* at all.'

'What is *mangal dosha*?'

'God knows. Just some made-up crap. But the sage said I had not one bit of it. He actually gave me a report on this cheap white paper, with the readings printed out. *Mangal dosha*: zero.'

'Shit.'

'They wouldn't approve the marriage, and her mother was afraid for Bhav's life, threatened to disown her if she went ahead against their wishes. Suddenly I was their daughter's potential murderer. It was all very dramatic. So we returned to London unmarried, and agreed to do it ourselves, in secret. But, for one reason or another, we didn't. We carried on living in Brixton, then I was given a chance to report on the war in Bosnia, which I took. For the next year I barely spent longer than a month in London, and Bhav moved to Greenwich to be near her hospital. And then we kind of drifted apart . . .'

Geoff is staring wide-eyed into the remains of the sunset. His stew is untouched, while Anna's plate is now empty, besides a few stony pieces that she thinks might be the shot that killed the rabbit. When she clears her throat Geoff startles, and looks about as if he doesn't know where he is.

'Sorry, I was miles away.'

'That's okay.'

'Years away, I should say. I got a bit immersed in the story.'

'I enjoyed it,' she says, honestly – her jealous feelings were manageable, easy to rationalise.

'Now you do some talking,' he says, taking his knife and fork. 'Tell me a story about *you*.'

'I can't compete with that.'

'Tell me anything. Just talk while I eat. When did you decide to be a journalist?'

Anna says it wasn't until fairly late, about four years ago. She did a twelve-week NUJ course, then got an internship at the website off the back of it. Eventually she was given a paid position as a sub-editor, then an assistant writer.

'I'd done bits and pieces before then. Freelance copy editing. Writing blogs. A six-week stint as a sub-editor at the *Hackney Gazette*. But mostly in my early twenties I was just bumming around, doing temp work when money ran low, and trying to . . . you know . . . do something *big*.'

'See? This is interesting,' he says, refilling both their glasses. 'What kind of things?'

She reminds him of the Community Shed idea, and he again says it's excellent, though he isn't sure about the name.

'You don't like Community Shed?'

'It's *alright*. But I think we could do better.'

They brainstorm quickly, each making puns on tool, shed, garden, ladder. After a minute some cogs turn in Anna's head.

'How about Tool Shared?' she says, and Geoff laughs.

'Perfect. Just perfect.'

'*The* Tool Shared? Or just Tool Shared.'

'Just Tool Shared. It's cleaner. What else have you got?'

Feeling energised, she tells him about the subterranean cycle tunnel in central London, and her idea for a gym where people's workouts would be turned into real power, to sell to the National Grid. Next she tells him about a combined old people's home and children's day care centre, where the elderly help look after kids, and her idea for transforming street phone boxes into charge stations for mobile phones. Geoff says they are charming, utterly charming.

'All the ideas have something societal about them,' she explains, 'or at least *social*. Even the silly small ones. I wanted to

produce this sling that would allow two people to sit opposite each other while leaning backwards, the opposing force
of each holding the other one up. Even that has a nice social
message at its heart.'

'It comes across loud and clear. You're a romantic. And an
idealist. So what happened?'

'Well,' she says, her mood becoming heavy. 'A few years
ago my dad died. And that kind of changed my outlook.' She
does her own wet-eyed stare towards the Tor, which is barely
perceptible now, and Geoff invites her to stop. But this time
she insists on continuing, and explains that her dad always en-
couraged her to be adventurous and take risks, and how he
used to send her bits of money – £300 here, £200 there – in
support. And then he died, and he transformed from a role
model into someone who just seemed like an overgrown kid.
He'd never settled down – Anna's mum was wife number one
of three – and for all his boisterous energy he never actually
did anything. At his funeral he was described as a teacher – a
supply teacher at that – and when executing the will she found
out how indebted he was: he owed money to banks, had mul-
tiple credit cards, used payday loan companies. She realised
that the bits of money he used to send her must have been bor-
rowed, perhaps thinking he was investing in something that
might eventually bring a return. 'That's when I signed up for
the journalism course and got serious. I decided I didn't want
to be like him. Not one little bit.'

By now the wine is finished and the last hint of daylight
has vanished; the table is no longer connected to the terrace
and garden and fields and hills beyond, but appears to be
floating in black space.

'Sorry,' she says. 'That was a bit much.'

'Not at all. I love the way you talk. You've got a writer's mind, and mouth.'

Anna can feel herself blushing, and makes a conscious effort to resist the urge to say something modest and deprecating, and instead to appropriate the compliment, to wear it like a piece of jewellery. She tells him that she is enjoying writing more. Even at work, she is enjoying writing more, and after her Sahina article she will be interviewing Gwyneth Paltrow, and maybe Meryl Streep.

'I don't mean *that*,' he says. 'That's not real writing.'

'Not this again. All writing is *real*. You still have to write words. And organise words into sentences, sentences into paragraphs.'

Geoff says it doesn't matter, that real writing has to be an expression of what the writer believes in, what they feel *inside*. He taps his fingers against his chest when he says this, pointing to his heart: a classic hippy.

'I'm doing the Twitter project as well. That was my idea. That came from *inside*.'

'Precisely. It's just a shame you don't really commit to it. That you don't do it full-time.' Anna tuts and rolls her eyes, but Geoff pushes onwards. 'Listen: I know you're concerned about money. But there are other ways of earning a living. For example, I was thinking about my project. We may well need some help with the writing. And there will definitely be money in that.'

She doesn't know what to make of this, and her face tells him as much.

'Surely you'll write it?' she asks.

Geoff appears bashful. He looks at his empty wine glass and says there might be an awful lot to write about, perhaps even enough for a book. 'We could really do with a female perspective. If you were interested . . .'

'And then you would be my boss?'

He shrugs.

'If that's how you want to put it.'

'I don't have a way to put it. That's the way it would be.'

He shrugs again, and then faces her with a hopeful, anxious expression that she hasn't seen before. For the first time he is saying something that projects an idea of the two of them together, maybe weeks and months and years in the future. She realises it is less of a job offer than a roundabout way of asking her to be with him, a step towards asking her to switch off.

'How much,' she says, and then stops – it has become difficult to speak, her lips feel strangely gummed up, immobile. 'How much work are we talking about, do you think? A few days? A week?'

'Oh, much longer than that,' he says, smiling at her, more sure of himself now, perhaps sensing she understands. The number 81 flashes above his head. 'We could string it out for months and months. Even years.'

'I'd have to see the contract,' she says, coyly, turning away from him.

'Come to my office and we'll write it.'

There is a silence now, and she knows the moment is upon them. She looks directly at him and tries to let her face go slack and blank, providing a large, neutral target for him to aim at. He inhales to speak and Anna's heart lifts further, but the air is exhaled as a sigh through his nose.

'More wine?' he says, scraping his chair backwards.

She watches him standing, unfurling his great height in

front of her, as the excitement suddenly collapses. The question couldn't be more different from the one she was braced for, but she finds she can use the same prepared phrase to answer it: 'I thought you'd never ask.'

Sunday

At around 1 p.m. the farmhouse is locked up and the key returned beneath the plant pot, and before leaving Anna and Geoff walk across the fields and then up the hill to the Tor. From close range the mediaeval tower appears less of an inland lighthouse than a steeple that has somehow become separated from the rest of its church. At the top of the hill they look back towards the red-brick farmhouse, about the size of a postage stamp. They stand like this for a time, a fresh breeze in their faces, his long arm around her shoulder. On the wave of an unusual feeling she almost tells him that she has been suffering from depression, that she has been taking pills for the last few months, and now plans to start weaning herself off them. But she keeps this inside and they ride the moment out in silence before heading back down the hill to the car. In Glastonbury town they wander around the lanes, Anna encouraging Geoff to buy the hippy and mystical tat on sale – tarot cards, a map of Camelot, a druid's hat. They have a roast lunch in a pub with several glasses of wine, Anna practising her questions for Gwyneth Paltrow in an American accent. On the drive home she is at first giddy – dancing with her fingers to Geoff's Ethiopian jazz and quizzing him on how much money he would pay her to join his project – and then sleepy. Near Salisbury she closes her eyes for a moment, and when she opens them the sky has changed colour and they are whizzing beneath an overhead sign for Heathrow, Slough, the M25.

'What?' she says, blinking, unsure where she is.

'There you are,' says Geoff, wearing sunglasses against the late afternoon glare. 'Since I have to do all the driving, you could at least keep me company.'

'Fuck,' she says, rubbing her eyes. Her tongue feels swollen, her head leaden, her mind clotted. She tries to rub the sleepiness from her eyes but she feels sedated, as if there is a weight pulling her downwards. 'I don't feel so good.'

Geoff makes another crack about Anna being selfish, but she isn't listening. As well as physical discomfort she has woken with a sense of unease, equivalent to having set off on a journey knowing you have forgotten something, but not yet knowing what that something is. She takes her phone from her jeans pocket and sees she has two missed calls from Pete and one from Zahra; it must have been vibrating against her leg while she slept. There is also a message from Zahra:

Pete called me and I told him you knew about the ring. I had to tell him something. You should go home as soon as possible.

The words burn away her drowsiness in seconds, and she knows the final blowout is about to happen, is already happening, without her. She feels a stab of displeasure that she hasn't signed off with Geoff yet, but perhaps it is naïve to try and stage-manage events like this; things will inevitably fall into place at their own speed.

'That's right,' says Geoff. 'Don't bother talking to me, look at your precious phone instead.'

Anna just stares through the windscreen at the factories and fields flickering by; she suddenly feels that the car is a cage, and that she is horribly late for something.

'My friend,' she says. 'She's in trouble.'

'Sounds interesting.'

'It's . . . a personal thing. I need to go and see her. Now.'

'You may have noticed I am driving us back to London.'

'Can you just drop me at the first tube station? I'll go on from there. This is urgent.'

Even as Geoff scoffs at this, she is searching on her phone for where this nearest station might be. She barely says another word to him for the twenty minutes it takes to get to Hammersmith, where he slows to a halt in the taxi rank outside the station.

'Just let me drive you home,' he says, perhaps for the tenth time. Anna doesn't even respond as she unbuckles her seat belt and looks around to check she has everything. Then she pecks him on the cheek – he seems helpless and confused – and says she will come to his after work tomorrow. Then she is out of the car and hurrying into the station. For the tube journey she wrings her hands and bites her nails, and then in Kilburn she almost runs along the pavement, swerving to overtake the dawdling pedestrians. But then, after rushing all the way home, she hesitates outside her own front door, with the key in her hand. She looks up at the two front windows of the living room, which glow red with the reflected sunset. Suddenly anything is possible. He might have done some thing terrible to the place, or to himself. She makes a conscious effort to control her breathing, then unlocks the front door. Inside, the hallway is gloomy, having darkened just beyond the threshold at which lights should be switched on.

'Pete?' she shouts. She strains her ears for a response but only makes out faint music that could be coming from David's ground-floor flat. As she climbs the stairs she sees that the kitchen and bathroom are empty, and can hear a more distinct version of the pop music playing in the living room.

'*Pete?*'

The door is ajar, and after taking three deep breaths she steps up and pushes it open. The room is empty. On the table is the usual arrangement of Pete's textbooks and notepads. A tinny version of 'Gypsy' by Fleetwood Mac is playing on the radio. Anna crosses the room to turn it off, and a small black something on the table beside the textbooks catches her eye. Immediately she knows what it is and her insides lurch like a vase pushed from a table. The small velvet cube fits snugly in her palm, and she pops it open and looks down upon the ring, just as she did that one time before, two months ago, and countless imagined times since. It looks different, somehow. The ring is darker in hue, almost bronze, and thinner than she recalls; likewise the diamond is sharper and less gaudy. It is amazing, how different it seems from the remembered image, despite the intensity of her recollections; perhaps each time she remembered the ring the mental creation must have been a slightly new imagined version, so that by tiny increments the memory diverged from the reality.

'Hello, Anna.'

She spins on the spot and sees Pete standing in the doorway. He is wearing his casual, stay-at-home jeans and T-shirt, and the lower half of his face is darkened with stubble.

'You scared me,' she says, with a hand on her chest.

'You did call my name.' He walks into the room but stops after a few steps and props himself on the arm of the sofa, still a good six feet from where she stands beside the table. 'Good time at your mum's?'

'Yes,' she says, the word sounding barely more substantial than a hiss. There is something sardonic about the way he is smiling at her, as if he knows she hasn't been to Bedfordshire, and she resolves not to let herself be cornered. She smiles back at him and says: 'And you? You've been revising?' She looks across at the calendar hanging above the television and sees the three squiggles of biro for each exam, the first of which is next week. But Pete doesn't answer this question, and instead nods towards her right hand, where she is holding the open ring box.

'Your birthday present,' he says. She holds up the ring as if it has just appeared in her hand and she is only now seeing it for the first time. 'But you knew that already, didn't you?'

She doesn't offer a reply, because it doesn't feel necessary; she just closes the ring box slowly, her fingers absorbing its clamlike bite. Eventually Pete sighs and says: 'We've always been nice to each other, you and me. We've always been . . . considerate. Whatever is going on, we should talk about it. It's not right, us living around each other like this.' He doesn't sound happy, by any stretch, but there is a solidity to his voice that makes him seem calm, authoritative. Maybe he was relieved to learn that she had discovered the ring, which to him must have instantly explained her recent behaviour. 'How did you find it, by the way?'

'Find what?'

'The ring.'

'Oh. I was looking for loose change.'

'In the pocket of my suit?'

'I was looking everywhere. I turned the whole flat upside down. I only needed 20p for some milk.'

'Milk,' he repeats brightly, as if he finds it amusing that all this should have been founded on something so trivial. 'It's quite amazing, actually. I only had it here for four days;

the rest of the time it was with Bean. Just *four* days. That was over two months ago.' Anna stares at her twined fingers and smart boots, says nothing. 'Two whole months. And you never thought to say anything.'

'I was trying to make a decision.'

'I see. So I suppose we can deduce that you weren't exactly bowled over by the idea?'

He says this with a brave smile, but there is an unmistakable sadness in his eyes, and for the first time she has the urge to go to him, to scrub out the cold distance between them. There is something inhuman about this empty six feet of space; this conversation – no matter how difficult and painful – should at least be delivered from a distance befitting the feelings that existed between them, that still exist. How nice it would be to go to him and make him smile by saying, quite honestly, that the answer was usually yes. In all the hundreds of times she posed herself the question, the answer was usually yes. But she can't do this. She is not that person any more. More to the point, he is not that man either. She thinks of Zahra's face blushing in the pub, the deleted messages on his phone. She places the ring box on the table and stands up straight to face him.

'I've had doubts.'

'About getting married?' says Pete, after a pause.

'About the whole thing.'

'See, this isn't so bad? We're *talking* about it. Good. So you had doubts. About what?'

This time Anna pauses, as she fumbles at a series of formulations in her mind; it is like they are speaking on a satellite phone. Eventually, she says: 'I doubted if we were happy. I doubted if we wanted the same things. I felt like we saw a lot of things differently. And I wondered if we were a good match for each other.'

'What made you think that?'

'I don't know,' she says. She senses that Pete is going to pump her for examples, is not going to allow her a single euphemism or generalisation. 'Loads of things. Our score.'

'Our score?'

'It's low.'

'No it's not.'

'Yes, it is; 70 is below the national average.'

'Well, what does that matter? It's just a computer-generated number. What matters is between me and you.'

'But the number is *about* me and you. You know it is. This is the first time we've mentioned the number in four years. It's like a taboo.'

'We haven't mentioned it *because* it isn't important. You're completely oversold on the whole thing.'

'Well,' she says, quietly, with a little shrug, 'I suppose that's one of the things we see differently.'

Pete doesn't reply to this, and it feels like she has won this point; he sinks into himself while searching for a new angle. And after a moment he does wag a finger, and reminds her that she used to say they complemented each other. She is ready for this, too.

'And maybe we did,' she says. 'But now I think we hold each other back.'

Predictably, Pete asks how so, and the only image that springs to mind is being in some sultry villa in Greece, drinking sugary espresso with silt at the bottom; she tells him she wants to travel and would like to live abroad.

'So do I,' he says. 'So does everyone.'

'But you want this *more*,' she says, moving her arm in a

vague sweep that is meant to encompass his textbooks, their flat, their entire lives in cold grey London. 'I'm serious. I don't want to wait until I'm retired to go on a cruise.'

He chews on this for a moment, and says: 'We could talk about moving overseas.'

'No, Pete,' she says, and she's had enough of this now, his questions, his demand for examples, his playing dumb. 'That's just one tiny thing. The point is we're different. We want different things. There are other people better suited to us. To you, as well. Girls that you have more in common with. Girls that want the same things as you. Surely you feel it too. I know you do.'

He makes a little disbelieving smile at her and asks if she's serious; she shrugs and says that she is.

'So let me get this straight,' he says, his smile gone. 'You're saying that you know – *for a fact* – that I'd rather be with other girls?'

His tone is pressuring her to doubt herself, but she thinks of Zahra and him at the dinner party, Zahra and him discussing botany and cooking, Zahra and him smiling and laughing together. She repeats that she does, and for the first time Pete loses his cool.

'How does that make any fucking sense? At all? To anyone?' He stands up from the sofa and takes a step towards her, jabbing a finger towards her chest. 'You found an engagement ring, and yet stand there accusing me of wanting to be with other girls. Please, explain to me how that works.'

The heat of his frustration is such that she turns away from him, and it takes her a moment to organise herself to respond.

'Because I found other stuff as well,' she says. 'I know about you and Zahra.'

His slow approach is halted as if he has walked into a pane of glass. There is a moment of blank confusion, as if time has stopped altogether, and then his face creases up and he says, simply: 'What?'

'Don't play dumb, Pete. I know you had a thing going on. And that you agreed to not see each other. I know all about it. She told me as much herself.' Pete looks like he's had the wind knocked from him. He takes a step back from her and begins rubbing his face vigorously. She thinks maybe this is the start of a blubbering confession, but when he removes his hands he just looks drained.

'Fuck me,' he mumbles. 'You've really lost it this time.'

'So you're denying it?'

'Yes I'm fucking denying it. It didn't happen!'

'Then why did you delete your messages?'

'What? You checked my phone?'

'There's a massive gap where the messages between you and Zahra should be. Why did you delete them?'

'I didn't delete anything.'

'Where are they, then?'

Again he stops and rubs his face, this time moaning in exasperation.

'We use WhatsApp as well. The same as everyone else.'

'You do?'

'Yes, Miss Marple. How does that fit with your genius theory?'

She scans her memory of him having WhatsApp back then, of them using it to track him down in Kew Gardens, but it doesn't seem to fit.

'Show me, then,' she says. 'Show me the messages.'

'No fucking way. You don't deserve it.'

'It will take ten seconds. Just show me the messages from last summer, and I'll take it all back.'

Pete turns away from her, and as he does so she sees a tension around his eyes, the same look of concern that Zahra wore in the pub. It seems that she has him cornered.

'Come on, Pete,' she says. 'What have you got to hide?'

Then he steps towards her, wearing a penitent look of sadness and contrition, and she knows it really is true, truer than she ever thought.

'Listen, Anna,' he says, his arms reaching out as if to take her into a hug. Without thinking about it she slaps him, for the first time ever – a good clean thwack.

'My best friend,' she says, her voice warped by a sob.

Pete is wincing in the wake of the slap, but then with a few blinks and a shake of his head he is back to normal, as if nothing has happened. 'Listen to me,' he says, through gritted teeth. 'I didn't do anything.'

He takes hold of her wrist, so she swings at him with the other one. He catches this as well, and now has hold of both of her writhing arms.

'Nothing happened,' he repeats, at point-blank range, his breath a hot wind in her face. 'You've got to trust me. We wouldn't do that to you. I promise. Look me in the eyes.'

He says many more things like this at high volume, as they step about the floorboards; David downstairs must be wondering what has got into the nice couple above him. Pete says the words 'love' and 'promise' and 'trust' over and over again, and also asks her to look him in the eyes. Eventually she does this, and they are close and wide enough for her to see the flecks of green around the pupils, and the tiny red veins in the white. He asks her to believe him, to trust him, and his earnest insistence is irresistible – she knows he isn't lying. After a time they stop their slow dancing steps around the floor, and her struggling arms fall slack within his hands.

Then they are just standing there, in a pose that could be thought of as affectionate. He says, softly now, that nothing happened, that he loves her and that he'd never do anything like that. Then he rearranges his hands so they are holding not her wrists but her clammy palms instead.

'Do you know what I'd like to do?' he says, in a new voice altogether, now forward-looking and friendly, as if he has just had a new idea. 'I'd like to go back in time. To turn the clock back to before you found the ring. No, even better: to before I even bought the ring. Can't we just do that? Can't we just pretend?'

She looks down at their hands and is surprised by how enticing this idea sounds.

'How about I just take the ring back and we forget all this craziness? We can use the money to go on a holiday instead. Perhaps Morocco or Sicily. Just you and me and the beach.'

The look in his eyes and his talk of a holiday has made Anna weak with nostalgia. The idea of lying on the beach and feeling the sun pressing down on their bare bodies like a dry weight fills her with such a powerful yearning that tears spill over her eyelids, and she is defenceless against Pete pulling her into his arms.

'Baby,' he says, kissing the damp side of her head. 'Baby, baby, baby.'

The room darkens as her face presses into the cotton of his T-shirt; through her nose she breathes air flavoured with sweat and the organic detergent he buys. Instinctively, her hands discover one another on the other side of his wide

317

back, and press into the padded flesh around his spine. Pete whispers that he has missed her, and Anna hears herself say that she has missed him too. It is amazing, to find that it still isn't over; despite all the supposedly irreversible decisions and actions, all she has to do is go upstairs with Pete, delete Kismet on her phone, and it will be as if none of this has happened. She searches within herself for the certainty that was hers an hour ago, or even a few minutes ago, that this life in Kilburn is merely a simulation, and that her real life with Geoff is just beginning. She pictures Geoff driving with stiff, fixed arms. She thinks of them looking down over London, the city a luminous cluster of stars. She thinks of kissing him under the awning of the jewellery shop. She thinks of the way he rotates his hand as he talks, and the dream of her dad, telling her not to be afraid. She thinks of the very first time she saw him standing before her, holding out his phone in front of him, showing her their number, the number 81. That does it. Heavy locks turn within her, and she is filled with the hardness and strength to end it, to end it now.

'Stop it, Pete,' she says. She pushes from his embrace and into clean air; the change feels elemental, like cresting the side of a pool. 'There's more. I've been using Kismet.'

'What?'

'I've been using Kismet. I wanted to test my feelings. To see how I felt about us. And I met someone.'

Pete doesn't even blink; he is utterly still. Before she has a chance to change her mind, she explains the rest. Feeling like her voice is coming from outside herself, she tells him she met an 81, that his name is Geoff, that he is a reporter too. These words sound unbelievable, even to her, so she takes her phone from her bag and shows him proof. She tells him she spent the night of her birthday with him, that she's spent most afternoons with him since, that she's been with him all weekend. She tells him he asked her to switch off, and she said yes. It only takes a moment to say and do all this, but a moment dragged out in a thicker, liquid time. When she falls silent Pete is seated on the sofa, his eyes pointing down to the space between his knees, as still as a statue.

'However you want to react,' she says, 'that's fine with me. It's your reaction.'

He still doesn't respond, and to fill the void she carries on talking. She tells him she didn't have a choice, that she's been depressed, that she doesn't belong in Kilburn or her job or her life, and that she needs to change. It is a long speech, bringing in her inventions and his love of food and her love of music and her dad and lots of other things beside. Then she tells him this is a good thing for him, too, that it is probably the best thing she could do to him; she has the presence of mind to recognise the absurdity of saying this to a man who appears frozen through shock. Eventually she crouches down in front of him, like a person trying to peer through the keyhole of a locked door. When she lays a hand on his knee and says his name, he finally reacts. He brushes her hand away and then pushes her whole body so hard that she falls on her side. Then he stands up and without a word leaves the room. The bathroom light twangs on and the toilet flushes and she can hear Pete coughing or heaving or maybe sobbing.

The next thing she knows she is seated on the sofa – time is moving strangely now – and listening to footsteps in the bedroom above. She hears the ladder creak and then Pete is standing in the doorway, a holdall on his shoulder.

319

'I don't know what to say,' he says, eventually. And then, as if to prove this, he opens his mouth and no words come out. Then he tries again, and says: 'I think you've made an awful mistake.'

Don't go, thinks Anna. For her part, she cannot speak at all, but despite her numb and mute state she still knows that it would be a terrible conclusion for Pete to leave with his holdall. It is late now, and if anyone leaves it should be her. But for some reason she is unable to turn these thoughts into words, and just stares listlessly at him.

'Goodbye, Anna.'

She wants to tell him to stay, but she's thinking at half speed, and before she's organised her thoughts she can hear him going down the stairs. She listens to each of his slow, heavy steps and braces herself for the slam of the door. But it doesn't come. There is instead a silence, and after a moment she realises he must be standing at the bottom of the stairs, thinking. After a moment she hears more footsteps, this time climbing up the stairs, and her whole body is flooded with relief to think that he is coming back, that it still isn't over. When he pushes open the living-room door she tries to conjure all her regret and contrition into her expression, but he doesn't see it. He walks straight to the table, picks up his textbooks and the ring, and then walks out again, without even looking at her. Then he is on the stairs again, this time taking them quickly and heavily, two at a time, before the door slams and he is gone.

Anna sits there with the same contrite look on her face, for the benefit of no one.

Monday

When Anna wakes she is alone in bed, and the room is filled with the pallid grey light of dawn. For a moment she doesn't remember what happened, and then she does: Pete is gone. She moans and turns her face into her pillow. Her bedside clock says 6.18 a.m.; at 11 a.m. she has to interview Gwyneth Paltrow. This seems a ludicrous idea; she feels barely capable of speaking to a ticket inspector or a cafe waitress, or even getting out of bed at all. It is like some vital organs have been wrenched from her, and the body that remains is merely an empty and fragile shell.

Last night she cried herself to sleep. She thought this was just an expression, but that's exactly what happened. When Pete left she began weeping, and the tears kept gathering strength and pace until they reached a kind of cruising altitude and refused to stop, even when she tried to distract herself with television, her phone, doing some washing-up. When they did finally abate she imagined it was because she had no more tears left. But when she climbed the ladder into the bedroom she immediately spotted the little dish of foreign coins, like a topological record of all their holidays, and a moment later she was lying face down on the bed, this time immersed in a fit of tears from which she didn't recover, but instead slipped directly into sleep.

Anna continues watching the clock move through 6.21 a.m., 6.22 a.m., 6.23 a.m., thinking she should text Stuart to say she is sick and that she will be staying in bed all day. But then, at 6.26 a.m., without consciously deciding to do so, she swings her legs from the bed and rises to her feet.

She goes to the toilet, showers, brushes her teeth, climbs back up the ladder, and around these modest achievements a sense of herself begins to gather; her insides regain their heft and shape. Once again she feels capable of basic tasks, such as walking down the street and buying things in shops and having conversations with Ingrid and perhaps even Stuart. But interviewing Gwyneth Paltrow? She pushes the idea to the side of her mind, to be dealt with in a few hours, and focuses on finding a clean pair of socks. There aren't any, and this discovery threatens to plunge her back into despair, until she decides to simply go without. Her feet are damp and swollen from the shower, and forcing them into the tough leather boots is a challenge – the fact that she succeeds is, Anna feels, another testament to her resilience and grit.

There is only one trendyish cafe on Kilburn High Road, and Anna orders poached eggs and asparagus, as a kind of conciliatory gift to herself. It is the same cafe where she and Pete came after being shown their flat by the estate agent over three years ago; she remembers him saying that this place was evidence that Kilburn was about to take off, that the high road would soon be filled with similar purveyors of the organic and free range, locally sourced and ethically procured. Being reminded of this doesn't bring the threat of more tears, and she is able to concentrate on reading through the Gwyneth questions, and then putting the list face down on the table and reciting them from memory. She does this without hesitation, and decides that the questions are better than the ones for Sahina, with the brand values more subtly placed – this time she will hold her nerve and ask each one, regardless of how Gwyneth responds.

It will be fine, she decides, and in the wake of this optimistic thought she notices that the coffee she is drinking is unusually delicious. Most of the dozens of coffees she drinks each week pass by without so much as a thought, but every so often one like this stands out and grabs her with how sweet and rich and fragrant it is – it feels like all those other coffees are justified by these rare moments of sensory delight. She raises the mug towards her face and studies the brown dissolving microfoam, as if within the evaporating pattern she might detect the secret of its quality. The remaining foam looks like a series of white and gold islands in a brown sea, as they would appear from a plane passing overhead, and maybe these two things – coffee foam and archipelagos – are indeed subject to the same natural laws, just on a scale several million times removed. This same pattern probably repeats itself at even more extreme scales as well, can probably be detected in entire galaxies and also molecules and atoms too small for even a microscope . . .

This thought feels like a miniature revelation, and the fact that it occurred to her at all is a sign that her best self is returning. Her mood lifts further when golden light creeps across her table, and she sees that the sun has burnt through the early morning clouds. She pushes away her half-eaten plate of food and asks for the coffee to be transferred to a paper cup.

There aren't any benches on Kilburn High Road, since no one besides weary shoppers would want to dwell there, so Anna sits in a bus shelter opposite the station, sipping her coffee and feeling the sun on her face, thinking that she must be over the worst. The despair of last night and early this morning has now passed, and her deeper instincts are coming to the surface. There are three other people at the bus stop, and she remembers the guy that looked like her dad and sang to her a few weeks ago. She would love it if he approached her again, right now, but something like that never happens in Kilburn, which feels exclusively reserved for the predictable, the drab. *Kilburn*, she thinks. It's like the name itself – along with Balham, Clapham, Dulwich – is a protective measure against anything interesting happening there. She imagines vocalising this to Geoff, knowing that he would reply with a ready-made speech on the topic, something about the dull nomenclature being a deliberate means of keeping the residents sedate. She pictures him sitting beside her at the bus stop and is filled with an excitement that makes her feel dizzy. She has barely thought of him since he dropped her off in Hammersmith, and for a second it strikes her as unusual that he hasn't texted her. But they have been in contact during this time, via some invisible and indefinable channel, and the idea of him is now returning to her stronger than ever. She knows, without the slightest doubt, that she's made the right decision. And not just for her – for Pete, too. Even if nothing did happen between him and Zahra, he should ultimately be with a successful and sensible middle-class girl, someone who wants the same things as him. On some level he knows this too.

This thought of Pete threatens to drag down her mood, so she takes a final sip of coffee and thinks of Geoff again. The weekend they spent together, the job he offered her, the fact that they could soon be living and working and planning a shared future, starting with their next meeting, just eight or nine hours away. This feels like a vast span of time that has to be bridged, and she impatiently stands up and throws away her coffee and hurries across the street, as if wanting to rush through the day to get to him quicker.

At 8.21 a.m. Anna enters her office building, and the fact she is greeted by the security guard rather than the receptionist proves this is the earliest she has ever arrived. And indeed, when the lift bears her upwards to the third floor, she is delighted to be met with an entirely empty office. The only movement and life is from the big board, which has been ticking away and refreshing all night, like traffic lights at a deserted junction. It is surprising to see that her Sahina article has vanished from the rankings entirely, but this just makes her more focused on the task in hand. She settles down with her questions and practises reciting them again, in reverse order, and still has time afterwards to answer some Twitter messages before Ingrid finally appears beside her.

'I did it!' she says, spinning her chair around to face Ingrid and holding her arms aloft. 'I've beaten you. I'd like to thank my family, my friends and most of all God.'

Ingrid smiles at this but doesn't say anything, and then puts both her hands on the back of her chair. She isn't wearing her coat or carrying her bag, and the screen of her computer has the little green standby light on.

'Wait, you have been here?'

Ingrid glances at Anna, her smile now gone, and then looks over her shoulder towards the meeting rooms at the end of the floor.

'You need to speak to Stuart,' she says.

'You've been with him this whole time? What's going on?'

Ingrid is still gripping the backrest of her chair with both hands, and her frown deepens and her lips purse tightly; it looks like she might cry.

'Oh, Anna!' she says.

It is clear that something is seriously wrong, and without thinking about it Anna is up and on her feet and walking towards whatever it is. As she strides across the clearing she can see Stuart sitting in the Quiet Room, his back to the glass, and then she is pushing into the room, her heart everywhere at once.

'Hey, Stu,' she says, taking a seat opposite him. 'Ingrid says you want to speak to me.'

He is sitting in front of his laptop, and for a second he holds the frozen pose of someone interrupted in the middle of a task. Beside him on the table is a black attaché case that she has never seen before. Then, still without looking at her, he bites his bottom lip and closes the laptop.

'Anna, Anna, Anna, Anna,' he says. 'Yes, I'm afraid that I do.'

His eyes meet hers for a second, then he taps his finger ponderously against his closed lips. Slanting sunlight is entering the window behind her and cleaving the room along a diagonal into two distinct halves: the light and the dark.

'Can we get on with it?' she says, checking her watch. 'I'm going to be late for my interview.'

'No, you're not. For once you're not going to be late for anything.'

'Oh?' says Anna, a tight feeling spreading across her chest. 'Why's that?'

'Because Ingrid will be going instead. Anna, we've had some issues over the weekend.'

He flips open the black attaché case and tosses a ream of

paper across the table to her. She turns it the right way round and sees it is a printed email from Paula to the guys at Romont and to Clem, saying they will be taking immediate disciplinary action against the journalist in question.

'What the . . .'

The next page in the ream is a much longer email, consisting of one huge paragraph in which many words and phrases have been capitalised and emboldened. Anna's eyes jump around the text, impatient to grasp the gist, and she has to turn the page again before seeing it is an email from Sahina Bhutto, addressed to Clem. It says that a major project she is planning in China is under threat because of offensive quotes about government officials that were EXPLICITLY OFF RECORD and that the writer HAD NO RIGHT WHATSOEVER TO REPEAT.

Anna's face is burning, her forehead especially.

'But it's not true,' she says. 'She never said—'

'Keep reading, Anna.'

Sahina explains that the quoted statement was made while the interview was interrupted by one of her employees, to whom the comments were addressed. The matter discussed was not initiated by the journalist and could IN NO WAY be considered part of the interview. It also says that the journalist appeared disorganised and distracted, and she suspects that this might be the reason for the mistake. She rounds off with a threat of possible legal action if the China project does indeed collapse, and a general reflection on the decline of journalistic standards.

'Is it true, that she said them to someone else?'

'Um,' says Anna. The pages are quivering in her hand. 'She kind of said them to both of us.'

327

He chews on this and folds his arms.

'She's not serious about suing, is she?'

'The legal team have been over it and they don't think she has grounds. The bigger problem is that she sent this to Romont, and now they are threatening to pull the whole series unless we take swift action.' He glances at her as he says this.

'You're going to fire me?'

'I'm sorry, Anna. My hands are tied. We have to suspend you, with immediate effect.'

Anna looks down at her knees, also shaking slightly. Official confirmation of disaster makes her feel nauseous. Beyond Stuart's head, the office is beginning to fill up. Mike and Beatrice are walking across the clearing, sharing a joke as they unbutton their jackets. Ben from sports emerges from the dark recess of the kitchenette with a filled cafetiere. The door to the landing opens and another guy enters, one of the many people she knows well enough to smile at but not to exchange any words. They all look so excessively carefree and cosy, inhabitants of a world that Anna has been ejected from permanently, never to return. In the centre she can see the back of Ingrid's head, beside her empty desk, and the sight makes her grief and shock harden into bitterness.

'You told me to put those quotes in,' she says. 'It wasn't my idea.'

'I asked if it was off the record.'

'You asked me if she said it.'

'You knew what I meant. Or at least you should have done. But listen: I do accept I am partly to blame. You clearly weren't ready to take on this kind of responsibility. Paula asked me at the start if you could handle it, and I said that you could. That was my mistake.' He smiles at her in a consolatory, pitying way. 'That's why we're not firing you. It is a suspension, perhaps for one month or two, until this blows over. Paula says she will try and find you something else, something less senior. Perhaps a team assistant role.'

'An assistant?'

'Most likely in another team, on another floor. But we don't have to make a decision now.' He is still smiling, and it occurs to her that he is happy; perhaps this is precisely what he wanted all along, for her to mess up so he could get rid of her.

'You don't have to find me something else. I'm going to quit.' This sends his chin backwards into his neck. 'I've been offered another job, anyway. A proper writing job.'

'Anna, I think you should take some time—'

'No thanks. I don't need any of your suggestions. As far as I'm concerned this is entirely your fault. I never wanted to include those quotes. I didn't want to even ask those questions. This is all down to you, and you're just blaming me because you haven't got the . . . balls to face up to it.'

He looks shocked and holds out a calming hand.

'Anna, please don't use that kind of—'

'No,' she says, almost shouts, standing up from the desk. 'I'll say what I want. Fuck you. And fuck this stupid process you call journalism. It isn't journalism at all, it's just prancing around to please corporate clients. You wouldn't know an interesting piece of writing if it was jammed up your arse.'

Stuart's eyes are wide in shock.

'I'm not going to be the assistant to anyone in this place. I'm going to be a real writer. Writing about things that actually matter.' She taps her finger against her chest as she says this, in the rough vicinity of her heart. 'See you around. And thanks for the chat.'

With that she rounds the table and pushes back through the glass door. As she crosses the clearing she sees that Ben and Jessica and Mike are all watching her, are not even trying to hide it; her voice must have carried out of the room. Before she reaches her desk Ingrid turns in her chair, a broken, tragic expression on her face. Anna smiles at her, then at all the watching faces, projecting total serenity. It feels fitting that she is the centre of attention; maybe this is how her life will be from now on. It would be nice to have one of those boxes to carry her belongings, but there is nothing of hers on the desk other than her phone, her accomplice in sin. She slips this into her bag in exchange for her ID card, and then takes her coat and walks across the clearing, perhaps for the last time.

'Don't look so sad, everyone,' she says, turning at the door, feeling the need to say something to all the shocked faces watching her, including Ingrid, who is following her out. 'You'll be seeing me again.'

Anna arrives back on Kilburn High Road just before 11 a.m. In one sense it feels strange to be back so soon, and in another rigorously simple: she left to go to work, and now is back again, having been fired. No: having quit, she tells herself. This makes her feel slightly better, though she is still irked by the sight of the shops and businesses and buildings of Kilburn that she had mocked just a few hours ago; they now appear to be laughing at her in revenge, their windows and doorways so many grinning teeth. She hurries along the street with her head down, and it is a relief to turn onto the quiet side street and then be encased in the silence of her flat. But once she has taken off her coat and dropped her bag and

sat down, she finds she cannot relax. Her nerves are singing, and the image of Stuart's face keeps forcing itself into
her mind. She paces around the living room and hallway and
kitchen, each room as silent and lifeless as a morgue, and feels
an almost physical need to speak to someone. Her instinct is
to call Zahra, but things are too weird between them at the
moment. She obviously can't call Pete either, and she tells
herself she should ring Geoff instead. But she doesn't want
to. It is far too early in their relationship to burden him with
such news, especially since they haven't even switched off.
This thought stops her still in the middle of the living room,
wondering why this is and what's holding him back. She can
sense panic rising within her, and she grabs her old laptop
from the bedroom and leaves the flat again, barely ten minutes after entering.

This time she confronts the high road head on and, to prove
that she's fine, goes back to the trendy cafe and takes the exact
same window seat as she did that morning. Keeping busy is the
key to blocking out thoughts of Stuart and Sahina, and first of
all she writes an email to the *Guardian* journalist, suggesting
that they meet for coffee sometime this week. Then she checks
Twitter, sees she has no new messages, and logs on to her online banking instead. She looks at the various numbers for a
long time. Standing orders. Direct debits. Overdraft limits.
ISA savings accounts. She does some rough calculations on the
laptop's calculator and realises she will have to ring Pete soon
to discuss mortgage repayments, and what they're going to do
with the flat. Then her phone buzzes with a message from Ingrid, saying she is so shocked and sad she can't think straight.
It is just a shorter version of what Ingrid said on the street two
hours ago, as they hugged goodbye, and Anna replies with a

shorter version of what she said then: that she really was planning to quit anyway, that she already has another job lined up, and a meeting with a *Guardian* journalist about the suitcase project. The message sends and she tells herself that these things really are true, that Geoff has offered her another job and that she will probably meet the journalist, but for some reason these facts don't diffuse calmness or satisfaction – there is something slippery about them, as if they lack foundations. Once again her thoughts are directed to the fact that Geoff and her haven't switched off, and she decides that this is what she needs to feel grounded. Never mind that it should come from him, and take place in a romantic setting – she wants it to happen right now, as soon as possible. Her phone is still in her hand, and she opens Kismet and calls Geoff.

'How are you?' he says, answering almost immediately. 'I was worried yesterday afternoon.'

'I'm okay, thanks. I'm . . . good.'

'Really? You don't sound fantastic. How did you get on with Ms Paltrow?'

Anna is silent for a moment, then says: 'Geoff, are you busy right now?'

'Unfortunately so. I'm in dratted Vauxhall.'

'I was hoping I could see you.'

'Is everything alright?'

'Yes, everything is fine. I just need to talk to you about something. Can you finish early?'

He still sounds concerned, but she assures him again that she is fine, and through a quick negotiation they agree to meet at his flat at 4 p.m. Without even dropping her laptop at the flat she heads to the station and takes the Bakerloo and Northern lines to London Bridge. Her plan is to first of all kill time at Borough Market, but this is a bad idea. Every single item on every single stall – the hanging legs of ham, the piles of dead fish, the stacks of organic vegetables – reminds her of Pete, and she instead buys a coffee and walks south towards Elephant and Castle. She wanders around the shopping centre by the station, past the brands – Clarks, Thomas Cook, W. H. Smith, McDonald's, Argos – that are as familiar and deep-seated as family members, as her earliest memories. This is the kind of place she belongs, she thinks, rather than Borough Market. This is an unfortunate idea, since it reminds her that she is a provincial nobody who has been pretending to be a smart London professional, and has finally been uncovered as a fraud. She leaves the shopping centre, as if chased out by this unpleasant notion, and browses instead the market stalls that spread around and below the station. She walks past scarves and saris and piri-piri chicken and mobile phone covers and cheap trainers and jogging pants, feeling totally invisible, vaporous. She tells herself that this is what Geoff said freedom feels like, and that in order to escape the confines of her old life she had to destroy it. She tries to project her thoughts forwards to some future idyll, Geoff and her in the villa on a Greek or Italian island, but these brave thoughts skim the surface of her anxiety and do not dislodge the sickly, nervous feeling. At one point she catches herself gawping at a stall of luminous sweets, and to justify her weird behaviour she buys a foot-long red liquorice lace, which she sits down on a bench to eat. When she finishes she resumes walking around, and can't stop grinding her teeth.

At 3.56 p.m. she enters the atrium of Strata SE1, and her stomach does an even more intense version of its usual

333

plummet as the lift bears her up to the twenty-second floor. When she knocks at flat 176 Geoff opens the door immediately.

'Darling,' he says, in a mock jolly tone, his white teeth gleaming. But his smile falters when he sees her, and he steps back from the door and says she'd better come in.

She follows him along the hallway and into the open living space, and he asks if she wants a drink. She says no, but he drifts into the kitchen anyway, leaving her standing with one foot in the tiled kitchen and one in the carpeted lounge. Geoff tells her to make herself at home, and she says thanks; there is so far a conspicuous absence of joviality. She takes off her coat and finds that removing her boots is a struggle; when they finally pop off she is surprised by her bare feet, and remembers not being able to find socks this morning. The white skin is a raw pink where the leather has pinched and rubbed. Geoff has gathered several bottles, a tumbler and ice on the kitchen island, and Anna grows impatient.

'I wanted to talk to you about something,' she says.

'I gathered that much,' he says, clinking ice into the glass. 'I'm not a complete idiot.'

'I've been thinking,' she says, unsure how to continue, 'about things.'

'It looks like you've been doing more than just thinking,' he says, carrying his drink, a short lemony something, to where she stands. 'You look a little . . . frazzled.'

'It's nothing bad.'

'No?'

'No. I've just been thinking about work. And about writing. And about what you said about us working together. On your project. And I decided that . . . I'd like to give it a try.'

334

His eyebrows jump in surprise, and he says right, and great, and comes to hug her.

'That's not all,' she says. 'I've been thinking that if we were to do that, it would mean us spending a lot of time together. It would mean us . . . carrying on what we've started. Carrying on . . . seeing each other. Being together.'

A new concern spreads across Geoff's face.

'And how do you feel about that?'

'I feel great about it,' she says, and he smiles. 'Really great.'

'Excellent,' he says. 'Me too.' He puts his drink down on a side table and comes at her with his arms ready for another hug, as if they have reached the resolution of the conversation. She steps backwards away from him.

'Geoff, there's still more. If we feel this way, about each other, then there's something we should do together. Don't you understand what I'm getting at?'

The dark cleft between his eyebrows indicates he does not, and Anna realises she will have to talk him through it; she regrets the unromantic circumstances, and wishes they'd done this in Somerset.

'Geoff. We met using Kismet.'

'I'm aware of that.'

'And, as far as I know, we're both still using Kismet.'

'I understand that.'

'So we're both still getting matches. Only I'm not looking for anyone else.'

Geoff blinks a couple of times.

'You're not?'

'No! Are *you*?'

'No. No, I'm not.' He smiles at her and she sees that, amazingly, he still doesn't get it.

335

'When people aren't looking for anyone else, they switch off Kismet. Together.'

'I've heard about that,' he says, nodding.

'So? Is that what you want?'

He appears to think for a moment before giving the question back to her: 'Is it what *you* want?'

Her annoyance is such that she can't bear to look at him, and she says, 'For God's sake,' and turns on her heel. Through the kitchen's glass wall she can see the Shard, the only nearby building of comparable size – the sight of lifts gliding up and down makes her insides wobble.

'It's just that you seem so *fraught*,' he says. 'I want to make sure you really mean what you say.'

'We're an 81,' she says, turning back to face him. 'Do you know how rare that is?'

'I have an idea, yes.'

Just saying the number makes tenderness replace her momentary annoyance, and she steps towards him and takes his hands.

'I couldn't be more certain,' she says. 'About anything.'

Geoff looks down at their joined hands and smiles.

'Okay,' he says. 'Let's do it.'

'Okay.'

'Now?'

'Yes. Now.'

Anna smiles back and follows him to the bedroom, where he says his phone is. She sits on the side of the bed with her phone in her lap, but Geoff can't find his, and leaves again. She sits watching the southern view of London, a textured map in which the west-facing walls are brightly lit by a resurgent sun.

'Found it,' says Geoff, coming back in with a chunky, red-backed device that surprises Anna, since it is different from the phone he had when they met. She realises she hasn't seen him hold a phone since those very first moments in Vauxhall.

'Right then,' he says. 'Talk me through it.'

He sits on the other side of the bed, and they face each other like card players, their phones held up to their chests.

'Okay,' she says. 'Are you on Kismet?'

'Not yet.'

'Well, get on it. Okay? Now, select options.'

'Right.'

'Do you see where it says "Close account"?'

Geoff peers at his screen, and Anna is struck by how old he is; she isn't finding this romantic in the least.

'"Close account",' says Geoff. 'Press that, do I?'

'And then press "Confirm". Now, see that it's asking if you're linking with one of your matches?'

'Uh-huh.'

'Click "Yes". Then find my name.'

'Anna 81.'

'That's right. Press that.'

'And you're doing this too?'

'Yes!' She turns her phone around to prove it. 'Then click "Confirm" again, and it's all over.'

'Just like that?'

A short silence as both make the final steps. Anna hits her thumb three times through 'Geoff 81', 'Confirm' and 'Double confirm'. Then her screen fills with a short animated congratulations, and the whole app shrinks and disappears from her screen.

'That's it?' says Geoff. 'We've done it?'

337

Anna nods, says they've done it, and Geoff sighs theatrically and falls back onto the bed.

'Well done, Anna,' he says. 'It's all over. You've done great.'

Hardly the words she had expected, but at least there is relief and happiness in his voice. It is hard not to think of the same moment she had with Pete, his proposition delivered with flowers and champagne. Eventually Geoff stands and walks around the bed, before kissing the top of her head and leaving the bedroom. Again, not what she expected, but who is she to judge, since she barely feels happy herself; she mainly feels drained and numb. She looks again at the glass wall and sees the shadows have risen like liquid up the eastern-facing walls since she last looked; in another hour or so the individual buildings will be invisible. She keeps watching the view for long enough for some of the buildings to become lost to shadow, but still Geoff doesn't return. She can't hear anything from the bathroom next door, and decides to give him another minute, before leaving the bedroom. She is surprised to find him sitting in an armchair in the living area, doing nothing. When he sees her enter he comes to life.

'Hello, Anna,' he says, in an unusual tone, as if this is the first time he has seen her today. 'Come and take a seat.' He aims a flat palm at the sofa opposite him. 'There's something I need to tell you. Something important.'

'What is it?'

'Please. It's really better if you sit down.'

She steps into the sunken, carpeted lounge area and sits on the sofa. Geoff studies her with a blank expression. Her first thought is of his daughter in Argentina, and that maybe he is going to say she actually lives in Bromley, or that he has a second wife and child elsewhere. Immediately she decides this is bearable, that she can cope with it, and that this is a natural time to exchange their secrets; once he's finished she can tell him about Pete.

'There's no easy way to say this,' he begins. 'So I'm just going to come out with it. But I think you should try and keep an open mind. And try and see how, on the whole, this doesn't actually make a difference to you and me.'

'It's okay, Geoff. Just tell me.'

'Very well. We're not an 81 match. On Kismet. In actual fact we have a much lower score. A 62.'

Silence. His words are nonsense, and as such they bounce off the plane of her consciousness; after a few seconds it is as if he hasn't said anything.

'What are you talking about?'

'I've been carrying out an investigation. My secret project has been about Kismet. My colleague, Dmitri, hacked the system so every match I get is an 81. I've been tracking the results.'

Another silence, into which Anna hears herself laugh.

'I don't believe you.'

'I don't suppose you do. But I promise, it's the truth.' He leans forwards and taps his finger against the glass coffee table. His eyes hold hers with calm authority; there is no apology or pity in them. '*This* is the investigation. We wanted to show the effect that the number has on people. So I made several 81 matches, and you were the one I decided to go with. For several reasons . . .'

Anna laughs and says she doesn't believe him again, but she is beginning to feel the world turn around her, as if the skyscraper is rotating or being shaken by the wind.

'You see why I couldn't tell you? And why you had to be

the one that suggested switching off? I know this is a shock, but try and think about it. I want us to work together on this, we could—'

'Why are you saying this?' she says, standing up from the sofa. Her voice wavers, while Geoff appears utterly calm. Without breaking eye contact his hand goes into his pocket and takes out a phone, which he passes up to her.

'See for yourself.'

She takes it from him and sees this isn't the phone he just had in the bedroom; this is larger and thinner, like the one she remembers him having in Vauxhall.

'Open Kismet,' he says. 'Go onto connections.'

She follows his instructions, and a list of names appears on the screen:

Josie 81

Elinor 81

Anna 81

Sita 81

Anne-Marie 81

The list goes on but Anna reads no further; the words blur as if sliding underwater and she lets go of the phone; it clatters against the table top and falls to the carpet. She thinks she might be sick, and turns and walks away from the sofa. Geoff asks where she's going but she doesn't answer, just keeps on towards the bathroom, but the sight of the glass wall and the city beyond fills her eyes, and the idea of the sheer drop down to the distant street hits her like a punch in the stomach, turns her legs to water, and she falls to the carpet. Geoff calls her name and a second later is helping her to her feet.

'Don't touch me!' she says. 'I'll scream if you touch me!'

She makes it to her feet and goes to the bedroom, thinking she will get her phone and leave, but once in there she feels dizzy again and decides to lie down for a moment. Perhaps she sleeps for a time, for the next thing she knows the light has changed – the glass wall is now dark, the city a spread of tiny white and yellow lights – and Geoff is sitting on the edge of the bed, in the middle of a speech. He is talking about Wikileaks and the Cypherpunk movement, how he's been vaguely involved with each for years, but never led any of his own projects.

'But as soon as they launched Kismet I knew this was what I wanted to do. It struck me as the culmination of our dominant ideology; the fulcrum, the godhead. It trades on the additional ghostly something that all commodities have, the intangible extra that all products share: "Just do *it*." "*It's* the real thing." "I'm loving *it*." This *it* is powering the profiles. All Kismet is doing is matching people with a few things in common; the rest just happens in a person's brain. Ask any psychoanalyst – the human mind can fill any shortfall with its own invention; it's a real chancer, an opportunist. So we set about hacking into the system to find a profile, to unpick the algorithm. But we couldn't find one! After almost a year of trying to find a hole in their system, Dmitri admitted defeat – we concluded that the profiles were so well guarded they couldn't be stolen or, even more interestingly, that they don't actually exist.'

Anna wants to get up and leave the flat, but she feels immobilised. He continues talking about how, for all their supposedly scientific evidence, Kismet has never been tested against a placebo, and they have never released a profile for independent scrutiny. He doesn't doubt that the European

Court decision to make Kismet release people's profile data will be overturned on appeal, as it has been many times before. He says that's why they decided to stage their own experiment, so that they could use the results as an exposé and put Kismet on the back foot.

'But that's why I need you to help me write it. It's *your* story, as much as mine. People will listen to you. Together we could dissect the whole system.'

Anna sits up against the padded headboard. She still feels nauseous, but is at least in control of her motor functions, and this makes her want to get away from him as quickly as possible. He is talking about ideology again, and Anna swings her bare feet off the bed, finds the floor, pushes herself upright.

'Where are you going?'

'I'm leaving.' Her voice sounds reassuringly solid. 'I don't want to be here.'

'I know you're upset,' he says, following her out of the bedroom. 'That's natural. But you have to keep an open mind and listen to what I'm saying. This is exactly what you said you wanted: to be part of an interesting project, to write something important. You're meeting that *Guardian* journalist; this is exactly the kind of story you could sell them.'

Anna walks away from him. The ground wobbles beneath her, but she manages to get to the sofa, though her boots aren't where she left them.

'And you have to keep in mind that nothing has changed between us,' he continues, following her. 'All the time we've spent together. The fun we've had. The sex. That hasn't changed at all. Unless, that is, all I am to you is the number.'

'Not just a number. You're a fraud, as well. I might call the police myself.' She looks behind the armchair and sofa, but still can't see her boots. He follows her around, tells her that it is definitely not illegal, that all the hacks happened in Russia and that the police couldn't touch him.

'Criminal or not, you're still a fucking liar.'

'But I haven't lied.'

The gall of this makes her stop still, and she wheels around to face him.

'You haven't *lied*? The whole thing has been a lie.'

'Only the number! And the number is a fabrication anyway. We just switched a made-up percentage for another made-up percentage. Why trust one over the other? The only real thing you can trust is the time we spent together. It was a person, *me*. I am the person you decided to be with.'

Anna considers this. The number 62 flashes above his head, and with it she sees more clearly the loose skin hanging from his neck, his arrogant demeanour, the simulated poshness of his voice. It is like these imperfections have sprouted from him in the last few minutes.

'Don't play their game and think of me as a number. Think of the time we spent. Think of the things we have in common. These are real things, experiences that happened between us, as two people. Don't let them interfere with that.' He continues talking, says that the only way to escape the ideology is to step right out of it, to go against what their numbers are telling her. His speech does send her mind back to the time they spent together, and one memory in particular – the loose skin around Geoff's neck becoming inflamed and rigid during sex. The image is repulsive. Anna stops listening before the end of his speech, wanders about, opens a squat wooden cabinet that might contain a shoe rack. Inside there are several bottles of spirits.

343

'Is that really all I am to you?' says Geoff, following her around. 'A number?'

'No, you're not a number,' she says. 'You're nothing to me. Now: where the fuck are my boots?'

Elephant and Castle is still busy, but has switched to its evening routine. The market stalls have been packed away and the shuffling old women have been replaced by swift, suited commuters, who rush along the pavement from tube to bus, bus to tube. Anna floats through them and into the brightly lit shopping centre. The vinyl tiles beneath her feet are refreshingly solid and strong, and it is a relief to be at ground level. The floor feels so robust that her legs are precariously flimsy in comparison; it seems possible that they might buckle beneath the pressure of each downward step. She proceeds, one step at a time, past the Body Shop and Clarks, and suddenly recalls those school shoes, with the Velcro straps and the ladybird prints, and another time when she went to buy Doc Martens with her dad in Bedford and burst into tears in the shop. She continues deeper into the shopping centre and her aimless drift is rewarded with a discovery: rather than ending after the long row of shops, the building opens up into a huge supermarket. Or maybe it is a hypermarket – it certainly seems as big as the French giants she was taken to on childhood holidays, with ceilings as high as a warehouse and shelves stacked well above head height. This surprising find makes her think of the gymnasium beneath Somerset House, and she laughs.

'Life is full of treasure,' she says, while taking a trolley. She glides past sloping banks of pears, apples, bananas, and then snakes in and out of the aisles – dairy, red meat, poultry and

344

fish – feeling she is turning corners in her own internal space, her own consciousness, which she decides is infinite.

Everything is relative, she thinks, and everything is up for grabs. She could do anything she likes, starting right now. She could take £100 from a cash machine and spend the evening raving at the Ministry of Sound, just over the road. She could slide a bottle of whisky into her bag and spend the night in a police cell. She could go back to Kilburn and order pizza and if the delivery boy is even remotely good-looking she could go down on him, right there in the hallway. She could go to Bean's house in Brixton and ask if Pete's there. She could go down to the tube and jump in front of the first incoming train. She could go back to Kilburn, grab her passport, get a taxi to Heathrow, buy a flight to Sydney on her credit card, fly there, get a bus to her brother's district, find his house, knock on his door and, when he answers, say, 'Surprise.'

'Excuse me, dear, is everything okay?'

A large woman in a luminous green fleece is blocking her way. Anna realises she is in Asda – another brand as familiar as an aunt or an old school teacher. Anna smiles and says she's great, but the woman steps towards her and puts her hand on her upper arm.

'Maybe you would like to sit down for a bit? We could go out the back.'

Anna tells her again that everything is fine, that there's nothing to worry about, but she does like the sound of going out the back. She abandons her trolley and follows the woman, telling her she worked at Sainsbury's as a teenager. They push through double doors to the supermarket's backstage, where it is suddenly as cool and dark as a church, and the pretence of cleanliness and order and cheerfulness falls away. Flattened

345

cardboard boxes are stacked next to a monstrous baler, and a forklift truck is parked next to a leaning tower of shrink-wrapped boxes. They step into the relative normality of a low, cramped office, and Anna is given a tissue, while the woman makes a cup of tea. Anna tells her about the last twenty-four hours – how she has lost Pete, her job and now Geoff. But she does so obliquely, using an elegant analogy that she is immediately proud of. She talks of an ivy plant that was attached to the side of the house she grew up in, and how it survived all weather for years, but one day, on a whim, she decided to give it one good tug, which snapped its roots and killed it. The woman places a cup of tea in front of Anna and sits beside her, pressing her dark fingers into Anna's forearm. She doesn't respond to the ivy story, and is studying Anna with a worried expression that seems entirely misplaced.

'I'm fine, really,' says Anna. To prove it she picks up the tea and takes a sip. It is surprisingly sweet; the woman must have stirred sugar into it. This makes Anna laugh and say that her dad made her tea with sugar, but only when her mum wasn't looking. By jerking her mouth to say this some of the liquid escapes, and warm sugary tea dribbles down her chin. This makes her laugh more.

'I can't even drink any more!' she says. She lifts the mug to take another sip, and again she laughs; more tea spills and follows the same tracks as the first, creating a waterfall.

'I have to start again from scratch,' she says, laughing with tears in her eyes. She will even have to learn how to put liquid in her mouth, she realises. And then how to keep her full mouth closed. And then, finally, how to swallow.

Monday

While the first week of April was a cold and blustery affair, the month settles into its stride, and by the middle weeks is fully delivering on its promise of light and stillness and warmth. Blossom is evident on most trees, the pale leaves set in sharp contrast to the endless blue sky, and memories of glorious summers past seem to hang in the mild air. Every night Anna goes to bed thinking it can't continue, but when she is woken by her alarm at 8 a.m. on Monday – the first time she's had something to get up for in days – she opens the blind and finds yet another clear expanse of blue.

At 9.50 a.m. she clears the dining table and sits down in front of her old cranky laptop. She has carefully considered the appearance of her face and torso – she has washed her hair and applied make-up and is wearing a favourite shirt, a black silken thing with loud African print shapes on – but her lower half, beneath the table, is clad in lounge pants and slippers. The clock in the corner of her screen hits 10.00, then 10.01, then 10.02, but nothing happens. Anna's eyes drift across the living room to the calendar hanging above the television. The date of her meeting at the *Guardian* – which has been postponed twice – is now eleven days away, marked with a big black X. Every time she sees it her attention is drawn to the preceding day's square, which also bears a mark; at first glance it might be a meaningless squiggle, the kind made when testing if a biro works, but on close, forensic inspection it says 'engineering exam'. It is one of the few visual reminders of Pete, most of which have been cleared and cleaned and packed away.

At 11.04 her laptop begins wailing. It is the distinctive sound of an incoming Skype call, more of a song than a ringtone, and the caller ident box reads *Andre_Vasselhom*. Anna shuffles and straightens herself on the chair, then clicks accept and the image of a blond man appears before her. More accurately, a jittery image of a blond man appears, accompanied by a scabrous crackling sound, and then cascades into a nonsense: the millions of glittering pixels fall apart, leaving a black screen and the blue/yellow/magenta/black colour card.

'No you fucking don't,' says Anna, slapping her laptop with her palm. It seems fitting for her to be deprived contact with this man at the final moment of deliverance, as if getting this far has been some grand cosmic tease. But a few seconds later the ringtone sounds again, and this time a perfectly serviceable picture of the blond man glows before her.

'Hey!'

'Hey!'

'Can you see me okay?'

'Sure,' she says. 'You look . . . great!' And he does: clean and tanned and healthy, with a handsome angular head and short blond hair; something about him is reminiscent of an army figurine.

'Thanks,' he says, his eyes twinkling; he looks like a man who fancies his chances. 'You look great too. I like your shirt.'

'You should see my lower half,' she says, not realising until it is too late how strange this sounds, and they both laugh.

The next few minutes are filled with a bland exchange of information. In an attempt to get settled, Anna asks what time it is in the Philippines (4 p.m.), where he's from in Sweden

(Malmö), and how long he's worked for the UN (eight years, on and off). She takes a screengrab of them both, to share later on Twitter. He speaks English with the confidence of a native, and barely an accent, but as with all Skype calls she struggles to keep the conversation flowing. It is frustrating that they cannot make eye contact due to the location of the tiny camera lens, and Anna is irked by the little inset window that shows how she appears to Andre – her eyes are averted, as if she is too shy to look at him.

'It's amazing to finally speak to you,' she says, moving them on to the main business. She imagines this archetypal modern-day Viking standing at the baggage carousel, and receiving the urgent news that made him abandon his bag and run through the airport. 'In some ways I feel like I know you already.'

'I suppose you've washed my underwear.'

'Exactly.'

'Which I'm grateful for. I can't imagine the state of those underpants. They weren't in great shape four years ago.'

'Well, that was my punishment for leaving it so long.'

They begin talking through the items in the case, and he confirms that he packed for every possible weather event; apparently he always has to. He says there was also a small velvet pouch of jewellery in the case, containing a ring and matching earrings, that he didn't see in the Instagram pictures.

'They weren't there, sorry. They must have been swiped by the baggage handlers.'

'Yeah,' he says, nodding with resigned sadness. There is a pause, and then he shakes his head and asks Anna why on earth she did this. She tells him that she thought the investigation would be an interesting spectacle in its own right, but that the main inspiration was to get to the story at the start of the lost suitcase: *his* story.

'My story?' he says. 'Nothing interesting to report there, I'm afraid.'

'Of course there is. I mean, why did you do it? Why would anyone leave their suitcase at the airport? Was it to catch another flight?'

'Pardon me?'

'I said, why did you—'

'I heard you. I'm just confused. You think I left my suitcase at the airport?'

'Well . . . yeah.'

'Of course not,' he says. 'It was lost on a connecting flight. I went from Mozambique to Stockholm via Addis Ababa – that's where the tag must have come off, and it was put on the wrong plane.'

'Oh,' says Anna.

'I think that most suitcases are lost this way.'

'Right. I suppose that makes sense.'

There is another pause, and he says that she seems disappointed.

'Um,' she says. She has a vision of Andre at the baggage carousel, but this time with the suspense and drama sucked out; rather than running through the terminal to Departures, she sees him trudging to the information desk to report a missing item. 'I thought you had to fly off to another war-zone or something.'

They lapse into silence, both looking away from their screen.

'Sorry to disappoint,' he says.

'It's my fault for not thinking of it. I thought there would be an interesting story at the end. That it would have a happy ending.'

'You've found me. Doesn't that make it a happy ending?'

'Yes, it does. But I thought it would be *meaningful*.'

'We could *make* it meaningful,' he says, coming closer to his screen. He is being so bluntly flirtatious that she blushes. 'I'm actually going to be in London next week,' he continues, 'so I could pick up the suitcase then. In person.'

'You don't have to do that. I'm happy to send it to Sweden.'

'No, I'd like to. I'm going to a conference anyway. I could take you to dinner.'

She can feel herself smiling, and is now glad that she doesn't have to look him in the eye.

'Okay,' she says. 'That sounds great.'

For the rest of the morning, Anna is in something close to a good mood, easily the best she has felt in the past fortnight. After getting properly dressed she makes herself poached eggs and fresh coffee, and eats in the living room beside the open sash window. Every few minutes a fly swerves in, buzzes about the room, then flies out again. Anna keeps reflecting happily on the call with Andre, and she has to perform a kind of manual override and tell herself that it was not a success: as there isn't an interesting reason for the suitcase being lost, she doesn't have a story to pitch to the *Guardian*. But still her good mood bounces back. It is true what he said, that finding him was a happy ending in itself, and meeting him will make it even more so. There was also something thrilling about being asked out like that – it was at once gallant and quaint, an abrupt proposal that seems more suited to old films than the real world. She tweets the

351

screengrabbed picture of them talking on Skype, under the heading 'Contact made!', and her mood is further lifted when her most loyal followers post congratulatory emojis – high fives and smiling faces and gold trophies.

After washing-up she heads out into the bright daylight, planning to walk all the way to central London. She has no destination in mind, just a vague goal of finding other story ideas to take to the *Guardian*, and in just over an hour she drifts along Kilburn High Road, Maida Vale, Edgware Road. She decides to give Soho a wide berth, and rounds Marble Arch and enters the park. She then heads towards Leicester Square, and doesn't stop walking until she is struck by the black statues of berserk, careering horses where Haymarket meets Piccadilly Circus. Tourists are there as well, taking photos and videos. Despite having passed this sculpture countless times, Anna has no idea what it represents. After a few minutes a group of Chinese or Japanese tourists arrive and a guide explains that the four horses are pulling the chariot of Helios – the Greek god who each day drags the sun across the sky. Anna contemplates the horses through the lens of this knowledge and feels suddenly richer.

She heads south along Haymarket, then walks up the steps of Hungerford Bridge. She settles against the railing halfway out and takes her sunglasses and notebook out of her bag. She jots down an idea for an article about how tourists, rather than being dumb, sheeplike creatures, are actually better informed about London than *real* Londoners. The piece will be based around a vox-pop quiz delivered to tourists and residents, testing them on landmarks, important events, historical figures. By the time she returns her notebook to her bag the pale skin on her forearms feels tight and is slightly pink.

The idea that summer is beginning is momentarily pleasant, but this broadens into a neutral recognition that the year is already a third complete, which sets off a resounding bass note of dread at how fast time is passing. In a few months it will be the height of summer, after which the nights will draw in and then the clocks will change and all will be plunged into darkness. The thought makes Anna's heart beat faster and sweat prickle in her palms and armpits; she fears her mood might plummet back to a wretched, dangerous low. She takes conscious control of her breathing, and with shaking hands retrieves her phone from her bag, eager for distraction. She calls Zahra, who picks up on the third ring.

'How are you feeling? What's going on?'

Speaking slightly faster than normal, Anna tells her that she had the Skype call with the suitcase guy; Zahra releases a flurry of congratulations.

'Well, actually it was an anticlimax. He lost the case because of a connecting flight. There's no dramatic story.'

'Huh. Connecting flight. I'm surprised we didn't think of that.'

At that moment a boat slides beneath the bridge, honking its horn; Zahra asks where Anna is and she tells her.

'You're on a *bridge*?' says Zahra. 'Why are you on a bridge?'

'Calm down. I'm here because it's nice. I've been walking around, trying to get ideas for stories. Listen to these.'

She tells her about the Tourists v. Londoners article, and also an idea for a series called 'Around the World in Eighty Dates', where Anna would go with a different man to a country themed restaurant each week – Afghan, Brazilian, Chinese, Danish . . . Zahra listens quietly and asks questions;

it was her idea that Anna should go to the *Guardian* with other ideas to pitch.

'It will be a celebration of the ethnic diversity of London,' continues Anna. 'As well as a retro celebration of pre-Kismet dating and good old-fashioned flirty gossip.'

'Now all you need is eighty men.'

'As it happens, I have a dinner lined up already.'

'Fuck off. Who?'

'Andre. The owner of the suitcase.'

'Get out! He's in London?'

'He's in Manila at the moment, but he'll be in London next week.' Anna tells Zahra that he was funny, and good-looking, and that it could be a perfect end to the story.

'You think he's single?' asks Zahra, doubtfully.

'Who knows? He travels the world with work. Maybe he doesn't have time.'

Zahra says it sounds like a crazy, ridiculous idea, and that it is a relief to hear Anna sounding like her old self. Then she says she has to go and that she'll see her on Wednesday.

'You're sure it's okay for you to take the day off?'

'Of course,' says Zahra. 'They encourage us to do pro bono work. And I'm looking forward to it. Listen, I have to go. Call me later.'

Anna's phone falls away from her face, the glass screen moist from where it was pressed to her skin. Her hand is dangling over the edge, with only air between her phone and the green-brown water, and it suddenly feels like a very easy thing to let it slip through her hand and watch it fall down and disappear. But this would be crazy and irrational, and she is trying to be neither of these things. Instead she holds the phone to her face and peers at her reflection, finding the glass to be a surprisingly effective mirror that gives back a clear picture of her smiling face.

Wednesday

Anna and Zahra are standing in the lobby of Kismet UK, beside the handrail that surrounds the grand centrepiece: a ten-foot man-made waterfall that plunges between two angled staircases. Anna has seen plenty of pictures of this water feature, itself a replica of an identical model in the global HQ in Seattle, but she still reads the information plaque attached to the lip of the pool. The flow of the falling water is in constant flux, increasing and diminishing in line with the activity on Kismet around the world – each couple that signs off is represented by a litre of water. On the far wall is their own version of the big board, but this time showing a single rolling figure, the cumulative number of couples that have happily switched off: 23,098,876, 23,098,877, 23,098,878. Beneath that are TV screens, showing Raymond Chan and other executives. Raymond looks delighted again, as he did when she last saw him, on a news piece announcing that the European Court of Justice had upheld the appeal from Kismet, allowing them to block the release of profile data to anyone.

'Looks like a suspiciously even flow to me,' says Anna, returning to the waterfall. The invisible spray coming from the green water is like tiny cold pinpricks on her face.

'Apparently it slows to a trickle sometimes,' says Zahra.

'Do you think they take numbers off the tally as well? For when couples split up?'

'I don't know. Let's ask them.'

Both of them stare into the pool for a time, the green water giving back wobbling versions of their own faces, until footsteps approach them from behind.

'You must be Anna,' says a surprisingly normal-looking man – short, with pink blotchy skin and a narrow face – who is coming at her with his hand raised. 'I'm Linden. We spoke on the phone.'

He shakes hands with Zahra as well, then leads them to a lift. Zahra asks Linden the question about whether failed couples have their number taken off the Kismet grand total, and Linden explains that the number is removed only when either partner switches off with a new partner.

'I suppose you don't know if people have split up otherwise,' says Zahra.

'Oh, we know if they've split up,' says Linden. 'But a significant number get back together. Much more than people seem to realise.'

At the eighteenth floor Linden leads them along the central aisle of an open-plan workspace, which has the same large and kidney-shaped desks as Anna's old office. The sight and sound of professional normality – the distant trill of someone's desk phone, the scuttling noise of a fast typer, the background static hum that is to her the very sound of thought – fills Anna with a sudden and profound shame, and she is relieved when the desks give way to an empty, carpeted space. It is unclear what purpose this area serves, but it must be some kind of antechamber or vestibule, for they turn from it into a marble corridor with floor-to-ceiling glass walls on either side. They walk past several grand meeting rooms, and Anna is glad to have accepted Zahra's offer to come with her, and not to be facing such a formidable corporation on her own. This feeling of advantage is short-lived, and disappears when Linden opens the door to yet another long boardroom, where no fewer than five men in suits are waiting for them.

'Anna,' says a baby-faced and American-accented man, who stands up from the centre of the table and comes round to them. He introduces himself as Tim, head of customer relations for Kismet UK, and says that it is a pleasure to meet her, and how sad he is that it's happening under such unhappy circumstances. Then he directs her to shake hands with each of the other men – Charles from legal, Ramesh from IT and tech, Duncan from communications, and Pablo, who will be taking notes. Anna says hello to each before taking a seat and looking again at this Tim, who is rubbing his hands and appears set to kick things off. She tries to work out his age. He can't be older than thirty-five, and it is incredible that he has risen to such a senior position. But his being North American helps explain this, as it did with Ingrid; Anna has always felt that New World people move through life at a different pace.

'Let's begin, shall we?' says Tim. 'I imagine we're all busy, and that's why we're going to make this as simple as possible. We feel terrible about what happened. And embarrassed. We have no knowledge of a breach like this happening before. We had no idea it *could* happen. But we have made sure that it will *never* happen again.' Tim pauses, his eyes locked with Anna's. There is a slight shine to the skin of his boyish face, which makes her think of a ventriloquist's dummy.

'I'm deeply sorry, Anna. I really am. And this apology comes from Raymond himself.' Linden passes her a printed email from Raymond Chan, addressed to Anna, saying he is shocked and furious at what happened, and has urged the London team to do whatever is necessary to make it up to her. 'He really is personally invested in this, and that's why we want to make you a simple offer of reparations, no questions asked. We have considered the case and believe that £30,000 is a generous offer.'

Anna blinks, surprised. It's more than she expected. She could live for a year for free.

'No questions asked?' says Zahra, suspicious.

'Well,' says Tim, smiling. 'Naturally, such a payment would be a settlement. As in, we would consider the matter closed.'

'You mean I wouldn't be able to write about it?'

'Exactly,' says Tim.

'Or document it in any recordable format,' says Linden, at the far end of the long table. He has a black attaché case in front of him, which gives Anna another jolt of shame. 'The terms of the settlement will prohibit you from discussing the nature or the details of the incident, or corroborating the claims of others.'

'A gagging order, essentially,' says Zahra.

'Call it what you will,' says Tim, smiling good-naturedly at her. 'But really we just want this issue closed, so we can all move on. You must agree it's a generous offer?'

'No, I don't agree that it's generous,' says Zahra, who told Anna they should negotiate, whatever is offered. 'This amount is insignificant compared to the profits Kismet makes on any single day. Whereas the damage done to Anna has been colossal. She's lost her job, her partner, and now her home is at risk. Her mental health was already fragile before the event, which could, from a medical perspective, be described as traumatic.'

'We appreciate these facts,' says Tim, with a calming, flat-palmed downward movement, as if he is squashing the air in front of him. 'And we accept that Kismet is, *in part*, culpable. This is precisely why we have made such a generous offer. But the bottom line is, from a legal perspective, there's no case to answer.'

'In a criminal sense. But we could still launch a civil case, citing corporate negligence.'

'Absolutely not,' says the guy to Tim's right, a bald man that Anna thinks was the one from legal. 'The possibility of this hack wasn't known during our last technology audit, which was only six months ago. No court would find us negligent for not protecting against a technology that we didn't know existed.'

Zahra accepts this coolly, lifting her eyebrows as if to suggest he shouldn't be so sure. Then she resumes her argument along a different tack: she speaks of Anna's profession as a journalist, and her links with major newspapers and broadcasters.

'She could easily spin this into a series of articles, even a book. Imagine the potential damage.'

'With respect,' says the man from communications, 'you're overstating the reputational risk of such a story.'

'This offer really is generous,' says Tim again, as friendly as he has been throughout. 'And, in addition, we're willing to add free use of the service, for as long as it takes Anna to sign off again.'

'You think she wants to go back on Kismet after what happened?'

'This won't happen again,' says the Asian guy from the technical team. 'If that's what you're worried about. We've tripled the firewall for this kind of attack.'

Tim smiles at Anna again, and seems keen to demonstrate more sensitivity to her mindset.

'I know it will take time,' he says. 'It could be several months before you feel comfortable going online again. But you shouldn't let this creep stand in the way of getting what you really want. His little test didn't prove anything.'

'You don't think it proved *anything*?' says Anna.

'Of course not. One-off examples are baseless, since we have always accepted that the matches aren't perfect anyway; there will always be outliers and surprising results. All he proved is that, in your isolated case, the figure of 62 was perhaps a bit low – it should have been higher, at least in the seventies. Hence why you were susceptible to believing it really was a super-high score.'

'Right,' says Anna.

'And, of course, he proved what a callous individual he is. Did you know he has been a tax avoider for decades? He has spent most of his adult life abroad to avoid paying tax on an inheritance. He was almost jailed for it ten years ago. He slipped away on a technicality that time, but we're confident we'll get him for this. Isn't that right, Linden?'

'Well . . . we're working with police to establish grounds for arrest,' Linden says.

For the first time there is a crack in Tim's composure, and he glares at Linden for a second before turning back to Anna.

'We'll arrest him, don't worry. And if he tries to harass you, be sure to let us know. Has he been in contact?'

'No,' she lies.

'Good. Well, let's hope it stays like that. And you can slowly return to something like a normal life. So . . .' He brings his fingers together and looks around the room. 'I feel like we're getting close to an agreement. Wouldn't you say, Anna?'

All the men watch her, and she turns to Zahra; Anna can tell she thinks it's a good offer, despite her tough talk.

'It would be good to think about it,' she says, and they all appear surprised. 'I am allowed to think about it, right?'

Each man around the table speaks over the others in their eagerness to agree with her, saying, 'Of course, of course,' and 'Take your time.'

Saturday

After the meeting at Kismet Anna suggested they go to a cafe to debrief, but Zahra was having none of it – she insisted they go to a bar, to celebrate. She ordered a bottle of champagne and wouldn't stop talking about how good the offer was, and how she thought they could squeeze them for even more. She wanted to go for dinner as well, but Anna didn't want to carry on drinking; she said she felt tired and went home. When she got there she changed into lounge pants and a hoodie, which she continued wearing for the next three days.

During this time she didn't say a word to anyone, other than a brief salutation to the man in the corner shop and the delivery boy who brought her a pizza. But keeping herself cooped up wasn't due to apathy and depression, or not exclusively. She actually felt okay on Thursday and Friday, in comparison to previous weeks. And on Saturday, there is even a moment when she feels happy: as she steps out of the shower, she is captivated by the sight of the bathroom window. It gives on to David's overgrown garden, the red-brick house beyond and the empty blue sky above, and these are obscured by the mottled glass into glowing banks of colour – green, red and blue – that blur into each other and appear to radiate their own energy, like an electrified Rothko painting. The fact that she can appreciate this proves that her brain still retains the potential for pleasure and happiness; perhaps this modicum of calm will grow, day by day, until her sadness is blotted out and relegated to being a mere memory. But just an hour or so later, something equally random – the sound of workmen drilling a few streets away, which she had already decided was the most lonely sound in the world – sends her mood into a nosedive, which turns into a tailspin when she unwittingly glances at the blue squiggle on the calendar. The fleeting moment of happiness was simply an illusion caused by the higher dose of Zoloft the doctor prescribed, which is also obscuring the fact that her whole life is going to unravel, is unravelling, has unravelled; Anna can no longer concentrate on mortgage repayment calculations, and has to go and curl up on the sofa and focus on her breathing.

Later in the afternoon, she returns to her computer to find an email from Geoff. She isn't sure where he is right now, or how he found her email address, though in a weird way she feels that the answers to these two questions are the same. It seems as if he has retreated to an ethereal space where he can watch everything from a safe distance, while also having access to all information; she imagines he has somehow gone *into* the internet.

It is a long email, perhaps the longest she has ever received from anyone ever, stretching to several thousand words. It is a manifesto as much as a message, a business proposal, written in a hasty, messy and often clunking prose. It begins with his life story, and why he wanted to do this in the first place, how he was always forced to be on the outside of the normal world, never felt included anywhere, and how his ultimate ambition was to tackle the global corporate elite which he feels is the main cause of unhappiness in the world. This turns into a kind of diatribe on why Kismet deserves to be targeted, how they are the worst of the worst, how they are exploiting people's mental fragility with a calculated mendacity that hasn't been seen before. He makes reference to psychological papers on 'confirmation bias', the series of forums that are full of disgruntled users, all of whom are silenced and paid off by Kismet, and the dubious professional credentials of the 'statisticians' who carried out the 'independent' research on which Kismet bases its claims. He even makes a lengthy diversion into Freud and the superego.

Reading all this provides the answer to why he wanted her help with the writing, and why he never made it as a journalist: his spelling and grammar are all over the place, and many of his sentences don't make sense at all.

In the second half of the email he sets out a proposal for the series of articles that they will write together – or, he clarifies, that *she* will write. It will be a dissection of their time together, their meeting on the South Bank, in Somerset House and beyond, with Anna explaining her thought processes in relation to the number and the psychological theories mentioned above. It will be a journalistic first, someone writing up the findings from an experiment they didn't know they were part of, that they didn't know was an experiment.

'I'm sure the *Guardian* would bite your hand off for something like this,' he writes, and says that they could serialise the articles over months to let attention gather, and put Kismet on the back foot. In the meantime, before the series gets picked up, he's willing to pay her a salary. It is only in the final paragraph that he makes reference to her feelings, and says that he hopes she is okay and that she hasn't taken the news too badly. He says that he understands if she is still 'cross' with him, and if she wants to work together they can 'archive the sex and romance stuff', or even just communicate by email.

'Though that would be a shame, I feel,' he says, in his closing remark. 'The truth is I miss you. Regards. Geoff.'

Anna is tempted to write back immediately. Something along the lines of 'fuck off'. But she doesn't. She scrolls up and down, marvelling at the spelling mistakes. She remembers what he said about failing his exams and not going to uni and her heart goes out to him for a second. Then she decides to ignore the email and do something else instead, something useful. She begins cleaning the kitchen, but thirty minutes later she is back at her laptop, reading his message again. This time she works through the links he sent, starting with the upset Kismet users in America. Many of the forum posts have links to local news stories, and while none of these repetitive cases is surprising – in fact they are similar to ones she has already read – she does notice something sinister. Someone talks of a Kismet settlement they received and a message they got from Raymond, and Anna sees it is identical to the one she was given just the other day.

Without wanting to, she moves straight on to the academic and psychoanalytic articles that Geoff sent her. She has cheese on toast for dinner, which she eats while reading, and then stays up past midnight, trying to get her head around the id, ego and superego.

On Sunday, despite having planned to spend the day exploring the options that £30,000 would give her for starting a business, going on a round-the-world trip, paying off a chunk of the mortgage, or a combination of all three, she is once again drawn to Geoff's email. This time she rereads the proposed structure of the articles – their initial meeting, going to Somerset House, spending the night together, their countryside break, deciding to switch off Kismet – and she is able to imagine them as words on a page, columns in a paper or website. She takes her notebook to the sofa and jots down her main memories of each meeting, trying to recall conversations that were especially interesting, or things Geoff did which seemed funny or impressive or attractive. All of the memories are tainted, and she views them as if through a dark smog, but they are not entirely negative. Neural pathways have been created in her mind, so that even if she isn't amused by the memory of their wrestling on the bed, or aroused by the idea of taking her clothes off in Somerset House, she nonetheless remembers *feeling* the feeling, can grasp its shadow, the imprint it left within her. These thoughts give rise to a sudden desire to look at Geoff's face, to see if he really is as handsome as she remembers, but she has no picture of him. This feels like a terrible shame, regardless of how things turned out. She tries to concentrate her mind on what his face was like, but for some reason the image slides from her mind's eye; she can remember him only in the act of turning, and his face exists for a flash before sliding away, refusing to stay still and be scrutinised.

As she thinks this her phone, resting on the arm of the sofa, starts ringing with a call from an 'unknown' number. She stands up and watches it from the centre of the room, wondering what the chances would be of him calling her right now, at the precise moment she was trying to picture his face. But she realises the odds are probably not that long, since she's been thinking of him all day, and yesterday too. The phone rings twice, three times, four times. Anna clenches every muscle in her body and grits her teeth, holding herself back from touching it. On the sixth ring, she considers that it might not be Geoff; maybe Pete is trying to call from someone else's phone, wanting to talk about the money and mortgage arrangements, or even just to see how she is. The phone rings a seventh, then an eighth time, and she senses whoever is on the other end is just as determined to speak to her as she is to resist the call. It rings a ninth, tenth, eleventh time. She stands there watching it.

Wednesday

Incredibly, the nice weather holds for another week; it is as
if it has become stuck on this one setting – warm and sunny
– and has forgotten how to be anything else. On Wednesday,
at around 5 p.m. Anna starts a serious but unhurried process
of getting ready, with the Velux window open to the empty
blue afternoon sky. She tries on two or three shirts and tops
before settling on black jeans and an oversize denim shirt and
hoop earrings. The outfit makes her feel young, as does getting
ready to go out when it is still broad daylight. In particular
it reminds her of those heady first big nights out in Bedford,
aged fifteen or sixteen, when whole gangs of them would attack the main club in town, Enigma, split into tactical dribs
and drabs, the most youthful boys paired up with the most attractive girls, all armed with fake ID, and always horrendously
early, 8 or 8.30 p.m., just after the club had opened, governed
by the untested theory that the bouncers were more lenient
before a queue had formed. After one such summer night she
went with Alex Brisindi to the sculpted gardens of Cemetery
Park, where they made a hapless attempt to take each other's
virginity, beset by torch-wielding passers-by, an inside-out
condom and finally a vanishing erection; this memory makes
Anna smile, and the fact she enjoys it without a sense of doom
at the passing of time is a good omen for the evening to come.

At 7 p.m. she hauls the suitcase – which she paid the dry
cleaners £20 to fumigate and cleanse – down the stairs and

into the street. It doesn't have rollers, and she has to swap arms every twenty metres or so and takes two long rests before finally reaching the station. At King's Cross she rides the escalators up to the open paved space between the station and St Pancras, and despite him being one man in a huge crowd she spots Andre immediately. His muscular arms and square jaw and close-cropped blond hair give him the look of an elite soldier, or a film star playing the role of an elite soldier, though he is shorter than she expected and, she sees when she reaches him, shorter than her. They hug and kiss on the cheek in greeting, before taking many selfies: Anna and Andre both standing behind the suitcase, Anna handing the suitcase to Andre, Andre crouching down beside the case. She posts these on Twitter immediately, under the sub-heading of 'mission accomplished', and they both watch as the first likes and notes of congratulations roll in.

'Can we get something to eat now?' he says. 'I'm starving to death.'

'Do you have a preference where?'

'That McDonald's is starting to look pretty good.'

She is pleased to be able to suggest the Afghan Kitchen in Angel, a ten-minute walk away. Andre heaves the suitcase up and says that it's fine with him, as long as the food is better than he had in the real Afghanistan.

'It's not nice?'

'It tastes nice enough on the way in,' he says, shifting the case to his back so he looks like Atlas bearing the globe. 'But going in wasn't the problem, if you know what I mean.'

By the time they reach the top of Pentonville Road the veins in Andre's neck are like rope beneath his skin and his forehead shines with sweat; he complains that she didn't say the ten-minute walk was straight uphill. But he dismisses the idea of getting a bus, and in another ten minutes they reach the restaurant, which is scruffier than it looked in Google Images, and doesn't serve booze.

'This is . . . *nice*,' says Andre, after they are sat at a rickety table, and a waiter has taken the suitcase to store somewhere out back.

'You don't have to be polite,' she whispers, looking down at the laminated menu. 'I actually just wanted to come here as part of a new project. Something to follow the suitcase thing.' She explains the idea of a weekly column where she goes with someone to a different country-themed restaurant in London each time: Afghan, Brazilian, Chinese, Danish, Ethiopian . . .

'Where did that idea come from?'

'From a pun, like most good ideas. The series would be called "Around the World in Eighty Dates".'

Andre smiles and says that this is a date, then – he is a man who not only fancies his chances but likes to get straight to the point. Anna hastens them onwards, telling him about the meeting she has with the *Guardian* on Friday, and her need to develop ideas to pitch to them. Andre is still smiling suggestively, so she changes the subject entirely by asking him his favourite country to work in. He limits his answer to culinary matters, and gives high praise to the cooking in South East Asia, apart from the Philippines, whose food is so sweet and salty and bland it is like toddlers have been allowed to dictate the national dishes. While he talks their meals arrive, and Anna is pleased to see her dish is like a hybrid between a curry and kebab, which fits nicely with where she pictures Afghanistan to be on the map.

371

'You're not going to reunite more people with their suitcases?' he asks.

'I was planning to. But your connecting flight bombshell has killed my idea. Now it's less of an interesting story and more of an international lost-and-found process.'

'If it's any consolation, losing the suitcase did feel quite dramatic at the time. In a sense it cost me a relationship. Or helped to end one, anyway. Maybe you could use it.'

Anna says that she's all ears, and he begins telling her about the floods in Mozambique, how it was the weirdest mission for him. For a whole year beforehand he hadn't been sent anywhere – the world had been unusually peaceful and calm – and during that time he lived in Geneva and worked in the headquarters and dated a girl called Iris.

'We didn't meet on Kismet, just naturally at a party, and things became really serious, really quickly. After two weeks we said we loved each other, by a month she was living in my flat, and by three months she started talking about marriage and babies.' Andre shakes his head at the memory of this time – his eyes focused on the air in front of his face – and says that he has never known an intensity of feeling like it. But when she spoke of marriage he was uncomfortable, and while not openly contradicting her, he didn't encourage the idea either, and began searching for subtle ways to put the brakes on. Iris noticed his change of tone immediately, and from then on every conversation about the future, especially to do with his going overseas for long periods with work, became a battleground.

'Finally she gave me an ultimatum: stop acting like a jerk and commit to something, at least tell her that I wanted the same things as her, or we should finish it before going any further.' He didn't like being cornered like that – has never liked being cornered – and reasoned that she couldn't be right for him if she felt it necessary to put him on the spot like that. But at the same time he couldn't reach a decision, and when the floods in Africa came it was like the decision was being made for him. He was deployed for three months, and Iris couldn't believe he was going, and was too furious and heartbroken to even say goodbye.

'After about ten seconds of being in Africa I realised I had made a mistake. And by the next day I knew this was about the worst decision I'd ever made, so dumb it was hard to convince myself that I'd really done it. It was like waking up after a night of drunken craziness, when you can't quite believe it was you that did those things the night before.

'Worst of all I had days and weeks without phone or even email access, so there was no way of keeping in contact with her. Do you know that feeling, of wanting to win someone back that you've driven away? And then being locked away from them, in the middle of fucked-up Africa without even email? You couldn't even post a letter! I could sense her thousands of miles away, hearing nothing from me, assuming I didn't care at all, getting over me one day at a time, eventually starting to go out, meet new people. It's crazy-making! Like standing at the side of the road and watching a car crash in slow motion. Do you know what I mean?'

Anna clears her throat, and with the solemnity and gravity of someone at the altar, says: 'I do.'

'But I decided to get her back, whatever the cost. Since I couldn't contact her, I decided I'd prepare a big gesture for when I returned to Switzerland. One of my colleagues showed me these amazing pearls he'd found – blue pearls they were called, though they were more purple – and he told me about this stretch of beach where I could get them at low tide. Iris loved anything to do with the sea – scuba diving, tropical fish, all that shit – so on my one day off in three months I went to find them. I walked on my own out of the little town we were staying in, which was against our security orders, and when I came to the right patch of beach I saw it wasn't deserted: there were dogs there, loads of fucking stray dogs.'

It occurs to Anna that she really should be recording this, that she might get something out of it, but thinks a notepad and pen would ruin the moment – she decides to commit it to memory instead. Andre says that his colleague had told him the pearls could be found in the smooth wet sand left by the retreating waves, but that's exactly where the dogs were skipping about; they seemed to be hunting for little fish. The dogs looked mangy and diseased and were just as aggressive as all the dogs in Africa. But he thought of Iris and went back up the path to the woods and found a fuck-off piece of driftwood, and went down to the water wielding it like a baseball bat.

'The dogs weren't shy, they started coming for me. I couldn't tell for sure if they were rabid, but I had to assume they were, and I swung the wood at them, swung it around and around like a madman. Hit one of them in the leg, probably broke it, but that did the trick; it whimpered off and the others backed away as well, but only for a minute. So I had to dance around in the shallows, looking for these little pearls while the dogs skulked about on the beach, trying to figure out the best time to have another go.'

At dusk he left with a pocket full of sand and three little pearls, which were actually tiny clams with perfectly spherical shells. Six weeks later, in the capital, Maputo, he had them made into jewellery – a pair of earrings and the ring he planned to propose with – before catching his flight home.

'The idea was to go straight to her place and get down on one knee when she answered the door. But in Geneva the bag didn't come out. Waiting there at the carousel, as soon as the bags stopped coming and mine wasn't there, I knew I'd fucked it. It was like my heart hadn't made the journey home with me. When I saw Iris I didn't propose, I didn't really say anything substantial. She said she'd joined Kismet and met someone else, that she'd given up on me. I pretended that I didn't care, and told her I already had my next posting lined up. This time in Haiti. I suppose I gave up on me too.' Andre sighs and blinks, as if surprised himself at how things turned out.

Anna says it's a decent story, that she'd love to write it up, and that it would make a great end to her suitcase project.

'I think we can make a better ending than that,' he says, smiling at her again. 'Let's pay up. I want to get a drink.'

They head to a large pub on Essex Road, where Andre proves his earlier flirting to be as nothing, just a process of warming up. He becomes chattier, more tactile, more flattering, and on his way back from the bar with their third drinks he slides into Anna's side of the booth, making it abundantly clear, if it wasn't already, that something is in train, and that she doesn't have to make anything happen; the momentum is already gathering, her options are to stop it or let it run. There is something about his confidence and the way he moves his body that makes her think he will be really quite fantastic in bed, like sleeping with a professional. He lets slip that he is flying to Sweden tomorrow, and that he is staying in the St Pancras Hotel tonight; Anna tries to work out if that makes it a better or worse idea to sleep with him.

'But what about your work meeting?'

'I made that up. I was heading back to Sweden for a holiday, and just added the London leg on to meet you.'

'Just to meet me?'

'Uh-huh. Something made me think it was a good idea.'

'That's a lot of effort to go to. On a long shot.'

'And that's pretty rich, coming from you.'

He kisses her, and she waits a few seconds before pushing him away.

'It would be a great end to the story,' he says. 'That's something you could sell to the newspaper.'

He kisses her again; she pushes him back even sooner.

'What is it?' he says. 'You don't like me?'

'No, I do.'

'Then what's the problem?' He asks this as if the problem naturally must be on her side, and Anna supposes that it is. She knows that spending the night in his hotel will be fun and sexy and exciting and almost certainly have no lasting consequences, but these considerations are massively outweighed, like a hugely imbalanced set of scales, by a countervailing consideration – it isn't the usual bottomless feeling of panic in her stomach, but something founded on a solid base. She just doesn't want to.

'Let me guess,' he says. 'You've already got someone.'

Anna just shrugs, as if to say: what can I do?

'I should have known. Every time I come back to Europe there are fewer single people. It's the way of the world.'

Like a radio tuned to a different frequency, Andre drops the physicality and compliments, and just becomes plain friendly. They have one more drink, a celebratory cocktail, before Andre says he should go and make use of his hotel room. Anna says sorry for making him spend the night alone in that big room, and he says he has no intention of being alone, that he has several old flames in London; Anna laughs out loud and calls him a slut. Then they are outside on the pavement, and hug on the street; they ask a solitary smoker to take a final picture of them posing with the suitcase. Then he is heaving it onto his back like Atlas again, and she watches him walking away from her like a tortoise or snail, the suitcase growing gradually smaller as it proceeds along the straight road, before finally turning a corner and vanishing altogether.

Thursday

In the early hours of Thursday morning she has a moment of untainted sensual delight that feels like another milestone in her recovery. When she returned to the loft bedroom the previous evening it had heated up like a pressure cooker, as it tends to on warm days, and she discarded her duvet and fell asleep beneath a single sheet, with the window open. At around 5 a.m. she wakes up shivering. She leans off the bed and grabs the duvet, noticing the dawn doing a spectacular light show for those few late or early birds lucky enough to see – a big rippling layered cake of orange and yellow and the departing cadet blue – and then pulls it back onto the bed and herself. The sudden warmth is delicious, as is the weight of it pressing down upon her, and she just has time to feel grateful for seeing such a nice dawn, and for experiencing such pleasure, before her thoughts curdle back into sleep.

She next wakes naturally at around 8.30 a.m., and the room is filled with a pleasing dusty sunflower light. She gets up, but only to make a cup of tea, which she takes back to bed and drinks while gazing out the window at the sky, reflecting on her evening with Andre. It was a success, she thinks. More than that: it was a triumph. It wasn't meeting him or handing over the suitcase or the gushing responses she's had from all corners of her social network, but the decisiveness she displayed when he propositioned her. This calm certainty seems to have solidified further during her sleep, so that now it is completely obvious what she wants, and how she should go about getting it. As if to test this new conviction, she gets up and goes downstairs and stands before the calendar with her hands on her hips. Tomorrow has the big X indicating the *Guardian* interview. Today has the blue squiggle of the engineering exam. The feeling of decisiveness is there again, even stronger, flowing through her like a form of energy.

After breakfast and coffee, Anna digs out her running shoes from the cupboard and slams out of the front door. She jogs east across Finchley Road and then down into Camden, where she zigzags between pedestrians and tourists and sometimes shimmies into the road. Camden Road takes her up the long straight hill to Holloway, and she is surprised to not yet be flagging. She deliberately left her phone at home, so she has no way of tracking distance; but it feels much further than she'd normally run, even though she seems to be getting more energised as she goes along. The pleasant springtime sights are another boost; in Finsbury Park dozens of trees in blossom line the paths like pompoms, and the far-off buildings are faintly obscured by a thin veil of mist, and look like a reflection of themselves in a glassy lake. From the park she picks up Green Lanes, where she slows into a steady bobbing rhythm that takes her back to her adolescent cross-country races, how she'd lose herself in a trance where the complaints from her muscles couldn't reach her. The long northward road takes her through Haringey and Turnpike Lane and Wood Green, where it finally splits and she is faced with a steep terraced street that ends in Alexandra Palace Park. With acid burning in her calves and her heart thrumming against her ribs, she climbs the hill at barely faster than walking pace, and only when the path flattens and she is beneath the entrance to the gutted, shell-like Palace does she turn and allow herself the view of the whole city spread beneath her.

It is all there, from the tilted arc of Wembley Stadium off to the west to the faux-Eiffel Tower of Crystal Palace way off in the south, and then in the east the river glistening as it widens and curls like a snake, surrounded by endless housing and industrial estates, then finally mud flats and a shimmering nothing. Between these marker points, a horrendous cluster of stuff. So many skyscrapers, landmarks, and whole districts that appear nothing more than a jagged mishmash of buildings. But it seems manageable, the city, because she knows what she wants. She thinks it is true, what Geoff said: it is our desires that make sense of the raucousness, the chaos. Whether she gets it or not is immaterial; the point is that she knows what she wants, and it is this that drowns out the noise of the city, that shrinks it to a manageable size.

When she finally gets home, having had to walk most of the way, she finds two missed calls, one from Zahra and one from an unknown number that also left a message; it is from Linden at Kismet, saying that he'd love to follow up with her about the meeting, and see if they can try again to reach an agreement. Instead of returning these she opens her maps and plugs in the route to Alexandra Palace via Camden, and is amazed to find she ran for thirteen miles. Then she sees it is almost 2 p.m. and she doesn't have time to attend to the missed calls; instead she has a bite to eat and a shower before getting dressed and leaving the house again.

The 139 to Waterloo arrives at the bus stop almost immediately, and she gets her favourite seat at the front of the top deck, another small victory. On the wave of this happy feeling she takes her phone out and calls Zahra, not just to return her call, but also to project her good feeling outwards and have it rebound back to her.

'Hey,' she says, when Zahra picks up. 'Something weird just happened.'

'Don't tell me. Another busker freaked you out?'

'No. I just went for a run and accidentally kept going for thirteen miles! That's a half marathon.'

There is a pause and then Zahra says: 'I don't understand why this is strange. You go running all the time.'

'I would normally run for three or four miles, max. But this time I didn't have my phone, and didn't know how far I'd gone, and just kept going and going and going. It's like not being able to measure myself opened up all this new energy.'

Zahra laughs and says, 'Far out,' and then that something happened to her as well: the guy from Kismet called.

'Why did he call you?'

'Because that's what legal representatives do. We represent. And maybe because you weren't answering your phone. Anyway, it's looking good: it sounds like they'll definitely increase their offer. Maybe to thirty-five or even forty K. I reckon we should go in hard, and ask for fifty. What do you think?'

'Actually,' says Anna, as the bus slides past a billboard for the Kismet Love Test, 'I've decided not to take it.'

'What?'

'I've decided to turn down the offer.'

'Are you crazy? Think of all that money.'

'Yeah . . . I have been thinking about it. A lot. And I've decided I want to write about it. I don't want to be silenced.'

'But what if the *Guardian* don't like the idea?'

'Then I'll take it somewhere else. It's easily the most interesting thing that's ever happened to me. Listen to this.' She explains how the series of articles will work, each one a breakdown of the meetings and how she led herself to believe she had a one-in-ten-million hit. She asks Zahra if she likes the sound of it, and she responds with a question of her own.

'He's put you up to this, hasn't he?'

'Well . . . he's definitely played a part.'

'Anna! Do not carry on seeing him! I forbid you to carry on seeing him.'

'Relax. I'm not going to. I don't need his help. Or his money. I'm going to do it myself.'

There is a frustrated huffing sigh from Zahra, and she says that Kismet will make it hard for her, that they will launch a media war on anything she tries to do, that any main broadcaster would be pressured not to take it – Anna interrupts her mid-flow.

'Zahra. Listen. I've made my mind up. And you have to trust me on this. And support me. Okay?'

'But what about all that—'

'Zahra. Trust me.' There is a pause long enough for them to pass the green expanse of Regent's Park, and Anna realises her stop is the next one. Finally, Zahra sighs again, this time in defeat.

'I suppose I'd better call them up, then. Tell them the matter is closed.'

'You don't have to.'

'I want to represent you.'

'Alright then. Thanks. Listen, I've got to go in a minute.'

'*You* have to go? I'm the one that's at work.'

'Unemployed people still have things to do,' says Anna,

ringing the bell and standing up. 'Important things. Want to have dinner tomorrow?' They quickly agree that Anna will go to hers, and then say goodbye to each other; without planning to, Anna says that she loves her, something she hasn't said sober in years, if ever. Then she climbs down the stairs and shouts a thank-you to the driver as she skips off the bus.

It is 3.45 p.m. when she arrives at Malet Street and the long, pedestrianised square flanked by grand university buildings bearing the names of SOAS, UCL and Birkbeck. She is a bit early, and waits with a coffee on a stone bench, her eyes on the grand doors and steps of a building called Toynbee Hall. Students of various ages and shapes and colours walk past, all giving the impression of knowing where they are headed and having the right books and notes to do what is required when they get there; it reminds her of being a student not a bit. A little after 4 p.m. the doors of Toynbee Hall open and a handful of people trickle out. He is one of the last to emerge from the shaded doorway, and lingers on the steps talking with a dark-skinned young woman; from the smile and his hand movements Anna can tell he is trying to make her laugh. Then they hug and walk off in separate directions. When Anna catches up he is still wearing the remains of the smile but this is wiped when he sees her angling towards him.

'What . . . ?' he says, stopping still on the pavement.

'Your last exam?' she says, forcing herself to look at him, and to appear happy and casual, offhand.

There is a silence as he holds her in a wide-eyed, frozen stare. Then he seems to make an effort to compose himself, and says, with dignity: 'That's right.'

'Looks like you made a friend,' she says, flicking her eyes

in the direction of the departing Asian woman – Pete neither smiles nor follows her gaze.

'What do you want?'

'To say well done, for finishing. And I was hoping to talk to you.'

'I'm meeting some friends for a drink.'

Anna nods and her eyes fall down to the pavement.

'But I don't have to meet them straight away.'

He says this and continues walking, and it takes Anna a few moments to realise he expects her to walk with him. She does a little run to catch him up. They walk in tandem into Russell Square, and she wonders if he is heading for the tube, and if she will follow him on if so. But he heads south, into Bloomsbury. After a few minutes of silent walking, Anna makes an abrupt announcement.

'I lost my job.'

'What?' he says, in angry disbelief. He stops walking and turns to face her. 'How the fuck did you do that?'

Anna is determined not to lie, or even exaggerate. She tells him about the Sahina article, the section she added in, the complaints that arrived, and how when Stuart tried to suspend her she said she didn't want to work there anyway.

'In theory I quit. So it won't look too bad.'

Pete stares along the street away from her and shakes his head.

'I don't feel like I know you any more,' he says, calmly. Then he carries on walking, and again she hurries to match his stride. They pass the British Museum and, in an effort to keep conversation ticking over, she begins asking questions about his exams and the work placement in Acton, but Pete gives stunted answers that allow no space for further questions –

yes, no, I don't know, maybe; it is like playing tennis with yourself against a brick wall, the ball flying back quicker and straighter than you want it. Conversation is eventually lost again, until he asks a question.

'You're still with that guy?'

'No.'

Pete doesn't stop walking or react in any discernible way.

'How come?'

'Didn't work out.'

'But I thought he was an 81?'

'Turns out that was just a number.'

She looks at his face in profile and again sees no reaction, but this is what is noticeable, his controlled lack of any expression, his refusal to respond. A few seconds later Pete's phone rings and he takes it out of his pocket. He has a call from his friend Finn, which he watches ring out.

'I can reschedule the drink,' he says. 'It would be good to talk.'

'Yes,' says Anna, tentatively, careful not to react as if this is a victory.

'I'm worried about you.'

'I can understand that.'

'And we need to talk about the flat. And money.'

'Yes.'

'And I'd still like to get a drink.'

'Definitely.'

They walk past some pubs but it is such a nice afternoon that Anna suggests they stay outside; Pete agrees. They buy four cans of San Miguel from a newsagent and take them to the nearest green space, which happens to be Soho Square. When they sit on a bench Anna winces with pain; every muscle in her body feels bruised from the morning run. She tells Pete that she ran all the way to Alexandra Palace, and for the first time he loosens up. Being on neutral territory is a relief, and they speak about running and the different routes they take from Kilburn until Anna's first can is almost gone.

'Is that what you're doing with your days?' he says, opening his second. 'Going for epic runs.'

'Most days not even that. But tomorrow is important. I've got a meeting at the *Guardian*.' He asks if she is going to talk to them about the suitcase project, and she says she wants to write about something else, then goes quiet. The need for massive tact is overwhelming.

'I want to write about my life,' she says, forcing each word out of her mouth against its will. 'I want to write about . . . what happened recently.' He asks what the hell that means, and after another long pause she tells him that a lot has happened to her, that it's been a crazy time.

'What did he do to you?'

'I don't want to explain it all.'

'You've started now.'

'Please, Pete. It's not really about him. Or about you. It's about me. I've been depressed.'

'You did tell me that.'

'No, clinically depressed. I take antidepressants, every day.'

For the second or third time in this short meeting Pete appears shocked, and releases an exasperated moan. He wants to know exactly how long she's been taking them, how long she felt down beforehand, why she never told him, why she never told anyone.

'I can't believe you kept this a secret from me.'

'I kind of kept it a secret from myself.'

386

'But why?'

'Because I knew you'd overreact. I didn't want you to think I was crazy.'

'You're the one that overreacted. It's really not such a big deal. Loads of people take them.'

'No they don't.'

'I know people who take them and keep it a secret.'

'Who?'

'I'm not saying. They're just as sensitive about it as you.'

He takes a long swig and sighs and says again that she should have told him, months ago, when it first started.

'It's not good for you, keeping these things all to yourself.'

'Well, they do call it an illness. But I am trying. To change, I mean. To be more open.'

This seems to round off the issue and for a long time they drink in silence, until most of their second cans have gone. Anna realises she will need to go to the toilet soon, and thinks of where she could go. The park is shifting into its post-work routine; all the benches are now taken, and dozens of people are lounging about on the grass, with beer cans and cigarettes. Anna watches a couple sitting with crossed legs opposite each other, and thinks of her Slinghy idea; she imagines her and Pete in one, sitting in the park with one sling wrapped around them, both leaning back against the stretchy fabric, each providing a counterweight to hold the other up. Then she thinks of her most recent idea, the theme park of human consumption, and holds up the can of beer to measure it with her eyes.

'How many beers do you think you've drunk in your life?'

The question makes Pete flinch in surprise, but then he very quickly gathers himself and says: 'Around seven thousand pints.'

'That was fast.'

'Ten pints a week on average since I was fifteen. That makes thirteen years. Thirteen times fifty-two times ten is around seven thousand.'

'Wow.'

'I've still got my engineering hat on.'

'Seven thousand pints. Imagine that, as a pond or lake.'

'Hardly. That recycling bin could probably hold that.' He points to a bin at the far side of the park, and explains that when it comes to volume people always underestimate how much can fit into a space.

'Remember those games when you had to guess how many sweets were in a jar? People always guessed way too low. All the water you drink in your life would fit into an Olympic swimming pool. All the wine you've drunk would probably fit in a barrel.' Anna's imagined theme park shrinks in her mind; an amassed bar of soap would be the size of a pillow; all the wine would fit in a bottle the size of a double bass; the totality of butter would just be a large block of butter. This doesn't seem so bad; maybe it would be cute that way.

'You're smart,' she says. 'I like the engineering hat.'

'Ask me more questions, if you like.'

She looks for inspiration, and just within eyeshot is a metal sign saying the park will close at dusk. She asks Pete when dusk is, and he laughs.

'Let's stay and find out. Whenever the man comes to tell us it's dusk, we'll disagree.'

They both laugh at the idea, but this happy moment only makes the subsequent silence feel sadder in comparison. They don't speak for at least five minutes, and it is getting late. The slanting sun is bringing out the character in each flagstone surrounding the lawn; in the flat light of day they appear as uniform grey slabs, but in this angled bronze light every one is shown to be uniquely dappled and mottled, of a slightly different hue, with its own pattern of lichen and moss, and set at a tilt away from its neighbours. Anna thinks on this and feels the real question she wants to ask Pete, the one that all the others have been revolving around, forcing itself to the surface.

'Do you think you could ever forgive me?'

'Is that what you want?'

'I think so.' She looks down as she says this, at her feet and the flagstones beneath the slats.

'You think so?'

'I mean, I'd like you to try.'

'But I thought I was just a 7o?'

'Yeah, well,' she says. 'I never really was a numbers person anyway.'

Without smiling he looks away from her and shakes his head. Then he crushes his second can in his hand.

'You're only saying this because things didn't work out with the other guy,' he says. 'Otherwise you'd still be with him.'

'It's possible,' she admits, 'but I kind of doubt it.'

He pivots towards her. 'Tell me why I should even take you seriously at all.'

Again she lowers her head and studies the flagstone beneath her boots.

'Because I've been thinking. *Really* thinking. And I identified some things about us that were good. Such as . . . such as that we always got on really well.'

'And?'

'That . . . we always had good sex. When we were having it. You know it was the pills that made me lose interest.'

'Anything else?'

She senses that he knows she finds this uncomfortable, and is enjoying it.

'That you'd be a good dad.'

This makes his head drop; she has never said it to him before.

'And . . . and that, you know, despite everything, I did always love you. And I still do.'

Pete's head remains hanging, and Anna looks out across the park. She watches a couple packing up their small picnic arrangement – they dust grass off their bums and knees, fold up a tartan blanket, put their shoes back on. Eventually Pete speaks.

'Like I said: I don't even feel I know you any more.'

Again they fall silent. Anna watches the couple walking from the park, and notices that many empty spaces have appeared on the lawn. Dusk must be approaching; a green keeper or warden in a boiler suit is going around and asking people to leave. She watches this man for a long time, and is startled by Pete jumping up and off the bench.

'Fuck it,' he says. He jumps up and down on the spot, shaking his limbs out, as if preparing his muscles for strenuous exercise.

'What's going on?'

'There's something I want to say as well,' he says. 'Something that's been bugging me. I wasn't entirely honest with you. When we last spoke in the flat.'

A shiver runs along Anna's tender limbs.

'Honest about what?'

She already knows the answer, which is further confirmed by the dark furrow between his eyebrows, the evidence of trouble that the topic causes him. Anna feels sick.

'It's about Zahra, isn't it?'

'Nothing happened between us. That much is true. But we did . . . there were *feelings*. We talked about it.'

Anna finds that she is shaking; her fingers are gripping the wooden slats of the bench, as if to keep herself upright. The diseased tooth is still there, at the dark recess of her mouth, has been there all along.

'But we never did anything. And we agreed that we shouldn't see each other. Because we both love you. That's when I decided – really decided – that I wanted to be with you forever. And that I was going to propose.'

Air swells painfully in Anna's throat, and she can feel her eyes coating with tears that she blinks away; she isn't sure if she is crying about Zahra and Pete having feelings for each other, or about Pete saying that they love her, or both.

'Say something, Anna.'

'I don't know what to say.'

She wants to ask where and how and why, to pick apart the full chronology of events, but dizziness swirls up within her. Like a seasick person trying to lock their eyes on the stabilising horizon, she looks out across the park. She sees the green keeper speaking to a couple, and thinks of the Slinghy again. This time she sees Zahra and Pete in the Slinghy, facing each other and laughing. Then she sees her and Zahra facing each other. Then she imagines a three-cornered Slinghy, with all three of them holding each other up. Her addled mind finds space to wonder if this would work, from a technical perspective, and she realises that yes, it certainly would.

'This is a lot to take in.'

'I know.'

'I don't know where to begin.'

'Well,' says Pete, retaking his seat beside her, 'we're in no hurry. We're here until dusk.' The next statement, a few minutes later, is Anna saying that she isn't sure they could work through all this stuff; Pete agrees, but says that at least they are talking about it, and trying to identify the problem.

'In engineering, they say that ninety per cent of the work is trying to find the problem. The solution then just flows naturally from that.'

'You really do love that engineering hat, don't you?'

He doffs his imaginary cap at her and says he might keep it on forever.

'It does suit you. So then . . . do you think we've identified the problem?'

'Are you joking? We're just getting started.'

More people get up and leave the park, and she can see the green keeper has worked his way across the lawn and is almost at their bench. In a few moments he will reach them, and in this time she thinks about meeting the *Guardian* journalist. And she thinks about Zahra and Pete. And she thinks about Andre the suitcase man. And she thinks about her articles on Kismet. The park warden is just a few metres away now, and he looks at her and they make eye contact, and he smiles, as if to say 'Sorry to be a spoilsport, but the party's over.' And she smiles back and tries to decide what to say when he tells her it's dusk, and this question mingles with all the others hanging over her, and she realises this business of making decisions is only just beginning.

Acknowledgements

I am incredibly grateful for the support and encouragement of Georgia Garrett, Louisa Joyner, and Julia Bell. Thanks also to everyone at Birkbeck and Splinter that read all or part of the book, especially Michael Button and Victoria Richards. More generally, thanks to Nathan Small, Robert Logan, Roisin Feeny, Gagan Rehill, Finn Smith, Rachel Brown, and everyone else that collaborated on random projects over the years.

Extra special thanks to Anne and the rest of my family for their interest and support. Most of all thanks to Sheena, for everything.